Hawker's Drift

Book Two

Dark Carnival

Andy Monk

The Carney King

Thomas Rum chewed the stem of his unlit pipe and peered out across the grass from behind half-closed lids. He'd never been one for the beauty of nature, but by all that was unholy this was a dull looking land.

Every year they trundled out here for the summer. Every year he ended up yearning for a tree, or a hill, or a river, or a pond, or a three-legged dog pissing in a ditch or any damn thing to break the monotony.

He closed his eyes again against the ferocious sunlight; it was too damn bright for his liking. He wanted to slither back into his cot, but the constant roll of the caravan would make him feel sick. For a man who had covered so many long, long miles he sure hated traveling; maybe he should look for a different line of work.

He smiled at that; he was far too old to learn any new tricks.

"How far to the next shit hole?" Tawny demanded through a yawn.

"'bout the same as it was last year I reckons," he replied, not bothering to look at the young man. He'd be hunched over the reins with a scowl etched above his too-wide eyes; Rum didn't need to look to know that.

"Maybes we should find some new places to go?" He could sense Tawny's eyes flick in his direction.

As if that would ever be an option...

"Hawker's Drift pays real well, and a deal is a deal."

"Still, such a bitch to get out here."

Rum rolled a bony shoulder, "Yeah, life's a real bitch... now keep your damned eyes on the road!"

"I was!" Tawny protested, "not that there's anything to see..."

"You pay attention, don't want you missing a hole and throwing a wheel. I hate it when that happens. Breaks all my goddamn crockery."

Tawny gave a snort; he was probably winding up to make some smartass comment about bringing good china on bad roads. Rum peeled open an eye and gave him a significant look. He'd heard it all before and was in no great hurry to hear it again.

Maybe he should drive his own damned wagon. It would save on the company, which, frankly, weren't much more inspiring than the view. But he was the king of this here carney and was therefore far too important to drive his own wagon. You needed boundaries when you were in charge. Though most folks seemed to have precious little regard for boundaries these days.

"Here comes sunshine..." Tawny muttered after a few minutes blessed silence.

Rum forced his eyes open again, even through the smoke-blackened glass of his spectacles he had to squint. He hated bright, hot days almost as much as he hated wet, cold ones.

A rider was coming back along the road towards them. He

2

wasn't coming hell for leather, so Rum guessed it wasn't anything too bothersome. He paid off the major brigands and renegades whose patches they had to travel through, but they weren't exactly what you would describe as honourable when it came to a deal. Plus there were plenty of transient bands of desperate men who might be stupid enough to think a convoy of carney wagons would be an easy target. So he sent some of his guns ahead of the wagons to make sure there were no nasty surprises waiting for them.

The rider reined in his horse fifty yards ahead and drank from his canteen as he waited for them.

"Trouble?" Rum asked.

Stodder Hope shook his head and wrinkled his big misshapen nose after he wheeled his horse around to come alongside. He was an ugly sonofabitch with a much-abused face partially hidden by a thick tangled beard. He'd cut his Granma's throat for the right price, but Rum doubted anyone would pay him more than he did, and stupidity was not one of Hope's long list of faults. So he trusted him about as much as he trusted anyone.

"Wagon ahead, thrown a wheel an blocking the road."

Rum glanced over his spectacles at Tawny, "Someone else who wasn't paying proper attention..."

Tawny scowled a bit more than usual but didn't reply.

"How many?"

"Man an two boys, might be more in the wagon – were a bit skittish so didn't get too close." Hope cracked a grin, revealing his missing front teeth, "think I made em nervous."

"See anyone else about?"

Hope took off his hat and wiped a hand across his bald

3

scalp, "Could have a small army squatting in this grass but didn't see anyone. Think they're just what they seem."

Rum nodded and settled back, a faint smile ghosting across his face.

Just like us then...

*

He made a show of climbing down from the wagon. First impressions mattered, and he liked to give the impression he was a harmless old coot, particularly to a man carrying a gun. Thomas Rum tried to avoid getting unnecessarily shot whenever he could.

He let Tawny jump off first so he could scurry around to help him, pulling a pained face as his feet finally found the ground. Rum stood holding on to the side of the wagon while the younger man recovered his cane. He straightened up with a wince, adjusted his battered top hat and brushed down the long black coat he wore before wrapping thin, crooked fingers around the cane's ivory handle.

When he was good and ready he turned towards the stranger's wagon, remembering to drag his right leg a little; Tawny poised at his elbow in case he stumbled. Stodder Hope stayed a couple of paces behind. Unlike Thomas Rum, he didn't look the slightest bit harmless.

"You folks look like you're having a bothersome day?" He called out, forcing his mouth into a friendly grin.

"You could say that," the man replied. He was tall and too skinny, with lank, unkempt hair that was retreating sharply from his temples; restless suspicious eyes squinted against the glare of the late afternoon sun. He cradled an ancient

4

rifle in his spindly arms. His attention flitted from Rum and Tawny to the long procession of wagons and the people clambering out of them. Mostly though, he stared at Hope on account of him looking like one mean sonofabitch.

"Thrown a wheel huh?" Rum asked. It was a rather unnecessary question given one of the battered wagon's wheels was lying in the road, but the man didn't strike him as being much of conversationalist.

"Yep," he replied, rather confirming Rum's impression.

Thomas Rum planted his cane in the ground, rested both hands on it and ran his eye over the wagon. It had seen better days. Several flaps of canvas were twitching in the breeze, scorch marks blackened the back half of the wagon, and it was peppered with what looked suspiciously like bullet holes. The two horses up front didn't look a whole lot healthier.

"Looks like you done some hard miles?"

The man nodded.

"Need a hand getting that fixed?"

"We got it."

Proud and stubborn, Rum thought, like so many of these people were.

There were two boys with him. One was a gangling youth who held a shotgun with the calm authority of someone who wasn't entirely sure which end did what, and a lad of ten or so who, thankfully, hadn't been trusted with anything more dangerous than a mallet. They both had the same look as the man, spare and hungry. Rum guessed they were his sons and that life hadn't been kind to any of em for quite a while.

"Pa?" The older one muttered, "we could-"

5

"We're fine." The man snapped.

Rum shrugged, "We don't mean no harm... we're just a carney, not a gang of desperados looking for mischief."

"A carney?" the younger boy asked.

"Indeed!" Rum beamed at him, showing off his striking white teeth. *"Billberry's Travelling Carnival,* the greatest show on the road between the Mississippi and the Rockies and I, Thomas Clyde Rum..." he doffed his hat and gave a suitably theatrical bow, "...have the honour of being the impresario, owner, master of ceremonies and custodian."

"He sells the candy too," Tawny added.

Rum put his hat back on and made sure it was at a suitably jaunty angle, before adding, "We all have to chip in."

"There many carnies out here?" The man asked, his tone softening a little.

"Not so many... the times I guess. Where you folks from?"

"Near Philadelphia... well, what used to be Philadelphia anyhow."

"You've come a long ways Mr..."

"Wheeter..." he lowered his rifle and held out his hand, "...sorry to be so..."

Rum gripped his sweaty palm and tried not to wrinkle his nose as he peeled it away.

"No need, lot of bad folks on the road. Lot of bad folks every damn where, truth be told."

"Yeah, we've met one or two..." his voice faded away, and he glanced at the oldest boy. Rum wondered where their mother was.

"These your boys?"

"Yep, Rolly..." Wheeter jerked his head at the older one

"...and Lucas."

Rolly nodded and waved his shotgun around more than was entirely necessary. Lucas grinned from ear to ear, craning his neck to see all the brightly painted wagons snaking back along the road as far as the eye could see.

"Well, Mr Wheeter, we're about done travelling for the day, so we're gonna get our wagons off this sorry excuse for a road and make camp. You folks are welcome to join us." He nodded at the wheel on the ground, "I got a lot of lads who can pop that back on and make it right. Have to be self-sufficient out here. We can handle most eventualities."

"That's mighty kind," Wheeter said, "but we really ain't got a lot to pay you with."

"Pay?" Rum waved him down, "there's nothing to pay. Won't cost me a dime. My crew are used to getting stuff put up, taken down, rigged, jigged, fixed and made good in no time. Just a good deed that's all."

"Ain't seen too many of them on the trail. Good deeds."

"Well, I'm an old fashioned kinda guy. I'll send a couple of boys over later."

Wheeter pulled a thin smile and nodded, "Much obliged Mr Rum... if there's anything we can do to help."

"Who knows...? I'll be sure to yell if I can think of anything." He nodded and raised a hand as he turned back towards his wagon, which was a dark red and held what meagre comforts he still owned. "Come on Tawny go get the wagon sorted, I need a nap."

Once Tawny had jogged off, Rum glanced at Stodder Hope, who had fallen into step beside him.

"When we make camp, make sure the black wagon is

7

nearest the Wheeter's..." he said in a low hiss as he looked over his darkened spectacles at the gunslinger, "...just in case..."

*

A campfire, a full belly, the first stars emerging from the darkening sky and a nip of whiskey in his glass. It was enough to bring a sense of contentment to most men. Thomas Rum, however, wasn't most men.

He watched the Wheeter's demolish their plates of stew, wiping them so vigorously clean with coarse black bread that he feared they might rub a hole clean through his least cherished plates.

He usually ate alone, perched on his canvas chair as the carney made camp. Keeping an eye on things, keeping his distance. You had to have boundaries after all. However, tonight, he'd invited the Wheeters to dine with him, if squatting on the grass and eating off a chipped plate counted as dining.

The carney wagons formed a rough double circle; a couple of Hope's men were perched on top of the tallest, keeping an eye out. Everybody else was inside, little knots of people gathered around cooking fires. The hum of chatter and laughter carried on a fitful breeze.

Rum hadn't said much and neither had Wheeter, his boys wide-eyed as they ate, looking around at the garish wagons and equally garish people flitting about between them.

"Much obliged Mr Rum," Wheeter said, finally putting his plate down on the grass, "for the wagon too."

Rum gave a little smile, "Really, just being hospitable. I'm

8

guessing it's been a while since you folks seen much of that. Where are you heading?"

"California."

Rum raised an eyebrow.

"We heard things are better out there..." he sounded like a boy still clinging to the hope that Father Christmas was real.

"Ain't as bad, I hear," Rum offered, not wanting to be the one to give him the bad news about Santa Claus, "but you'll never get there."

Wheeter was sitting cross-legged on the ground, and his mouth took on a hard line. Stubborn and proud, Rum thought again.

"We can do it."

Rum took a sip of whiskey and shook his head, "Not on your own. You might make it across the plains if you're lucky. But the mountains? Bad land to cross, even if you know the terrain; and that's without the renegades, outlaws an savages. Need more than a couple of guns to get through that." He jerked his head towards the Wheeter's now repaired wagon, "you look like you had plenty of troubles already?"

"We started out with a wagon train," Wheeter sighed, "got a couple of hundred miles and they trebled the price to take us further... some of us struck out on our own. We run into some... bad men a week later. We lost a few people. The others decided to turn back. We carried on."

"You've done well to get this far."

Lucky more like.

"We had a few scrapes."

They sat in silence, the two boys staring at the small fire that they didn't really need on a warm summer's night. Rum

9

always had a fire though; it reminded him of home.

"Plenty of land here to farm," Rum sniffed eventually.

"Heard it's better in California."

"Maybes..."

"Where are you going Mr Rum?" the younger boy, Lucas, piped up suddenly. His father shot him a look.

Little boys should be seen and not heard, eh Mr Wheeter?

He would get Giselle to run her eye over young Lucas later and see if he had anything of worth about him. Rum was pretty sure he knew from the way the hairs on the back of his neck tingled whenever the boy spoke, but Giselle was more sensitive than he'd ever been.

"Heading west to a town called Hawker's Drift; we pitch up there every year."

"Never heard of it," Wheeter said.

"No reason why you should have. It's a long way from anywhere, but it's a peaceable town. Never much trouble. Other than getting there in the first place of course."

Wheeter's ears picked up, "Never any trouble?"

"The Mayor is an old, old friend o' mine. He runs it tight, don't stand for nonsense. Upholds the law. Not so many places like that left in the world."

"I guess not."

Rum ran a hand over the scrubby bristles on his chin, "Look, we're heading in the same direction. Why don't you hitch along with us as far as Hawker's Drift? Run your eye over the place. Real good land there. A place a man can make a fresh start."

The two boys were looking pointedly at their father. They had no dreams about California. They were sick of the road, with its hardships and dangers. Rum thought they were both a lot smarter than their old man.

Wheeter avoided his sons' eyes but chewed it over for a minute all the same, "Well, guess it can't hurt to take a look."

"Oh, I'm sure you'll like it," Rum beamed, "most folk find Hawker's Drift a real hard place to leave..."

The Gunslinger

"What makes you think she has anything to do with me?"

"Well... there's... a resemblance."

John X was leaning against the door frame; he looked at Amos out of the corner of his eye before replying, "I'm not responsible for *every* dark-skinned child in this town."

Amos raised an eyebrow.

"This one is *nothing* to do with me."

Molly looked up from the bed and put a finger to her lips. She was glowering. Again. Amelia shuffled under the blankets before settling back with a wheezing mumble.

"She don't look too good," the gunsmith muttered as Molly leant over the girl to dab her brow with a damp towel.

Amos indicated they should leave with a jerk of his head.

"Rudi seen her?" He asked once they'd reached the kitchen.

Amos nodded.

"What did he say?"

"She's got a fever.... keep her in bed, keep her warm."

"And how much did he charge for that piece of wisdom?"

"More than Molly can really afford..."

"I should have been a doctor..." John X snorted, staring out of the window while Amos sat at the table. "Sorry I can't be of more help, but honestly, I don't know the girl."

It had seemed a possibility that Amelia might be connected to John; a visiting relative's child who'd wandered off perhaps. The gunsmith, however, didn't have any guests (or relatives for that matter) but had asked to look in on the little girl who'd been found lost in the street all the same.

"Thanks for coming anyway."

"You're welcome; to be honest I've always hoped I'd get into Molly's bedroom one day..."

"Well, if the Mayor gets his way..."

John X turned back from the window and leaned against the sink.

"You still trying to help her with that?"

"Trying..."

"Well, whatever you decide I hope you ain't going to be poking around the Mayor's business no more – you see where that nearly got you?"

"You mean you don't think that was all just an unfortunate misunderstanding?"

"Dunno, but glad they didn't hang you all the same. Heard about the other thing too..." John X pulled a face and whistled "...sorry... must be..."

"Yeah..."

"Yeah."

John X was one of those people Amos could never get a sense of, just a blank page or a closed door. Even so, he still felt him wince.

"Guess it explains why you're so odd and uppity though."

Amos snorted a little laugh.

"What you going to do with the girl?"

"Not much we can do for now. She's sick, can't kick her back into the street."

"Plenty of people that would," John X dropped his eyes and stared at his scuffed boots.

"Molly isn't one of them."

"Makes things even more complicated though?"

"Yeah..." Amos sighed, "...just have to find out who she belongs to. She can't have appeared out of thin air."

"Guess not... look sorry I can't be of more help, but I gotta get back to the store."

"Sure," Amos nodded, rising to his feet.

Instead of heading for the door however John turned back to the window and folded his arms across his chest, "By the way, does Molly know she's got a clown in her backyard. He seems to be juggling apples?"

"Yeah, he ran out of eggs... Molly put him out there so he wouldn't stink the house up."

"That bad, huh?"

"Mr Wizzle's got lots of fizzle..."

John X grunted, "I try to keep downwind of clowns for a whole variety of reasons. Looks like Molly is opening up a refuge for the lost, broken and... downright weird folks of Hawker's Drift."

"We'll keep a room free for you."

"The clown found this girl then?"

"Amelia, yeah."

"Taken an interest in her?"

"As puzzled as the rest of us."

Amos followed John into the hall just as Molly came down the stairs. He could feel her concern, but asked anyway.

"No better?"

Molly had pulled her hair loosely up and a few more ringlets worked their way free as she shook her head, "She's so hot... I just don't know what to do."

"Kids can be tough, she'll pull through," John X sounded confident though Amos wasn't sure what experience he had with children beyond producing them.

"I need her to eat something at least, I'm going to run down to the store and get some bits, can you keep an eye on her?"

"I'll go, I tend to scare kids," Amos offered.

"Really, it's fine... just keep an eye on her."

She's worried what might happen if I go out on my own, Amos realised, after all, who knew what the Mayor might be cooking up next.

"It's ok Molly, I can probably make it to the store and back without getting shot or thrown in the cells."

Molly looked like she was going to protest that wasn't what she been thinking, but settled for giving him a mild scowl.

"There's always Mr Wizzle?" John offered, "he could watch over the girl..."

"You go Amos; I'll make a list..."

*

"Oh..." John X muttered out of the corner of his mouth "...this is gonna be interesting..."

Amos thought about crossing the street. However, it was a small town and he was going to walk into Ash Godbold sooner or later anyway.

16

They'd almost reached Pioneer Square and the town was largely going about its business. He was still eliciting curious glances, but at least they weren't trying to hang him anymore. He hoped Ash felt the same way.

Ash was coming straight towards him, a blonde woman Amos assumed was his wife at his side. Her eyes were red and puffy while Ash's were so distant there was a fair chance he wouldn't notice them at all.

"Afternoon Ash... Kate..." John barked as they drew close.

So much for that hope.

Ash blinked and looked like he was struggling to focus; Kate jumped half out of her skin.

Amos, who'd never been much of a student of etiquette, wasn't quite sure what the situation required and settled for touching his hat and nodding.

The realisation of who he was came upon Ash suddenly, his face flushed and his eyes dropped away. At least he didn't think Amos had anything to do with Emily's assault anymore.

Amos was about to pass the couple without comment, but Ash stuck his hand out in front of him, which at least proved to Amos that people could still surprise him.

"I owe you an apology..." Ash's words were mumbled and his embarrassment was so vivid Amos almost had to squint against its glare.

"Not needed..."

"I don't make a habit of attacking people with a razor... *please.*"

Amos stared at Ash's still outstretched hand, he wasn't reluctant to take it because he bore a grudge, he just didn't

17

like touching people. He never knew what he might see and feel. The man's emotions were raw, painful and etched deep enough into his face for anyone to see, touching him would be like picking up a glowing coal.

"In the circumstances... I'd have done the same." There was no way he could ignore Ash's offered hand without insulting him. That wouldn't usually bother him in the slightest, but he didn't need any more trouble, both for his sake and Molly's.

"Still..."

Amos took his hand and tried not to grimace as the man's pain and anger lanced up his arm and engulfed him, guilt-fuelled furies dancing around his head. Ash was like a wounded beast in a cage, desperate to lash out because he didn't know what else to do.

"It wasn't your fault," Amos said, his hand springing open.

"Huh?"

"When bad things happen to people we love... we blame ourselves for it regardless."

"You don't know how I feel," Ash's voice was suddenly cold and Amos wished he'd kept his mouth shut. He couldn't deal with his own pain, let alone help salve another's.

"He's only trying to help," Kate shushed, squeezing her husband's arm as her eyes darted between the two men. She was frightened by her husband, by what she saw in his eyes, the uncharacteristic, impotent rage streaming through his veins. Frightened by what he would do...

...if he ever found out...

"Sure... everyone's real eager to help..." Ash spat, shrugged off his wife and stomped off down Main Street.

"I'm sorry," Kate said, pulling a long downcast face, "...he's not really himself at the moment."

"How's Emily?" John X asked before Amos could reply.

Kate blushed slightly and dropped her eyes to the ground, "Hurt, confused, withdrawn..."

There were a few things Amos wanted to ask Emily about, but he guessed it wasn't likely he'd get the chance.

"I'd better catch up with Ash before he bites someone else's head off..."

"Of course."

She nodded and hurried off after her husband.

John watched her for a moment, before turning to find Amos staring at him.

"What?"

Amos didn't say anything, but at least he now knew why Kate had never heard the attack on her daughter...

*

There were only a handful of customers in *Pickerings*, but they all stopped talking and started staring too intently at things that didn't need much staring at as soon as Amos walked in.

Well, at least they're not trying to hang-

He cut the thought short; he was starting to wonder if this *was* better. At least if they tried that again he could shoot his way out of it, which wasn't something he could do when a woman was just staring with bulging eyes at a can of beans.

Amos stood in the doorway and fiddled with the list Molly had given him until John plucked it from his hand.

"Leave it to me," he whispered with a wink, "I get a discount."

"Afternoon Bernie, you're looking as sweet as pie!" He boomed, bounding over to the counter.

Bernie, despite being in her forties, giggled behind her hand as her plump cheeks flushed like a teenage girl trying her first flirt.

"Oh, I'm full of plums today and no mistake," Bernie said, in an unnecessarily loud voice, as she leaned over the counter towards the gunsmith.

Amos had intended to ask John how he got a discount but decided he really didn't need to.

After John X had handed the list over the counter and added a couple of items he needed, Bernie hurried off to fill a bag with groceries.

"Are there any women in this-"

"One or two."

"How long you been here?"

John looked at the ceiling and screwed up his nose, "half my life I'd say. Give or take. Why?"

"And they tried to string *me* up in less than a week?"

The gunsmith laughed.

*

They stood on the corner of Pioneer Square, Amos wasn't sure why, but John seemed to be dragging out going home. Perhaps his bed would be too empty. Sometimes it was more convenient just to know what was going on in someone's head. It saved an awful lot of time.

"So... you staying with Molly permanently now?" John

asked, in what sounded awfully like small talk.

"Nothing's permanent."

"Sounds like a man avoiding a question."

Actually it was a man avoiding small talk, but Amos just pulled a fleeting smile and kept an eye on the good folk of Hawker's Drift wandering by. Just in case.

The gunsmith shuffled a brown paper bag holding his groceries from one hand to the other. For a man who lived alone, he'd bought a lot of food.

"Well, I'd better get back," Amos hoisted up his own smaller bag.

"You still got stuff in *Jack's*?"

"No, moved it all to Molly's.

John X gazed across the square to the saloon and shuffled his feet. He looked like a small dog that wanted to gnaw a chair leg but knew his master would clip his ear if he did.

"You planning to go back anytime?"

Amos frowned, he was usually glad when he met someone that he couldn't read, but this was starting to get irritating.

He shrugged. He had few plans to leave Molly's house until they'd either fled town or paid off the Mayor.

"Keeping a low profile, huh?"

"Is there something you want to say?"

John looked down, a troubled expression dancing across his face, "That girl, Amelia, she's pretty sick."

"Seems that way."

The gunsmith glanced both ways, but nobody was in earshot, "Mention it to the new girl in the saloon. The singer."

"Cece?"

21

"Uh-huh."

Amos peered at him, "Why?"

"Just mention it to her... just don't mention me."

"But-"

The gunsmith shook his head and wheeled away, "Just do it!"

Amos watched him cross the square and disappear into his store.

The Widow

Amelia was sleeping. Or at least Molly hoped she was. How fine a line was there between sleep and unconsciousness?

The girl's eyes were moving behind closed lids and an occasional groan bubbled up from her throat as she shuffled beneath the sheets. Sweat covered her face like fat dewdrops on a spring morning. Her skin was acorn-brown, but there was a sickly, waxy pallor beneath it as if her colour was fading with her life.

Molly rested her palm lightly against the girl's forehead. She was burning.

Dr Rudi had checked her for lesions and had ruled out The Reaping, which was something at least. Still, plenty of other things in the world could kill a little girl just as effectively.

Hearing footsteps on the stairs she half turned towards the bedroom door. She tried not to look disappointed when Mr Wizzle heaved laboriously into view.

"Golly, those are steep stairs," he panted, waving his derby in front of his face, which was even redder than normal.

Molly stood up and offered him her chair; she didn't want

another patient, especially one that smelt of stale sweat and old eggs; a combination that even Guy Furnedge had yet to try.

"No, no, I'm fine," he wheezed.

Molly pushed the chair towards him and gave him a look.

Mr Wizzle slumped into it without further argument.

"How is little Amelia?"

"Burning up."

"She suffers, but she will overcome."

"I hope so," Molly moved to the other side of the bed and sat on the edge, "I just wish there was something I could do."

"Do?" Mr Wizzle frowned, "You have taken the child in, given her comfort and succour. What more could you do?"

Molly shook her head, "It just feels... inadequate."

"She isn't going to die."

Molly shifted on the bed and glanced at Amelia, but she was too far under to have heard the old man's words.

"Of course she isn't..."

"God did not send her here to die, we just need to have faith and he will provide. As always."

"You think God sent her here?"

"Oh yes."

"Why?"

Mr Wizzle pulled a long face and turned his palms upwards. "I have no idea. God doesn't share his plans with me, but it was his intention that I found her outside your house and brought her here."

"It was?" Molly wasn't convinced by the idea of divine intervention. "If God wanted someone to look after a sick little girl I'm sure there are far better choices he could have

24

made than me."

A frown creased Mr Wizzle's flustered brow, "Admittedly, you wouldn't have been my first choice, given your moral failings. But God is a lot smarter than me."

Molly sat up a littler straighter, "Moral failings?"

"The drinking and fornicating. Your language is quite inappropriate too. Bad words are entirely unnecessary, especially around a child."

"I-"

"No need to apologise," Mr Wizzle beamed, "none of us is perfect, after all."

"I wasn't intending to apologise," Molly said carefully, ignoring several bad words that had sprung to mind.

Mr Wizzle just smiled. It was the kind of smile that suggested he knew better; in other words it was the kind of smile that usually made Molly want to hit someone.

Before she could decide whether or not to slap the old man, Mr Wizzle took off his hat and looked up at her, "I'm sorry about your husband. I didn't know him of course, but still..."

"Thank you."

"It must have been a shock."

"Yes, it was..." Molly muttered, turning back towards Amelia.

"Lots of people die suddenly in this town. I've noticed."

Molly paused, "They do?"

"Oh yes. Most don't fall off their horse mind, but even so...."

"Like who?"

Mr Wizzle stared at Molly, tilting his head slightly, "You

have very beautiful hair."

"Erm... thank you..."

"It's like rust in the sunset."

Molly's eyes narrowed, "What?"

"Your hair, it's the colour of rust in the sunset."

Tom had told her that once, as they'd lain together in some cheap hotel room long before there'd ended up in Hawker's Drift. She was pretty sure he wouldn't have said it to anybody else given he'd usually been as descriptive and poetic as a fence post.

"Why do you say that?"

"You'd think I was mad if I told you."

"I already think you're mad," Molly said before she could stop herself.

Mr Wizzle continued smiling and looked at Amelia, keeping whatever passed for thoughts to himself.

"I can look after her..." Molly said, after a few minutes of heavy silence punctuated only by the phlegmy wheeze of Mr Wizzle's breath "...if you need... to get home?"

"Oh, I have nothing to go home for," Mr Wizzle looked down at the hat that lay in his lap. He interlaced his fingers and rested them atop the derby.

"Well, there's not much to do but wait."

"I'm good at waiting. Patience is a virtue, remember..." he peered across at her in a manner that suggested he considered virtue to be a bit of an alien concept to Molly.

"So is cleanliness."

"Indeed it is," Mr Wizzle agreed, missing the barb entirely.

Molly sighed, short of physically dragging him to the door and throwing him onto the street it seemed she was stuck

26

with the strange old man for the time being. She got up and opened the window.

"Splendid idea," Mr Wizzle beamed, "fresh air is a marvellous curative."

Molly leaned out and looked down to the street. Would he survive the fall if she could somehow manage to manhandle him out of the window?

When she turned back, Molly found Mr Wizzle staring at her, "I understand the Mayor wants you to work in the whorehouse?"

"Word gets around, huh?"

"I hope you're going to say no, it is a den of iniquity."

"I may not have a choice."

"You can *always* say no," Mr Wizzle insisted.

"Sadly, I think that would just get me more customers."

Mr Wizzle blinked and looked bemused. Or rather, more bemused. "Why?"

"Oh, you know how some men are."

"I do?"

Molly decided to put it in words he might understand, "Full of wickedness."

"Oh yes," Mr Wizzle settled back in his chair and nodded hard enough to wobble his chins, "that is very true."

Molly was saved from further moral guidance as Amelia suddenly stirred, kicking at her blankets and muttering.

"She's getting hotter and hotter..." Molly said, placing her hand on the girl's forehead.

"Perhaps s little water?" Mr Wizzle suggested, rising to pour some into a beaker, but Amelia just jerked her head away when Molly placed it against her lips.

For a moment, Amelia opened her eyes, which were gummy and bloodshot, "Where's my Mommy?" She asked in a croaky rasp.

"I don't know, hun..." Molly whispered, stroking her hair, "...really I don't."

*

Molly put a plate of oatcakes in front of Mr Wizzle; she'd sweetened them with honey and soured them with her smile. He stared at the plate, before frowning and looking up at her, "You sure you don't have any eggs?"

"Not till Amos gets back, no."

He looked uncertainly back at the oatcakes; perhaps he suspected she'd poisoned them. To be fair, the thought had crossed her mind.

"I like eggs," he muttered, taking a tentative bite.

If he spat it out she was going to drag him to the door, no matter what. Instead, after some consideration, he smiled and took another bite.

Molly put her own plate down and sat opposite the old man. She glanced at the ceiling, she didn't like leaving Amelia alone, but she needed to eat and she'd rather keep Mr Wizzle where she could see him. He seemed harmless, but it didn't feel quite right leaving the little girl alone with a strange and smelly old man. Especially one in a clown's cast off suit.

"What did you mean earlier, about a lot of people dying suddenly in this town?"

"I've been here a long time... just something I noticed."

"How long?"

Mr Wizzle screwed up his face as he took another mouthful of oatcake, showering the front of his shirt with crumbs, "'bout thirty years I suppose, give or take."

"Not a local then?"

"No... most of the town are not local."

Molly raised an eyebrow.

"A lot of people turn up here from all over. Just look at little Amelia."

"Yeah, wherever she comes from."

"Mississauga."

"Huh?"

"That's what she told me."

"Before you brought her here?" Molly asked. The girl had been too feverish to do much but sleep since Mr Wizzle had turned up with her in his arms.

The old man hesitated then nodded.

"Is it anywhere around here?"

"Don't think so. We're a long ways from everywhere here."

"Yet people keep turning up, you reckon?"

Mr Wizzle polished off an oatcake before raising his eyes to meet her gaze, "You did?"

"Well... yes, but we didn't *plan* to come here."

"You just... arrived?"

Molly frowned. Why had they ended up in Hawker's Drift? She couldn't recall any conscious decision. They'd had to get out of their last home after, inevitably, one of Tom's get rich quick schemes had turned into a get out of town quick or get thrown in jail scheme.

She supposed the first stage they could get had been coming here, but Tom had handled that. She'd been busy making sure none of his newly found creditors got hold of their meagre savings by hiding them somewhere that was safely out of sight – if somewhat uncomfortable.

She'd never asked Tom where they were going, he'd turned surly and introspective like he usually did when one of his schemes went horribly wrong. It was a look she'd seen quite a bit of during their six years of marriage.

Instead, she'd watched the land bounce by for hour after bumpy hour. They'd been a string of overnight stops in places she never bothered to find out the name of before they'd been deposited in Hawker's Drift. The end of the line.

"Yeah... we just arrived... nowhere left for us to run I guess."

"Lot of folk like that here."

"Lot of folk end up here... and a lot of folk end up dying suddenly?"

"Yes"

"Why?"

"Oh..." Mr Wizzle raised his shoulders till they touched his ears "...I dunno. Just something I noticed. Strange huh?"

"I suppose."

"Then there are the ones that just disappear..."

Molly's oatcake hovered in mid-air as she frowned, "Disappear?"

Mr Wizzle held up a closed fist then splayed his fingers wide, "*Poof...*"

"Who?"

He raised his eyes to the ceiling and mumbled under his breath before announcing, "Thirty-three."

"That's a very precise figure?"

"I keep notes on this town."

"Notes?"

"Oh yes, all kinds of shenanigans happen here..." he leaned in and lowered his voice a notch as he added knowingly "...between you and me, all kinds of *godless* shenanigans..."

Molly polished off her oatcake, "Well I haven't noticed."

"People don't. People try real hard to not to notice, but I do. Once a year, more or less, someone just vanishes." He splayed his fingers quickly twice this time.

"People come, people go..." Molly sighed; she should be getting back to Amelia.

"Oh sure, but I don't count people who leave. You know, the ones that pack up a wagon and go, not even the ones who do it in the middle of the night. I mean vanish. Into thin air."

Molly collected the plates and stood up, wondering how likely it was the Mr Wizzle might suffer the same fate.

"People don't just vanish into thin air," Molly insisted, putting the plates into the sink. She'd wash them later. She heard Mr Wizzle's chair scrape on the floor.

"Clara Pierre did."

"Who?" Molly looked back at Mr Wizzle, her heart sinking a little as he came scurrying over to the sink.

"Clara Pierre," he repeated, his tone low and urgent, "twenty-two years old, pretty lil' wisp of a girl. Went to bed one night, an hour later her husband finished writing a letter and went up to join her..."

Mr Wizzle splayed his fingers in front of Molly's eyes suddenly enough to make her blink.

"Poof?"

Mr Wizzle nodded, "It's shenanigans Molly, there's definitely godless shenanigans going on in Hawker's Drift..."

"Well..." she sighed, stepping around the old man "...she probably just run away. People do that, jeez, I did that! I'm sure there's an explanation."

"Sure there's an explanation," Mr Wizzle insisted as she made for the door "and that explanation wears fancy suits and a tatty eye patch..."

The Manservant

"Will there be anything else, sir?"

"There will always be something else…"

Symmons looked up from the tea he had just placed on the Mayor's desk, which was as empty as it usually was.

"Are we feeling a touch wistful tonight?" Symmons asked, straightening up.

The Mayor made a little snorting noise but didn't look back from the window. He was watching the dusk settle over Pioneer Square; the Mayor had a tendency to do that when he was feeling reflective. Or when he was pissed at something.

Symmons hovered, but when the Mayor said nothing further he decided the mood was thoughtful rather than angry. Preacher Stone, he assumed, but it wasn't his place to comment. His master would let him know when he wanted his opinion.

"Will you require any of the young ladies this evening, sir?"

"No… not tonight."

Very reflective. Clearly.

The room was unlit and Symmons could make out little of his master's face mirrored in the window, but he suspected he had one of his brooding faraway looks. Best to leave him alone, it would pass by morning. It usually did.

He turned and moved towards the door, he even got as far as curling his hand around the doorknob before the Mayor spoke.

"We have a new arrival in town I hear..."

"Yes, sir..." he let his hand fall away from the doorknob "...a little nigger girl I believe."

The Mayor let out a slow, measured sigh and half turned away from the window so Symmons could see his profile against the twilight. Definitely brooding.

"What have I told you about that kind of language?"

"To only use it in front of the locals, sir."

"Please try to keep it that in mind. I find such language quite distasteful."

"I'm sorry sir," Symmons gave a slight and perfunctory bow; "I sometimes forget we're quite the enlightened despot these days."

The Mayor turned back to the window, "She appeared in town it seems."

"Interesting, if true."

"Rudi has no reason to lie."

"Has he taken blood?"

"Not yet, but I've given him instructions."

Symmons took a step back into the room; it seemed the Mayor was in a talkative mood after all.

"Do you believe she will be of use, sir?"

The Mayor twitched his shoulders, "Possibly."

"She must be *very* attuned."

"In which case she will be of use."

Symmons felt his tongue slither along his lips before he could stop himself, his master hated him doing that, "She would be-"

"Too young," the Mayor interrupted, "there is no need to be hasty. The sweetest fruit is best left to ripen on the vine."

"Of course sir, you know best."

"We are here for the long ride, remember?"

"How can I forget?"

The Mayor turned away from the window, shoving his hands deep into his pockets.

"You seem troubled sir?" Symmons ventured once the Mayor had perched himself on the corner of his desk.

"I was thinking about Preacher Stone."

Ah, I was right...

"The evil old rapist sir? Better for everyone that he's dead, isn't it?"

"You see things so clearly, don't you Symmons?"

"I just serve sir, it is what I was bred to do after all."

"I made a mistake."

Symmons raised an eyebrow. This was new. "You did?"

"With the gunslinger... I tried to be too clever."

"You weren't to know sir."

"And Preacher Billy had to pay the price."

"He was dying anyway."

"Even so."

"He would have died long ago without your... help. It wasn't a bad deal. I assume he didn't suffer, in the end."

The Mayor stared at his spotless black shoes, saw something he didn't like and rubbed the left one against the back of his right calf. "No... he didn't."

"Then all is well."

The Mayor raised his eye, "I was quite fond of him you know. Our little theological debates were rather entertaining."

"You told me everything he believed in was complete twaddle, sir."

"Well, yes, obviously, but still…"

"I know, the little monkeys can be quite endearing," Symmons said, pursing his lips, "particularly the ones with large breasts I find…"

The Mayor's lips twitched with a brief smile, "Indeed, the earthly pleasures of the flesh have been an unexpected bonus, I must admit."

Symmons walked over to the desk and poured his master's tea.

"It was a necessary evil; you know that, don't you sir?"

"Everything I do is necessary… whether or not it is evil is all rather subjective."

"Of course sir. One sugar or two?"

"Three."

Oh dear…

Symmons looked up from the tea as he scooped sugar into the cup, he wasn't concerned for his master, but he was curious.

"What will you do about the gunslinger now?"

"I'm not sure. I will have to think on it."

"Is he really that dangerous?" He passed the porcelain cup to his master, who accepted it without acknowledgement.

"He has… unusual talents."

"You already have a small army of gunslingers."

"No... not that. There is something else about him."

Symmons raised an eyebrow, but the Mayor didn't elaborate and slurped his tea instead. Sometimes his master could be distressingly uncouth.

"So, kill him then. I'm sure Mr Blane is more than capable of arranging that."

The Mayor shook his head, "Tom McCrea and Preacher Stone have both died suddenly in the last few weeks, plus young Emily Godbold's rape. People will get nervous. People will notice."

"But he's just a stranger, strangers come and go..."

The Mayor looked up at him pointedly.

"Well, in most towns..."

Another slurp of tea.

"He could just disappear, sir? I doubt it would cause much of a stir."

"I suppose."

"And he is proving an inconvenience in regards to Mr Furnedge and Mrs McCrea."

"Well, there is that too." *Slurp.*

"The numbers are very encouraging in that regard."

"Yes, we mustn't forget the numbers, eh Symmons?"

Symmons smiled, "We are here for the long ride..."

The Mayor took a final slurp of tea before mercifully putting the empty cup down beside him.

"Mr Rum and the others are due soon. Have you had word, sir?" Symmons ventured when the Mayor remained perched on the corner of his desk.

"They'll be here on the same day and at the same time; as they always are."

37

"With bounty?"

"Let us hope."

"And the Dark Carnival."

The Mayor snorted. He hid his displeasure from the others, but not from him. He was the most faithful and most loyal. The one who had never left his side through it all. He felt a flutter of pride and stamped it down. Such feelings were foolish and unnecessary though he knew the Mayor prized him above all others and that was all the reward he'd ever wanted.

"Will you go?"

"It is expected though I would prefer they were less open with the natives."

"Then why don't you put a stop to it, sir? You are the boss after all?"

"Are you criticising me Symmons?"

"Heaven forbid sir," he gave a little bow of the head, "Just playing Devil's advocate sir. As always."

"I must give them something. They have lost so much after all and they have always been fond of rituals."

"Our only desire is to serve and I believe the others only wish for an opportunity to adore you with their minions..."

The Mayor looked sceptical but held his tongue.

Symmons walked to the window when it was clear his master was going to say no more. He stared out at Pioneer Square as his master had been doing a few minutes before, "The little monkeys are heading for their waterhole..."

"Miss Jones has proved quite a takings booster."

"Who would have thought free whiskey and plentiful whores wouldn't already have filled the place to the rafters every night?"

"The novelty will wear off when the Dark Carnival arrives in town."

Symmons felt his master move to stand behind him and watch the steady stream of locals heading across the square from all directions towards *Jack's Saloon*.

"And what are we going to do about her?"

"Miss Jones? Oh, we can't possibly part with her."

"The numbers?"

The Mayor chuckled, "Yes. She will be bountiful."

"But she knows, doesn't she?"

"It would appear so."

"That could be a problem."

"What people know can be forgotten."

Symmons turned back towards his master, "If she imbibes enough."

The Mayor nodded, "I have taken steps."

"Let us hope she has a taste for your candy..."

"If it doesn't work... well, there are other uses for her, aren't there?"

Symmons smiled, nodded and licked his lips again...

The Lawyer

He was free.

He was rich.

He was desperately unhappy.

How long had he waited for this moment? It seemed like it had been his entire life. Of course, that wasn't true. There had been a time before he had met Lorna. He'd been young and had enjoyed a young man's dreams, but that had been more than a lifetime ago, surely?

He ran a finger over the papers spread across his desk. Everything was as it should be, as he'd hoped and prayed it would be. Every "i" was clearly dotted, every "t" was precisely crossed and every last cent was his. Everything was absolutely tickety.

Apart from the one thing he wanted most.

Carson had arrived on the stage from Fellowes Ford. He'd checked the paperwork, he'd spoken to Doctor Rudi and Sheriff Shenan, he'd sniffed around, he'd asked questions. He'd endured Lorna's coven of friends, he'd questioned Amy, he'd even suffered Miss Dewsnap's infernal baking. He'd shoved his wet, pink snout into every conceivable crevice.

The man was thorough, Guy Furnedge had to give him that.

At the end of his enquiries he'd been satisfied Lorna had died of natural causes, that Furnedge had been a dutiful and loyal husband right to the last and there was nothing to stop the will being read and executed.

It was all his. Every last cent.

And there were a lot of cents.

He'd always feared Lorna had squandered the money somehow. Drunk it away, given it away, frittered it away in one final act of spite, but no, it turned out she hadn't. The money had rolled in year on year from her late father's estate and it seemed she'd barely touched it.

He was rich; stinkingly, filthily, stupidly rich.

He could buy the whole town, pretty much. But he didn't want the whole town, he just wanted Molly. Sadly, it seemed she had other ideas.

A gunslinging eunuch, no less.

Perhaps she just felt sorry for him. He could only be staying with her because she pitied him. That had to be the explanation, mustn't it?

It had all seemed so promising on the evening Amos had been arrested and hauled away to the cells. It had been foolish to make the proposal before Carson had signed off on Lorna's will, but he been unable to resist the temptation. He was only human after all, while Molly, well she was...

He leaned back and closed his eyes.

Had he ever wanted anything more? If he had, he certainly couldn't remember it. If it took every last cent he inherited from Lorna to get her, it would be worth it. After all he had suffered, didn't he deserve her?

He snorted.

Of course, he did. And she had been conducive.

Perhaps they'll be other times for coming in...

She had seemed so tantalisingly within his grasp, then Amos had been released and had taken up residence in Molly's home, which wasn't at all appropriate. Cock or no cock.

He remembered the first time he'd seen her, she'd been with that brash, uncouth husband of hers, walking down Main Street. The sun had been setting and her hair seemed to be afire as she threw back her head and laughed loudly at something Tom had said.

That laugh; so rich and earthy and full of promises.

He'd stood outside his office, keys dangling in his hand as he gawped at her. He'd always enjoyed looking at women, but he was a man of standing and decorum, so he could only afford to look discreetly. A furtive glance here, a sly peek there, but that first time in the street he had stared at her like a simple-minded bumpkin at his first county fair. He hadn't even realised his mouth had been hanging open until they'd turned the corner.

He'd hoped she would glance back at him; a smile, a flick of her wild, flowing hair. Just a little encouragement. But of course, they'd been nothing. Women didn't really notice Guy Furnedge. Not women like Molly McCrea anyway.

He'd daydreamed about her all the way home, wondering who she was and praying fervently that she wasn't just a transient visitor to Hawker's Drift. He'd imagined her laughing like that at his jokes; nose wrinkled, eyes half-closed, head thrown back, riotous hair rippling down her back. He'd had a faint, faraway smile on his face all the way home. In fact, he'd had it right up to the moment he'd sauntered into the Throne Room and Lorna had started screaming at him.

However, it had completely vanished by the time she'd thrown an empty bourbon bottle at him.

He remembered crawling into bed that night, burying his face in the pillow and weeping. The linen must have been freshly laundered as he'd been able to faintly taste the soap as he'd bit the pillow to stifle his sobs. Even from across the landing and beneath the haze of another day's booze Lorna might have heard and he hadn't wanted to give her the satisfaction.

Had that been the lowest point of his life? Possibly, though there were so many to choose from, he couldn't entirely be sure.

He collected the papers up and shuffled them into a neat little pile. Now Lorna was gone, there was no one to shout at him, to scream at him and throw things at him. He should be happy, but he wasn't, thanks to that wretched gunslinger.

He slipped the papers into a folder and filed them away. The drawer clicked shut and that should have been that. A closed door on the past. Everything was done, dusted and tickety. Time to move on.

Furnedge stood up, rubbed his neck and looked out of the window. He was late for work. So what? Miss Dewsnap would flap around like a headless chicken, of course, but otherwise, who cared? Things were different now. He'd never been late for work; he'd always prided himself on being a punctual man, a reliable, conscientious man. A man people could rely on. It had also been a good excuse to get out of the house and away from Lorna. Now the house was empty and quiet. The Throne Room was vacant, filled with light and air instead of smoke, darkness and his own personal tyrant. Now he could do what he liked.

The morning was bright and warm. It was shaping up to be a hot summer. They usually were in Hawker's Drift. Hot summers, cold winters. Furnedge found both oppressive, but, unlike his wife, there wasn't much he could do about the weather. Even the Mayor's influence didn't stretch that far. Probably.

His eye caught a woman strolling by, Nancy Milligan, her face shaded by a wide-brimmed hat, the rest of her body by her skirts and blouse, long sleeved and done up to the collar. He thought about what lay beneath. Milky white skin, smooth and soft. He closed his eyes. She was passably attractive and married to a brainless dolt with a flattened nose and no front teeth. Another woman who never noticed Guy Furnedge.

He took a deep breath. That would change.

"This is the first day..." he muttered "...and things are a changing."

He would go and see Molly soon and make it clear to her, in no uncertain terms, what he could offer her. He could pay her debts off; he could give her comfort, security, respectability. He could also offer her an impeccably intact and working cock too. What could that worthless gunslinger offer her? Nothing. And that would mean the whorehouse for her.

He pushed his despondency aside. That should be in the past. That should be in his desk drawer with Lorna's will and

45

in the ground like Lorna's body. He didn't need to sob into his pillow anymore. The future was going to be a better country.

Guy Furnedge smiled to himself as he spotted Amy coming up the street. She would be surprised he hadn't gone to work yet. It wasn't the only thing she was going to be surprised about when she got here. Guy sniggered and felt his heart beat faster. It was high time she was told the terms of her employment were going to be renegotiated. He rubbed his fingers over his groin.

Yep, times were definitely a changing...

The Secretary

"Mr Furnedge!"

Eudora Dewsnap's jaw and the files she's been holding both hit the floor at the same time.

"Whatever happened?" She cried, trailing him into his office.

"Nothing," he muttered with a shake of the head, dropping his case casually enough for it to topple onto its side. Which wasn't like him at all.

"But your face?"

He touched the livid and swollen skin beneath his eye and winced, "It's nothing..."

"Mr Furnedge, it most certainly isn't nothing. Have you been... *assaulted?*"

"Assaulted?"

"You look like... well... like someone has punched you in the face?"

He stared at her, touched his eye again and eased himself into his chair, "Punched? No, no... I... I... slipped. Slipped coming down the stairs and banged my face. Too much hurry Miss Dewsnap," he sighed and looked, for a moment, utterly forlorn, "far, far too much haste."

"Oh dear..." she wrung her hands and hovered over him.

As if the poor man hadn't suffered enough already. The loss of his wife had evidently left him bereft, he'd been so devoted to her after all, and now he'd fallen down the stairs. Something that could happen to anyone she supposed, but it was a worrying sign. He had endured his loss so manfully and resolutely, but now, alone in that house with so many painful memories anything might happen. Grief was a terrible thing after all.

"Shall I call for Dr Rudi?"

"No, no... " Furnedge shook his head and waved his hand, "...it's just a bruise Miss Dewsnap. It looks far worse than it is."

She smiled and nodded, "Of course."

That was Guy Furnedge. Never one to make a fuss. It was just one of his many admirable qualities.

Eudora leaned over and righted his case, it looked messy and out of place lying on its side, "Then I will go and fetch some ice, it will help with the swelling."

"There's no-"

She raised her hand. Being brave was commendable of course, but foolishness most certainly wasn't.

"It will help with the swelling" she repeated, sometimes it was necessary to put one's foot down, "a black eye does not look... professional."

"I suppose not... thank you, Miss Dewsnap."

He opened his case and pulled out some files.

Still taking work home with him.

He was a hardworking man was Guy Furnedge. Another admirable quality. She would have said he was busying himself to keep his mind from his recent misfortunes, but

48

then he'd always done that. Caring for his wife through her... illness. Of course Eudora knew, like the rest of the town, the exact nature of Lorna Furnedge's problems, but there was no need to think ill of the dead. A less admirable man than Guy Furnedge would have walked away long ago if half the things she'd heard had been true, but not Mr Furnedge. No, no, he had remained loyal until the very end.

So, utterly, admirable.

Of course, he deserved better. Not that it was her place to say of course. He was a married man and he'd upheld his vows. Not many men in the world like that, mores the pity. Of course, he wasn't a married man any longer.

She pushed *that* particular thought aside.

"Can I get you anything else?"

"No, no... really... thank you."

She remained at the edge of his desk, turning her hands one over the other. It was something she often found herself doing when she was worried or concerned and it always annoyed her to find herself doing it again. She took a breath and folded her arms.

"Is there anything you would like to talk about... Guy?"

Furnedge stopped rummaging in his case and looked up at her, a little frown wrinkling his forehead. She hadn't intended to be so familiar, but she liked to think of him as her friend as well as her employer.

And he is an unmarried man now after all...

"Talk? About?"

"You have suffered a terrible loss. A trauma! A tragedy! I know you are not a man who wears his heart on his sleeve. And that is very... admirable. But a burden shared..."

49

Furnedge's face twitched as if he were biting down on his tongue. Instead he sat back, pulled out the little cloth he kept in his jacket pocket and took off his spectacles. Which Eudora had always thought made him look much younger.

"Indeed Miss Dewsnap, but, truly, I am coping... life goes on after all."

"Yes, it must," she agreed, "but if there is anything you ever need... anything at all?"

"Thank you, Miss Dewsnap. I know I can rely on you."

He gave his spectacles a vigorous rub.

She smiled and noticed she'd started turning her hands over again. "Well, I'll get that ice for you." She'd been prattling on too long while poor Mr Furnedge suffered stoically. She couldn't cure his grief; time alone would do that, but a nasty bruise. That was something else entirely.

"Oh, there is one thing Miss Dewsnap," he called, slipping his spectacles back on.

"Yes?"

"I need a new maid... do you know any suitable women looking for work?"

"Oh... er... I can ask around. What about young Amy?"

"I had to let her go..." Furnedge shrugged "...she wasn't working out at all..."

The Gunslinger

Molly was sleeping next to Amelia when he got back; sitting on the bed, her chin on her chest, hair about her face. Amos stared at her, then he realised he was smiling, though he wasn't sure why. Amelia was curled up next to Molly, her breath wet and ragged. Even from the doorway he could see the sweaty sheen on the girl's skin.

His smile faded and he backed carefully out of the room. Molly hadn't slept much since Amelia had turned up on her doorstep.

He padded down the stairs; Mr Wizzle was in the rocking chair by the drawing room fire, his chins also on his chest as he snored. Amos gave him a rough shake as he passed before slumping into the chair opposite.

"Huh?" Mr Wizzle muttered, blinking and looking about him.

"We need to talk," Amos said, stretching out his legs and hooking one boot over the other.

"Of course, we must," Mr Wizzle nodded and leaned forward, before asking in an urgent hiss, "Did you get any eggs?"

"Yes."

"Pickled?"

"Fresh."

"Oh," Mr Wizzle settled back into the chair, "shame."

"Amelia?"

"She's still poorly, but she will recover."

Amos run a hand across his rough chin. He needed a shave though that wasn't his most pressing concern.

"I remember what you said, that day we found the dead animals."

"You do?"

"You met an old lady."

"Uh-huh."

"Called Amelia."

Mr Wizzle remained silent.

"Amelia Prouloux."

"You remembered? I'm so forgetful, just the other-"

"Something of a coincidence?"

Mr Wizzle hauled himself out of the chair, stretched his arms above his head and gave a long theatrical yawn, "Gosh I'm tired."

"Who is she?"

"I have no idea," he retrieved his derby which he'd hooked on to the back of the rocking chair, "other than that God sent her to us."

"What did the old woman say to you?"

"Oh..." he shrugged and put on his hat, "...I wasn't really listening. She babbled on like some folk do. A nice old lady, but she wasn't talking much sense."

Amos stared at him, "Don't lie to me. It doesn't work."

Mr Wizzle drew still and the smile faded from his lips, "No, I don't suppose it would."

"Out at the crossroads, you said she'd talked about me?"

"Oh, she rambled on about *someone* called Amos; I have no idea if it was you though."

He was still lying.

"What else did she say?"

"Just an old woman's recollections... probably didn't mean anything. Between you and me I think she was a little bit mad."

"Was she a black woman?"

Mr Wizzle nodded.

"They must be related, her grandmother?"

"Maybes..."

Mr Wizzle shuffled towards the door, "Well, I should be going home for a bit..."

Amos sprang up and put his palm flat against the door before the old man could open it.

"What aren't you telling me?"

"Nothing."

"You were happy enough to chat about this old woman a few days ago. Why so reticent now?"

Mr Wizzle just smiled and looked blank.

"Where did she go?"

"I don't know."

"How can you not know? You can see for miles out on the grass!"

"I dozed off, when I woke up she was gone..."

"And she wasn't with anyone?"

"Nope. I'd have noticed. Even an itsy bitsy little girl..."

Amos blew exasperated air out of his nostrils. There was something the old man wasn't telling him. Something important. He could almost taste the deceit in the air.

He stared into Mr Wizzle's bloodshot eyes that peered out from behind folds of ruddy flesh and gripped his shoulder. He hated doing it, but sometimes, just sometimes, it had to be done. He needed to know what this old clown was hiding. He knew something about Amelia in whatever passed for his brain and Amos needed to know what it was.

Mr Wizzle made no move to pull away, returning Amos' stare with a look of faint bemusement.

Sometimes it came easy, sometimes it didn't come at all and sometimes what you got wasn't of much use to anyone.

Amos sighed and let his fingers slip away.

He'd got something from Mr Wizzle, a memory that was solid, clear and almost overpowering. Something that was important to the strange old man, something Amos suspected he thought about an awful lot.

A jar of pickled eggs...

*

Amos paced through the house. It wasn't a large home and it didn't take long. He should just sit down, take a book from the shelf and wait for Molly to wake up, but he'd never been one for reading. Or being in a house. He felt contained within the walls and at a loss as to what to do.

Strange really.

He could spend hour after hour in the saddle. He could go days without talking to another living soul. Sometimes even seeing one. He never got bored. Never got restless. Never stared at his hands and thought he should be doing something useful. But here, he didn't have a clue.

He just wished Molly would wake up.

He'd warily climbed the stairs a few times, but Molly and Amelia were both sleeping, the girl curled up against her. He'd stood in the doorway and watched them. Or rather he'd watched Molly.

How had this happened, exactly?

He asked himself the same thing each time he watched her, and then hurried away when no obvious answer came. None he liked the sound of at any rate.

It would have been pretty obvious what he was doing if he'd still been a man. But he wasn't. He was something else entirely now. Was he even still a human being? Technically, he supposed, but he didn't feel like one. He didn't feel like the people he passed on the street or stood next to at the bar in *Jack's*.

He felt he was a lot less than any of them.

He should be alone. In his saddle staring at an empty horizon, where he couldn't do any harm. Till someone paid him enough to do some harm at least.

Instead, he was here. In this little house. With Molly and a sick girl who'd apparently appeared out of nowhere. His own peculiar little family.

He pushed the thought away. It was too painful.

Mr Wizzle, who he supposed qualified as the eccentric uncle, had hurried out of the house promising to return later. All of his questions unanswered.

Whoever Amelia was, he needed to find who she belonged to. There must be somebody in town, the old woman Wizzle had met he presumed. Amelia's grandmother. Perhaps they'd become separated from a wagon train, or were the survivors of an attack. An old woman and a little girl. Maybe some robbers might spare them, possibly...

Perhaps he should go and ask Shenan. If anything had happened close to town he would have heard. And it had to have been close to town, a little girl and an old woman couldn't have travelled far without horses or provisions. It had to be the answer. It made sense and Amos always liked things to make sense. Particularly in a world that generally made little.

He looked up at the ceiling, but Molly and Amelia were still asleep, he would talk to Shenan, maybe see if he could bump into Cece too. He didn't know why John thought she might be able to help, she could undeniably hold a note, but he doubted she could do much more than Molly in terms of healing the sick. Still it was another avenue to explore.

They needed to get Amelia back to where she came from because he was damn sure Molly wouldn't be leaving town with a sick little girl in her bed. He could see that in her eyes clear enough.

He grabbed his hat and headed for the door; he only needed an hour and would probably be back before Molly was awake.

Amos hadn't even got his hand around the latch before he realised he'd been wrong about that.

Molly's scream told him that much.

The Widow

Molly was still staring at Amelia when Amos burst into the room.

"What's wrong?" He demanded, looking around, one hand on his holstered gun.

"Amelia…" Molly whispered.

Amos frowned as he came over to the bed, leaning across to rest a hand on her forehead, "She's still hot," he muttered, eyes flicking from the unconscious girl to Molly.

"She…" Molly shook her head; she couldn't say it. He'd think she was fucking crazy.

Amos eased himself onto the edge of the bed. She wanted him to hold her, but that was probably asking too much.

"It's nothing," she shook her head, "I was just having a nightmare."

He stared at her, in the way he did when he thought people were lying to him.

She climbed off the bed and crossed to the window, her hands were shaking. It had been a dream hadn't it? It must have been. Of course. She was tired, stressed and worried. Nothing more.

Little girls, sick or otherwise, didn't disappear in front of your eyes did they? Not unless you were going mad at any rate.

The world outside seemed ordinary and sane enough. The window was open and a warm breeze was ruffling the curtains, Bruno was barking at something. Harry Shultz was carrying a couple of planks of wood down the street. The sun was shining and little girls did *not* fade away.

Amos stood behind her. Close for him, she wanted to feel his hand on her shoulder, his fingers, coarse, hard and reassuring. But of course, he didn't.

"Molly…"

"It was just a dream. Really."

"Molly…"

Damn him. Could he really know what went on in her head? That had to be bullshit didn't it? Mr Mysterio. She remembered that moment in the cells when she'd doubted him. When Shenan was describing exactly how Emily Godbold had been assaulted. The way he'd looked over at her, like he'd heard it and she'd let him down, just like the rest of the world. Had that been her imagination too, just like Amelia shimmering and fading, becoming as translucent as steam in sunlight? Fading till she could see the rumpled sheets beneath her.

"For a moment…" *oh hell this is going to sound crazy as hell* "…I thought Amelia was fading away."

Now he did put a hand on her shoulder, as light as a falling leaf, but there all the same.

"She's a strong little thing, she'll pull through."

Molly closed her eyes. That hadn't been what she'd meant.

"I know."

But it would do.

58

She reluctantly let his hand slip away and eased herself back into the chair by the bed.

"You should take a break."

Molly shook her head, "I'm fine... besides, I haven't got much else to do, have I?"

Amos shrugged and leant against the wall by the window.

"I can't leave," she murmured, "not while Amelia is... here."

"I figured... we got plenty of time."

"If the Mayor keeps to his word."

"And what happens when Amelia is better?"

"I don't know."

"We can't take her with us."

"And I'm not leaving her here. Alone. Not in this town."

"You don't know her Molly. She's not your responsibility."

She stared at him, feeling her features harden without quite knowing why, "She's in my bed, so she's my responsibility... till we find her people."

"I was going to see Shenan, see if he's heard anything. A wagon train being attacked... or something."

Molly nodded, "You think that's where she came from?"

"I dunno, but she doesn't seem to be from town, and she couldn't have come far on her own."

She pursed her lips, before asking in a hesitant voice, "Could you find out?"

"Well, I'll see Shenan like I-"

"No," she insisted, "can *you* find out?"

Amos looked at her blankly.

"Your... *Mysterio* thing?"

He raised an eyebrow.

"You said you can... pick things up?"

"Sometimes."

"Or was that just some rubbish to impress me?"

Amos' eyes widened slightly, "Molly... it doesn't impress people, it scares them. Scares me half the time..."

"Can you?" She insisted.

"It doesn't work with young children; their thoughts are too jumbled to read... even worse than women's."

Molly was going to swear but caught herself in time. She didn't want to cuss around Amelia, even if she was too far under to hear much.

"Thought as much," she said instead, sniffing.

"Thought what?"

"So much bull."

Bull didn't count as swearing. She was pretty sure about that.

"Molly, I don't really care if you believe me or not, I don't even know why I mentioned it in the first place. I feel enough of a freak anyway."

"You're not a freak," her voice softened and she smiled, "just tell me what I'm thinking."

Amos shuffled from one foot to the other, "I have no idea."

"Go on try; show me what you can do."

"Molly, this isn't some... fairground trick."

"I understand, but... I want to know if you really can do this... stuff?"

"My word isn't enough?"

"Of course not, you're a man."

"Only just."

"Don't."

"Ok," he said, coming over to take her hand, "think of a number."

She looked up at him and smiled, squeezing his hand in return, "Any number?"

"Anything between one and a million."

"Don't think I know that many numbers."

"Molly?"

"Alright." She screwed her eyes shut and thought real hard.

"Molly..." Amos sighed, "...I said a number, not a turnip."

Her eyes sprung open as she jerked her hands out of his, "Jesus fucking Christ!"

For the first time in days she completely forgot about Amelia.

*

Molly looked at Amos warily across the table.

A little girl that goes transparent and a cockless man who can read my mind.

Jesus, she used to think some of the scrapes Tom got her into were screwed up.

At least the old fat guy in the clown's suit had uprooted himself for the time being.

"You're spooked now, aren't you?" Amos asked.

They'd drunk coffee in silence, not that she really needed to say anything of course.

"You tell me?"

Amos pulled a pained face.

"Can you hear everything that goes on inside my head?"

"It doesn't work like that. Just bits and pieces, now and

again."

"Fuck..."

"Doesn't work with some people... usually stronger when I touch someone, though."

"Guess that's why you keep your distance then huh?"

"One of the reasons."

"One?"

"You know why?"

"We can't all read minds."

Amos sighed and scratched his chin, "Molly I like you..."

"I like you too."

"I mean..." he sat back in his chair "...I *like* you."

She looked at him blankly.

It must be so much easier if you can just read someone's mind.

"The kind of like that wouldn't be a problem if I was still... whole."

"Oh."

"Yeah. Oh."

"I *like* you too... if that is any help."

"I kinda figured that," Amos smiled, "and, no it isn't. Not really."

They shared an awkward moment's silence, before Molly asked, "When we're in bed, is it difficult?"

"I've spent the last thirteen years trying to be as far away from women as possible. So yeah, it's difficult."

"I meant the mind reading thing actually..."

"Oh... er, no. I don't pick up things when people are asleep. No thoughts I guess."

"Surprised you pick up anything when I'm awake – never

too many thoughts in my head."

Amos smiled, but it melted as quick as snow on a sunny morning.

"I should move back to the saloon, it might-"

"No."

"No?"

"I don't want that."

"Does it matter what I want?"

"No, not really," Molly smiled sweetly.

"You sure? Always wondering if I've picked up your thoughts?"

"There's nothing going on in my head that I've got a problem with you knowing."

Amos looked pointedly at her.

"Well, not much. I've always been a lousy liar anyway."

"Dunno about that."

"Bastard."

Amos snorted a little laugh and leant forward to fold his arms on the table, "I saw something else in your head when I took your hand, apart from a turnip."

"Really? I'm surprised. It's by far my favourite root vegetable."

"You couldn't just have picked a number?"

Molly shrugged, "I'm contrary."

"No argument with that."

"Bastard. Again."

"I saw Amelia…" he frowned, "…when you said she was fading away I thought you meant dying. You didn't, did you?"

Molly shook her head, "I must have been dreaming… I thought I woke up and when I looked down at her, I could see right through her. Like she was a ghost or something. But it must just have been a dream, right? I couldn't have been awake," she gave a little laugh. It seemed quite ridiculous now in the bright kitchen with empty coffee mugs in front of them.

"I don't see dreams Molly; only thoughts, feelings and memories."

Or maybe not so ridiculous.

The Gunsmith

Women are a foreign country to me.
A realm of mist-sheathed trees and half-remembered hills.
Of blue, glacial lakes and red, fiery mountains.
Women are a distant, distant, oh so distant land...

John X Smith sat in the darkness and thought about
women.

In truth, it wasn't an entirely unusual way for him to pass
his days. Never had been. Even when he'd been a busy man,
with responsibilities and duties, with weights upon his
shoulders; even when he'd had a future to think of.

A cute smile, a lingering look, the lightest of touches, the
heaviest of silences; tendrils of perfume snaking through the
air to twist about his limbs and ensnare him. Again.

He smiled at that. As if women had cast their mischievous
spells to trick and deceive and he was but a helpless,
innocent creature. Better to believe that than accept that he
was but a pawn to his lust and desire. The problem had been
that he hadn't *only* been a pawn to his lust, if he had of
been, then he might never have strayed from his bed and the
women he had decorated it with. He really hadn't needed to
do anything else; he'd been rich after all. He could have

spent his time bedding beautiful women and enjoying himself utterly. Most of his rich wasted friends had done that.

But he'd been cursed with a terrible curiosity that ran far beyond what lay beneath the folds of a woman's blouse and the turn of her smile. It would have been better if it hadn't.

He wondered how many people had died, in the end...

He ran a hand across his chin, his skin felt rough, like well-used sand paper. His face was thinner. Age fattened some people, others it hollowed out. It had hollowed him, in more ways than one. He looked younger than he actually was, a lot younger, but time was catching up with him all the same.

He stared into the darkness, little green lights looked back at him, steady, unblinking.

How many women had he been with over the years, here and before? A lot; more before than here, of course, but even in this little town...

He'd given up counting a long time ago.

Some he had liked; he'd even cared for a few. Most, though, had just been a pretty thing to use and amuse. All save for one of course. The one who had walked away and left him. The one who had broken the heart he'd never dreamed he'd possessed.

All so long ago, yet he had waited for her all the same. So many roads he could have run down after he'd done what he'd had to do. All the roads of the world. Yet he'd come here and grown old and become hollow.

He doubted she'd even recognise him now. He did look different; Bald, thinner, older, haunted...

He'd waited until he was a man she'd no longer know. Maybe for the best. She'd despise him if she knew what he'd done. When she found out what he'd done.

Maybe it was the punishment he deserved. Hawker's Drift was just a big prison after all, one with women to distract his mind and his guilt, even if its bars were cast from his own spurned love rather than iron.

He rose from his chair, his knees clicked and his spine was sore. He winced and rubbed the small of his back as he crossed to the window. As if he needed to be reminded that time was catching up with him at last.

A few people were about, going to and from the saloon mostly. He didn't venture inside much himself. Drinking had never been one of his major sins. A little nip from his flask usually sufficed. He didn't care for prostitutes either. Never had to. There was no pleasure to be had had from paying for a woman's favours. It had always been their desire that had inflamed him. Take that away and what was left? Mechanical, empty rutting as you stared into distant, uncaring eyes. No, that had never been for him.

He wondered where Kate was. Stupid thought. She was home with her family of course. Trying to mend what couldn't be mended. And ignoring the monsters that walked among them. That was a sin all the good folk of Hawker's Drift shared, but probably himself more than any of them.

There was a figure crossing Pioneer Square. His face was just a suggestion, the brim of his hat keeping the moonlight from his face, but John X recognised him well enough from his long canvas coat and slow, almost stiff-legged stride. Blane. Some men had a propensity for violence. Some chose it. Some liked it. Some couldn't resist it. And some, like Blane, were born to it. It crackled about him, a raw nervous energy that he tried to hide from the world. Most people were easy to fool, particularly those who wanted to be fooled. By the gunsmith saw it well enough. He saw all the monsters well enough.

Blane was heading towards the Mayor's pile. Town business no doubt. John X smiled, cold and humourless. No doubt at all.

He looked away, he'd become good at doing that during the long years he'd spent waiting in Hawker's Drift.

He threw open the window and leaned out. It was a warm night; a breeze caressed his skin, like a lover's breath. He stared across at the saloon. Distorted figures moved behind the frosted glass, hazy ghosts in the sallow glow of oil lamps. He could make out a voice singing above a piano's lament. Sad and distant like a love you knew you should better recall.

Cece Jones. She sang at this time every night.

He'd seen her in the saloon just once, through clouds of smoke, shuffling bodies and nodding heads. He hadn't gone back. Her voice broke his heart, which reminded him he was still human at least. There was way too much knowing in that young girl's voice. Too much heartbreak and loss for this world and any other. Couldn't anybody else hear it? Understand it? Feel it?

He closed his eyes like he did every night.

Had anybody seen him? Standing in his window, mumbling the words like a crazy, old fool trying to recite poems he'd learned as a schoolboy.

The love and hope that had brought him here were but an echo lost amongst the mountains of his past. The woman he had once loved, still did love he supposed, wouldn't know him anymore. That man was gone and only this hollow shell remained, lost and alone, closed off from the men and monsters of Hawker's Drift.

He could barely remember now, who he'd been and why he had done the things he had. He didn't understand women. Never had. Didn't know what they'd ever seen in him because, in truth, he'd never seen much himself. But now... now he didn't know himself anymore either, he was fading to nothing, held together by a memory he knew now he would never revive.

The man he had been was gone; he'd waited too long for a dream and a ghost from the past. Women had always been a distant land to him.

Now he was too.

The Farmer

I love her. I love her. I love her.

And what had she said, exactly? Her life was too messy. They were just friends. He was really nice.

Such a dull, unimaginative word isn't it? Nice?

Yeah, the Mayor had been right about that. It was dull and unimaginative. Seemed how Cece felt about Sye Hallows though. Poor old Sye. Losing out again.

To some less deserving fellow...

Sye shook his head as if that would be enough to shake loose the Mayor's words rattling around inside. He opened his eyes. The pile of horse shit hadn't gotten any prettier.

The stable was hot and stuffy, dust motes, illuminated by shafts of sunlight that snuck through ill-fitting planks, filled the air. There was a constant hum of flies darting around him and Sye was continually flicking them away from his face with agitated swipes.

The horses were out grazing, but they usually spent the night in the stables. The weather could turn foul quickly out here and they were safer from horse thieves locked in the stables too. Animals had a habit of disappearing if you left them on the grass long enough.

Keeping them in the stables also afforded him further shit

shovelling opportunities of course. And horse shit was a far nobler and more useful commodity than mere cow shit.

He threw his shovel aside in disgust and wandered outside to find something more appealing to stare at. Cows, grass, sky, fence, barn. The options were as limited as ever. He settled for the sky. At least the clouds changed and, unlike him, they were going somewhere. Even if it was just to rain on someone.

He vaulted a fence and took a couple of strides into the field beyond then plonked himself down on the grass after checking there was no dung to dunk his backside in.

Why couldn't she just want him? Why, just for once, couldn't life be easy?

Instead, he had to fall for a girl who wasn't interested in him. Fall? Crash was a better word; crashed headlong through a plate glass window and straight into the welcoming maw of a meat grinder.

He sat, cross-legged, in the grass with his eyes screwed shut, listening to the wind and trying to think of something, anything, other than Cece Jones. He failed miserably. When he opened his eyes, he found the Mayor's little black bottle resting in his palm.

Love potion indeed!

Sye snorted, what kind of a fool did the Mayor take him for? He should toss the silly thing away. It was bad enough being the town's resident lovesick halfwit without everyone sniggering at him as well for falling for some absurd little prank that the Mayor had decided to play.

He stared at the bottle nestling in his palm. Yes, he should definitely throw it away. Instead, he found his thumb was gently stroking it.

He couldn't actually remember taking it out of his pocket, but it had found its way into his palm regardless. Actually, come to think about it, he couldn't remember putting the bottle in his pocket either. Hadn't he left it nestling at the bottom of a drawer? Cocooned in his misbegotten collection of worn, darned, hole-riddled, sweat sullied old socks.

Surely the perfect resting place for a love potion?

Love made you forgetful, he supposed. As well as bloody miserable.

Sye turned the bottle over in his hands. It seemed heavier than it should, for such a little thing. Warmer too. It had been in his pocket while he'd been working up a sweat rearranging horseshit, but it always seemed warm, even when it had been nestling in his sock drawer. Odd.

What if it really was... what the Mayor said it was? Something to make his heart's desire come true. Would he even want that? What if she swooned into his arms after he'd put a few drops in her drink? More likely she would just puke spectacularly over his shirt. That was more in keeping with the way his particular world worked, but if she did... then what? It wouldn't actually be real; she wouldn't truly love him, would she? It would just be a trick. A trick that would fool the world, but most importantly a trick that would fool him too. Could he be happy with that?

Sye laughed, despite himself and tossed the bottle from one hand to the other. A love potion. *Really!*

It had come to a sorry state of affairs that he'd even consider such nonsense. Why was he sitting on his ass weighing up the moral dilemmas of using a love potion? It wasn't a love potion, it was a little bottle full of - he held it up against the sunlight and gave it a little shake – *something.*

A little bottle full of nothing more likely.

Sye hauled himself to his feet and shook his head along with the bottle. Whatever was sloshing around inside, it wasn't going to make Cece fall in love with him. He guessed only he could do that. After a moment's hesitation, he pulled back his arm and hurled the bottle across the field, squinting against the sun as it spun beneath the bright blue sky before disappearing into the grass. Perhaps it would help one of the cows find love.

He snorted and headed back to the barn, it wasn't going to help him find love and it certainly wasn't going to help him shovel horse shit.

*

Cece was laughing; her nose wrinkled and her sparkling eyes half-screwed shut. She was leaning forward; close enough for a few soft curls to brush against his face. The sunlight was making a halo through her hair. Her fingers were resting lightly on his arm. She tilted her face towards him; her laughter subsiding to a gossamer smile. Her eyes opened wide to stare at him, before closing as she tilted her head to one side and leaned up to brush her –

"Sye!"

He opened his eyes with a start. Ma was standing over him. It had just been a dream. Damn...

"Don't just sit about snoring, if you're tuckered out get off to bed with you!"

Tuckered out. Hell, he was always tuckered out. He heard the old timers in *Jack's* bemoaning the fact they were always tired and wistfully recalling when they were young and so full of energy they could work all day, drink all night and be able to jump out of bed with the cockerel's first cry to do the same again the next day. Either Sye was old before his time or they were all full of bullshit because he was permanently as tired as a fat old dog during the swelter of a summer's afternoon.

His neck ached, his back ached, his arms ached, his head ached. Not forgetting his heart of course. That ached worse than the rest put together.

He pulled himself up from the chair. Bed was the one place he could be sure to be left alone to find a few hours' peace at least.

"You sickening for something boy?" Ma peered at him as he brushed past her.

"Just a hot day... drained me dry," he muttered.

"Well, an early night will see you good... you been going into town too much of an evening. That's the root of it."

Cece would be singing now of course. He paused and looked back at his Ma, wishing he was there. Sitting close to her, letting her soft, haunting voice wash over him. A sea of honey to soothe away his cares and salve his pains.

"Yeah, maybes..."

"Sye..."

"Huh?" He turned back from the doorway. Ma looked fretful. He didn't need a lecture tonight. Really he didn't.

"I was talking with Mrs Monza this morning... she said you were seeing some girl from the saloon?"

Connie Monza, a woman who gnawed at gossip like a cow chewed the cud. No doubt she'd come galloping across the grass eager to let his Ma know her son was up to no good with a saloon floozy.

"I'm not seeing anyone Ma..." he wanted to leave it at that, but she would only keep worrying at it till she got the truth of the matter. She had a habit of working herself up into a lather of anxiousness. Which would just make his life even more miserable.

"There's a girl there. She just sings, nothing else, she's not... you know... She's a nice girl."

His Ma raised an eyebrow and looked unconvinced.

"I like her, she..." he shrugged "...only *likes* me. Ain't nothing else..."

"Well..." she sighed and Sye braced himself for the lecture "...I'm sorry to hear that."

"You are?" Sye blinked.

"Mrs Monza says she's a helluva pretty girl and sings like an angel..."

"She is... does..."

"...and that everyone can see how smitten you are with her."

Oh great...

He wasn't entirely sure what to say, so settled for wrapping his fingers around the door frame and letting his eyes slide away from his mother's.

"Don't give up hun, you'll find someone real nice."

"I guess."

"You sure this girl ain't interested?"

"Pretty sure."

76

"Sometimes... sometimes a girl don't necessarily mean what she says. Some girls like to be... *wooed?*"

Hadn't the Mayor said something similar?

"I think she's a straight up kind of girl, anyways, don't think she knows anything much about cows or farms or... anything useful."

His Ma took a half step forward, "Sye, I just want you to be happy."

This seemed like news to Sye.

"I thought you wanted me to find a good practical girl, who knows how to roll her sleeves up and do a day's work."

"Of course!" his Ma's eyes softened, "don't mean she can't be pretty though."

"You feeling ok Ma?" Sye wondered if she'd been at the whiskey.

She scurried across the room and placed a hand on his arm, "You'll find someone, just you see."

Sye felt himself blushing, "Sure Ma... night..."

His Ma dug her fingers into his arm, "Why don't you ask this girl out again. You never know..."

"I... didn't think you'd approve of her... working in the saloon an all."

"She ain't a whore is she?"

Sye felt his blush deepen, "No course not, but still..."

"I'll have my opinions boy and I'm happy to share em. You know that. But the thing I really don't approve of is you being unhappy. And you been as miserable as an unmilked cow these last few days."

"I guess,"

"So?"

"So?" Sye repeated with a frown.

"So go get your udders pulled boy!"

He felt like his face was going to combust.

*

Sye placed the candle on the little table and let out a long, slow sigh as he flopped down on his bed.

What had gotten into Ma?

He would have put serious money (if gambling weren't such a sinful business) on Ma being horrified that he had been trying to woo someone like Cece Jones. A sweet slip of a girl who looked like she wouldn't know one end of a cow from another and made a living by singing in a saloon. Yet, she had seemed... encouraging?

Pity it all counted for nought.

Ma could be as encouraging as she liked, but it wasn't going to get Cece to fall for him. Nothing was.

...the sweetest candy anyone ever did taste...

Sye found his eyes drawn to the dark window though he could see nothing but his blurry reflection. The bottle was gone and good riddance. He wasn't going to go crawling around in the grass to find it. He wasn't quite that big a fool.

Maybe he would go and see Cece again though... maybe Ma was right and she just needed a little more wooing. Probably not, but best to be sure. At least he'd get to hear her sing again and that was something. Not enough maybe, but certainly something. Yeah, he'd go and listen to Cece sing tomorrow, Ma could hardly complain, not with her encouraging him an all.

Sye thought about listening to Cece sing and for the first

time that day felt something that might just have been in spitting distance of happiness.

Silly fool.

He dragged himself to his feet, stifling a yawn as he did. Lord, he was bushed. He was going to sleep like a baby tonight.

He pulled his jacket off and tossed it towards the chair in the corner as he battled with another yawn. Sye glared at the traitorous garment as it slid off and crumpled on the floor. He was half inclined to leave it there, but after pulling off his shirt and pants and throwing them over the back of the chair he bent over and scooped the jacket up. He froze, jacket hanging from his hand.

There was a little black bottle standing upright on the floor.

The jacket fell forgotten from his grasp. The bottle must have slipped from the pocket, except, of course, the bottle hadn't been in his pocket. He'd flung it away. He remembered throwing it; he remembered watching it turn head over tail as it had sailed off over the grass, black glass glinting against a cornflower sky.

He remembered the little tug of protest as he'd flung it away and he noticed the distant flutter of relief deep inside him now too.

With hesitant shaking fingers he picked the bottle up. It was slightly warm. It was familiar. It was comforting. His thumb stroked the smooth, perfect glass.

It was very, very wrong.

Sye sagged down on the edge of the bed. He had thrown it away... he had. Except, he couldn't have. Could he? It had been in his pocket all the time. He must have just dreamed he'd thrown it away. That must be what had happened. He'd sat in the grass and nodded off. Just for a few minutes, just to have a funny little dream about throwing the Mayor's bottle away. A peculiar little dream that's all...

And a damn realistic one too...

He closed his fist around the bottle and lifted it to his forehead.

Sweet candy.

It was probably just a joke, but everyone was laughing at him swooning over Cece anyway. So where was the harm? Maybe it would work. Maybe she would be his and then he...

...could get his udders pulled...

...would be happy and everything in the world would be perfect. As it was meant to be. Sye Hallows and Cece Jones. Together. Now that would be a thing. Wouldn't it now?

Sye closed his eyes.

I love her. I love her. I love her.

The Songbird

She kept thinking about Sye. Why did she feel guilty?

He liked her; she didn't feel the same way about him. It wasn't exactly the first time that had ever happened. The first time she'd ever used someone because of it though. She thought back to her university days. Probably.

What was she supposed to do? Let him fuck her by way of a thank you?

She thought back to her university days...

Cece let out an exasperated sigh and rolled over onto her side. Her sorry excuse for a bed groaned in protest but managed to stay intact.

She needed to get out of town again; there was more land to check. A lot more. The sooner she could get it done, the sooner she could get home. Or at least try to get home.

Sye might want to go riding again?

No. It wasn't fair.

Yeah, being fair had been a real big part of her training, hadn't it?

She rolled over onto her back again. Now she was having conversations with herself.

Cece let her eyes drift across her little attic room. Nothing much had changed. What if she couldn't get home? What if she got stuck here, forever?

Guess you'll have to learn some more songs.

And not spend so much time hiding in a pokey little room with nothing but dust motes for company.

She shook the thought away. She'd get the job done, she'd get home and Quayle would be waiting for her. Did the last one matter so much? If she really loved him why did she leave in the first place? Why take the chance that she'd never see him again?

She suspected it had never really been love, more infatuation; he was smart, successful and worldly wise. He was also pretty amazing in the sack. When he'd asked her to marry him she'd said yes without much thought. Then she passed all her tests and got accepted and being Mrs Quayle suddenly seemed a lot less important. And maybe even a bit more frightening than coming here.

A tentative rap on the door pulled her thoughts away from the past.

Cece frowned. She wasn't due to sing for a couple of hours yet and nobody came to see her up here; unless it was Monty trying to persuade her to dress like a slut again.

"Coming!" She called after taking a moment to decide whether or not she wanted to pretend to be out. She patted down her hair, made sure her skirt wasn't tucked into her knickers and nothing was hanging out that shouldn't be. Just in case it was a customer looking for one of the saloon girls. Cece shuddered at the thought.

"Miss," Amos nodded as she peered around the door.

"Amos! How are you?" She said, far too brightly.

He seemed to think about the question, turning his hat

over in his hands a couple of times, "I'm quite well."

"Can I help you?"

"Sorry to trouble you Miss, but could I have a word."

"Of course, I'll come down..."

"In private?"

"Oh?"

"I don't mean to impose-"

"No, no..." she swung open the door and beckoned him in. Of all the men in Hawker's Drift she could invite into her room Amos was the least likely to jump on her. All things considered. She smiled and felt guilty for the thought. She was doing a lot of that lately.

"Cosy," Amos said after she'd closed the door and he'd found a spot he could stand in without having to stoop.

"That wouldn't be my first choice of words to describe it," she sighed and sat on the edge of the bed, waving her hand at the room's one chair.

Amos gingerly lowered himself into it; thankfully it didn't collapse under him.

"I'd offer you a drink..." Cece shrugged, "...but the amenities are fairly basic here."

"I've stayed in worse."

Cece decided not to speculate how.

"I'm glad that... other business was sorted out."

"Me too."

"You'll have to forgive me... it's been a while since I entertained a gentleman in my room."

Amos raised an eyebrow and Cece laughed, she was forgetting where she was. Again.

"Just a joke, I'm a nice girl really."

"Oh... I didn't think..."

"It's ok, I'm sure my reputation will survive. You're not staying here anymore?"

Amos shook his head and looked at his feet, "No... I moved in with... a friend."

"Mrs McCrea?"

Amos nodded.

"I heard. You pick up all the gossip in a saloon."

"I bet."

She wondered if she should mention the other thing she'd heard about him, but thought better of it. She supposed it didn't really count as polite conversation. Poor man.

Amos looked up and gave her a little smile. His eyes seemed incredibly sad.

"So..." she coughed, "...is this just a social call?"

"Social call?" He frowned.

There I go again.

"Just... dropping in to say hello?"

"Erm... no... look, this is probably a waste of your time and you'll think I'm crazy but..."

Cece's eyes widened slightly.

Oh god, he's not going to ask me out is he?

Amos paused, frowned even more heavily and looked deeply uncomfortable.

"I'm sure I won't think you're crazy," Cece offered.

"There's this little girl..."

"Little girl?"

"She's staying with Molly... Mrs McCrea... and me I suppose. She was found lost, wandering in the street. She's really sick, some kind of fever, been unconscious for days and she's not getting any better. Not sure how much longer she can last. She's just a little slip of a thing really..."

"Where are her family?"

"Don't know. No one in town seems to know her. Anyway... I heard... you might be able to help?"

Cece stared at him blankly, "Me?"

"Uh-huh."

"I'm a singer, not a doctor."

Amos sighed, "That's what I thought."

"What makes you think..."

"Just something someone said."

"Who?"

Amos scratched his ear and stood up, "It doesn't matter... look I'm really sorry to trouble you."

Cece climbed to her feet, "No trouble... this girl, how old is she?"

"Seven or eight. Maybes. I'm not real good with kids..."

"Me neither." Quayle had been terribly keen on kids. Another reason she'd left him she supposed. "Someone in town must know her; she couldn't have walked here on her own?"

Amos gave a twitch of his shoulders as he turned for the door.

"That's what I thought, gonna see the Sheriff again, see if he's had any word of travellers being attacked nearby, but no one in town knows a thing about her. It's like she appeared out of thin air."

"Thin air?" Cece felt cold all of a sudden.

"Well, not literally."

"Hang on," she said, "let me get my bag."

The Gunslinger

Cece was puzzled and confused. It filled her mind like a cloying autumn fog. He'd thought the gunsmith had sent him on a fool's errand, but it seemed she did know something about Amelia after all.

Once she'd grabbed her satchel, Cece wanted to know everything about Amelia. Which didn't really amount to a great deal. He recounted the story as they hurtled down the stairs, though he didn't mention the bit about the girl becoming transparent (too crazy).

She almost ploughed into Monty on the final flight of stairs.

"Hey!" he shouted, "Where are you off to? You're on in an hour or so."

"Monty, I'm your employee, not your damned prisoner," she shot back with a glare that Molly would have been proud of.

"Sure, sure," Monty threw up his arms as they hurried by, "Just make sure you're back in time."

"You gonna dock my wages if I'm not?"

Monty just scowled by way of a reply.

"Miserable old skinflint," Cece muttered, not *quite* loudly enough for him to hear.

The saloon was filling up for another evening's drunken debauchery. The usual suspects flopped against the bar, while the other drinkers, diners, gamblers and fornicators were scattered around the tables. Amos recognised most of them from the mob that had wanted to lynch him last week.

This evening he elicited no more than a few cursory glances. It appeared he'd gone from the mysterious stranger who'd been seduced by a sex-mad widow, to an evil child rapist, to a freak show curiosity. He was looking forward to returning to obscurity.

As they reached the bottom of the stairs, Amos noticed one figure sit up and take more than a cursory interest in them; Sye Hallows. The young man's face was a mask, just not a particularly convincing one. He was trying to conceal his shock and anger, though if he clutched his beer any tighter the glass was liable to explode.

Amos sighed to himself. Coming down from the bedrooms with Cece, he could see how that might look, especially to a young man who thought he was in love. Easy enough to put two and two together and come up with five. Or even six given he was physically incapable of fucking the love of Sye Hallows' life even if he'd wanted to.

As misfortune would have it, they had to pass Sye's table to get out of the saloon. Amos didn't like the expression on his face, which was about as dark a look as a man got without a gun in his hand. Or a cut throat razor.

Surely he wasn't going to have two men trying to kill him in the same saloon in a week?

"What's the rush?" Sye painted a smile on his face and slowly uncurled his fingers from his beer.

Cece jerked around, "Oh, Sye didn't see you there... just gotta run an errand before I sing."

"With him?" Sye demanded, eyes bouncing back and forth between them.

Cece's smile faltered a little.

"With me," Amos replied when Cece didn't.

"Well, have a great night," Sye sneered, reaching for his beer again.

"Sye, we're not on a date!" Cece snapped.

"I'm just concerned about you," Sye said carefully, "being your *friend* an all."

"I'm touched, but I'm a big girl and who I spend my time with is my business, not yours. C'mon Amos," Cece turned on her heels and stomped out of the room.

"Least you didn't get your face slapped," one of the barflies quipped, rubbing his cheek to a smattering of laughter.

Sye was going a pronounced shade of red. Anger and embarrassment were never a good combination. Amos leaned over the young man. He wasn't well qualified to give relationship advice on account of being an itinerant killer. His dealings with other human beings hadn't stretched much beyond whether to order the pie or the stew over the past thirteen years. However, he'd enough shit to deal with already without having to worry if this jealous lovesick pup might take a shot at him.

"Son," Amos hissed (advice always worked best when you started by patronising the person you were giving it to) "if you want that girl, you're going the wrong way about it."

Sye half rose, mouth opening to protest, but he caught sight of something cold and hard in Amos' eyes and slumped back down.

"It's none of your goddamn business, but there's nothing going on here. In case you ain't heard I'm not exactly equipped for it even if she was interested. Which she ain't. So don't be giving me any more of your shit, I've put men in the dirt for a lot less. Understand?"

Sye gave a curt little nod.

"Understand?" Amos repeated with a hiss, knuckles resting on the table as he loomed further over the young man.

"Sure, I understand."

"Good, now just buy the girl some damn flowers and start acting like a man."

Amos nodded and wheeled away.

Cece was waiting for him on the boardwalk.

"What did you say to him?" she asked as Amos let the doors slam behind him.

"Just a bit of advice, I think I've put him straight on a few things."

"Really?"

"I think so."

As they headed off Amos tried to figure out why Sye had been thinking so intently about a little black bottle...

*

"People keep looking at us..."

"Welcome to the world of notoriety," Amos muttered.

"But you didn't have anything to do with that rape."

"Yeah, funny huh? You'd have thought they'd be used to cockless men moving in with drunk, foul-mouthed widows by now."

"Oh," Cece winced, "sorry."

"Don't worry, after thirteen years of having to pretend I'm a fully functional male it's almost refreshing to have everybody know otherwise. Almost..."

Cece stared at her feet as they walked down Main Street

Boy, do I know how to kill a conversation...

After a couple of minutes of trying to pretend nobody was hissing whispers to their companions about the former evil sex fiend and the beautiful songbird...

How does he get all the good-looking ones anyhow? Him with no... you know?

...Cece looked at him out of the corner of her eye, "How are things with you and Mrs McCrea?"

Sometimes silence and stares aren't so bad...

"You're doing that thing women do, aren't you?"

Cece's eyes widened, "Pardon me?"

"Taking an interest in... *relationships*."

"Or being nosey – boy how my days drag when I have no new gossip to amaze the drunks slung along Monty's bar with."

"You'll have to excuse me; it's been a long time since I've been in anything within touching distance of a relationship."

"How close are you to one now?"

It was Amos' turn to stare at his feet, "I dunno, kinda... difficult."

"I can imagine," Cece winced again "...sorry, that's shit, I can't even begin to imagine."

"First time I've heard you swear. I thought you were a nice young lady."+

Cece laughed, "Oh, you have no idea."

For an instant an image of writhing, naked bodies flashed into Amos' mind, their laughter and cries so loud that he half stumbled.

"You ok?"

"Yeah..." Amos coughed, feeling his face flush slightly.

God, he hated knowing what went on in people's minds. For the most part it was mundane, banal crap, but sometimes you caught sides to people you never would have dreamed of.

"I don't mean to pry," she smiled, before adding, "I've said that before haven't I?"

"Yep," Amos nodded, "didn't believe you the first time neither."

"Mrs McCrea has something of a reputation – from what I hear."

"Her bark's worse than her bite."

"She's not going to start screaming at me – is she?"

Amos laughed, "No, she's..."

Just how do I think of her?

"...rather sweet."

Cece just smiled.

Oh for pity's sake.... Sweet?

"Seems a bit scary to be honest..."

"She's not scary at all. I'm sure you'll like her once you get to know her... really..."

The Widow

I don't like her at all...

She was too pretty by half, for a start, even with the dowdy clothes. Did she think she didn't even have to try?

Quite what Amos thought he was doing in bringing her home with him she couldn't imagine, not that she ever had much idea went on in that strange old head of his anyway. She'd just seen off Doc Rudi when Amos got back, the little singer from the saloon in his wake.

"He have anything to offer?" Amos asked, nodding in Rudi's direction as he disappeared down the street.

"Fussed around, took some blood and tutted. Not much more."

"Took blood?" Cece frowned once Molly had ushered them into the drawing room.

"Erm yeah... for tests he said."

Molly shot Amos a look.

W*hat-is-she-doing-here?*

"Molly this is Cece... I think she might be able to help with Amelia?"

"You're from the saloon, huh?" Molly asked, her voice was as cold and unwelcoming as a collapsed roof in a blizzard.

Cece beamed, "Just for the moment – lovely home you

have."

"Thank you, so you help sick children as well as sing?"

She could feel Amos staring at her, he obviously hadn't been around her long enough to work out she hated surprises. He'd said he was going to check in with Shenan about Amelia and had come back with this too pretty by half singer instead.

"I used to work in a hospital... back east."

"Really?" Molly felt her eyebrow arch.

"Look, I need to get back and sing soon or Monty will... explode or something. Can I take a quick look at this girl?"

Molly bit her tongue.

Oh, I'm sorry, so grateful you could squeeze us in though....

"Sure," Amos stepped in, "she's upstairs." Molly noticed the way Amos lightly touched the girl's arm as he steered her towards the stairs.

He's never so keen to put his hands on me.

Perhaps he liked what he saw in Cece's head more.

Amos glanced back questioningly at her.

She was being a bitch, she knew. But knowing something and doing something about it were not the same thing at all.

How much of this was Amos getting she wondered as she trailed up the stairs, Amos' ass bobbing up and down in front of her. Was she so sure there was nothing in her head that she wanted to keep out of his?

Cece stood by Amelia, tying back her blonde hair before leaning over the girl. Amos hovered at her shoulder while Molly remained in the doorway and fought down the urge to demand to know why the fuck Amos had brought this little slip of a girl into her home. Apart from the fact she was disconcertingly pretty of course.

She shook the thought away. It wasn't fair. She couldn't, off the top of her head, think of another man such a thought would be unfair of, but in Amos' case she was sure whatever was behind this it wasn't good old familiar male lust.

Of course if it was, she'd scratch the bastard's eyes out.

She frowned.

Really?

Just how much *did* she like this guy, exactly?

"Well?"

Cece was resting her hand on Amelia's damp brow and Molly fought down the urge to tell her Doc Rudi had already done that. Or that she'd already done it too, pretty much every ten minutes since Amelia had washed up at her door in Mr Wizzle's arms.

"I don't know," Cece offered, straightening up. She had a satchel across her and she was fidgeting with the strap as she turned towards them.

"Just like the rest of us then?"

"Can you give me a couple of minutes alone with the girl?"

Molly took a step into the room.

"Why?"

"I need to examine her properly."

"That little girl's got nothing I ain't seen before."

"Please," Cece insisted, eyes flicking in Amos' direction, "just a minute or two."

"Sure," Amos replied before Molly could spit anything else out.

Cece nodded her thanks and turned back to Amelia as if the matter was settled.

She felt Amos's fingers clamp around her forearm before she could protest, "We'll be downstairs."

Molly opened her mouth to object to being ordered out of her own bedroom for no obvious purpose, but Amos pushed a finger against his lips and manoeuvred her out of the door. She considered kicking his shin but decided to hold fire until they were downstairs.

"What the fuck is going on?" She demanded once they were back in the drawing room.

"Cece's just trying to help," Amos hissed, he sounded annoyed, which wasn't like him at all.

"That girl's no more a doctor than I am – what's going on?"

Amos gave her a long look, the kind he gave out when he was doing that thinking stuff of his.

"John suggested it."

"John X? The gunsmith?"

"Uh-huh."

"You mean the biggest sucker for a cute face in Hawker's Drift?"

"I don't think this is part of a scheme to bed her Molly."

"I wouldn't be so sure, from the things I've heard-"

"And the gossips of Hawker's Drift are such reliable judges of character. Aren't they Mrs McCrea?"

She puckered her lips, he had a point. She really hated it when someone had a point.

"Even so... what can she do?" Molly waved her hand at the ceiling "and why does she need to do it alone?"

"I don't know," Amos muttered and slumped into the rocking chair by the fire.

"What do you know about her?"

"She's got a great voice."

"Don't be facetious Amos. I do it a whole lot better."

"I trust her."

"What do you *know* about her," Molly repeated, "and don't give me that crap about women's minds again," she snapped as Amos started to speak.

"You sure you can't read minds too?"

"Nope. Just female intuition and a lifetime of listening to men's bullshit."

Amos looked pained, then thoughtful. Thinking. Again. What the hell *was* the attraction with doing that?

"I've seen... things..." he offered, eventually.

"In her head?"

Amos raised his eyes to the ceiling as if he could see where Cece was, which she was pretty sure he couldn't do. At least he hadn't mentioned that being one of his unlikely talents anyway.

"Uh-huh."

"What kind of... things?"

"I dunno..." Amos sighed, "...strange stuff."

"Stranger than turnips?"

"Much stranger."

"Fuck," Molly muttered, "the sick bitch."

A smile flitted across Amos' face and he looked at the window.

"You going to tell me more?" Molly asked, easing herself into the free seat by the fire and hunkering forward.

"No."

"Why not?"

"Would you like me to tell people the stuff that goes on in

your head?"

"Most people aren't that interested in turnips."

"Even so... besides I'm not entirely sure I understand what I saw anyway."

"Now you're intriguing me."

"I only get fragments, usually... sometimes what I see doesn't mean what it seems to."

Molly looked at him blankly.

"Like reading one random page from a book and trying to work out what the whole story is about."

"I understand. I think... but what have you seen that makes you think she can help Amelia?"

"I don't know. Honestly. But John thought she could help... and he knows more about this town than he lets on."

"More mind reading?"

Amos shook his head, "John X is a blank."

"A blank?"

"Someone I get nothing from..."

"Like the Mayor?"

Amos shifted in his seat and looked troubled, "The Mayor's not a blank... he's just... *different.*"

"He's an oily little creep, but that ain't entirely unique."

They both looked up as the bedroom door opened and closed, followed by footsteps on the stairs.

"It seems the beautiful and comely young doctor has finished her rounds," Molly muttered, hoisting herself to her feet, "I wonder what her prognosis is?"

Amos gave her a dark look, "Don't be-"

"Such a bitch?" she finished for him. "Why ever not? I'm rather good at it."

He settled for giving her a dark and lingering look by way of a reply as Cece opened the door, distractedly flicking a stray hair from her face.

"Well?" Molly demanded.

Cece puckered her lips and gave a series of rapid little nods, "She's going to be fine."

"Fine? Really? Oh, that's reassuring, I can stop worrying now."

Cece's smile faltered, "She has a fever, it will pass. It's not as serious as it looks," she turned her big, blue eyes towards Amos, "trust me."

Well, no doubt that cute smile and the bright eyes worked on most men, but Amos wasn't most men.

"Thanks... we really appreciate you coming to take a look," Amos almost gushed.

Men! For fuck's sale!

"Look I've got to get back to the saloon, but if anything... strange happens with the girl. Let me know."

Like becoming transparent?

Molly glanced at Amos, had he told the girl about that? She didn't want the town thinking she was barking mad on top of everything else.

"Sure, we'll do that."

Amos saw her out; Molly went as far as the foot of the stairs and forced a smile until Amos closed the door.

"Well, that was a complete waste of time... at least she didn't want any money, just an amateur charlatan I suppose."

Amos shrugged, "It was worth a try, there's no harm done."

"We'll see about that," Molly snorted as she climbed the stairs, "I'll have to check my knicker drawer first."

"You have one low opinion of that girl, don't you?" Amos replied, trooping up the stairs behind her.

"Just sceptical about pretty faces."

Molly opened the bedroom door and Amos almost piled into the back of her as she came up short.

Amelia yawned and blinked several times as she sat on the edge of the bed.

"Where's my Mommy?"

The Barber

Despite Hawker's Drift's sole barbers being closed for over a week there had been no queue of people clamouring to get their hair cut, whiskers trimmed or face's shaved when Ash had finally gone back to work.

He'd wanted to be busy; he thought it might have helped. At least a little. Instead, he'd spent the morning sitting and staring at the hollow-eyed reflection in his grandfather's mirror. Perversely he found he had even less to do here than he did at home though at least he didn't feel completely useless in his barber's shop.

He stared out of the window. How hairy would the men let themselves get before putting their necks under his blade again? He held up his hand, at least he wasn't shaking anymore. Not all the time anyway. That was something, wasn't it?

Probably shouting at everyone who came near him hadn't helped. Well, to be fair he hadn't shouted every time and not at everyone, but enough all the same. Enough for folk to worry.

Is this a man I want to let put a razor against my throat? Is this a man I want to put scissors an inch or two from my eyes? What if I say the wrong thing? It could be messy. Best not take the chance, a little more hair won't do me much harm, not as much as a grief strangled father who is slowly unravelling at the seams anyhow.

Ash didn't think he looked much different, a little darker around the eyes maybe, but otherwise the same as he had before Emily had been attacked. A fool, in other words.

Ash let his head loll back, the ceiling looked a lot better than he did.

He should have got his family out of Hawker's Drift a long time ago. Instead, he'd fooled himself into thinking it was safe here. So a few people went missing from time to time, it had been nothing to worry about, he'd told himself. Even if most of them had been girls and young women. Just like Emily.

Except... except he couldn't actually remember ever thinking that. Not even a peripheral little worry that he'd shrugged off from time to time. A girl would go missing; he would shake his head and tut with Kate and that would be it. He'd never asked himself why? Never asked himself what had happened? Never asked himself if it was really as safe for his family here as he thought it was?

And now it was too late.

Nobody else had said much either for that matter. There might be search parties and a few flyers if no plausible explanation came forth, but after a few days people stopped looking. In a few weeks they stopped mentioning it and in a few months all that would be left would be a torn flyer or two turning yellow in the sun. Then the next year it would happen again, but nobody connected the dots, nobody exclaimed, "Hey, it's happened again!"

Everyone save that mad clown, of course, who would stand on any street corner he could find to preach it was all the Devil's work. At least till one of the Deputies wandered by and kicked his ass down the street.

Perhaps William Stone had been whisking girls away for years, perhaps he'd been disturbed and had left Emily battered and bleeding, but still alive and not in some unmarked grave out on the grass like all the others. Then again, perhaps Preacher Stone had nothing to do with the disappearances.

Perhaps Hawker's Drift still wasn't safe for Emily and Ruthie.

Ash jumped up, grabbed his jacket and flipped over the closed sign on the door as he hurried out.

The men of Hawker's Drift could carry on getting hairier for another day.

*

It was a simple single storey little house; modestly furnished, neat and tidy, clean, functional and unfussy. An ordinary and unremarkable home in other words.

Ash wasn't sure what else he had expected.

He'd broken a window to get in, but the glass on the floorboards was the only thing that looked out of place. He'd assumed Sheriff Shenan and his men would have searched the Preacher's house tucked behind the church after he'd run off and hung himself, but nothing seemed out of place save for a few torn strips of paper in one corner of the drawing room. They looked like they'd come from a Bible. Ash turned one over a couple of times before letting it float back to the floor.

He wandered into a little study between the bedroom and drawing room. What was he looking for exactly? A signed confession would be good. Something that said unequivocally that Preacher Stone been responsible for Emily and all the disappearances that had blighted the town. Something that would tell Ash it was safe to stay in Hawker's Drift. Too much to hope for, he supposed.

Ash frowned and stared at the old roll top desk that sat beneath a window looking out onto a tiny rose garden. Was it really? If you were going to commit suicide, why not confess your sins. That's what normally happened, wasn't it?

Preacher Stone had been found hanging with a scrap of paper pinned to his jacket bearing a single word. *Sorry*. Which to Ash's mind explained nothing.

He eased himself into the chair and lightly drummed his fingers on the scuffed edge of the desk. He didn't know much about suicide. Old Kenny Neyack had blown the top of his head off with a shotgun a few years back and he hadn't left any kind of note as far as Ash knew. His brains all over the ceiling of his outhouse, but no note.

A Bible sat atop a stack of assorted letters, bills and notes on the desk. Ash shuffled the papers into a rough pile and hesitantly flicked through them. He was unsure whether he wanted to see what the mad old man had been working on, perhaps afraid that he might somehow catch a dose of lunacy if he exposed himself to the late Preacher's thoughts.

Ash let out a little snort. Damn stupid idea. Besides he was half way to losing his mind already anyway.

The papers seemed to be mostly sermons, nothing crazy

looking, just the regular kind of stuff William Stone had spouted from the pulpit every Sunday. Ash remembered those times he'd taken Kate and the girls to church, shuffling at the back and trying not to look bored while feeling guilty for being bored. Kate had always been the one for the church. He'd never seen the need to spend his one day a week off work being told he was going to burn in hell for this sin or that sin. Especially, as far as he could see, his only sins had been the occasional beer, a game of cards once in a while and the chance glimpse at a pretty woman's ass. And if a guy got to burn in hell for such misdemeanours then there was gonna be even more room in heaven than there was out on the grass.

Even Kate had lost her enthusiasm for it over the last six months for some reason and they'd only been a handful of times. He wished they'd never gone.

Had Preacher Stone looked out over his congregation and noticed Emily blossoming into a young woman? As he'd lectured them about God's love and God's mercy had he been thinking about raping her? Thinking of what he would do to her? How much he'd hurt her? Of beating and fucking her? Had his cock grown stiff in the pulpit as he'd watched Emily sing hymns and smile at all round her like the happy, bright girl she'd once been?

Ash found he'd crumpled the sermons in his shaking fist.

He slowly unpeeled his fingers and tossed the Preacher's words away. How could he have sat here and written about love when... when all that shit had been in his head?

He flicked through the rest of the pile, there were a couple of invoices for some work the Morten brothers had done on the church roof, some bills from *Pickerings*, but otherwise nothing. As he tossed the papers away with a snort of disgust, he noticed something sticking out from beneath the Bible. A letter.

It was addressed to Cornelia Stone, in Bridgeton, a place Ash had never visited a couple of hundred miles away over the grass. A relative presumably. The kind of person you confessed to?

Ash turned the envelope over in his hands. Was the answer in here? In this little off-white envelope? A confession of all the old monster's sins? That he'd been doing this for years, driven by whatever sickness made a man do such terrible things. That Hawker's Drift was safe now?

He ripped the envelope open and unfolded the letter inside, his eye running over the neat, precise lines of tight script. He read it once quickly, then again a second time to be sure before tossing it aside to rest on the sermons.

Nothing.

He would like to visit, but he was busy. His stomach was bad. His roses were lovely this year. He hoped her daughters were well. He missed them.

I just bet you fucking did...

Ash bent down and opened the desk drawers one by one; books, papers, stationery, boxes of neatly folded letters, a collection of coins in an old candy tin. He checked the papers; mundane, routine, common. Like any man might write. Any normal, sane man. Ash sighed; he supposed it had been naive to think anyone, even a madman, would simply record all of his crimes.

The final drawer was locked.

He looked about the desktop, but there was no sign of a key.

There was nothing at hand he could use to jimmy the drawer open and he hadn't brought anything with him to help in the business of thievery. He found a heavy bladed knife in the kitchen, which was as neat and well-ordered as the rest of the house, and used it to prise open the lock, which came apart easily enough.

There was a tinkle of glass as he wrenched open the drawer. Ash frowned. The drawer was full of little black bottles; they'd seemingly been thrown inside with no order or care to rattle around on top of each other. Each bottle appeared identical; blackened glass, without a label or marking of any kind.

Ash picked one up and turned it in his hand. Empty and uncorked. He pressed the rim of the bottle to his nose. There was a faint lingering smell of something that was far too sweet. Like overripe fruit. Medicine of some kind he guessed, it sure didn't smell like booze. Whatever the stuff was, Preacher Stone had got through an awful lot of it.

Instead of throwing the bottle back into the drawer, he slipped it into his jacket pocket. Maybe he'd ask Dr Rudi about it, he thought distantly. He ran a hand through the pile of bottles, all empty. The glass beneath his fingers was strangely comforting, so smooth and dark. He stared absently into the drawer and fought down the urge to collect the bottles and line them all up across the desk like soldiers on parade. The bottles clinked as he moved them, just the way you'd expect empty bottles to sound, yet Ash couldn't help but think of insects chirping, like crickets on a hot night.

Distantly he heard a wooden creak, just the boards settling or a footstep? Ash turned his head and told himself Preacher Stone wasn't going to come hurtling through the door, dead eyes bulging and blackened tongue lolling from his mouth, axe raised over his head. Back from the grave to protect his precious collection of empty bottles.

He turned his eyes back to the bottles, they sure did look pretty for some reason he couldn't begin to fathom.

Ash found something else amongst the bottles. He pulled out a small pocketbook, black and unremarkable. There were only three words written inside.

Sweet. Black. Candy.

Repeated over and over again, filling the entire notebook. Preacher Stone's usually neat, precise script became more disjointed and ragged with each page. It was as if every word had been scrawled into the little book with slightly more ferocity than the last until, by the final page, the words were slashed across the paper with a furious and shaking hand. The hand of a madman.

Ash let the notebook fall back amongst the empty bottles, the words hissing across the back of his mind in a demented chant.

Sweet. Black. Candy. Sweet. Black. Candy.

He kicked the drawer shut, the bottles rattling like a disturbed hive and jumped to his feet.

The Preacher had been mad, he'd known that already, but now his hands felt unclean from touching that book and those words hung before his eyes like the afterglow of a blown out candle.

"You can't catch madness," Ash whispered, eyes lingering on the desk drawer.

He searched the rest of the study. There were shelves heavy with books, a mixture of religious texts and novels. Nothing noteworthy as far as Ash could see. He flipped through a couple of volumes, some of the religious scripts had notes and annotations scrawled in the margins, but nothing you wouldn't expect to find in a Preacher's library.

Beneath the shelves was a sturdy oak cabinet. The doors were locked and the mechanism was much less flimsy than the desk drawer had been. It took a couple of minutes work to force the lock, which finally gave way with a resigned crack.

Inside were card file boxes, all filled with the same type of pocketbook he'd found amongst the bottles.

Sweet. Black. Candy

He couldn't have filled them all with those three meaningless words could he? That would have been one damn big steaming pile of madness.

Ash pulled out a notebook at random and skimmed through it, crouching on his haunches between the open doors of the cabinet. Each page was filled with tight, precise handwriting, with a date before each notation. Ash thought it was a diary at first, but quickly realised it was a record of the Preacher's conversations with his parishioners.

May/ 17/ 32

Mrs Vickery – fears her father-in-law is becoming soft-headed and forgetful. Left milk on the stove yesterday, boiled to nothing and ruined her best pan. Doesn't know what to do –

admitted would be better if he died than became demented.

May/19/32

Bob Gratis – has been having lustful thoughts about his neighbour, has been looking out of his window at night after catching sight of her getting undressed one evening. Fears he will go to hell.

Ash snapped the notebook closed. This was worse than the mad rambling in the other notebook. The Preacher had recorded every confidence he'd been told; every worry and concern, every fear and petty sin. All the crap people kept a secret from everyone bar themselves and their Preacher. Everything. Ash stared at the neat pile of boxes, each filled with thin, black notebooks.

Years and years' worth.

Mostly mundane, some silly, some downright crazy no doubt. All hugely embarrassing. Why on earth had Stone recorded everything he'd been told? There was a whole town's worth of little secrets in those boxes.

A board creaked again and Ash jerked around, startled like a little boy caught going through his mother's underwear drawer. The doorway was empty, the house quiet. He was getting skittish.

He stared down at the rows of notebooks. Had he ever said anything worth a shit to the Preacher? He couldn't recall anything he'd regret other people knowing and was grateful for that. He might have discussed the weather and whined about Kate's cooking a couple of times when the Preacher came into have his hair cut, but nothing worth writing down and nothing worth bothering about if the sick old fucker had.

Had Kate ever said anything to the Preacher? Just moaned about her husband's snoring and smelly feet probably.

He ran a finger along the neatly filed notebooks. Would he want to know? He was pretty sure Kate had no secrets, but everyone was capable of spitting venom at something or other when the wind blew wrong and she'd always been more of a one for the church than him. Bearing her soul to God an all – not knowing this old fucker was recording every word for posterity or some other no good reason.

There was crap here about the whole damn town. All his friends and neighbours most likely. Part of him felt like settling down, cracking open a beer or two and having a good read. Instead, he pulled himself to his feet. Maybe there was something about Emily or the other girls in there, but what else would he have to wade through to find it? How many tawdry secrets and impure thoughts? How many petty sins and dark whispers? Some shit was best left alone.

He half closed the cabinet doors.

Maybe he wouldn't read them, but eventually someone would, even if it was just the new preacher, whoever he might be. And someone could do a lot of harm with what was in those books. If they had a mind to.

He should burn them. It was the best thing to do; else the sick legacy of William Stone might end up haunting Hawker's Drift for a long while to come. He'd find a bag in the kitchen, pack em up and burn them in his yard. Best thing.

He gave a little gasp as he turned to the door. A figure was leaning against the frame, thumbs hooked into his gun belt, watching him intently with cold slush-grey eyes.

"Shit!" Ash managed to say, taking a step back and banging into the cabinet doors.

"You really shouldn't be here," Deputy Blane drawled, finally.

The Mother

It was like a piece of Emily was missing.

Whatever spark gave a soul its life and vitality seemed to have died within her. She never smiled and her eyes saw nothing around her. She just slumped on the back porch, blanket wrapped around her whatever the temperature, staring at the laundry flapping in the breeze.

She wouldn't enter her own room anymore, so she'd been sharing with Kate while Ash slept in her bed. Every time Kate awoke in the night she found Emily on her back, glistening, unblinking eyes fixed on the ceiling. The rare moments that her daughter did drift off, she endured a fitful, restless sleep that brought her no peace. It was the only time her eyes seemed to move, twitching behind closed lids, the occasional moan escaping her lips as demons pursued her into the land of dreams.

One particular demon anyway.

Kate had tried to talk to her daughter about what had happened. She'd tried giving her space to be alone, she'd tried sitting with her in silence and holding her hand, she'd tried hugging her so tight she could barely breathe. Nothing had worked. Emily was becoming no more than a ghost and Kate feared one day she would be able to see right through her.

Emily had talked when she'd first came around, told them who had hurt her. Later she'd talked to Shenan and, in a croaking pitiful voice, told him what had been done to her. Using words Kate hadn't thought her little girl would even have known.

Now she said virtually nothing.

Kate watched her through the window, shrunk into the big old rocking chair Ash had hauled outside years ago so he could sit and watch the girls play in the backyard. Emily was rocking back and forth, the wooden joints creaking softly, blanket pulled up to her chin and looking nowhere but inwards.

Kate hated the silence that had enveloped her daughter. It seemed there was nothing left inside Emily anymore; she'd become a clockwork toy with all its gears smashed up, frozen in one final position for eternity. But when Emily did speak Kate hated it even more because now she said only one thing. The same words, whether in answer to a question or mumbled in her sleep. Occasionally she'd just shout em out loud for no apparent reason, vomiting the words up like bad eggs.

It was Amos – the gunslinger...

It had seemed so simple to begin with. A sick, evil stranger had broken into their home and raped her beautiful daughter. Terrible and heart-breaking, but simple. Ash had tried to kill him, thankfully the Sheriff had got there in time and justice could be done. The gunslinger would hang, Emily would recover and life, or something close to it, would eventually return.

But none of those things had happened.

The gunslinger hadn't done it. Kate hadn't believed her ears when Sam Shenan had turned up, looking as awkward and uncomfortable as a man could be with his clothes on, to tell them the gunslinger *couldn't* have done it.

She'd heard Emily describe what had been done to her, in that terrible, hollow voice she had now and she knew damn well a man with no cock couldn't have done any of them. Then Preacher Stone had run away and hung himself out on the grass. Hung himself from the old Judas Tree with a scrap of paper stuck to his jacket, a note that bore a single word. *Sorry.*

The man who had sat by Emily's bedside and prayed for her to recover with Kate and Ruthie. The man who'd been there when Emily's eyes had finally flickered open The man who'd been there when Ash had asked her who had hurt her. The man who had raped and beaten her.

Kate turned sharply away from the window, tears welling up again.

Of course, it was her fault. If she'd been home where she was supposed to be instead of rolling around in John X's bed...

She cut the thought out. She had tried not to think about John, as if simply forgetting him would be enough to change the past. Other than bumping into him briefly on the street she hadn't seen him since that night. She wasn't sure she ever wanted to see him again though she suspected deep down that wasn't what she wanted at all. But what she wanted didn't matter anymore; the only thing that mattered was getting Emily back. Making her better. The bruises were fading, the welts healing, but the wounds on the inside? Those were still weeping and she didn't have the faintest idea how to bind them.

Kate wiped her face, blinked back her tears and went outside.

"Do you want some lunch, Hun?" Kate asked. She didn't expect a reply; she'd just make up a plate and leave it by Emily. On a good day she'd take a couple of little bites. Most days she didn't.

Emily continued to stare at the sheets on the line, her hair limp and lank about her face, her fingers clutching the blanket to her chin despite the warmth of the sun.

Kate stood over her, trying to keep her smile from faltering, trying to act like everything was normal, everything was as it had been and her daughter just had a bit of a head cold. She didn't know what good it did, pretending everything was normal wasn't going to make Emily forget what had happened to her. However, Kate suspected the alternative would be her screaming and wailing and begging Emily's forgiveness for her own selfish lust which had allowed this to happen.

If only I'd been here...

She placed a hand on Emily's shoulder and forced her smile a little wider, "Hun?"

Emily slowly looked up at her, as if the drying sheets were the most fascinating thing she'd ever seen and it took a physical effort to pull her eyes away.

"Mom..." she croaked, her voice the dry, withered rasp of an ancient crone rather than a young woman's.

"Yes, Hun?" Kate crouched down beside her, placing her

hand on the rocking chair to still it.

Emily's flat empty eyes fixed on her for a moment, "It was Amos – the gunslinger..."

There was no emotion in her voice, no pleading, no insistence. Just flat, hollow words, as meaningless as a tune you couldn't shake out of your head.

"Emily..." Kate managed to say, but her daughter had already turned back to stare at the sheets.

She bit her lip, swallowed, then stood up.

"I'll fix some lunch then," she announced, as brightly as she could.

The only reply as she hurried back into the kitchen was the rhythmic squeaking of the old rocking chair.

*

She'd fallen asleep in Ash's upholstered chair by the unlit fire, Bible still clutched in her lap. She didn't want to open her eyes. She just wanted to sleep some more, she'd been dreaming. She couldn't remember what about, but it hadn't been a nightmare so she'd take whatever it had been over the anguish that poured into her mind as soon as the dreams melted away.

She felt the Bible beneath her hands and thought of John. Had she been dreaming of him? She sometimes did. It was hypocritical even to be holding the Lord's words and the thought of her lover made her feel dirty and ashamed. Kate let the book slip from her lap and thump to the floor.

Distantly she wanted John to be here, to feel his arms around her and his voice whispering in her ear again. Even now. What a selfish bitch she was. He wasn't going to come of course. Him or anyone else. Strange how the stream of neighbours and well-wishers had dried up now the excitement was all over.

She guessed none of them wanted to see what remained of Emily.

Had she ever felt this alone? Emily was so broken she wasn't even sure her daughter knew who she was anymore. Ash had become consumed by anger and impotence. He was as desperate to make things better as Kate was but even less able. He'd retreated into brooding silence and he only seemed to notice her when she caught him staring darkly at her out of the corner of her eye. Blaming her, she supposed. Wondering how she could have slept through Emily's attack. A mirror to her own guilt.

Even Ruthie had developed a haunted expression, jumping at every noise, staring at every shadow, trusting no one.

Was Preacher Stone coming for her too?

Kate let out a long, slow sigh, rolled her shoulders and grimaced. Ash would be home soon; she should start cooking. Another tasteless meal to be pushed around the plates before being scrapped into the trash. She gripped the arms of the chair and peeled open her eyes.

Then gave a strangled little scream.

"Good afternoon Mrs Godbold…"

The Mayor was standing over her, resting easily on his cane. He wore an immaculate pinstriped grey suit.

Have I ever seen him in the same suit twice?

The thought bubbled into her mind and she fought down the urge to giggle.

"What... what are you doing here!?" She wanted to leap from her feet and push him away, but instead she slumped back into the chair under the weight of his gaze.

"I didn't mean to startle you," the Mayor smiled, taking off his derby, "You must forgive me,"

"For...?"

"For not coming sooner."

"Oh," Kate wasn't at all sure what to say.

"I did not want to intrude... at such a difficult time for your family," his smile bled away as he bent down and rested his hand on her shoulder, "...but I thought it was time I popped in to see how things were. If there's anything I can do to help..."

"Maybe knock before coming in..." Kate hissed.

"I did... but when there was no answer I became concerned. I thought it best to come in a check that everything was... alright."

"Oh..." Kate felt the weight of his lingering hand upon her shoulder and strangled the urge to throw it off. She wanted to scream at him that absolutely nothing was alright, given what had happened the last time a man had let himself into her home.

She didn't know the Mayor particularly well. She knew he visited Ash once in a while to have his hair cut and beard trimmed, but otherwise he'd had little to do with them beyond the occasional nod and smile in the street. She'd heard the stories of course. The little whispers. She hadn't paid them much heed, life was good in the town, compared to most other places anyway, and what the Mayor got up to in private was very much his own business.

"After such a terrible, terrible thing, whatever comfort I can offer..." his hand moved from her shoulder to gently cup her cheek "...is yours for the asking."

His touch was cool, smooth and wrong for a reason Kate couldn't quantify. She wanted to jerk away from his fingers, partly because such familiarity was inappropriate, but mainly because his skin felt repulsive. She felt too warm and too lightheaded; she found she was unable to utter anything more coherent than a soft grunt.

"How is Emily?" Kate heard him ask, his hand twisting around as he softly stroked her cheek with his knuckles.

Why is he touching me like this? Why am I letting him?

"Upstairs... asleep..."

"The poor lamb... sleep is the best medicine, though."

"I hope-"

"Oh, it is Kate, it definitely is. Time and rest will cure most ails. Right most wrongs. You see if it doesn't?"

He cracked a smile. Wide and bright; too wide and too bright in truth. He let his hand fall away and looked up at the ceiling.

"I should look in on her. To see if there is anything she wants?"

Kate blinked; grateful he was no longer touching her.

"She shouldn't be disturbed."

The Mayor's nostrils twitched and he lowered his gaze,

"Of course... you know best."

Kate struggled to her feet and tried not to cringe as she brushed up against the Mayor, who made no effort to move aside.

"Would you like coffee?" She asked, patting down her hair

and wriggling past him. He smelt faintly of perfumed smoke, sweet and slightly sickly.

"Oh, that would be delightful, but I don't want to take up your time and I have so many things to do," he smiled that bright too wide smile again, "there really is no rest for the wicked."

"Well, I'm very grateful for your concern."

"No need, but if there is anything you think of that you want... you only need to ask. I will move heaven and Earth for you, Kate, if I can."

"All I want is my daughter back the way she was... and unless you can turn back time there's absolutely nothing you can do," her voice sounded colder than she'd intended, but better that than disintegrating into furious sobs.

The Mayor pursed his lips and turned his palm upwards, "I'm afraid that is beyond even me. I can do no more than bend time I'm afraid."

He stared at her, or, rather, he continued to stare at her. She assumed he was making a joke, but neither of them were doing much laughing.

He replaced his hat and gave her a little nod, "Well, I will see myself out."

Yeah, you saw yourself in easily enough...

"Did he do it?" Kate spurted the words out as the Mayor turned away.

He paused by the door and looked back.

"Preacher Stone?"

"You doubt it?"

"Emily... she keeps saying it was Amos... I know he couldn't have done it. But, why does she keep saying he

121

did?"

The Mayor tapped his temple, "The human mind. A strange thing. Capable of so much, but it can be... manipulated. We'll never know what games William Stone played, but your daughter was under his spell. A trusted man and a young girl unfamiliar with the ways of the world... He did things to Emily's mind, despicable things that convinced her, somehow, that another man did those terrible, bestial things to her. Unfortunately, he picked the wrong man," the Mayor pursed his lips, "...the best-laid plans..."

"I suppose..."

"Preacher Stone is dead and even the greatest monster's powers cannot survive the grave. Eventually, she will remember the truth of things..." his eyebrows flicked up as his head lowered. "You see if she doesn't..."

"You think it'll be that fucking easy?" Kate snapped, anger suddenly boiling up inside her before she could slam the lid down on it.

"I understand-"

"You understand nothing!"

She marched across the room and stood before him, fists clenched at her side fighting the urge to punch him, to pummel his chest and spit in his one good eye.

"I can see that you're upset."

"I'm sure you mean well, but the next time you let yourself into my home I'll call the Sheriff. Now get the hell out!"

The Mayor stared at her, his easy smile evaporating into a tight hard line. His eye seemed to burn and an unfamiliar flush touched his cheeks. She supposed he was used to a bit more deference, but she really didn't care who he was, she didn't want him in her house with Emily upstairs, alone and vulnerable again.

"You seem to have quite forgotten your manners Mrs Godbold..."

"Get the fuck out of my home you slimy one-eyed fucker!"

She thought he was going to hit her then. She could see it flash in his eye like lightning momentarily illuminating the black heart of a thunderhead. Instead he just muttered, "Quite, quite forgotten... how unfortunate."

He raised his cane and Kate flinched, certain that he was going to strike her. Instead, after the barest hesitation, he tapped the cane against the brim of his hat before swivelling on his heels and stomping out of the room.

Kate found she was holding her breath until she heard the front door click shut behind him. The fury that had boiled up inside her was gone as quickly as it had arrived and she hugged herself to stop shaking. Where had that come from? The same rage that was burning Ash from the inside out she supposed.

She bit her lip, sniffed and tried to regain her composure. She didn't want to cry, she was so, so tired of tears.

How long had she been asleep and how long had the Mayor been in the house? She couldn't shake the image of him standing over her, watching her snore and wondering what fun he could have in the meantime. She caught her reflection in the mirror. The top couple of buttons of her blouse were undone. Had she loosened them? She supposed she must have. Did she really think the Mayor had crept into the house so he could fondle a tit while she'd slept?

It was a crazy thought, of course. He was only trying to help as much as he'd pissed her off. Of course it was. He certainly hadn't groped her in her sleep. Nonsense.

She took the stairs two at a time all the same.

Emily was stretched out on her back, almost lost within the big double bed, sheets pulled up to her chin, staring at the ceiling.

"Hun?"

Kate took a couple of tentative steps into the room and tried to paint that useless little smile on her face again.

Emily's head lolled to one side, her glassy eyes finally focusing on Kate as she came towards her.

"How... how are you doing?"

Another dumb, useless question.

"Mom..." she whispered in her empty faraway voice.

"Yes, Hun?" Kate leaned in towards her daughter, her throat catching as she did.

"It was Preacher Stone..." she croaked "...he did it."

Kate bit her lip and took a step back, her hands suddenly shaking. Partly at her daughter's words, but mainly because the room smelt ever so faintly of sweet perfumed smoke...

The Deputy

"My, my, is that a little something for me?"

Mrs Thurlsten had been drinking again. Not a lot, Blane judged, but enough.

His eyes flicked down to the box he was carrying and back to Liza Thurlsten, who had draped an arm over the balustrade.

"Just work," he replied. He moved to step around her, but she was way ahead of him.

"Work? At this time of night? Tut, tut Arthur…"

He hated being called Arthur; he should never have told her his first name. Deputy Blane was good enough for most people. The Mayor got away with just being "the Mayor", which would have suited him even better.

"It is a twenty-four-hour job," he said.

"You sure are always hard at it…" she purred, "…why not put your feet up for five minutes and have a drink with me?" She sloshed her glass under his nose before knocking it back, her eyes lingering on him.

Blane had never been much for understanding what people were about and he generally didn't give a shit one way or the other. However, he knew exactly what his landlady was about and it didn't have anything to do with cheap booze.

"I'm not much of a drinker," Blane replied evenly, glancing up at the dark landing and wanting nothing but to get to his room. This was starting to sound suspiciously like a conversation, which was something he managed to avoid most days.

"Haven't you got any vices, Deputy?"

"Not really."

Save for rape and murder of course...

"Shame..." she fluttered her big overly blackened eyes at him and continued to resolutely block his path. No so long ago he would have simply shown her the back of his hand and barged past, but he was a more responsible individual these days.

He'd been lodging with the Thurlsten's for a few months now and it had quickly become apparent one of Liza's hobbies was going to be getting in the sack with him. This wasn't particularly surprising, or even flattering, given all her pastimes involved getting into the sack with the men in her lodging house. Sadly, at the moment, Blane was the only lodger and so was the sole recipient of her attention.

It was so typical of the irony of life that when he'd been drifting along the road and would have been delighted to find such easy prey none of his landlady's had been anywhere near so obliging. Now that he was settled and his pleasures had to be far more focused and restrained this fat old tramp would probably gladly kneel at his feet and let him throttle her.

"I really should be getting to bed," he insisted. A smile flickered over her bright red lips and he thought she was going to invite herself to join him.

Instead, she reached over the cardboard box he was holding and slipped a hand onto his arm, "Nonsense," she breathed, squeezing his bicep, "Come have a little drink with me... I insist."

This really was intolerable. He should have sorted out a place for himself long before now. He was paid well enough and hated company, but it had just been easier to lodge given all he needed was a bed to sleep on. Getting his own place also seemed a bit too much like a commitment for a drifter like him. Even though he knew he'd never get a deal as sweet as the one he had in Hawker's Drift, the call of the road still occasionally tugged at whatever he had in place of a soul.

He'd had to move out of his previous lodgings when his landlady, who'd been old, short-sighted and utterly disinterested in him, had invited some half-witted cousin to come and live with her. The Mayor himself had recommended Mrs Thurlsten.

"Well, perhaps just the one..." That was what people said, wasn't it? To be polite. It was one of the downsides of his new life, having to be polite. However, it seemed to be the only way he was going to get her to shut up without using his fist.

Mrs Thurlsten glowed, "Yes, just a little one, don't worry. I wouldn't think of leading you astray!" She giggled in a manner she probably thought of as girlish though to Blane it sounded closer to demented.

He tramped reluctantly into the parlour with Mrs Thurlsten's fingers still biting into his arm.

The parlour was as gaudy and tasteless as Liza Thurlsten herself. Every nook and was cranny stuffed with unnecessary clutter; china ornaments, potted plants, oversized dressers, acres of velvet drape, a multitude of overstuffed chairs and huge mirrors framed in baroque swirls of rosewood and mahogany.

"Why don't you put that down and make yourself comfortable Arthur?" She breathed in his ear before sliding away to pour some drinks. He'd planned to keep the box on his lap, partly for protection, partly to ensure she didn't try to peep inside. She was almost as nosey as she was lascivious.

Instead Blane carefully placed the box by the door, before turning to sit in the nearest chair. Unsurprisingly Mrs Thurlsten had other ideas.

"Uh-ah," she tutted, nodding towards an oxblood leather couch, the upholstery worn smooth by the backsides of her countless victims. This was tiresome. However, it would be quicker to let her have her little thrill and then she'd be out of his way all the quicker.

She sauntered over to him, the booze in each glass sloshing in time to the exaggerated sway of her hips. She stood over Blane after handing him his drink, rolls of cleavage pouring out of a corset so tightly bound he was surprised she could actually breathe.

Liza Thurlsten was clearly of the opinion that the ravages of time and excess could be cleverly disguised by the application of as much makeup as possible and wearing outfits the whores in *Jack's* would baulk at.

Eventually she eased herself slowly down next to Blane,

her leisurely descent was either meant to be alluring or she was worried that something might snap if she moved too quickly.

"Well, here we are..." she held up her glass and Blane clinked his own against it rather than smashing it into her face. He sipped booze. It might have been brandy, but he wasn't entirely sure. He generally tried to keep his face as expressionless as possible, but even he struggled not to grimace.

"Well, this is a nice way to end the day, don't you think Arthur?" Mrs Thurlsten flicked a few strands of greying blonde hair away from her face.

"Yes, Ma'am."

"Please... call me Liza... you've been here long enough for us to dispense with formalities. Haven't you?"

Blane suspected she was more interested in dispensing with clothes than formalities, but he gave a little nod all the same and sipped some more. It was harsh on his tongue and burned his throat, but it at least masked the fruity stink of Mrs Thurlsten's perfume.

"Of course."

"You don't say much do you, Arthur?"

"Only when it's required."

"How mysterious you are – I'd so love to know what makes you tick?"

Oh, I'm pretty sure you wouldn't...

Mrs Thurlsten was leaning in towards him – as much as her corsetry allowed anyway – the great pale stretch of her cleavage quivering with every movement and gesture. Blane, however, was more interested in the soft, delicate meat of her throat, the excess flesh hanging in curtains of skin. She wore a thin velvet choker about her throat. Blane wanted to run his thumbs along it as he squeezed the warm, yielding flesh of her neck, all the time watching her eyes bulge from beneath her garishly painted lids, little bubbles of drool escaping her fat red lips, her-

"Arthur? Are you alright?"

Blane swallowed and nodded.

"Yes. Why?"

"You looked... a little strange for a moment?"

"Just the drink."

And the thought of killing you.

Blane's balls were tingling and he shuffled slightly away from Mrs Thurlsten as his cock stiffened. He didn't want to give her the wrong idea.

"I think I make you a little nervous."

Blane levelled his eyes at her, forcing them away from her saggy throat.

"No, not really."

"What about when I do this?" She reached over and rested her hand on his knee.

"Wouldn't Mr Thurlsten object?"

Liza snorted, "Oh he knows I only like real men and if he doesn't like it he can go find his drinking money somewhere else."

She raised her glass and kept her dark-ringed eyes fixed on his as she squeezed his knee harder, "There's no need to worry about that little prick Deputy."

He liked the way she'd called him Deputy. She was showing some respect at last. He'd like the sound of it even

more if it were the last word she ever breathed...

Would the Mayor really be upset if he slaughtered this old fat sow?

Sadly, he suspected he would be.

"You fuck a lot of the men who stay here, don't you?"

Her hand froze. "I don't know what you mean?"

"I hear you sneaking about at night, into the other rooms. The walls are thin and the beds creak."

She smiled and her fingers started to move up his leg, "I like to ensure my guests have a memorable stay."

"And if a guest only wants a bed to sleep in?"

"His loss," she grinned, "though I don't get too many who turn down the chance to have their bed warmed."

"I prefer my bed cold."

Mrs Thurlsten was running her nails back and forth across his thigh, slow, languid little scratches between slurps of booze.

"And I like a challenge, Arthur..."

"I prefer it when you call me Deputy."

"How do you like the sound of Sir?"

"Better," Blane admitted.

What am I doing?

He swallowed and let his eyes drift away from Mrs Thurlsten. He didn't want to sit here and waste his time drinking cheap booze and enduring this stupid woman's clumsy flirting. But he knew that anyway, so why had he agreed to drink with her? Why hadn't he brushed her advances off like he usually did?

Because he was aroused and excited and he really, really wanted to kill...

She leant in close to him, close enough for him to see the ravages of time she tried so clumsily to conceal beneath the dust and powder. The faint lines etched into the corners of her eyes, the loose, puffy bags below them and the puckered creases surrounding her lips.

"You can do anything you like to me, sir... I'm very obliging..."

Blane realised he had screwed his free hand into a fist, hard and tight enough to whiten his knuckles.

"Anything?" His voice wavered a little, which was irritating.

"Oh anything you like sir," she bit her lower lip and raised an eyebrow, or at least the pencil line where her eyebrow was supposed to be.

Blane was mildly surprised to find his hand around her throat.

"How about this?"

Her cloudy blue eyes had widened and her lips had parted, but she didn't struggle.

"If that is what... you like..." she croaked.

What he liked was having her life in his hand and the power to snuff it out like a spent candle whenever he chose. If this had been a few short years ago, back when he was just dark tumbleweed being blown from one ramshackle town to the next, he would have done it without a second thought. His only concern would have been how much time he had to enjoy himself before he needed to scurry off and disappear back into the road dust.

But now... now he couldn't. Not without the Mayor's permission.

He eased the pressure on her throat and she took a shuddering breath. He didn't release her, though. Instead he just ran his thumb back and forth along her choker, feeling the velvet on his skin, then he slid his thumbnail along the edge. How much would he have to tug it for it to come away? How much would it hurt her?

"You have dark tastes, don't you?"

His thumb became still. He didn't like that. He had let his mask slip. Damn booze; that was why he didn't drink. It took away his control and let the demons run free. Above all things, Blane prized control. Control was what set a man apart from beasts and he was most certainly not a beast. Although, perhaps, not entirely a man either.

"No."

"You don't have to lie to me... I've always known..."

Blane's eyebrow twitched and he fought down the irritation he always felt when the echo of an expression found its way onto his wooden mask of a face.

"You are mistaken."

"Then why is your hand still about my throat?"

Blane reluctantly let go, he'd enjoyed the feel of her throat even more than he'd expected.

"I lose my temper sometimes. Forgive me Mrs Thurlsten."

She laughed, "I've never met a man less likely to lose his temper than you. I reckon you got a whole river of ice water in you, young man..."

Blane stood up, knocked back the rest of his glass and placed it on a table between a collection of ugly little china dogs.

"Thank you for the drink, but I shouldn't have anymore.

As you can see, liquor can get the better of me..."

"We should do it again though. It was fun..." Mrs Thurlsten jiggled her glass in front of her nose "...the drink that is..."

"Goodnight, Mrs Thurlsten," Blane scooped up the box and hurried out of the room, her throaty laughter pursuing him up the stairs.

*

His room was sparse, tidy and without fuss.

He spent very little time in here, so it didn't need to be anything else. There was a small square table in one corner that served for eating meals – he tended to avoid Mrs Thurlsten's dining room when he could – and as a desk at other times.

Blane sat, straight-backed, at the table. A lamp cast a pool of yellow light around him, beyond were only shadows. The box he had brought from Preacher Stone's house sat in the middle of the table, the little notebooks he'd taken out and sorted into piles, each one a different year.

He found they made compelling reading.

All the poison and lies, all the bitterness and bile, all the hatred and jealousies meticulously recorded. It seemed there was an awful lot more shit in Hawker's Drift than even he'd been aware of.

People were an endless puzzle.

Why did so many of em feel the need to spew out their pathetic, tawdry secrets? Just because a man wore a dark suit and carried a Bible, did that mean he could keep a secret? And even if he could, a secret shared was a loss of control, like a bird released from a cage; it might fly away into the deep blue sky never to be seen again. Alternatively, it might come back and shit on your head someday.

And there was a lot of shit in Preacher Stone's notebooks.

Lust, theft, avarice, greed, hatred. Sordid affairs, petty crimes, dark suspicions. All the stuff that made people human. All the stuff that made them interesting.

Of course, there was a lot of drivel to wade through, but some real gems too. Knowledge was power. The Mayor had taught him that.

He guessed the Preacher had been recording the town's dirty little confessions for the Mayor's benefit. It made sense. The Mayor loved to know everything – or at least give the impression that he knew everything.

He'd have to take them to the Mayor, of course, in a day or two, but not before he'd read some of them. A perk the Mayor wouldn't object to – not after all the dirty little jobs he did for him.

Blane glanced up at a small mirror hanging above the table. His flat, expressionless face stared back, no hint of the smile he felt on the inside. How many hours had he spent standing in front of mirrors perfecting that blank, unreadable look? Time well spent however long it had been. Other fools might rush to tell Preachers about the filth in their minds or let that shit bubble up and settle on their ugly twisted faces, but not him. No, he was a smarter cookie indeed. He kept everything under lock and key.

His gaze fell back to the pocketbooks. A lucky find. He'd had a hunch he should follow Ash Godbold when he'd seen him stomping up Main Street, all his anger and loathing painted on his face like it was the side of a barn. Fool.

He knew how to follow someone discreetly when he wanted to. Discreetly enough for Godbold to break into the Preacher's house without noticing he was being watched. He'd had a smoke and walked around the square to give the barber a chance to have a good little root about before slipping into the house and catching him red handed.

His dumb slack-jawed face had been quite the picture.

He should have arrested him and thrown him into the cells. That probably would have riled Shenan right up, but he'd seen those notebooks and had been intrigued. Of course, they might just have been the Church accounts, poetry or some God blathering nonsense, but he hadn't thought so. He had an instinct for the darkness in men, or a nose for shit if he wanted to be more prosaic.

So he'd told Godbold to clear out and be thankful he wasn't throwing him in a cell.

He'd been dead grateful, the stupid fuck. Showing him a kindness on account of his daughter he'd probably thought.

Blane looked at the mirror again. Was that a twitch of a smile? Some things were just too much of a struggle for even him to contain...

There was a knock on the door.

"Yes?"

The only reply was another rap.

"A minute."

He had no intention of letting anyone in, but it was best to be careful. Dark, strange fellows like he needed to be prudent. Always. He quickly filled the box with the notebooks and kicked it under his brass bed.

136

He wasn't surprised to find Mrs Thurlsten standing outside. He wasn't even surprised to see that she had struggled out of her dress and corset and was now almost wearing a long flowing nightgown of black silk.

"Mrs Thurlsten..." Blane said, pleased that his voice betrayed no hint of annoyance or resignation.

"Deputy Blane..." she replied, her hands were behind her back and she'd allowed her greying blonde hair to hang loose to her shoulders.

"Is there something I can do for you?"

"I was thinking more along the lines of what you could do to me?" She fluttered her eyelashes, which were still heavy with makeup even if she had discarded most of her clothes. She was still wearing that choker, though...

"It's late. I need to sleep."

"It's very late," Mrs Thurlsten agreed, "there are no other guests and my husband couldn't care less what happens to me, if he hasn't passed out already anyway."

Her gaze never wavered from his as she brought her hand out from behind her back; she was holding a belt, the leather old and cracked. Blane watched it swing back and forth from her outstretched hand.

"In other words, no one will hear me scream..."

She cocked her head to one side and held the belt out towards him.

Blane's eyes moved from the belt to her cleavage, to the black velvet choker around her throat. Slowly he reached out and took the belt.

After all, despite everything else, he was only human...

The Gunslinger

"There's a man on a *horse!*" Amelia exclaimed, as if it were the most wondrous thing she'd ever seen, before turning back to press her nose against the glass.

Yesterday she'd been unconscious and apparently slipping away from the living world. Today she was eating Molly out of house and home. In between rushing from room to room and window to window, jumping around and waving her arms about at every mundane thing she came across.

"She seems... better," Amos offered.

"Dunno what that girl did for her, but I could do with some of it," Molly replied in a half whisper, leaning in towards Amos slightly.

"Maybe Cece didn't do anything."

Molly looked pointedly at him.

Yeah, sure...

"Well, that's something we can wonder about another time. We still need to find out where she came from," Amos rubbed his chin.

They watched as Amelia climbed down from the window and hurtled past them out of the room.

"Gotta catch her first..."

"Do children usually have this much energy?" Amos'

experience with children was about as extensive as his experience with embroidery.

"Not when they're recovering from a fever."

"If this is her recovering..." Amos winced as a crashing sound came from the kitchen "...you might want to think about a bigger house when she's all better."

They hurried through to find Amelia standing over a shattered plate with Molly's freshly baked biscuits scattered across the floor, save for the one Amelia was clutching in her hand.

"Uh-oh," she said, looking up at them with an apologetic grin stretched over her face.

"Don't worry hun, accidents happen," Molly said, shooing Amelia away from the broken china.

If I did that, I'm pretty sure I'd be on the end of some more rudimentary language...

"Let's go outside while Molly cleans up," Amos said, opening the back door.

Amelia took a bite of her biscuit and looked back and forth between them.

"Go on hun," Molly encouraged as she squatted on the floor recovering the bigger fragments of the plate.

Amelia trooped out, still nibbling the biscuit, eyes not leaving Amos.

He didn't need any gifts to know she was wary of him. He didn't have the kind of face children found reassuring.

The sun was bathing the yard in fierce sunlight; it was another hot day, the heat pressing upon the earth from an almost painful sky. Amelia squatted in what little shade there was and attended to her biscuit. Amos eased himself down beside her.

"Are you a cowboy?" She asked as she chewed.

"Erm. No, not really."

"You look like a cowboy." Amelia insisted.

"Do I?"

Amelia nodded vigorously, "You got a gun like a cowboy."

Amos touched the butt of his holstered weapon. With Amelia running around putting her nose into every nook and cranny, he'd decided he'd better keep the pistol on him.

"Lots of people carry guns, they're not all cowboys."

Amelia didn't look convinced, "You got a horse?"

"Yep."

"Yep," Amelia mimicked, finishing the biscuit.

The little girl was lost in one of Molly's old shirts; the strange clothes she'd been wearing when Mr Wizzle had found her were drying on the line. Her long frizzy hair had been tied with ribbons into two bunches. Amelia had given Molly precise instructions as to how she liked to wear her hair.

"Can I ride your horse?"

"Well... it's a pretty big horse."

Amelia shook her head emphatically, "I'm not scared of heights!"

"Well, maybe... we'll see."

"That's what Mommy always says when I say I want a pony," Amelia pulled a face "actually she says that about most things."

"So..." Amos asked gently, "where is your Mommy?"

Amelia shrugged, "Dunno."

"When did you see her last?"

"When she read me a story."

"And when was that?"

"At bedtime of course."

"How did you get here then?"

Amelia looked at him, her expression blank. Somewhere beneath the folds of Molly's shirt her little shoulders twitched.

"You remember being in the rain? Where Mr Wizzle found you?"

Amelia leant a little towards him, "That strange man who looks a bit like a clown?"

"Yes."

"Yeah... I remember."

"And before that. Where were you before then?"

Amelia screwed up her face, "It's kinda fuzzy."

"Fuzzy?"

"Makes my head hurt to think about it... are there any more biscuits?"

"Erm... I think Molly will have to make some more."

"Is Molly your girlfriend?"

"Well... it's... complicated."

Amelia gave a little nod of worldly experience, "I think she likes you."

Before Amos could think of a reply, which admittedly might have taken some time, Molly appeared in the doorway, "All tidied up."

"Molly! Molly!" Amelia scrambled to her feet and run across to her, "Amos has got a horse! And he's going to let me ride it!"

They both turned to look at Amos with wide-eyed stares.

Amos managed a smile.

*

"What's his name?" Amelia's voice was hushed as she looked up at the horse.

"He hasn't got one," Amos admitted, patting the gelding's neck.

"But everyone has a name?" Amelia insisted.

He'd never felt the need to name his horse, it seemed a sentimental thing to do and a horse was just a means of getting from one place to another. Sure you had to care for it, but a name had always seemed entirely unnecessary to Amos. You gave names to things you became attached to and it had been a long time since he'd wanted to be attached to anything.

He glanced at Molly.

A real long time...

Molly hunkered down next to Amelia and rested a hand lightly on the girl's shoulder, "Why don't you give him a name?"

"Can I!?" Amelia looked wildly from Amos to Molly and back again.

"Sure... I've never been good at giving things names."

Amelia screwed up her face as she gazed at the horse that was disinterestedly staring out of its stable in the livery. It was hot and clammy, the air thickened with the smell of horseflesh and dung. Molly had been carefully guiding Amelia around the horseshit; she didn't want to soil the shoes and cotton dress she'd only just bought the girl.

"Silver!" Amelia announced, with a decisive nod of the

143

head.

"Silver," Amos repeated, staring at the midnight black gelding.

"Like the Lone Ranger's horse!"

"The Lone Ranger?" Amos asked, glancing at Molly, who shrugged.

"He's a cowboy like you. Can I ride Silver now?"

"Well, maybe we can take him for a walk; you'd like that wouldn't you... erm... Silver?"

Molly didn't look entirely convinced, but Amos fitted the horse with its bridle before leading them all out into the square, Amelia trotting alongside him, eyes never leaving Silver.

The sun was dipping towards the west, casting long, soft shadows across Pioneer Square. The heat of the day had lifted and a half-hearted breeze had begun fluttering across the town, strong enough to toy with Molly's hair.

There were several curious glances cast their way, mainly at Amelia this time. He supposed they were a gift that just kept on giving for the wag-tongues of Hawker's Drift.

"Here," Amos handed the reins to Amelia, why don't we take Silver for a walk."

Amelia wrapped the reins around her hand and gave a little tug, "C'mon Silver... good boy..." she grinned.

Amos walked one side of the girl and Molly the other. Molly was staring at the girl, a faint little smile dusting her lips. She looked happy, properly happy for the first time since he'd met her. He could feel it coming off her like warmth from the embers of a burnt out fire on a cold morning. Amos found he was smiling too and he looked away

144

sharply.

John X had wandered out onto the boardwalk in front of his shop, a mug in his hand. He grinned broadly and lifted his finger to his forehead in greeting. Amos nodded in return.

They did one slow circuit of the square, Amelia constantly chatting, mostly to Silver, who was content to be led by the little girl without complaint.

"Can I ride him now?" Amelia asked when they returned to the front of the livery.

"Well, he's a very big horse for you, hun," Molly said.

"But Silver's my friend, aren't you Silver?"

Silver looked blankly down at her and twitched a fly away with his ear.

"See?"

"Why don't you give him this first," Amos fished a dried apple from his pocket and gave it to Amelia.

Silver suddenly looked more interested

"Look Silver. Dinner!" Amelia beamed, holding the apple up at arm's length and then bursting into giggles as the horse plucked it from her fingers in one go.

"Now I can ride him?"

"Just for a little while," Amos chuckled. The girl's enthusiasm was infectious. Had he ever been like that? He couldn't remember.

Molly started to say something, her concern palpable, but Amos scooped Amelia up and boosted her onto the horse's back before she could say anything. He gave her a reassuring grin, but she continued to glower at him. He'd never been good with reassurances.

He handed the reins to Amelia and made sure she was

settled. Wide-eyed and grinning from ear to ear, but settled.

"C'mon then Silver," Amos said, taking hold of the bridle. He'd never been a skittish horse and Amelia weighed only a fraction of the weight he was used to with a saddle and Amos on his back, but he didn't want the animal to suddenly bolt. They'd only just fixed Amelia after all and Molly wouldn't be happy if she got hurt again.

He looked at Molly, who was staring coldly at him.

In fact, she would probably try to kill him.

He winked at her. Which didn't help any.

"Hi-ho Silver!" Amelia cried as they started off around the square again, giggling furiously as she leant forward and clutched the horse's neck.

"She's too small for this," Molly hissed.

"I was much younger than Amelia when I first rode a horse," Amos insisted.

"Yeah, and look how you turned out."

As usual he didn't have much of answer to that and let it go.

They plodded slowly around the town square again, Amelia squealing and laughing, Molly scowling and Silver probably hoping for another apple or two out of all the unexpected attention.

"Again!" Amelia cried, releasing the horse's neck and clapping her hands together once they'd returned to the front of the livery.

Molly was still glaring.

"Oh, I think it's time for Silver to get some sleep." Amos decided not to push it.

"Awww, but it's only early."

"And it's time for your dinner and sleep too," Molly chipped in before Amelia allowed herself to be plucked from Silver's back by Amos.

"Now you sound like my Mom," Amelia sighed, with a weary resignation that only the very young can quite pull off.

A strange little expression flitted across Molly's face before she forced it away with a smile.

Amos looked back across the square, not wanting to feel what was coming off Molly. Instead, his eye was drawn to the Mayor's residence. A figure was standing in an open window, almost lost in shadow, but Amos both knew who it was and that he was staring intently at them. Even if his eyes had not been sure the way his skin prickled like a spiteful north wind was cutting his flesh would have told him that they'd caught the Mayor's attention.

"Can't I have one more ride? *Please?*"

Amos pulled another apple from his pocket and pushed it into the girl's hand. "Silver needs his dinner too and then..." his eyes flicked momentarily towards Molly, "...we really need to get home..."

The Widow

Despite the animated protestations Amelia was asleep within a few minutes of her head touching the pillow.

Molly had spent so long staring at the girl when she'd been unconscious she didn't quite understand why she still felt the urge to sit on the edge of the bed and watch her some more. Eventually she leaned over, ran a hand gently over her soft wiry hair and kissed Amelia's forehead.

"Sweet dreams hun..." she whispered.

She'd been happy today, with Amelia and Amos. She couldn't quite remember the last time that had happened. Not without the aid of a substantial amount of whiskey anyway.

What would it have been like?

She'd often wondered. Would life have turned out differently if she'd been able to give Tom a child? Would fatherhood have brought an end to his stupid schemes, would responsibility have halted their nomadic life? Would they have been happy? Or at least content? Or at the very least still both alive.

Questions that can never be answered...

She sighed, pushed her hair from her eyes and left Amelia to whatever dreams might come her way. Ones with horses in them, she suspected, smiling as she carefully closed the door.

Whoever she was and wherever she'd come from she was a robust little thing.

Amos was sitting in the kitchen, staring into his coffee, his eyes far away until she slid out the chair opposite and eased herself into it.

"So..." she sighed, once Amos' eyes eventually focused on her.

"So?"

"So, what do we do with her?"

"Find her folks, I guess."

Molly nodded. Of course they should.

"Yeah... just do a little good huh?"

Amos jerked his head up and stared at her like she'd just slapped his face.

"What did you say?"

"Ermm... we should do a little good? Find her folks I mean."

Amos suddenly looked pale. The last light of the day was kissing the kitchen through the windows, a warm and friendly glow, but he looked like he'd just staggered in from a freezing midwinter evening. Or had just seen a ghost. Molly wanted to glance over her shoulder and see if Tom's angry shade was standing behind her. He wouldn't be happy about a man moving in with her, cockless or otherwise. He'd always been the jealous type.

"Are you... alright?"

She wasn't going to look over her shoulder. She really wasn't.

Amos forced a smile, taut and grudging, onto his face, "it's... it's nothing."

"Oh..." Molly returned a flickering smile of her own. "Tomorrow?" She asked eventually.

"Tomorrow?" He blinked.

"We try and find her people again tomorrow?"

"We'll have to try and talk to her again. Now she's settled in... maybe she'll be more forthcoming."

"You think she's hiding something?"

Amos shook his head, the colour slowly returning to his face, "She's what? Seven? Eight? How duplicitous can she be?"

"You haven't been around kids much, have you?"

Amos gave a little snort and went back to staring at his coffee, "No not much. But I'm pretty sure most little kids would be crying for their mommy right now."

She couldn't argue with him about that. Instead, she went to the stove and poured herself some coffee.

Amos looked at her as she sat back down, blowing into her mug.

"No whiskey tonight?"

"I'm not a complete drunkard."

"No... you haven't drunk much... these last few days."

"You counting?" Molly arched an eyebrow.

"I'm not your dad."

"You wouldn't be sleeping under this roof if you were," Molly muttered, trying to repress a shudder. She noticed the way Amos' eyes lingered on her like they always did when he saw more than he should, and she forced the image of Bert-Bert's snarling face back into the shadows.

151

Amos returned to staring into his coffee.

"Have you... sensed anything about Amelia?"

"No... nothing."

The clothes Amelia had been wearing when they'd found her were folded up on the kitchen dresser where Molly had left them after collecting them off the washing line.

"You ever saw anything like these before?" Molly stood up and grabbed them. They were kind of furry to the touch, but not any kind of actual animal fur as far as Molly could tell. Not that she could think of any pink animals anyway. She held up the little trousers and pulled at the waist to demonstrate how they stretched and sprung back into shape.

Amos shook his head, "No... something new I guess."

Molly turned them inside out and showed him a little label inside.

Made in Taiwan.

"Where's Taiwan?"

"Back east I guess."

Molly sniffed and folded the clothes up again.

She stood over Amos for a moment, he seemed distant tonight. Or, rather, more distant than usual. If anyone asked her opinion, something that rarely happened, she'd say he spent far too much time thinking. Little good ever came of too much thinking. You just ended up asking questions that could never be answered.

"You alright sleeping down here?"

Amos gave a little nod, "Can't really share a bed with you and Amelia."

"Not with your snoring. She needs her rest."

152

"I don't snore."

"Yeah, right," she leaned over and kissed him gently on the forehead, much the same as she had to Amelia earlier. Maybe for the same reason too.

Though the little girl hadn't flinched when she did it to her...

*

Molly was reading by the lamp. Or at least pretending to. It was a romance though it wasn't much like real life. The hero wasn't a eunuch, the heroine wasn't a foul-mouthed drunk and no strange little girl had appeared out of thin air.

She glanced over at Amos. He was sitting by the unlit fire, fingers curled around the arms of the chair. Eyes distant and glassy. Looking at things he couldn't see. He did that a lot. Go quiet and just stare. Not moving, not a scratch or a shuffle in his seat. Like he was asleep with his eyes wide open. Tom had often been quiet, but his had always been a restless, fidgety silence and it had always been born out of his worries. When things had been going well, or rather, when he thought they were going well and hadn't noticed the large bucket of shit that always seemed to be hanging over them, he'd chatted away ceaselessly. Amos never did. Every word was considered and weighed before he uttered it. Like there was a price he had to pay for each and every one.

Thirteen years he'd been on the road, he must have a few stories to tell, something to fill the silence of the house during the night. Though maybe they weren't the kind you told to make people chuckle.

She gave him a little smile, the kind she usually used

153

when she wanted a man to do something. Something like kiss her or put his arms around her. Then she remembered who she was with. Amos just continued to stare blankly at nothing. Her smile melted away. She probably could have ripped her dress off, run around the room buck naked whooping like a savage and his expression wouldn't budge an inch.

A frown crossed Amos' face and the life flowed back into his face.

Fuck... another stray thought I should have avoided...

Before any further images fluttered across her mind, there was a sharp knock on the door. Now it was Molly's turn to frown.

"Who the hell is that?" She muttered, tossing her book aside.

"The Mayor..."

"You're just full of uses aren't you?"

Amos didn't smile.

"How can you tell?"

"There's a wrongness about him... something dark and empty."

"I really have to learn to stop asking you things."

Molly stood up and wondered whether it was too late to simply hide.

The knocking came again. More urgent this time.

"He's not going to go away," Amos offered.

"Will you promise to shoot him if he's mean to me?"

"Will you promise to bad mouth him if he's mean to me?"

"You know, you're far less of an asshole when you lighten up a little," Molly threw him a lopsided grin.

The knocking came again. Hard enough to rattle the door.

Molly spun on her heels; she suspected nothing in the house was big enough to hide her from the Mayor.

"Alright! Alright!" She shouted, settling upon a suitable scowl to mask her unease as she tugged open the door. Molly wasn't in the slightest bit surprised to find that Amos had been right.

"Why, Mrs McCrea, I was starting to think you weren't home," the Mayor stretched out a smile that revealed teeth that seemed both too numerous and too white as he doffed his hat.

"You feeling unwell?"

The Mayor's smile faltered a little, "I'm in fine health, why do you ask?"

"You don't usually bother knocking..."

"Why-"

Molly wheeled away, leaving the door open behind her. She'd rather slam it in his face, but she supposed she had to offer some deference to the oily toad.

Amos was standing in the corner of the room, hand not far from his gun, eyes hooded and unsmiling. He seemed even less inclined towards deference than she did.

The Mayor had already followed her down the hall and into the room by the time she reached Amos and turned back to the door.

"I sense a little hostility..." the Mayor puckered his lips and cocked his head in their direction.

"What do you want?" Molly demanded.

"You know, I always imagined you to be a far more convivial host..." the Mayor waved his hat towards the

155

rocking chair Amos had been sitting in earlier, "...may I?"

Molly gave a little shrug.

The Mayor sniffed and looked around the room once he'd settled in, "No whiskey?"

"Not tonight."

"Strange, I'd always envisaged you getting slowly drunk every night" He glanced at Amos, "It's not as if there's much else you two can get up to, is there?"

"What do you want?" Molly repeated, grateful that Amos was next to her, unmoving eyes fixed upon the Mayor, his hand still not wandering far from the butt of his gun.

"Want? Oh, I want for little Mrs McCrea. It's just a social call. I like to make sure my constituents are well. Even the transitory ones."

"We're not planning on going anywhere." Amos' voice was little more than a growl.

"No? I thought you might be off across the grass one night. You know how debt can give some people itchy feet."

"You'll get your money. Don't worry."

The Mayor smiled. "Well, yes I will. One way or another."

"I'm not working off the money on my back."

"That's only one option. I'm prepared to listen to all reasonable offers. So long as you don't try to skip town."

"The thought hadn't crossed my mind, I wouldn't even know how."

Tom had always been the one for running away...

"Well, I suppose that was more your late husband's forte."

Molly tried not to shuffle her feet and avoid the Mayor's roving eye. Was Amos the only man in the room who could read her mind?

The Mayor began to rock back and forth. The gentle creak of the chair was the only sound to fill the room as his eye played back and forth between them, a distant, knowing half-smile upon his lips.

"I understand you have a guest?"

"Yes..." Molly whispered, wishing she could deny it without quite knowing why.

"A lost little girl I hear. Where do you think she came from I wonder?"

"No one seems to know," Amos replied before she could, "do you?"

"Hard to say. All kinds of people wash up in Hawker's Drift, all kinds of people from all kinds of places. Like you two for instance."

"We know where we came from."

The Mayor's only reply was to stretch his smile a little wider and rock himself a little harder.

Molly had never really paid any attention to the way the chair had creaked before. Actually, she wasn't entirely sure it *had* creaked before. Just another of those familiar little sounds that wrap themselves about you, so common and every day that we pay no heed to them. But suddenly, to Molly's ears, there was now something faintly carnal about the sound. Like a bed creaking beneath two lovers. Or a whore and her latest client who'd climbed aboard in return for a couple of coins that chipped away at a bigger debt.

"Is the girl well? I heard she had a fever."

"She's much better," Amos answered. Molly found she couldn't hear much above that damn *creak, creak, creak...*

"That's good to hear. Her folks will be relieved. Where ever they are..." he took a long slow breath "...of course, whether it is entirely suitable for a young girl to be in such a house as this. That is another matter entirely."

"What do you mean?" Amos stiffened slightly.

"Well, a killer and a drunken, foul-mouthed fornicator, no offence, people might think you entirely inappropriate guardians of an innocent child. I do have the moral welfare of the town and its citizens to consider."

"She-"

"She's going nowhere." Amos snapped, cutting Molly off before she could say the same thing, albeit more colourfully.

"Well, we shall see about that. I would have thought it would be in your interest to see her elsewhere. She must quite cramp your style. No to mention make midnight flits across the grass quite... impractical."

"The girl's going nowhere, till we find her people anyway."

"And what if her people are far too far away for you to find them? You're not particularly good at finding people, are you, Mr Amos?" His eye snapped back to Molly, "And you can't really take her to the whorehouse can you Molly? I don't allow that kind of thing in my town at all."

"Why don't you just go and fu-"

"I couldn't sleep," Amelia said from the doorway, "I had nightmares." Her eyes were wide and she seemed even smaller than usual in the old shirt she was wearing as a night dress.

"Well, you must be little Amelia," the Mayor rose from the chair and turned toward the girl.

She nodded, her eyes widening, "Amelia Prouloux."

"Amelia Prouloux, it's a pleasure to meet you," the Mayor

crossed the room and crouched down in front of Amelia. There was something in his voice Molly didn't like. Or rather, liked even less than usual. He held out his hand, but Amelia didn't take it. Instead, she shuffled towards Molly and Amos. As she moved the Mayor's head swivelled to follow her, like a cat in the long grass, hunkered down on its belly watching a small bird. His eye had grown still, fixed upon the girl.

"My, you are a pretty little thing aren't you?" His tongue slithered out and darted along his lower lip; pink, sinuous and serpentine.

Amelia scurried across the room and found refuge in Molly's skirts; she put her arm around the girl and pulled her closer still.

"Strange," the Mayor muttered, straightening up, "children are usually fond of me."

"I think it's time you left," Amos said, moving in front of Molly and Amelia. The Mayor's eye moved from the little girl to the gun on Amos' hip and his fingers that twitched an inch from the grip.

"And are you going to gun me down if I don't? Dear, dear, are you really so keen to put your scarred neck back into the noose?"

"I tend to deal with one problem at a time."

The Mayor laughed; a dark, husky chuckle that carried absolutely no humour.

"Don't ever pull that gun on me; I can assure I'm a problem that your lead will never solve."

He retrieved his hat and once it rested upon his head to his liking, he gave a little nod, "A pleasure. As always. If the powers that be decide yours is not a suitable refuge for an innocent young girl, I'll let you know."

"And who are "the powers that be" exactly?" Amos moved forwards until he was toe to toe with the Mayor and staring into his unblinking eye.

"Well, I think we all know the answer to that," his head jerked around toward Amelia, his smile wide again, "Even little Amelia."

He stared at her for far longer than was necessary and Molly felt the girl pressing herself into her skirts as if she could disappear amongst their folds.

"Good night. I shall see myself out."

They stood, silent and unmoving, until they heard the front door close, only then did she feel Amelia relax and pull away from her.

"Who is he?" Amelia asked, looking up.

"He's the Mayor here hun... he runs things in this town."

Amelia thought about that for a moment before saying, in a faltering voice, "He's a very bad man, isn't he?"

Molly exchanged a glance with Amos.

"Oh don't worry about him," Amos said, a thin tight grin stretching across his face, "His bark is worse than his bite."

"You shouldn't antagonise him," Molly snapped, not that she was upset with Amos, she just needed someone to snap at.

"What does *an-tag-o-nise* mean?" Amelia asked, wide eyes switching between the two adults.

"It means... pick a fight with."

Amelia nodded and looked squarely at Amos, "Molly's right. My Mom always told me you shouldn't pick a fight with the Devil..."

The Farmer

He found his hand had wrapped itself around the little bottle in his pocket. Again.

Sye had stopped asking himself what he thought he was doing, there seemed no good purpose in a question that didn't have an answer. Best just roll with it and see where you end up.

Instead, he focussed on Cece, singing at her piano. How could any human being produce such a sound? Such beauty, such perfection, such sweet, sweet...

...*candy*...

...music to fill the soul. Sye sipped his beer though he barely tasted what passed his lips. Someone behind him brayed laughter. The kind of laughter that was usually accompanied by spit, bad breath and bulging eyes. Sye fought down the urge to go tell him to shut the fuck up. He doubted the oaf would listen and he'd have a fair to middling chance of being clubbed round the ear for his trouble if he did.

Jack's patrons were certainly being less polite than when Cece first started singing in the saloon though most still hushed to listen to her.

What would happen if people got bored of her? That

seemed a fairly absurd idea, but what if they did? Would Monty send her packing? Would she be gone as unexpectedly as she'd arrived?

She half turned during an instrumental break in her song, Sye drank in her beauty and felt simultaneously elated and dashed. She would never be his. If she stayed in town some other...

...less deserving...

...fellow would eventually sweep her off her feet and even the thought of her being with another man broke his heart to splinters. If she left, he would be distraught, but, he supposed, in time, without her around life would eventually go back to how it had been before. She would become just a memory that he might not even trust to ever have been real.

His hand was squeezing the little black bottle in his pocket again.

Or he could try and do something else...

There was something comforting about the bottle. It fitted perfectly in his hand; the glass was so smooth against his palm. Not like glass at all really, not cold and inanimate, it was more like... skin? Impossibly smooth, utterly hairless skin, but that's how it felt in Sye's palm as he rolled it back and forth, forth and back. Of course it wasn't skin, he knew that, it tinkled like glass when he tapped it, it looked like glass, it was a bottle. What else could it be?

Would Cece's skin feel as smooth? Her stomach? Her thigh? Her breast? Obviously she would be soft and not hard like the strange, little bottle, but, otherwise, maybe she would. Sye felt a sudden urge to take the bottle and rub it gently against his cheek...

He blinked. People were clapping and Cece was rising from the piano. He dropped the bottle back into his pocket and joined in.

She noticed him as he took a step towards her once the applause had faded into the blur of voices. She gave him a cold look.

He gave her a faltering little smile in return, "Cece, I just wanted to apologise..." he blurted out before her cold eyes could be replaced by a cold shoulder "...for the other day. I was an ass."

She regarded him for a moment in an is-he-worth-slapping kind of way.

"Yes, you were."

Sye swallowed; at least she hadn't walked off or hit him. Yet.

"I... shouldn't have behaved like that about Amos..."

"No, you shouldn't..." Cece shuffled from one foot to the other before her face softened, "...it was rather childish."

Sye managed to keep his smile in place. How was being in love childish? He only wanted what was best for her. Amos was a gunslinger, a killer, a rough-handed oaf. Maybe not a rapist, but certainly not-

Stop it.

"Yes... I don't really know what came over me. Jealousy I guess."

Cece tilted her head to one side and offered him the thinnest sliver of a smile.

Slap the patronising bitch!

He blinked and found his own smile faltering. Where had that come from? He didn't want to hurt Cece, whatever else,

165

the last thing he wanted to do was hurt her. He loved her, after all, but the voice had been so clear in his head and the urge so overwhelming he found he'd shoved his hand into his pocket to stop himself striking her.

He found the little black bottle and caressed it with his thumb, it was as warm and smooth as a woman's thigh...

Cece was talking, he suddenly realised, she was doing the "I like you, but..." thing again. Nothing was going to change her mind. He wasn't going to woo her with his decency or his jokes or his goofy smile or his undying goddamn love for her. So he was going to have to try something else because he knew he wanted her more than anything he would ever want in all the years he would have on God's sweet Earth.

"Can I get you a drink – just as an apology and to say I understand we're just friends..." The words cut his mouth like gargling razors, but he smiled through the pain of them all the same.

"I don't really drink."

"Everybody drinks?"

She stifled a little laugh, "Alcohol."

She was laughing at him. Wasn't she? Laughing *at* him.

"A coffee then?"

"The stuff here is rotting my stomach."

"Anything, *please*," Sye's voice sounded suddenly high-pitched and desperate to his own ears. He wanted her to drink from the little black bottle he realised. No, he *needed* her to. Nothing would ever be right until she'd supped some sweet, sweet, candy...

Sye coughed, as if clearing his throat, before trying again, "Anything, just let me say sorry for being such a complete ass. I'm so embarrassed Cece... please..."

She nodded and her smile was fuller, warmer and his heart melted a little more, "Okay... a coffee would be great, thank you."

"Right, coffee it is!" Sye backed away a few steps, not wanting to wrench his eyes away before spinning around and shouldering his way to the bar.

His heart was thudding like she'd just agreed to sleep with him rather than letting him buy her a coffee. Though, of course, she was going to get much more than just coffee. He sniggered. Literally. Waiting at the bar trying to catch Sonny's eye he'd sniggered like a dirty old man catching an illicit glimpse of a girl's titties.

Sye put a hand over his mouth, as embarrassed as if he'd just realised he was standing in a puddle of his own piss. Nobody seemed to have paid much heed. A wayward snigger wasn't ever going to be the oddest piece of behaviour in *Jack's* even on a quiet night, but it was odd for him.

He stroked the bottle; he was just stressed and excited. Not enough sleep and too much unrequited love. Could do strange things to any man, but that would be a changing soon. Unless the Mayor was playing him for a fool of course.

But he wasn't.

For the first time since the Mayor had conjured up that smooth, beautiful little bottle, he didn't think it was a joke, or nonsense or some charlatan's game. Standing here, about to slip some of the Mayor's candy into Cece's drink he really did think it was going to work. That she was going to be his. And even if it wasn't real, that was only the start. She just needed a nudge, nothing serious, something to give her a chance to see how right they were for each other. How *utterly* perfect. Then she wouldn't need any potions, once she saw the depth and intensity and truth of his love, then she would feel the same. He was sure of it.

After what seemed an interminable age Sonny finally poured him a coffee and a beer. Cece might not drink booze, but he sure as hell needed one. His hand was actually shaking when he dropped the coins into Sonny's palm.

"You feeling alright?" Sonny asked, rubbing the coins together as if they might not actually be real.

"Fine, why?"

Sonny shrugged, "You look a little... sweaty, ain't got nothing have you?"

Sye wiped his hand over his forehead and was surprised to find his fingers came away wet.

"Bit of a cold... maybes."

Sonny nodded and quickly tossed the coins into the brass till behind the bar, wiping his hands on the beer-stained apron he wore as soon as it snapped shut.

Sye took the drinks to the end of the bar where there was a jug of milk and sugar; it was also behind a pillar that kept him away from prying eyes.

He sniffed the milk to make sure it wasn't rancid before splashing a drop in Cece's coffee. He glanced up, but no one was paying him any attention and he pulled the little black bottle from his pocket.

What are you doing?

The question was just a distant echo. Sye found it remarkably easy to ignore.

He pulled the stopper from the bottle and resisted the

urge to sniff the contents. Had the Mayor said something about not drinking it himself? He couldn't quite remember, but it seemed best not to. He didn't know how this stuff worked, but if it made you fall in love with the first person you saw after drinking it... he looked up at the collection of wrinkled, toothless barflies scattered about him. Definitely best not to.

Just a couple of drops. No more. He swallowed and felt giddy. His palm was so sweaty he had to be careful the little bottle didn't slip from his fingers, which would be just like him to find a way to screw this up. Another furtive glance but no one was pointing, staring, shouting or demanding to know what he was slipping into Cece Jones' drink. But if he lingered long enough that might change.

He tipped the bottle and the candy flowed; a slow, black droplet that, for a moment, looked like a slimy finger curling around the lip of the bottle. Sye almost expected to see the other fingers appear, followed by a hand and an arm and then... he blinked and one, two, three big, fat drops dripped into the coffee.

He feared the potion was stealing itself to gush out like a wary beast from a cage that hadn't been locked properly. Sye rammed the stopper back in, but, for just an instant it felt like the candy was pushing up against it, trying to burst free from its confinement.

He stared at the coffee; three grey-black rings were dissipating outwards before they slowly sunk down into the drink. He caught a whiff of something sweet and rank, but it was gone before he was sure it was even there. He stuffed the bottle back in his pocket; she needed to drink the coffee quickly. Had the Mayor told him that too? He couldn't remember, but supposed he must have because he was pretty sure she needed to imbibe quickly for it to work.

Imbibe?

Odd, he didn't think that was a word he'd ever used in his life. Not that it mattered, all he had to do was get her to knock back a coffee and then she would be his. Would she swoon immediately? Would she touch him? Smile at him? Would it happen instantly or would –

"Sheet!"

The figure had appeared out of a cluster of men and walked straight into Sye, knocking both beer and coffee to the floor. A chorus of ironic cheers echoed around the saloon.

"Sorry about that," the man said, holding out his hands.

Sye just stared at the coffee. Jesus, couldn't he do any damn thing right?

"I guess I was rushing too much," Sye mumbled. He wanted to kick the ass in the shins, but that wasn't going to help matters.

"Let me buy you another?"

"It's okay, really."

The man leaned in enough for his forehead to brush Sye's, "But I insist..."

Before he could protest the man slung an arm around his shoulders and led him back to the bar.

"Hey, Sonny, beer and a coffee!" He said, his voice slightly slurred.

"Sure John," Sonny glanced at the pair of them.

Sye stood as awkwardly as you do when a man you don't

170

know very well was being a bit too familiar. He wanted to push him away, but there was no need to upset the drunken fool.

He had barely spoken to him before, though he'd heard a few lewd and unsavoury stories. None of them had mentioned he was a drunk to boot.

"It's Sye Hallows ain't it?"

Sye nodded, always vaguely surprised when someone knew his name, even in a small place like Hawker's Drift.

"And you know me I'm sure?"

"Mr Smith."

"John X people calls me."

"John X," seemed a damn stupid name to Sye, but he probably wasn't at his most charitable.

"You gonna clean up that mess?" Sonny interrupted as he shoved the drinks towards them.

John X grinned and flicked a coin back at him, "Nope. Only adds to the welcoming environment of your fine establishment."

Sonny did a decent impression of being thoroughly unamused.

"Sorry about that, but no harm done, eh?"

"Accidents happen," Sye nodded, eager to get the coffee enhanced and back to Cece."

"They sure do," John X gave him an unexpected squeeze of the shoulder and patted his side. He had one strong grip for an old fella, Sye thought, trying not to wince.

"Enjoy your night..." John X pulled away, fixing a long steady eye on him before melting back into the crowded shadows of the saloon. It occurred to Sye that, actually, he didn't look at all drunk.

He shook the thought away and hurried back to the milk jug, gave the coffee another derisory splash before reaching into his pocket while glancing about again to make sure he was still unobserved.

He frowned, patted down his jacket pockets with an increasing sense of alarm and disbelief.

The little black bottle was gone.

The Clown

Mr Wizzle thought it had been a good sermon. He nodded in satisfaction and run his hands down the lapels of his jacket. His fingers came away feeling slightly greasy.

Given the town had no official preacher at the moment he had, perhaps a little foolishly, thought people might be more prepared to listen to him now. But during his sermon, despite it being a *very* good sermon, they had drifted past him just as disinterestedly as they usually did. Perhaps the last preacher having hung himself after apparently raping that poor girl had put people off God a bit for the time being.

It was indeed a terrible world.

Still, he would count his blessings. It was warm and pleasant evening, the sky was a vivid blue, the sun's heat had faded to a gentle warmth carried on a kissing wind and nobody had thrown anything at him today.

He stepped off his preaching crate with a huff of breath. It was starting to look a little sorry, the wood cracking under his weight. He would have to get a new one from round the back of *Pickering's*. It wouldn't do to put his foot through the crate just as he was preaching about God's power and fury. That might look a little inopportune.

Of course, it could be argued he didn't actually need to

haul around a crate. It's not like he ever got a crowd big enough that the people at the back couldn't see him. Actually he never got anything that could be remotely described as a crowd. A few heckling drunks, sniggering children and the occasional curious newcomer didn't really constitute a crowd. His small congregation of regulars, Gilbert Hox, Mad Milly James, Kendal Bratt and his dog Wally didn't really constitute a crowd either.

Mr Wizzle puffed out his cheeks and looked up and down Main Street; even Gilbert, Mad Milly, Kendal and his dog Willy hadn't shown up today. Which was a shame. These were important days.

Amelia Prouloux.

A portent, surely? He wished he'd paid more attention when he'd met the old woman on the grass. It was a lesson, obviously. Always have your wits about you, particularly in times like these. God wasn't in the business of making an appointment with the likes of Mr Wizzle when he'd something important to tell him. He'd expect, quite rightly, that you'd be paying due attention.

But what he did remember troubled him greatly. Perhaps it was better not to know what was coming. Wasn't ignorance supposed to be bliss?

He puffed again as he bent down and scooped up his preaching crate. He was by the Corner Park, the sun was warm on his face and it was easy to think that all was right in the world. If you didn't know better.

He shuffled over to an unoccupied bench and slumped down onto it. He was tired. And old and fat. Too old and fat for shenanigans, that was for sure. He would go and see

Molly McCrea and Amos later. Check in on Amelia. He didn't think Molly liked him much, but then most people didn't seem to like him much. Most folk laughed at him, called him bad names and occasionally threw stuff at him.

He didn't think Molly would do any of those things. Molly was one of those people who hid their true self behind bluster and bad words, maybe because the world had hurt them or had scared them or done something to crush them. But God had chosen her to care for Amelia all the same, maybe not the obvious choice, but he could see the wisdom of it now that he'd spent a little time with her. The woman on the grass, Old Amelia, had spoken warmly of her too...

"May I join you?"

He hadn't even realised he'd closed his eyes to enjoy the warmth of the evening sun and he opened them with a start to see a hulking form silhouetted against the dazzling golden light. It wasn't until he squinted and raised a hand to his eyes that he recognised the figure.

"Mr Godbold – of course!"

Ash Godbold lowered himself onto the bench with the air of a man who strongly suspected he should be somewhere else. Pretty much anywhere else in fact.

Mr Wizzle turned and expectantly waited for him to say something. Instead, Ash just stared into the light, eyes hooded against the glare. Perhaps he'd just wanted to admire the view.

"Pickled egg?" He offered, producing a greasy bag from his pocket.

Ash shook his head, glancing at Mr Wizzle with dark, distant eyes. They looked empty and terribly sad. He shrugged and put the bag back in his pocket. He didn't feel so peckish all of a sudden.

"I always thought you were mad," Ash said suddenly, returning his gaze to the setting sun after a long silent minute.

"Most people hereabouts tend to," he admitted.

"Now I'm not so sure…"

Mr Wizzle raised an eyebrow but didn't reply.

"Things happen in this town, don't they? Bad things. Every now and again, infrequent enough for people to pretend they don't, but you see it and you don't pretend otherwise." Ash blew out his cheeks, followed by a slow, almost anguished sigh, "perhaps it's the rest of us that are mad after all."

"A man can fool himself about most anything if he tries hard enough. Don't make him mad though."

"No," Ash admitted, "just makes him a fool…"

Mr Wizzle smiled, a faint little ghost of one anyway, "Who'd listen to a man who wears an old clown suit anyway?"

Ash half turned to face him, the bags under his eyes like old bruises in the soft glow of the falling sun, "Why *do* you wear an old clown suit?"

"Reminds me of where I came from?"

"Which was?"

Mr Wizzle grinned, "The circus of course!"

"Once a clown always a clown huh?"

"People constantly mocking you keeps a man grounded. Stops you taking yourself too seriously and helps to knock the pride and foolishness from your bones. If everybody could see that, underneath everything else, we're all just clowns, all ridiculous and petty and liable to walk into a fencepost at any moment, maybe they'd see the world for what it is and just what people really are."

"Which is?"

"Small, insignificant and of no great consequence to the Great Show; just a little act on an enormous stage."

"Sounds a kinda depressing view of things."

"I find it quite liberating," Mr Wizzle winked, "but then I'm mad remember?"

Ash tried to smile, but it was a feeble stillborn thing that convinced neither of them.

"Are my girls safe in this town?"

"Why ask me?"

"I've heard the things you say on your little box. Heard em, but never paid em any heed. Never thought about em even. Just a mad old fool spouting off nonsense about the Devil being among us and snatching people away, but since Emily..." His voice had slowly dropped towards a hoarse whisper with each word although there was nobody within a hundred paces of them, "...I've started to think about them a lot. So, I'm asking you. Are my girls safe in this town?"

Mr Wizzle looked away from Ash's troubled, pleading eyes, out across the grass that moved ceaselessly under the breeze, making the land look like a living thing. Out to where a long column of wagons, just black dots against the endless green, were trundling towards Hawker's Drift. *Billberry's Travelling Carnival* was rolling into town, just like it did at this time on this day every single year.

"No, they're not," Mr Wizzle said, his voice as much a

whisper as Ash's had been, "Nobody is safe in this town…"

The Carney King

"Thomas Rum."

"Mr Mayor."

They regarded each other for a moment, comfortable with the silence; they had known each other for a long time after all. Way back to when they had other names entirely, names they no longer used, names that didn't fit comfortably into a human mouth.

"You look older," the Mayor said at last, he was reclining on a couch, one of his floozies curled at his feet, all blonde hair, tits and vacant eyes.

"It's what's supposed to happen," Rum took off his top hat and smoothed back his thinning hair, "you look exactly the same. As always."

"My girls keep me young, don't you Felicity dear?" The girl's eyes were half closed, lids weighed down by all manner of excess Rum assumed. She offered the barest twitch of a smile in response.

"People will notice."

The Mayor raised an eyebrow. He wasn't used to being challenged and didn't much care for it, but who else was left to do it but him?

"People see what they want to see." His fingers brushed

the top of Felicity's hair, finding a few blonde strands to turn about his finger, "or at least what I allow them to see."

"Can we talk?"

"Of course."

Rum stared at the girl, which was easy as she was the kind that drew the eye well enough. The Mayor had always liked to surround himself with pretty things. Mostly useless, but pretty all the same. His eyes flicked to the doorway where Symmons still stood after ushering him through the Mayor's gaudy little palace.

Well, almost everything was pretty.

"You can say anything in front of Felicity; she is far too hollowed out to understand much." Felicity's eyes drifted about the room as if she distantly recognised her name, but couldn't quite work out what it meant.

"I'd rather not discuss everything in front of your latest cunt," Rum growled.

"Is such vulgarity truly necessary Thomas?"

Rum offered a thin smile by way of a reply. He'd always considered vulgarity entirely necessary when dealing with sanctimonious pricks.

"Why don't you go and have a lie down my dear," the Mayor said, eventually.

"But I am lying down already, silly..." Felicity murmured, her words as distant as echoes in the mountains, as she stretched out at the Mayor's feet.

"Symmons..." the Mayor snapped his fingers and his flunky came scurrying over.

"Comfy..." Felicity pouted, arching her back and tossing an arm out over the floor towards Rum.

"Off to bed now," the Mayor insisted, his voice taking a harder edge.

Felicity allowed Symmons to pull her unsteadily to her feet, before taking a chiffon covered arm and leading her towards the door.

"Make sure you take her to the right bed," Rum grinned.

Symmons' lip quivered, but his only reply was a fleeting sneer. He had a face well suited to the sneer and he'd perfected its use a long time ago. Symmons had never liked him. In truth, he didn't think Symmons liked anyone much, save for the Mayor of course, who he loved utterly. Perhaps when you poured all your devotion into one vessel, particularly a vessel as bottomless as the Mayor, there just wasn't anything left for the rest of the world.

Rum didn't really know, he'd only ever had hate in his heart.

Once Symmons and Felicity had gone Rum straightened his back, cracked his neck and strode over to slump into one of the Mayor's plush leather chairs. Both limp and stoop vanishing in the handful of paces it took. He tossed his hat onto the floor.

"Man got a pour his own drink in this fine 'n fancy house of yours?"

"Please, allow me," the Mayor rose and threw some brandy into a glass.

"Obliged."

"So... how is the big, bad world out there?" The Mayor asked once he'd eased himself back into his seat.

Rum sipped his drink. It was excellent, which was no surprise.

"Dying," he replied, savouring the drink before having to sour his mouth with the word. "Little by little," he added eventually.

"The folly of men."

"Lucky you're here to save them then." Rum took another sip and swilled the booze around his mouth. "Luckier still they don't know the price."

"Have you become... *demotivated* Thomas?"

Rum stared into his glass and sucked his teeth, "Seems a long road and one not likely to ever get us home."

"We will prevail."

"We?"

"You followed me willingly enough?"

"Yeah, I made my choices and we lost."

"Death is the only defeat that matters and we yet live."

"Sometimes death seems the better option."

"We *will* go home."

"There is no going home. We were cast out... Actually you were cast out; the rest of us damn fools..."

"Then why are you still here... still serving me?"

A familiar coldness crept into the Mayor's voice, a coldness Rum knew well enough. It would have terrified him once, but time had weathered the fear from him long ago. He finished his drink instead.

"A fool's hope is better than no hope. Mind if I help myself?"

The Mayor laid out his palm towards the bottle.

"How was this year's harvest?"

Rum poured a long measure and didn't answer until he'd taken another hit. It really was rather splendid.

"The black wagon's nearly full."

"Nearly, Thomas?"

"Can't bring you more than there is... Mr Mayor."

"I suppose quality is more important. Have you brought me quality?"

"One we came across a few days ago is a deep well, the others... not so much."

The Mayor pinched his bottom lip as his eyes glazed in thought. Calculating.

"I was hoping for more."

"There will never be enough."

"There's a whole world, they'll be enough. In time."

"There's a whole *dying* world. Do you even know how many you need?"

The Mayor's nostrils flared slightly. He was getting under his skin, he usually did, "It's an imprecise science. We must be patient."

Rum snorted.

"Something you want to say, Thomas?"

He looked about the room, stuffed full of finery from across the world. No expense spared for the Mayor's comfort.

"Patience is easy when you got your ass on soft leather, your cock in softer women and," he rocked his glass back and forth "your mouth full of hard liquor."

"We all do our part..."

"Yeah, and some of us spend all year travelling the world collecting souls..."

"It is what is required. You know that."

Rum wasn't sure he knew any damn thing. Seemed to him what they were doing was about as effective as breaking down a six-inch steel door by throwing eggs at it, but he kept his peace as he knew what the Mayor would say. Some shit about the wind wearing down a mountain to sand if you gave it long enough.

"And how are the cattle here? Getting fat on all this grass you have?"

"The livestock is flourishing."

Rum flashed a sour grin. He just bet it was...

The Gunslinger

It was a familiar dream. He had several and this was far from the worst, though he always awoke from it slick with sweat and his heart a drumming all the same.

There was a grey horse ahead of him, a tall stallion with a figure slumped in its saddle; his head lowered, long soiled coat rippling in the breeze, dust-smeared boots in the stirrups. Going nowhere in a hurry. Amos was following on foot, breathless and desperate, thrashing through the undergrowth. Screaming at the rider. Screaming at him to stop. Screaming at him to come back and face him. Screaming like he had when Megan had died in front of him. Screaming so hard he could taste the blood in his throat.

But the grey stallion just trudged on. Unhearing or uncaring. It didn't really matter which. Amos' gun belt was empty, the holster flapping uselessly against his thigh; otherwise he could have shot the bastard from the saddle. So, instead, he run and he run and he run, but the grey stallion never got any closer. One hoof plodding after the other, head down like its rider. Uncaring, unhearing. Exhausted like it had been traipsing across the world forever, or at least for the last thirteen years

Amos blinked at the darkness.

Some dreams were nonsense. Some had hidden meaning. Some told stories you didn't want to hear. This dream was easy enough to read. It had been his life these last thirteen years. Forever running after a figure he could never catch.

He closed his eyes again. There was nothing to see in the night but the ghost of a grey stallion in the formless shadows.

Time heals, his mother had always said. Time heals or time kills. Kitchen sink wisdom maybe, but true enough in most cases. Just not in his. The cuts Severn had sliced through his flesh may have healed, after a fashion, but the wounds inside had never knitted back together. Time had not staunched the flow of blood, it had not dried or scabbed them, not hardened them to scars. His life still dripped out with every day that crept by, but he didn't die.

Time didn't heal and time hadn't killed.

He was still following that grey stallion.

Amos wished he could cut the memories out of him. Of what had happened that day. Of why they had happened. Maybe then he could stop running and watch the grey stallion finally fade into the distance. But memories were harder to cut away than human flesh.

And even if he could, what then? What would be left of him? What was a man if he was not his memories? Flesh and blood, bone and muscle, piss, shit and bluster. No different to a horse or a dog or a crow picking at the carrion.

His memories made him and they had made him a man he hated.

He thought of Megan, running a hand through her wild tangled hair, curling a little smile at him and offering a shrug when he brought her a dilemma he couldn't resolve.

Just do a little good.

That had always been her answer to any problem. Do the right thing. Follow the bright path; make the world a fraction better. Just do a little good.

But he hadn't and she'd died and he'd become something less than a man.

Not just less than a man because he only had a twist of scarred gristle between his legs, but because of the things he had done since. The choices he'd made. The men he'd killed. Some no better than Severn for sure, but some no worse than most. Amos the Gunslinger. Killer and gun for hire. Pay the piper's price and send him off to do whatever dark works needed doing.

He told himself there was nothing else he was fit for. Nothing else that would pay for him to search for Severn. Nothing else that would take him to the hard, dark places the likes of Severn might slither under.

He was fast with a gun and looking into a man's soul made him faster still. He killed because he was good at it. He killed because it paid well; he killed because he couldn't kill Severn so he took his vengeance on other men instead. Maybe he just killed because he enjoyed it.

Or perhaps because he hoped that next time he might not be quick enough and a bullet would finish what time could not.

And now he was in this strange little town so far from anywhere. For the first time in thirteen years he had something else in his life, something that reminded him of the man he had once been. He had Molly and Amelia. A peculiar little family they made. He could save Molly; maybe he could even get Amelia home, wherever she had come from. Make them safe and do a little good.

But whenever he stopped and thought about what he could do, what he should do, all he could hear was the distant plodding hoof beats of a grey stallion that forever walked ahead of him. Just over the horizon. Calling him away. He didn't know what to do anymore. Part of him wanted to stay. To stay with Molly and little Amelia but part of him heard the grey stallion still and knew there was a slumped figure on its back, long coat whipping in the breeze, waiting for him to follow. A figure that never looked back and who if he ever caught would send him mad, because he knew it wasn't Severn on that horse.

Severn had never ridden a grey stallion.

If he ever caught up with that grey horse, the rider would twist around in its saddle, slow as old bones, and look down at him. In the shadow beneath the battered brim of its shit brown hat, the empty black sockets of a skull would peer and its laughter would ring out.

Severn didn't have a grey stallion, but Death rode a pale horse and Death wanted him to keep moving on because there was still plenty of dark work for Amos the Gunslinger to do. Plenty more souls to put in the ground. Plenty of flesh in need of lead.

Time had not healed and time had not killed. He had lain on the cusp of death for days after Severn had finished with him. Maybe he had crossed it once or twice. But the rider on the grey stallion had sent him back. Sent him back with the gift of reading souls to go with his fast hand and good eye.

Sent him back with dark work to do.

Just do a little good?

He truly didn't know how anymore...

The Widow

Molly hadn't slept. She would have tossed and turned, but she didn't want to wake Amelia so eventually she'd crept downstairs. Amos was stretched out on the floor, a blanket half over him, snoring loudly into her thin spare pillow.

She stood in the darkness and watched him for a while. Wanting him in a way that she knew he could never satisfy and then feeling guilty for thinking it. It was a thought she guessed she really should stamp down on in future. Amos had been hurt about as much as it was possible for a man to be hurt, but picking up on that thought would cut him pretty deeply too she would imagine. He might seem distant and cool on the surface, but even without his strange gifts she knew there was another man beneath all that. A man she really didn't want to hurt.

She half turned towards the door but hesitated, looked back at him before muttering half under her breath.

"Oh fuck it."

She lay down on the floor next to him, pulled the blanket over herself and wriggled up against him. He stirred a little but didn't wake. She lay for a moment and listened to his snoring, her head on the edge of the entirely inadequate pillow, before twisting around, finding his arm and pulling it over her. She pressed her backside against him and wrapped her fingers around his. He still didn't wake.

She'd always had a strange fancy to learn to play the trumpet. Perhaps that might work.

She sighed. Let him sleep, at least this way he wouldn't jump away from her like a scalded cat.

Molly closed her eyes, the floor was hard (not exactly a surprise). The pillow was thin to the point of pointlessness (she really should get another). But she felt his breath, warm and slow, against her hair and the steady, constant beat of his heart. They gave her more comfort than the softest of mattresses and the deepest of pillows ever could.

The house was silent and the world beyond too. Save for Amos' snoring of course. If she tried really hard, she could almost believe that everything was right in the world.

If she could live with the fact she was sleeping on the floor with a man without a cock whom she was feeling increasing drawn to, that she owed a fortune she couldn't repay, that the Mayor was still threatening her with the whorehouse and she'd now somehow found herself responsible for a lost little girl who might end up being snatched away from her by the said creepy one-eyed civic dignitary.

Perhaps snoring was the least of her worries.

She pulled Amos' calloused hand to her face, pressed her lips against it and tried to ignore the nagging feeling that there was another woe she had somehow managed to forget.

*

"Mr Furnedge," Molly managed to smile. Just.

Amelia had insisted on seeing Silver again. She was

192

worried he might be lonely and in need of apples, so Amos had taken her to the stables while Molly had popped into *Pickerings* to buy a few groceries. Furnedge had been waiting for her on the boardwalk. She rearranged the bag of shopping just in case the lawyer wanted to stare at her tits.

"Mrs McCrea," Furnedge beamed. Though leered would have been an equally accurate description as he doffed his hat and dipped his head. She wasn't entirely sure whether he was being polite or trying for a better angle to look around the groceries. Probably both.

"You look... *radiant!*"

"Thank you," her eyes darted towards the stables, but there was no sign of Amos, "how are you?"

"Splendid," Furnedge beamed/leered again. He looked anything but. He'd never been a particularly fetching man, but now he looked awful. Dark rings imprisoned his eyes and his skin had the waxy, flaccid appearance of a hastily embalmed corpse. He also appeared to have a bruise under one eye. His suit was quite nice though. His wardrobe had improved considerably since Lorna's death, even if nothing else about him had.

"And you?"

"Good..."

"And what brings you out on this delightful morning?"

Molly juggled her groceries.

"Shopping?"

"Yes."

Furnedge's smile stretched a little further like he'd just figured out something terribly difficult.

"I haven't seen you around town much these last few

days?"

"No..."

A lock of hair chose that moment to start bobbing in front of her eye as if fate had decided she didn't quite enough irritants to deal with.

"...I've been busy at home. I have a guest."

"The gunslinger," Furnedge muttered, his smile evaporating instantly.

"Well, yes, but I'm looking after a little girl too. She was rather poorly."

"Ah yes, I had heard A black child isn't it?"

"A little girl. Amelia."

"Very charitable, very Christian I must say," Furnedge's head bobbed up and down a little, before leaning in a little closer, "is she any better?"

"She's fully recovered, thank the Lord," And Cece Jones, she thought, only slightly begrudgingly.

"Well, best keep an eye on her now then," Furnedge leaned in even closer. Was he really trying to peer over the bag? Molly clutched the groceries a little tighter to her bosom.

"Keep an eye on her?"

"Well, you know how light-fingered those people can be?"

"Those people?"

"The blacks. Not their fault, of course, not really, just...well... their low intelligence I suppose. That's why most of them are in chains down south after all."

"Our gunsmith seems singularly bright to me. And I'm not aware of him stealing anything either."

Where the hell is Amos? I can't afford to waste a perfectly good bag of shopping on this fool's head.

"Well, from what I hear, he's stolen a few wives." Furnedge straightened up, chuckled and looked too pleased with himself by half.

Well, I suppose I didn't spend that much...

Fighting down the urge to find out if Furnedge would look more appealing covered in eggs and flour, Molly manufactured a smile and tried to step around the lawyer. Instead, she found his stubby fingers wrapped around her upper arm.

"No need to hurry off, we have things to discuss my dear. Remember?"

Molly swallowed. Really. How could she have forgotten?

"We do?"

"My proposal?" Furnedge bristled. More than a little.

"Oh... that."

To be fair most men probably wouldn't take kindly to their proposal of marriage being brushed aside so offhandedly, but Molly really didn't like the way his eyes narrowed even further than usual. They were contracting till his pupils were all but lost amongst the puffy bags and dark lids that encased them.

"You seemed... *conducive*... before..." his fingers tightened on her arm.

"Well, I've had some time to think-"

"I suggest you think some more..." Furnedge's words hissed from between his pressed lips like steam from an overheated kettle, "...you wouldn't want to come to a decision you'll later regret."

"Take your damn hand off me!" Molly's voice sounded both calm and cold to her own ears though she felt anything but inside.

Furnedge squeezed harder before his fingers sprung open and he offered her a faltering smile.

"I apologise; I didn't mean to hurt you... it is just... I love you!"

"I'm sure," Molly snapped. Now her tone was irate and hot, which was much more in keeping with her mood.

"I want you to be my wife. I will make you happy... I can give you... *everything!*"

"There's nothing you have that I want."

Furnedge blinked and took a step backwards as if she'd slapped his face.

"But... but you were conducive!" He spluttered.

"A girl can change her mind," Molly moved to brush past him with all the dignity a woman juggling a bag of groceries could muster, but Furnedge stepped across her.

"Molly, don't be so hasty. I can keep you out of the whorehouse!"

"But only if I marry you?"

When Furnedge didn't answer, she gave a little snort. She felt another response rising in her throat, something short, pithy and imaginatively using the word fuck, but it wouldn't come. What if there was no other way? Her eyes flitted towards the stable, but Amos and Amelia were nowhere to be seen.

"Mrs McCrea! What a lovely day it is!"

Molly looked round with a start. She'd never been so glad to see a fat old man in a stained and smelly clown's suit before. Actually, she'd never been glad to see one before full stop. But these were particularly trying times.

196

"Mr Wizzle!" She beamed, nodding at the old man as he doffed his battered derby in return. "Mr Furnedge." He turned his attention to the lawyer as he produced a grubby old rag that might have been a handkerchief in a previous life and mopped the shining liver-spotted pate between his tufts of red hair.

"I don't believe we've been introduced..." Furnedge took a step back.

"I'm Mr Wizzle..." he slammed his derby back on and stuck out a hand, "I'm a guy with a lot of fizzle!"

"I'm sure..." Furnedge peered at the offered hand as if the old man had just pulled it out of a latrine.

Mr Wizzle raised an eyebrow, his smile not wavering as the lawyer pointedly ignored his hand, "Pickled egg?"

"I'm sorry?"

He fished out a greasy paper bag from his pocket and thrust that at Furnedge instead, "You look a bit pale if you don't mind me saying. Perhaps a little something to eat?"

"I've eaten. Thank you."

Mr Wizzle shrugged and fished an egg out for himself, biting it in half with relish, "A man alone can easily overlook the importance of good food."

"I am coping with being a widower without recourse to such... delicacies."

"Really?" Mr Wizzle wolfed down the remainder of his egg with lip-smacking delight, "Have you found a new maid yet?"

"Pardon?"

"I heard your last help... had to find alternative employment. I hate to think of you alone in that big house. Solitude can turn a man's thoughts to maudlin. I should know..."

"My welfare is of no concern of yours," Furnedge, turned towards Molly abruptly. "Good day Mrs McCrea. I will call on you soon to discuss matters. I suggest you think about my proposal carefully in the meantime..."

Mr Wizzle turned, pulling a slightly pained face as Furnedge stomped away, "Don't you think he is a most peculiar man?" He asked with a sigh, thrusting his hands deep into the pockets of his soiled, baggy, yellow and black checked trousers...

*

"Amelia seems much recovered," Mr Wizzle gave Molly a sideways look and flashed a grin that suggested there had never been any doubt about the matter.

Molly nodded and smiled in return as Amelia belted across the square. Amos was holding her hand in the vain hope he might prevent her scampering in front of a horse, but it seemed more likely the little girl would only drag him in front of one too.

"Silver ate all the apples!" She declared breathlessly.

"Silver?" Mr Wizzle asked.

"Silver's a horse," Amelia explained, peering up at the old man, "he's a very *hungry* horse."

"Sure is," Amos confirmed.

"Do you feed him enough?" Amelia demanded, turning challenging eyes on the gunslinger.

"Sure..." Amos looked slightly abashed, "a man has to look after his horse..."

Amelia didn't look entirely convinced and span back

around towards Mr Wizzle, "Do you have any apples? Amos didn't bring enough; Silver still looks hungry."

"Horses are always hungry," Amos muttered, but nobody was listening to him as Mr Wizzle patted down his suit.

"Seems I'm plum out," the old man confessed, "does Silver like pickled eggs?"

Amelia wrinkled her nose, "Nobody likes pickled eggs apart from you."

Mr Wizzle could only nod and offer an expression that suggested he thought the world was a very peculiar place.

Molly looked away as the old man bent down with a puff so Amelia could tell him more about Amos' poor undernourished horse. A commotion was coming down Main Street, like music, but only just. There was nothing to see, however, apart from Furnedge, who was standing outside the Mayor's residence. Even in the bright sunshine his face seemed dark and overcast. A sky before the thunder arrived.

She couldn't run, not with Amelia and the clock was ticking down till she had to repay the Mayor. Or face the consequences. She glanced at *Jack's*, where a couple of the saloon girls were shooting the breeze outside, drooping feathers in their hair and cleavage spilling from the tops of skin-tight corsets. She tried to imagine herself dressed like that. Then tried even harder not to.

A weather-beaten rancher in a sweat-stained cotton shirt took off his hat and shook out the dust against his ass as he climbed the steps towards them. The girls smiled as he stopped to talk to them. One of them, a blonde in a ridiculously tight dark green dress, eventually took his arm and he led her inside. As soon as they turned away the smile evaporated from the other girl. She stared across the square and looked relieved.

Molly wondered how she would feel, rigged and bedecked to attract a man's favours. Would she look relieved if a man chose another girl, or would she see it as a few more coins she would miss out on chipping away her debt with?

"You alright?"

She snapped round, Amos was by her side. Looking concerned. Was her face so easy to read? Then she remembered. Of course. Every damn stray thought...

She was going to say sure and manufacture a smile. The kind she'd found distracted most men, but, of course, Amos wasn't most men.

"Furnedge..." she whispered, though Amelia was too engrossed with the old clown to hear her.

Amos glanced across the square at the loitering lawyer.

"He wants an answer."

"What one are you going to give him?"

She bit down on the lie that came instinctively to her lips. "I dunno..."

"You can't marry him, Molly."

"Can't I?" She jerked her head towards *Jack's*, where the saloon girl was still enjoying the sunshine and being vertical. "Would it be worse than..."

An image of herself dressed like a whore in front of a queue of filthy, leering men came to mind. Instead of stamping down on it, she focused as hard as she could on it.

Amos blinked and blushed faintly before dropping his eyes to his feet.

Hey, this is actually easier than finding the right words!

"I can't run away, not with Amelia..."

"Doubt you can take her to the whorehouse either."

"No... but you can look after her."

"Me?"

"She likes you."

"I'm lousy with kids!"

Amelia glanced over at them and flashed a big, happy smile.

"You see?"

"She likes my horse."

"Well, she likes the horse more than you, admittedly. The girl has some sense..."

The noise was growing louder, a brash, discordant sound, brass and drums played by people not entirely familiar with the concept of music. Mr Wizzle had risen to his feet and was staring down towards Main Street, one hand resting lightly on Amelia's shoulder.

"You can't marry that man!" Amos hissed, focused entirely on Molly.

"You going to stop me?"

"I'll do whatever is necessary." Molly wasn't entirely sure whether to be touched or chilled by Amos' tone.

"You're not going to shoot him are you?"

"The thought hadn't crossed my mind."

She was leaning more towards chilled.

People were starting to gather in the square as the source of the piss poor attempt at music hove into view. A colourful ragtag procession led by trumpeters and a small man almost lost behind a huge bass drum which he was whacking with gusto but little evident rhythm.

The musicians, if that wasn't too kind a word, were followed by jugglers, tumbling acrobats, a tall wisp of a man spitting fire through a flaming brand and a collection of gaudily dressed face-painted clowns. She glanced at Mr Wizzle, but if he was having any wistful thoughts about his circus days, he wasn't showing it.

At the very front of the procession was a gaunt old man in a battered top hat, so jauntily pushed to one side Molly wasn't entirely sure how it was staying on his head. He walked with a limp and a slight stoop, but he was still setting a fair pace as he waved to the gathering town's folk. Occasionally tossing his walking cane into the air and catching it deftly with his opposite hand.

"Looks like the carny has arrived in town," Molly muttered. She'd never paid them much heed. She vaguely remembered them doing this before, but it hadn't seemed interesting enough for Tom and her to drag themselves out of the saloon for. Though plenty of others clearly thought differently as they poured out of *Jack's* to clap and holler.

Women were walking along the edge of the boardwalk. Each one in the shade of a parasol, handing out flyers to the onlookers though most of the men were too busy gawping at them to read the handbills. They were all young and startlingly beautiful. It looked like the carney offered more than just juggling and sideshows to bring in trade.

"*Billberry's Travelling Carnival...*" Mr Wizzle spat.

Amelia was wide-eyed as the procession drew close. "Do they have elephants?"

"They have nothing of worth," the old man replied, drawing the little girl closer.

The man leading the parade was smiling broadly, a thin, long stretch of a smile that looked well practiced and entirely insincere. Molly grasped for his name, she was sure she'd heard it before, he was the Carney King, but his name wouldn't come. She'd never felt the need to pay it much attention.

As he drew level with them his head turned, she couldn't make out his eyes as he wore round spectacles with blackened lenses, but she got the impression he was inspecting them closely. After a moment, his smile stretched a little further. Adjusting the long black coat he wore in spite of the summer heat he swivelled towards them, his right leg dragging slightly behind him.

"Well, I do hope you good folk will be coming to see my little show while we're in town?"

Mr Wizzle's fingers dug deeper into Amelia's shoulder while his usually cheerful plump face wore an uncharacteristic sneer. Amos was just staring blankly at the carney man.

"I'm sure we will..." Molly replied when she realised neither of the men were going to answer him.

He gave a little nod, but it was a fleeting, perfunctory response. His gaze was locked firmly on Amelia and he crouched down in front of the little girl, with a fluid ease that didn't entirely fit an old man with a limp and a stoop.

"And who might this young lady be? I don't think I've seen you in Hawker's Drift before?"

"I'm Amelia Prouloux... I'm not from here."

"She's visiting." Molly offered, drawing closer to Amelia. The man's face was long, like something made of wax that

had been left just a little too long in the sun and had begun
to run.

"Is that so?" And where are you visiting from Miss
Amelia?"

"Mississauga," she said, with a giggle and a little shuffle of
her feet.

"Mississauga, eh? That's a mighty long ways from here
little lady. Just how'd you get to be so far from home?"

Amelia screwed up her face, "I just found myself here..."

"Happens..." His smile stretched again. Or the wax melted
a little more.

"What's your name, Mister?" Amelia asked.

"Why, I completely forget my manners, must be that
dazzling little smile of yours! I'm Thomas Clyde Rum... and I
have the singular honour of being the impresario, owner,
master of ceremonies and custodian of *Billberry's Travelling
Carnival*, the greatest show on the road between the
Mississippi and the Rockies. Here in Hawker's Drift for one
week only!"

"Do you have elephants?"

"I'm afraid we don't Miss Amelia, but I do have something
you'd like..." Rum pulled off his hat, revealing long grey hair
greased back over his scalp. He held it before the little girl,
"...why don't you put your hand in here and see if you can
fish it out?"

Amelia looked uncertainly towards Molly, who nodded,
doubting there was anything worse than some cheap candy
hidden in the hat as a treat to entice kids to come see the
show in the hope of more. Mr Wizzle was glaring at the hat
like he wanted to kick it out of Rum's hand. Professional

jealousy?

Amelia cautiously rummaged around a bit before frowning and pulling her hand out again, "There's nothing in there?"

"Really?" Rum pouted, shook the hat and peered inside over the top of his darkened glasses. His irises were such a light grey they were only marginally darker than the whites. "Silly me! I forgot the magic word."

"What's the magic word?" Amelia asked in a hushed tone.

Rum shook his head and pressed a finger to his pale lips, "Can't say it out loud. Too powerful. Anything could happen if I did. You might even turn into a frog."

"I don't want to be a frog!"

"That's why I'll just say it up here," Rum tapped his forehead and then shook his hat three times before tilting it towards Amelia again. "Ah, now there's something in here for you to share with a friend..."

Amelia tentatively reached into the hat, her expression suggesting she thought the carney man was full of some sort of bullshit. Though, admittedly, being eight she might have phrased it slightly differently to Molly. Her frown quickly returned, followed by a giggle as she pulled out an apple.

"Wow!" She gasped, head turning back and forth between the three adults standing over her and the showman crouching in front of her. "How'd you do that?"

Thomas Rum straightened up, put his hat back on and then tapped his nose, "It's just magic, Little Miss Amelia. Just plain an simple magic..."

The Lawyer

The carney was putting on the same brash, gaudy little parade it did every year, just to make sure everybody knew there'd rolled into town again. Making an awful din and interrupting people's proper work. There really wasn't any need for it at all as far as Guy Furnedge could see. Just a bunch of tricksters, shysters and whores set on parting people from their hard-earned money. Wasn't there enough of them in Hawker's Drift already?

A good-looking girl in a flowing white dress drifted by, smiling at him from beneath the shade of a matching parasol as she wafted a cheap handbill under his nose. He shook his head and tried hard not to stare at her. He knew as well as everybody else that the carney had pitched up in town, where it was and how long it would be there. It came as regular as Christmas and the first winter snows. The girls weren't advertising the carney anyway; they were advertising themselves.

Maybe some people went to laugh at the clowns, gawp at acrobats and throw balls at coconuts. Most of the men, however, went to enjoy the whores and the other darker pleasures the carney offered. He'd heard tales of what went on at the carney after dark...

They were certainly far prettier than the girls in *Jack's*. But a whore was still a whore.

He turned up his nose and looked pointedly away.

How could any man want to plough such well-furrowed soil?

The girl wandered away, her eyes distant. Why should she care? There were plenty of men in town who didn't share Guy Furnedge's moral backbone.

He liked women well enough. God knew he loved women more than most men. But not for a few coins, a few grunts and a bit of acting. His gaze returned to Molly McCrea, standing across the square with her peculiar little entourage. No, he wanted something else entirely.

So, it sadly appeared, did she.

To be precise; she wanted to waste her life away with a violent, half-witted eunuch, a stray blackamoor brat and a fat old man who preached from street corners in a filthy clown suit. It wasn't suitable company at all and the fact that she apparently preferred such companions over what he could offer her was all the more galling.

This was not how things were supposed to have been. Perhaps a lesser man might fall into despondency, or even concede defeat. But Guy Furnedge was not a lesser man. He'd worked hard; he'd been diligent, selfless. He had endured and, by God, he had suffered. He was not going to forgo his due that easily. And when she finally came to her senses and married him he would put a stop to her consorting with such undesirables straight away.

Whoever the gunslinger was and whatever Molly saw in him he could be dealt with. He was a boil on the world, on

Guy Furnedge's world, on the world as it should be with Molly his loving and devoted wife. But no matter how big and ugly a boil might be, it could still be lanced.

And Guy Furnedge knew just the man for lancing boils...

*

"What a pleasure!"

"Something has to be done!"

The smile, which admittedly hadn't exactly reeked of sincerity, dropped from the Mayor's face. It wasn't quite how Furnedge had intended to start, but after almost an hour of clicking his heels waiting to see the Mayor, his mood had slowly burned to a blistered and prickly black. He was, after all, a *very* busy man.

"Does it indeed?"

"That damnable eunuch!" Furnedge didn't approve of coarse language as a rule, but in such trying circumstances he thought the lapse was entirely forgivable.

"You mean Amos the Gunslinger?" The Mayor was slumped in his enormous leather chair. At least he hadn't hooked his boots up onto the mahogany desk. That had never seemed particularly professional.

"Yes. Amos!" He spat back. Reluctant to even speak the man's name. It left a bitter taste on his tongue.

The Mayor offered a little shrug, "Women's hearts... such strange and fickle things don't you find?"

"You said you were going to deal with him?"

"I am..." there was a stillness about the Mayor suddenly, a stillness that wanted to make Furnedge fidget and squirm, made him want to be somewhere else. Anywhere else.

"I... wasn't... complaining..."

"One would hope not, after all I've done for you Guy. That would be ungrateful."

Furnedge twisted the brim of his hat. There had been no chair for him this time and he stood before the great expanse the Mayor's desk and felt very, very small. Did it mean anything, not being given the courtesy of a chair?

"Oh, I'm very grateful. Truly... and I am your man forever."

"I'm very glad to hear it Guy," a slow cold smile cracked the Mayor's beard, "after all, I didn't kill your wife out of the goodness of my heart..."

Furnedge swallowed and shuffled his feet. Those words, when spoken out loud, sounded cold and cruel - like he had done some terrible thing. Of course, in truth, it had just been a kindness, for both Lorna and he, but still, he didn't like those words. They made him sound like some heartless, cold-blooded monster.

The silence stretched out between them and Furnedge fumbled for something to fill the void. The anger that had been stoked by his long wait was no more than a smouldering pile of damp wood. The Mayor could be a passable bucket of icy water when he wanted.

Furnedge swallowed, "It is just... Molly... I love her. As you know. I thought..."

The Mayor raised a hand and the faltering words dried in the lawyer's mouth.

"You will be together. It is only right and proper. It is the best thing for everyone. She will see that in time Guy. She will see you as the knight in shining armour that you are."

Furnedge, despite himself, glanced down at his slight

frame and the modest paunch that poked out of his open jacket. He didn't feel like much of a knight in shining armour.

"You will slay the dragon of the whorehouse for her," the Mayor said, his voice dropping to a sonorous whisper.

"But, this gunslinger... I fear she has feelings for him."

"Feelings? You have money, you can protect her, keep her safe. That is what Molly McCrea wants above all other things. To be safe."

"Perhaps..."

The Mayor rose smoothly, unfolding himself from the embrace of his huge leather chair he came around the desk to stand before the small lawyer.

"Do not worry about Amos. He will not be here for long."

"That is what you said before." The words escaped Furnedge's lips before he could stop them. There was still a flickering flame within him after all.

"That didn't work out as I had hoped, but trust me, Guy, Molly and Amos have no future together. Her destiny is with you." The Mayor tapped his battered leather eye patch, "I can see it clearly."

Furnedge nodded and smiled and tried to look reassured.

"How are you otherwise Guy?"

"Otherwise?"

"You appear to have a black eye. Have you upset someone?"

Furnedge touched his swollen eye and tried not to wince. Amy had packed a surprisingly powerful punch for a slender little thing.

"Oh, it's nothing. Just a stumble."

The Mayor gave the kind of smile you conjured when you couldn't be bothered to challenge a lie, "Domestics these days, they can be so ungrateful. Can't they?"

"I suppose..." Furnedge mumbled. Why did he ever even try to lie to the Mayor? The man, somehow, seemed to know everything.

"Don't worry Guy. You will get all of your rewards in time. Just be patient and loyal. That is all I ask. I shall see you attain your heart's desire."

"I am loyal. To the hilt! To the last!!"

"Of course you are..."

The Mayor returned to his desk and Symmons appeared unsummoned to show him out.

He managed a gracious "Thank you," and scurried out after the Mayor's manservant.

The sun was still shining out on the square and he was absurdly grateful to feel it upon his face.

He turned on his heels and hurried across the square and down Main Street. Miss Dewsnap had finished for the day and his office was blissfully empty. His home was equally empty, but he'd found himself spending more time here than in the house. Too many memories, he'd told himself. Too many creaking floorboards, too many little sounds, too many little smells and, occasionally, too many things he thought he saw out of the corner of his eye. All things he knew weren't there. Just guilt. Of course, guilt and stress. But still, a man needed to be comfortable in his own home. Once he'd sorted out a new maid and Molly had moved in, well, then things would settle down. Things would be better.

Furnedge slumped into his chair, for a moment he stared

across his own modest desk, which, unlike the Mayor's was scuffed and scratched through years of use. He unlocked one of the lower drawers and pulled out a bottle of whiskey. He kept it mainly for clients, a little something to settle nerves or seal a deal. Now he just needed one for himself.

His hand was shaking a little as he poured himself a glass. Usually, he drank in small measured sips, but this time he drained the glass in one.

That didn't work out as I had hoped…

Furnedge had assumed the rape of Emily Godbold and Amos' subsequent arrest had just been a fortuitous coincidence. It was quite believable that this itinerant drifter, who was a gunslinger and a killer for hire after all, would rape a young girl. When it conspired he couldn't have done it, Furnedge had been disappointed of course. It would have been convenient.

All very convenient.

He poured himself another glass. This one he did sip. The Mayor had killed Lorna. Poisoned her. He hadn't actually considered what else the man had done in this town. What he might do. What he was capable of.

That didn't work out as I had hoped…

Had that poor girl been raped simply to help him? So that he and Molly would be together? And had Tom McCrea, odious oaf that he'd been, really just fallen off his horse in an equally convenient accident?

Furnedge stared at his whiskey and found that his hand was still shaking, so he curled it into a fist and dug his nails into the palm. It didn't really help any, so he drained the glass again. He let the booze warm his throat with hot, smoky, fumes.

"Just who have I sold my soul to...?"

The Sheriff

The carney folk were an odd bunch.

Sam Shenan mopped his head and squinted up at the sky, it was 10am and the day was already pumping up to be a fearsome one, the kind where heat hazes would shimmer and shake the grass from horizon to horizon by mid-afternoon, as if the land could no longer bear the weight of the vast sky above. Best time for a man to do his labours was early morning or early evening when the sun wasn't so damn mean. The carney folk, however, had other ideas.

How long had it taken them to haul their wagons across the grass to get here? However long it had been they were in no hurry to get the carnival rigged now that they'd arrived – most of them seemed to be still snoring in their cots.

The town looked forward to the carnival rolling into Hawker's Drift and, eventually in their own sweet time, pitching up on Hooper's Fields, but they always made Shenan uneasy.

Partly due to their propensity for heavy drinking and rowdiness he supposed, but mainly it was just a nagging sense that bad shit seemed to happen whenever they were in town.

Maybe he was just a bigot; they were strange folk, with

strange clothes and stranger manners and anyone who was different was easy to blame for bad shit. But even so, every year he liked to come down early so he could run an eye over em and remind them that there was law in Hawker's Drift.

Thomas Rum's chief hired gun, Stodder Hope, was about. He gave the barest of nods as he saw Shenan approaching. The Sheriff nodded but didn't approach the man. He was one ugly mother; even with half his features obscured by a thick tangled beard he still had a face that would curdle milk.

Probably the kind of man that was useful when you were hauling wagons through bandit-infested badlands. Still, Shenan thought he would rather take his chances if he ran into a pack of cutthroat outlaws than have a man like that at his back.

Even the killers the Mayor had hired as town deputies were scared of the carney's gunslinger and steered clear of him. Shenan was relieved when Hope returned his attention to the slim effete Chinaman he was standing with.

The wagons were lined up along the far end of Hooper's Small Field. The actual carney, the tents and booths and rides designed to part the good folk of Hawker's Drift from their money, would set up in the Big Field nearer to town. Beyond the wagons, the carney folk's horses were corralled and grazing on grass that was still just about green.

A few of the more industrious carney guys were beginning to haul gear down to the Big Field; he gave them all a nod and a good view of his gold star. They all pretty much ignored him. Save for a wispy looking fellow in a red top hat garnished with sagging feathers who stuck his metal-studded tongue out at him before returning to his business of howling like a loon. Carney folk...

He reached the wagons and gave them his eye as he sauntered amongst the haphazard rows they'd been drawn up in. A few bleary-eyed souls were huddled around cooking fires, frying bacon and swigging coffee – at least he assumed it was coffee, in his experience carney folk didn't much believe in abstinence.

Nobody paid him much heed save for a heavy breasted young woman hanging out of the open window in a large green wagon that bore the sign *Mallory's Fine Strumpets* along the side.

"An hour for the price of thirty minutes hun..." she drawled, the Sheriff was pretty sure her breakfast had included something other than coffee too.

Shenan forced a smile and moved on without reply, she didn't bother calling out after him.

Nothing seemed out of place, nobody was rounding up other people's cattle or planning to rob the Old Union Bank. But Shenan had the same sense of unease he got every year. Never had been able to shake it and he'd never been able to find a thing to give it any substance.

He reached the end of the double row of wagons, drawn up to make the impromptu main street of Carey Town.

Why do you give a shit anyway?

It was all a bit late to care wasn't it? All he wanted was his retirement, so why come looking for trouble? He'd spent a good long while as Sheriff of Hawker's Drift doing his damnedest trying not to see it.

Yeah, things happen, but nobody really sees them, do they?

They had been Ash Godbold's words, spat in his face as they'd been waiting for Emily to come round; to come round and accuse a man who couldn't possibly have raped her.

Bad shit.

Last year, a girl went missing, *another* girl went missing. No one had noticed till the carney had rolled away. Donna Bloom had been her name, nineteen, too skinny, slightly pretty, completely unremarkable. The general consensus had been that her father was an asshole with an excessive fondness for his daughter since his wife had passed and she'd run away with the carney to escape him.

Jez Bloom had been a bit of a drunk and a frequent patron of the upstairs girls at *Jack's*, but had he been abusing his daughter? Who could say? Jez Bloom couldn't, he'd keeled over with a heart attack a few days after his daughter disappeared.

A year had gone by and everyone had forgotten about Donna and Jez Bloom. In truth, everyone had forgotten about them in much less than a year. These days, however, Sam Shenan was finding things much harder to forget. So, he thought, he'd mosey around the carney and see if Donna Bloom was about or anyone had anything to say about her. Just to put his mind at rest.

Beyond the main drag in the corner of Hooper's Small Field was a final wagon, set apart from the others; an old battered flatbed with a tattered canvas covering. The back of the wagon was scorched and peppered with bullet holes.

Shenan peered into the back of the wagon through the open flap that was twitching in the breeze. It was empty save for shadows, though the floor was darkly stained in places.

Looked like blood to the Sheriff's eye.

"Can I help you?"

Shenan twisted around with a start. He hadn't heard anyone come up behind him; although that was no particular surprise given his hearing was getting as dull as all his other senses.

"Morning ma'am," Shenan touched the brim of his hat. The woman was tall and striking with dark hair pulled sharply back, she wore a black silk dress embellished with lace. She watched him curiously, but without hostility. Her eyes were partially hooded against the glare of the morning sun, accentuating the crow's feet around her eyes. Shenan suspected the woman was maybe ten years younger than he was though she seemed to be aging a whole lot better than he'd managed.

"You had some trouble out on the grass?"

"Trouble?" Her eyebrow, which he realised, was just a thinly drawn pencil line, twitched upwards.

"This rig..." he jerked his thumb towards the wagon, "...looks like it's seen some trouble."

"Not with us, the previous owners I believe," her voice was rich and smoky, the kind you wanted to keep listening to.

"Hope you got a good price for it?"

She laughed; a deep, throaty chuckle as she glided past the Sheriff to examine the wagon for herself.

"Some settlers we came across, the poor folk had suffered a torrid time, they travelled with us for a while."

"What happened to them?"

"Found some land near Fellowes Ford and decided it was a better bet than California. We always need more wagons, so bought it from them."

"Lot of blood in the back. Looks like."

The woman placed a hand on the side of the wagon and closed her eyes, "A woman died in there, in childbirth, screaming in pain and fear, and anger too. Anger at her husband for bringing them out here, anger at herself for letting him... the baby died too."

"This happen when they were with you?"

She opened her eyes, and turned them towards Shenan, "No, long before. I have certain gifts..."

"Gifts?"

"My name is Giselle, I see the future and the past."

"Ah-huh..."

Giselle smiled, "You should come and see me, Sheriff... perhaps you have questions I could answer?"

"Not sure there's anything you could help me with."

"A sceptic? I suppose a lawman has to be."

She held his gaze in a way that seemed entirely inappropriate before lightly patting his arm and turning away, "If you change your mind..."

"Donna Bloom," Shenan blurted out.

Giselle turned, her painted eyebrow raised once more, "Who?"

"She left Hawker's Drift last year with the carney. We think. Just wondering if she's still about?"

"See. I knew you would have questions."

"Yeah... I guess."

"Donna Bloom... I believe she travelled with us for a while, a few months, but the carney life wasn't for her. It isn't for most people."

"Do you know where she could be contacted?"

Giselle shook her head, "No, I don't. Why?"

"Her father died just after she left town."

"I think that is news that would make her very happy."

Shenan nodded, "Well, thank you for your time Ma'am."

"My name is Giselle..." she repeated taking a couple of steps backwards before turning away.

Shenan watched the sway of her hips despite himself. When she'd disappeared back into Carney Town, he took off his hat and scratched his head as he took another look inside the battered old wagon. Sure, childbirth, helluva a lot of blood lost in childbirth, especially if there's no one about who knows what to do with a woman giving birth. He raised his eyes to the inside of the canvas and the dark elongated splatters that stained it in several places.

"That, however..." he muttered to himself "...looks more like someone had their throat cut..."

The Songbird

There was something hypnotic about the grass. The way it constantly moved, undulating as far as the eye could see; a living ocean without end.

It also gave a fairly good place for her to hide, at least if she hadn't have had a dirty big and rather obvious horse with her anyway. She'd ridden out to the Mayor's ranch again, looking over her shoulder at regular intervals, but there had been no town deputies, Sye or any other unwanted strange men trailing her.

It had been blistering hot; each day seemed to be hotter than the previous one. Shade amounted to no more than whatever you'd chosen to put on your head out here so there was little you could do to escape the sun. Her temples had throbbed all day from lack of sleep and her throat was raw from too much singing in other people's smoke. The heat had helped neither.

She'd done all she could in the time she had. Neither of which had been enough. She had seen nothing save a huge, ungainly black wagon trundling towards the Mayor's Ranch. It had been pulled by a team of six sweating horses and escorted by half a dozen grim riders who made the town's deputies look like sweet-faced babes.

She'd warranted a cursory glance but no more.

By the time she rode back into town the throbbing in her head had become the pounding fist of a madman clambering to get out of her skull. She wondered what the chances of Monty giving her a night off might be...

After she'd laughed that idea off as a sign of dehydration, she returned her horse to the livery. They seemed to have decided that, as a regular customer, she could now ride one of their less dead nags now.

As she walked back across the square towards Jack's a man was crossing Pioneer Square. He caught her attention only for the fact that he was the only black man she'd seen in town – something that had jarred her given the ethnic melting pot she'd grown up in.

She'd seen him in *Jack's* a couple of times, but she'd never gotten much of a look at him. He'd stuck to the shadowy corners of the saloon save for when he'd bumped into Sye and sent her coffee flying the other night. Which had been something of a relief, until Sye scurried off to buy her another one at least. By the time he finally came back with a lukewarm coffee however his heart no longer seemed to be in making amends for anything much and he'd slunk quickly off with a black scowl twisting his face.

Love, lust, infatuation - call it what you liked - really could make men act damned peculiar.

Cece stared at the man; his features softened in the shadow of his hat and wondered what his story was. He suddenly changed tack and veered sharply away from her, his pace picking up noticeably. Perhaps he'd forgotten something, but he looked mightily like a man trying to avoid someone. She glanced about her. Nobody else was crossing Pioneer Square save a mangy but otherwise harmless little dog.

Perhaps he didn't like dogs.

She watched him jump up onto the boardwalk and by the time she'd reached *Jack's Saloon* he was disappearing into the gunsmith's across the square.

"John X Smith..."

She shook her head as she laboriously trudged up the stairs towards the saloon door.

Maybe he was the type who got nervous around women...

The Gunslinger

"Well, he is a very busy man…"

Eudora Dewsnap raised her chin and crossed her skeletal arms across her chest as she looked down her nose at him.

Amos had been sitting across from Miss Dewsnap for precisely three hours and had no intention of leaving until he got into Guy Furnedge's office. The lawyer couldn't hide behind his desk forever. He couldn't see into the room thanks to the frosted glass pane in the door, but he had a pretty good idea that's what he was doing.

"Happy to wait," Amos nodded.

The poor woman clearly had instructions to ensure he never got to see Guy Furnedge and was becoming increasingly fretful at Amos' continual refusal to drag his butt from the chair and disappear.

"But I'm not sure Mr Furnedge will have time to see you today. He is *very* busy. Town business. He is a very busy and important man."

"I'm sure he is."

"If you'd like to make an appointment for another day?"

"Nope, I will wait. It might not be town business, but it's important to me."

She exhaled pointedly and dropped her hands in front of

her, turning them one over the other.

"Well, perhaps if you could tell me what it is about?"

"It's a personal matter."

"Of course... sir, but I have Mr Furnedge's confidence in most matters. We work very closely. Perhaps I could be of some assistance?"

Whenever she spoke his name she glowed; a faint, warm irradiance that flickered in time to her heartbeat.

Amos wanted to tell her the lawyer was worthy of neither her love nor her devotion, but that was for her to find out.

"But if you could just give me an idea, it might help?"

Amos smiled, which people generally seemed to find a not in the slightest bit reassuring gesture. Miss Dewsnap was apparently no exception.

"Just trying to do a little good..."

She didn't look convinced.

Amos settled down to wait.

*

"Well, *really*, this is most inappropriate!"

Furnedge had finally decided to make a bolt for the door.

"I only need five minutes."

"Well, you'll have to come back tomorrow."

"I've been waiting..." Amos glanced at the clock above Miss Dewsnap's desk "...for seven hours to see you."

"Well, you were told I wasn't available," Furnedge bristled, heading for the door. At least until Amos moved to stand in front of it anyway.

"Five minutes."

"This is really most improper!" Miss Dewsnap squealed,

positioning herself between the two of them.

"Well, I could go to your home Guy. Would you prefer that?"

"Are you threatening me?"

"I need to talk to you about Molly McCrea."

"Well, that is none of your business," Furnedge snapped.

"Your marriage proposal has... troubled her."

"*Proposal? Marriage?*" Miss Dewsnap's eyes widened and she turned to stare at Furnedge. The glow coming from her changed to a dark, throbbing violet.

"Well... really... this isn't the time or the place-"

"You proposed to *that* woman. And so soon after your poor wife's death?"

Amos suspected it wasn't the timing of the proposal that upset her the most.

"That dreadful, vulgar, woman," she gasped.

Furnedge was changing colour too, but he had no spectral glow about him. It was just his skin that was going bright red.

"Well... erm... perhaps I can spare you a minute," Furnedge ushered Amos into his office. He hesitated then, stuck his head back out of the door.

"It's very late Miss Dewsnap, please finish up and run along."

He slammed the door shut and turned on his heels to glare at Amos, "That was private... *extremely* private... you had no right to blurt that out in front of... my staff!"

"You could have seen me seven hours ago... in private."

The lawyer slammed his case down, retreated behind his desk, thought about sitting and settled for wheeling his chair

229

our and standing behind that too.

"Well?" he demanded, once Amos had swivelled around to face him.

He had planned a reasonably civilised speech about the distress he was causing Molly and how wrong it was to try and use someone's debt to leverage them into a marriage they did not want. Instead, after seven hours of kicking his heels, he settled for a more pithy and Molly-esque approach.

"Keep the fuck away from Molly…" Amos stood up, placed his knuckles on the desk and leaned forward enough for both lawyer and chair to shuffle back a pace.

"Are… are you threatening me?"

"Of course not."

"I'm not afraid of you. I shall do as I wish!" The high pitched squeal of Furnedge's voice would have told Amos he was very much afraid of him even if he couldn't feel the fear pouring out of him. There were other things too, echoes and reflections all but lost beneath the noise and glare of his distress.

"There's no reason to be afraid of me," Amos said, straightening up and trying to sound as reasonable as his own desire to pummel the creep to a pulp allowed. "I just want to discuss this. Man to man."

Furnedge didn't look convinced, "I really don't see what we have to discuss." His fingers were digging into the back of the chair hard enough to make the leather dimple.

"Molly… Mrs McCrea has just lost her husband, she has… the matter of the money he owed the Mayor, she now has a small child to care for too. She does not need your attentions as well."

"I don't see what business it is of yours?"

"I am her friend."

"Perhaps my attentions are inconvenient to you own! Huh? Huh?" Furnedge made little thrusting motions with his head.

"I can't give Molly – or any other woman – much attention. I'm sure you've heard that?" Amos held the man's eye, and the lawyer returned if for all of a second before hurriedly finding something else to look at.

"Well, that's as maybe, but Molly is very dear to me. And I intend to make her my wife."

"Regardless of her wishes?"

"I am not forcing her to marry me, sir, I am a gentleman!"

"A gentleman who has found himself very rich all of a sudden... just at the moment Molly finds herself both widowed and poor. Quite a coincidence?"

"I don't know what you're suggesting!" Furnedge protested, but he looked mighty uncomfortable.

Amos held up his hands and slowly moved around the desk towards the lawyer, who less than discreetly made sure the chair was still between them as he edged away.

"I'm not here to make trouble, just to see if we can come to an understanding. Like civilised men."

There was something Amos couldn't quite focus on, a memory or a thought that wouldn't solidify enough for him to comprehend, like a dream slipping from the mind in the dawn's grey light.

"What kind of understanding?"

"I'm sure you only want the best for her... but don't hurt her. Don't leave her with a choice of marriage or the whorehouse. You must know if you do that she will only end up hating you."

"She will come to love me..." Furnedge said, but his voice didn't seem to hold much conviction, "...in time."

"Your reward for saving her from the whorehouse?"

"It is not a matter of reward – I care deeply about her."

"But if she refuses your proposal, you will let the Mayor whore her out to the whole town?"

"I care deeply for her," the lawyer repeated, jutting his chin out like a stubborn child.

"If you cared deeply for her you wouldn't treat her like this. If you were her friend you'd help her regardless."

"Molly will be my wife. It is for the best. If you are her friend, you would help her see this."

Amos puffed out his cheeks and looked at the ceiling; there was no reasoning with the man. But then he hadn't really expected to. That wasn't why he'd come to see the little lawyer.

"Well, for Molly's sake let us both at least think about what is best for her... and act like gentlemen in the meantime."

Amos held out his hand and, after no little hesitation, Furnedge reached over and accepted it...

"

The Widow

"Amelia is still asking about the carney."

Amos was trying to worry the crust from atop one of her pies. She was pretty sure Tom had stashed a hammer away somewhere...

He'd been out for most of the day and had returned home late, silent and slightly surly.

"So, how was your day hun?" She asked, in a cheery, too-bright voice, "I taught Amelia how to ruin a pie. She seemed to enjoy it."

Amos paused, his surprisingly still unbent fork hovering over the monstrous shell, "It's good pie."

From anyone else she would put the comment down to politeness, but Amos' strange and inexplicable enjoyment of her half-assed attempts at cooking always appeared to be entirely genuine.

Molly eased herself into the chair opposite; she and Amelia had eaten earlier and the little girl was snoring in her bed upstairs. As she watched Amos chomp through the pie, she tentatively wiggled a few teeth to make sure they'd been no lasting damage.

"So, where have you been?"

Amos pushed his now empty plate away and a moment of

contentment flitted across his face, followed by a sigh.

"I'm not sure we should take Amelia to the carney."

"Well, I won't be. Outside of the town limits. Toss as much as a single ball at a shy and I'll be whisked off to put on my amusement show for the town."

"Ok, I don't think I should take Amelia to the carney."

"You try telling her. She's still not convinced there won't be elephants."

"She's quite stubborn, ain't she?"

"You noticed that huh?"

"She should have red hair..."

Molly stuck out her tongue and Amos got one of his faraway looks for a moment.

"So... where *have* you been?" It was a question he seemed to be avoiding, and an avoided question always made her extra inquisitive.

"I went to see your suitor... the lawyer."

"You had some legal business?" She let the suitor remark pass.

"Nope."

She raised an eyebrow and folded her arms. This was getting extra interesting. Just like avoided questions tended to.

"Thought I'd appeal to his better nature... and then shake his hand."

"Let me guess. He ain't got no better nature and his palm was as slippery and cold as a dead eel?"

"I think he actually does love you, Molly."

"I think I'm more comfortable with the idea of good ol' healthy lust and obsession."

"Well, those too."

"Great. You get that from what he said or the handshake?"

"From the words mainly, they glowed the way they do when someone's in love."

"Words glow?"

"Not always, not with everyone, but the stronger an emotion, the more it seems to manifest itself. Love is a pretty strong emotion."

"I guess," Molly shifted in her seat and stamped down hard on wondering what *her* words looked like to Amos, "...what did the handshake tell you?"

Amos pursed his lips for a moment before answering in a low voice.

"It told me that he killed his wife..."

*

"But there *might* be elephants!" Amelia insisted as she poked suspiciously at her porridge. It was fair to say porridge wasn't her favourite.

Molly shot a knowing look at Amos. There was no way they were going to get out of taking her. Thomas Rum and his apple had made quite an impression on the little girl.

"You sure you got no Frosted Pops?"

"Erm, pretty sure hun."

Amos looked as blank as she did. Neither of them had a clue what Frosted Pops were, but Amelia asked for them every morning. She never seemed particularly happy to get porridge instead.

She wasn't sure why Amos was so adamant that Amelia shouldn't go to the carney, he'd been his usual reticent self when she'd tried to ask him about it. She assumed he was no more taken with Thomas Rum than Mr Wizzle had been. He'd seemed harmless enough to her, but given her record when it came to assessing a man's character, that didn't mean any damn thing.

While Amelia half-heartedly ate her breakfast, Molly led Amos out into the backyard. The morning was already warm and only a few cotton wool clouds interrupted the blue vault of the sky.

"Are you going to see the Sherriff?"

Amos shook his head. It was a question she'd asked several times the previous night and she perfectly understood his reluctance. However, Lorna Furnedge had been her friend – well, kind of – and if her death hadn't been from natural causes then something needed to be done. Just like it needed to be done about Tom's death. She wasn't overly optimistic on either count but sitting and doing nothing grated on her. Particularly when the only other alternative, running away from this strange little town, wasn't open to her anymore.

"You don't think he'd believe you?"

"Molly..."

"Yeah, I know, one of my dumber questions."

"And, I don't even know for sure that he did – like I said last night I just got a memory of him pouring this little black bottle into her booze and a sense of guilt. I don't know if it was poison or medicine."

"You don't pour medicine into a bottle of booze."

"Guess not."

"Or feel guilty about it."

238

Amos nodded again.

"Could you find out... more?"

"I don't know. It's not like picking up a book and turning to a particular page. This stuff just pours randomly out of people. Sometimes I see stuff, sometimes I don't. Anyway, justice for Lorna isn't my priority. I went there to find out what Furnedge actually wanted. Now I know."

"And that helps us how?"

"Tom dies, leaves you in debt, the Mayor threatens you with the whorehouse, Furnedge is in love with you, Lorna dies suddenly leaving Furnedge a pile of money. Don't you think that's all a bit too... neat?"

Molly sighed and leaned against the back wall of the house, "The thought had crossed my mind."

"Maybe we can use this though..."

"How?"

"If Furnedge did kill his wife then that might give us leverage, might help convince him to be more charitable... more *generous...*"

Molly looked up at Amos, his eyes were half closed against the glare of the morning sun and his mouth was downturned. It made him look cold and, maybe, just a little bit dangerous.

"You mean blackmail don't you?"

"That's another way of putting it... I take it you don't approve?"

"No, I don't approve at all..." Molly shook her head hard enough for her curls to shimmer and bounce, "...I fucking love it. Let's make that bastard squirm..."

She reached up and pecked him on the cheek. For once he

didn't look in the faintest bit surprised...

The Gunsmith

The workshop was something of a mess.

He'd never been one for tidying up; he'd always preferred to leave that to the women in his life. It wasn't a misogynistic thing, he'd been equally happy to have men clean up after him too. But he'd lived here a long time now and nobody got past the store downstairs and, occasionally, the bedroom upstairs. The workshop was his alone, unsullied by another's presence in decades.

And it showed.

Assorted tools, machinery, materials, books, guns, bits of guns and things that might once have been guns lay scattered, piled, stacked, discarded, forgotten and heaped all about him. John X had long since become immune to clutter, along with dust, questionable smells and most states of domestic dishevelment.

He was hunched over a convenient piece of table from which he had swept aside the remnants of whatever project had ground to a halt and died in that particular spot months before. Illuminated by a single lamp most of the rest of the workshop was no more than a collection of ill-formed shadows. He could see all he wanted to see.

A small black glass bottle.

Now, why would a man want to spike a girl's drink?

There was one fairly obvious answer to that question, but it didn't look much like any narcotic he'd ever seen.

He'd poured a little into a glass dish that still bore the stains of previous experiments, but was cleaner than anything else that came to hand. The bottle's content was viscous, with a consistency somewhere between molasses and tar. Not knowing what the hell the stuff was he was wary of touching or tasting it, but it seemed barely a fluid itself when he poked it with a spatula. It appeared far too dense and heavy to easily dissolve into another liquid, which was a fairly basic requisite for the spiking of a girl's drink.

He flicked a gob of the stuff into a glass of water. For a second it floated on the surface and then slowly sunk downward, one moment a small black slug of goo, the next... it was gone; dissipating into a grey cloud before vanishing entirely.

John X sniffed the water. There was a hint of something far too sickly sweet to be healthy but it faded away in a few seconds. Then it smelt just like water should. He slid it across the scored surface of the worktop and made a mental note that, in this instance, he *would* remember to throw something away.

He picked up the bottle and twisted it around. There was no label, just plain, unadorned opaque glass that lay snugly enough in the hand. Sealed with a cork stopper. Completely unremarkable.

And yet...

The glass was slightly warm to the touch and it felt heavy too. Or at least heavier than it ought to. John held it up against the lamplight. Not a glimmer made it through the glass.

He found himself stroking the bottle with his thumb and finger. Almost lovingly.

I wonder what it tastes like. I bet it is reeeeal sweet...

His fingers snapped open and he let the bottle drop to the table. It gyrated back and forth on its base before settling. The last thing he was going to do, or wanted to do, was put any of this concoction in his mouth. But for just a moment the urge had been almost overwhelming.

He sat back on his stool and pinched the bridge of his nose. It was late and he was tired, he should crawl into his bed and look at this shit in the morning, but he had a feeling sleep would come grudgingly. He shouldn't have gone to the saloon again; he shouldn't be getting involved. He was too old. Too much time had passed and he should just stay in his store until things returned to normal. Whatever normal amounted to in Hawker's Drift anyway.

It was just fear, of course. He knew that. But he'd waited so long he didn't have anything else left and the woman he had loved would not even recognise the shell of the man he'd become. And if she did, she would be appalled.

He twisted on his stool with a start. There were only shadows behind him, but he thought he'd heard a footstep.

"Anyone there?"

A dog howled in the distance, faint and mournful, but no other reply came. He thought about taking the lamp and having a good look. It sure had sounded like a footstep, but he could see that the door was still closed. There was no other entrance to his basement workshop other than a couple of narrow little skylights that only the scrawniest of children would be able to wriggle through.

"Old fool", he muttered, turning back to the little black bottle, "scared of the dark too now, eh?" He'd made enough modifications to the house over the years that nobody was going to get in without him knowing about it.

He picked up the spatula and tapped the side of the bottle; it tinkled, just like glass should. But why was it warm? And why did it feel smoother than it should?

The particular smoothness of the glass was probably just an illusion, but the warmth could only be coming from the liquid. A chemical reaction of some kind, perhaps?

"Alchemy..."

He gave a little snort.

If he distilled it, he could break the stuff down into its constituents and work out what was in it – and then maybe what it did. Which was probably nothing, just some old witch's brew sold to a love-struck boy. That, at least, was easy enough to deduce. The way that farm boy looked at Cece...

Had he ever been like that?

He went a rummaging and came back with a glass vial and a lamp burner. Tomorrow he could set up a proper condenser, but for now he'd just see what a little heat did to it and work out its boiling point.

Creak

John's head snapped round. That definitely sounded like a footstep on a floorboard. Except... his basement workshop had a stone floor. He looked up. A footstep upstairs? In the shop?

Always people looking to get themselves a free gun, but he'd only had one break in before, an itinerant drifter who thought that where there were guns there was money. He hadn't done much damage when John caught him. He'd been wild-eyed with whiskey and desperation. He'd had time to sober up before they'd got around to hanging him out in the square. He'd cried and begged and John had wished he'd just thrown some coins at him and told him to get out of town.

Strange how he'd felt so bad about watching a thief hang considering how many lives had been lost because of him. Still, he hadn't actually been around to see them die...

He shook the memory away even if the guilt clung more stubbornly. He was sure the noise had been in the basement anyway. The far corners of the room were gloomy; the lamp's light doing no more than dusting the darkness with grey. The workshop was sizeable, the basement running the length of the building above, but not so big that anyone could be in here with him. And he definitely would have heard the door open.

He relaxed at that. It was either his imagination or a rat. Preferably his imagination.

He dropped another slug of black sludge into the bottom of the vial and watched it trickle reluctantly to the very bottom.

It sure does look sweet, don't it?

John shook the voice away. Damn, he must be tired. Maybe he should have left this shit in Sye Hallows' pocket. Maybe he should have let her drink it.

Maybe the bitch deserved whatever she got...

245

John put the vial in a stand and fumbled with the oil burner to get it to light. Creasing his brow as he worked and telling himself the voice he kept hearing, just like the creaking footstep, was definitely only in his head.

He really hadn't been sleeping at all well, with one thing and another. He should take a few days and stick to his bed. Alone. Get some good sleep. Stay away from Kate and Ash. That was sensible. Keep clear of Amos and the delightfully foul-mouthed Molly as well, that was clearly not going to end well. Amelia too. He'd done what he could, hadn't he? Sure he had. Molly's business now. Not his. And that damn carney was in town again, always a good time to keep to your own business. And the saloon? Yeah, above all, keep out of that dump.

The flame was burning as hot as it was going to get and he moved the vial over the flame.

There was a faint hiss... and then it screamed.

The black gob started to thrash in the vial, flinging out little tendrils like flailing arms as it tried to claw its way up the side of the glass tube away from the heat.

John, who had straightened up, hands gripping the sides of the table, saw something moving out of the corner of his eye. It was the bottle. Rocking back and forth on its base, slowly, but getting faster and more agitated with each movement.

The stuff in the vial was jumping wildly, trying to escape but not being able to get far enough up the tube before sliding back towards the heat of the flame.

And all the time it screamed.

Was that a mouth? A gaping little maw in the thick, black

slug? A mouth that was screaming?

We burn! We all burn!

John X stood up violently enough for his stool to topple over and crash to the floor.

Why do you burn us?!

His heart was thumping violently and he suddenly felt hot enough to burst into flames himself. A thin twist of smoke had started rise from the vial. A sickly, too sweet smell that seemed vaguely familiar. Perfumed smoke...

We burn... like all the others you burned!

The scream was becoming more intense, high-pitched and shrill. More desperate. More pained. Did he hear a voice too? Surely not? It didn't really sound like a suffering, distraught child. Did it?

The bottle was rocking violently too now; something inside was desperate to get out.

John X knocked the vial away from the burner; it clattered from its stand and rolled into the clutter strewn across the table. The screaming stopped. The bottle became still.

"What the fuck..." John whispered, making a fist of his shaking hand.

He turned to the wall where various tools were hung on hooks. The ones he'd bothered to put back in the right place at least. He grabbed a hammer and stood with it poised over the little black bottle, shifting his weight as if he were faced with some snarling and hungry beast that was about to pounce.

He'd been born with an abundance of curiosity. He'd never quite decided if that had been a blessing or a curse. It had landed him ass deep in trouble more than once and if he hadn't been born with it, he certainly wouldn't have ended up here. He had a curiosity about how the world worked, from the stars blazing across the sky to the bugs scuttling in the grass and all the wonders in between. But sometimes, even he realised, there were things best left alone.

Mainly when they left an aroma of sweet, perfumed smoke in the air.

He brought the hammer down on the bottle, once, twice, three times, then flung it aside, locked the door behind him and took the stairs up to his store three at a time.

At least the bottle hadn't screamed when he'd smashed it. Even if he had...

The Deputy

"Ash Godbold found em in Preacher Stone's house…" Blane nodded towards the box he'd just deposited on the Mayor's oversized desk.

"And what was he doing in the Preacher's house?"

"Reading notebooks."

The Mayor offered a little smile, "I assume some law breaking was involved in Mr Godbold's actions?"

"Yes sir."

"Is he in the cells?"

"No."

The Mayor flexed his shoulders and threw his head back in the manner of a man who hadn't slept entirely comfortably.

"Why not?"

"Under the circumstances… I thought it best."

"That's quite… considerate Deputy. You know I do believe law enforcement is helping you grow into a more rounded human being."

The two men regarded each other for a moment before the

Mayor laughed heartily.

"Should I have left them there?" Blane asked once the laughter had subsided.

"No... best with me."

The Mayor had made no move to open any of the notebooks. Blane was pretty sure he knew exactly what they were,

"Did you read them?"

Blane thought about it for a moment. He'd found lying was a pointless exercise around the Mayor. The man seemed to have quite the nose for deceit.

"Yes."

"Were they entertaining?"

"Eye-opening."

"I just bet – people can be fascinating; don't you find?"

Usually only when they scream...

"Yes, sir..."

The Mayor steepled his fingers and his eye grew still. There weren't many things in life that made Blane uncomfortable, other than small talk and children, but he had to force his feet to remain in one place and his eyes to return the Mayor's gaze.

"How have you settled in at Mrs Thurlsten's?"

"It is satisfactory."

"And Mrs Thurlsten?" The Mayor's expression was almost as impassive as his own, "Is she satisfactory too?"

"She is... very... satisfactory."

Now the Mayor chuckled, "I'm aware she has certain proclivities... I thought she might be able to settle you in better."

"Settle me in?"

"You're a creature of the road Blane; this isn't your natural environment. But you are useful to me and I want you to be content. You gave me your fealty, your body and your soul. In return, I'll feed your heart's desires. Within reason."

"I'm grateful for the opportunities you've given me here, sir."

"And I'm grateful for the work you've done for me. The special work."

"I enjoy taking care of your business."

The Mayor smiled and gave the faintest of nods, "I like a man who is happy in his work. So long as you remember you are my creature, you serve me, not your own desires."

No one had ever known about the desires that drove him. He had no doubt people thought him a cold fish and a strange fellow, but no one knew what he really was, what he needed, what made his blood pump and his heart sing. No one still alive anyway. No one save the Mayor.

He still wasn't sure how the Mayor had known, but he had taken him from the road and given him another life, a better life. He had always thought his life would be short and, probably, brought to an end beneath a gallows, but here... here in Hawker's Drift he had the chance to thrive. He needed to show restraint, control, like he had with Liza Thurlsten when she came to him in the night to be hurt. He'd controlled his desire to kill her and managed to find some measure of fulfilment in her suffering.

If he could do that, then he could enjoy the dark work he did for years, maybe decades. Not as often as he would like, and only when the Mayor pointed him in a certain direction, but he had a feeling the Mayor had lots of business that needed attending to. His type of business.

"I serve you," Blane said, a rare little turn of a smile twisting his mouth, "forever."

"I'm glad to hear it." The Mayor rose smoothly from his oversized chair and came around his desk to stand in front of Blane, close enough for the faint hint of perfumed smoke to tickle the Deputy's nose.

"Any news of my friend the gunslinger?"

"He is living with the McCrea woman and the black child. Happy families."

"Quite. No signs that they are going to run?"

"Nothing – the child seems to have complicated matters."

"They usually have that effect."

"Do you want me to kill him?" His voice was as even as ever, but he felt his heart beat a little faster at the thought. He'd enjoy killing the gunslinger, for reasons he couldn't be bothered to fathom he disliked the man even more than he did most people.

"No, not for now, but keep an eye on him," he lifted a finger "and *nothing* happens to Molly McCrea or the child. Understand?"

Blane nodded.

The Mayor half turned towards the box that sat behind him on the desk. He reached out and dipped a languid hand inside without looking. He pulled a single notebook out and handed it to Blane.

"A reward, for bringing these to me. And for your good service," he grinned and winked his good eye, "Someone who needs teaching a lesson in manners. A little treat for you... just nothing too obvious eh?"

Blane looked at the notebook, which the Mayor had plucked seemingly at random from the hundreds of little books inside.

He flicked it open, he had read some of them, but this was one he'd missed.

He glanced up at the Mayor, who had already retreated back to his desk.

"Nothing too obvious..." he repeated, "...just a little fun. We all gotta have a little fun sometimes, don't we Deputy?"

Blane smiled then, a broad, carnivorous smile, the kind he usually kept hidden inside as he had no doubt it was the kind of smile that would unnerve most people. But the Mayor wasn't most people and he knew now he didn't need to wear a mask for him.

The Mayor knew what lay beneath and he seemed to like it well enough...

The Mother

She saw less of Ash every day.

He was going to work early, much earlier than he needed to in order to get the shop open, and each day he came home a little later. If she didn't know better she would have thought he was having an affair or had developed a taste for strong liquor straight from the bucket. However, she did know better.

He was avoiding her.

She could see it in his eyes. He couldn't stand to be around her. He blamed her for everything but was too much of a gentleman (or a coward if you preferred) to confront her. So he hid in his barber's shop and avoided her.

Kate could imagine him sitting in one of his chairs, staring blankly at the reflection in his grandfather's mirror, slowly scraping a razor back and forth, back and forth across a leather strap. Probably thinking about her throat too...

The house was silent and nobody was there to see the tears squeeze out of her eyes. Ruthie was at school, Emily was in her bed staring at the ceiling, Ash was sharpening his razors... she was alone. As usual.

It wasn't that she could really blame Ash... after all it *was* her fault. It was all her fault.

She sucked in a couple of shuddering breaths, before wiping the back of her sleeve across her eyes and then her nose. Very ladylike, she sniffed, checking her reflection in the old hallway mirror between its black spots. She needed to go to *Pickerings* and get a few things, but she couldn't leave Emily alone. Maybe she could get Mrs Sloane to sit in again, but she had the feeling her neighbour was starting to regret the "Absolutely anything I can do darling," speech she'd given in the immediate aftermath of Emily's attack.

She probably spent half the day glancing out of the window, poised to dive behind a chair if she saw Kate coming towards her door.

Kate knew she couldn't spend the rest of her life watching over Emily, but she was damned if she was going to leave her daughter alone again anytime soon.

A rap on the door pulled her thoughts back to the present. Frowning she opened the door; the short list of people who might come calling hadn't included the dour young Deputy Blane.

"Ma'am," he said, with the slightest of nods.

Kate ushered him in. Never looked good to have a lawman hovering on your door, they rarely brought good news.

In truth she'd half expected a call from the Sheriff or one of his Deputies – Ash's bottled rage was going to get the better of him sooner or later.

...back and forth, back and forth...

"Is something wrong?" She asked once they were inside. She was in no mood for pleasantries, "has Ash done something?"

"Done something ma'am?"

"He... has been... it doesn't matter."

Blane took off his hat and cast a slow eye around the room, which was immaculately clean. She'd found housework was the only thing that did anything to empty her mind – even when everything was already spotlessly clean.

Once he'd finished looking about, he turned his eyes to Kate. He had such cold, expressionless eyes. They reminded her of two muddy winter puddles skimmed with ice.

"Are you alone?"

"No, my daughter is upstairs," Kate said, finding she was edging away from the Deputy without really knowing why.

"The one that was raped?"

The tone was flat and expressionless, nothing judgemental or accusatory in it, but Kate hated it all the same. It was as if that was all her beautiful daughter now was and ever would be. The one that was raped.

"Emily," Kate said, trying to calm herself. She didn't want to lose her temper with the young Deputy as she had with the Mayor, "her name is Emily."

"Of course," Blane said, no hint of either awkwardness or apology. He was a cold one and no mistake. Kate waited for him to say something, anything to explain his visit, but he remained silent and impassive. His muddy eyes fixed upon her.

"What can I help you with?" Kate asked eventually, both the silence and the staring unnerving her.

"Just a few questions," without invitation he ambled over to Ash's upholstered chair and eased himself into it.

She supposed she should have offered him a seat, but she didn't want the company for any longer than she had to stand it. The Deputy, however, seemed to be making himself at home.

"About?"

Blane raised his eyes as he stretched his long legs out and hooked one scuffed boot over the other.

"I ask the questions, you answer."

She blinked, not entirely sure how to take the young lawman. She'd always thought him a cold, inscrutable man, but she hadn't taken him for being such a rude one. Perhaps he was having a bad day. She could relate to that at least.

"Where were you when she was raped?"

Kate had been moving to take a seat herself, but his words speared her to the spot, "I'm sorry?"

"Where were you when she was raped..." Blane wrinkled his nose and clicked his fingers, "you know... what's her name? Emily."

"I think you should leave."

"I ask the questions, you answer," Blane repeated.

"I wasn't asking you a question, I-"

"Where were you? What were you doing? Why didn't you hear her being raped?" Blane's cold eyes moved up and down her before a shallow parody of a smile distorted his face. She couldn't recall ever seeing him smile before. "It must have been quite the racket..."

"Get out Deputy, before I report you to the Sheriff."

"Report me? For what exactly? Just asking questions ma'am. Just doing my job."

"Get out!"

Blane pushed himself out of the chair, unfolding himself slow and easy before taking a step towards her.

"Well, as you're choosing to be uncooperative, let me fill in the blanks. You didn't hear your daughter being fucked because you weren't here. You weren't here because you were off getting the same thing. Though I guess, unlike little, sweet Emily, you liked what you got real fine..."

He deftly caught her hand as she tried to slap him.

"Striking an officer of the law is a real serious offence ma'am. You want to spend some time in our cells?"

"Get out!!" Kate pleaded, somewhere between a scream and a sob.

Blane twisted her wrist behind her back and spun her around in one smooth movement. When she tried to struggle he pushed her arm up further and pain lanced all the way up to her shoulder, she screamed but found the Deputy's coarse hand clamped over her mouth.

"Now, now," he whispered in her ear once her scream had subsided into a sob "we don't want to wake poor Emily. Do we?"

Kate's mind was racing, different thoughts, sensations and feelings surging through her body; confusion, incomprehension, the roughness of Blane's hand, the faint smell of old, stale tobacco, the easy strength in his arms.

Why is he doing this? What is he doing? Is he going to hurt me?

But above all was fear. Not fear of what Blane might do to her; she was so full of self-loathing she almost didn't care, but that he knew. Knew where she'd been the night Emily had been attacked, who she'd been with and what there'd been doing. But that was impossible, nobody knew but John, and he, surely, wouldn't have said anything.

When Blane didn't say or do anything more, she stopped struggling, there seemed no point, she didn't think she could get away from his grip without yanking her arm from the socket. He didn't look an unusually powerful man, but she could feel he had a taut, wiry strength in him. A strength he knew how to use, especially against a petite middle-aged woman. So she grew still and concentrated on drawing short snorting little breaths through her nose.

"You going to be a good girl now?" He whispered in her ear.

She tried to say yes, but it came out as a wet, muffled whimper.

Blane eased the pressure on her arm a little. When she made no move to pull away, he slowly peeled his fingers from her mouth.

"See... you do know how to behave, don't you?"

When Kate said nothing, he gave her arm a sudden, sharp twist, enough to make her cry out and her knees almost buckle.

"I asked you as question ma'am?"

"Yes! I know how to behave!"

"See. This is real easy," Blane said, in his slow monotone as he eased up on her arm, "I ask a question and you answer it. Think you can manage that?"

"Yes."

"Now we are making progress."

A gentle little tug on her arm

"Yes!!"

"Now, where were you when your daughter got fucked for the first time?"

The words hurt her as much as the way he'd twisted her arm; nasty, mean words, without a hint of compassion. Is that how people spoke behind their backs? Did the pained expressions and talk of Emily's "attack" fall away to be replaced by gleeful sniggering about her little girl getting fucked?

"Where. Were. You?"

"Upstairs! Asleep!"

Blane exhaled, deep enough for his breath to stir the hair around her right ear.

"And I thought we were coming to an understanding. But no. You have to go lie to me."

"I'm not lying!"

Oh yes, you are.

"I know where you were Mrs Godbold..." his voice was a soft hiss, and each word cut a new wound in her soul "...and I know what you were doing."

Those words chilled her more than anything else. More than the pain in her arm, more than the fear and confusion about what was happening, more than anything she had ever experienced in her life, save for finding Emily beaten, bloody and abused.

Ever since the moment she had kissed John X Smith for the first time and had known she would become his lover. They were the words she had feared.

"I was asleep!" her protest sounded just like the hollow lie that it was, but she had nothing else to cling to.

She felt him move, one hand still pulling her arm behind her back while his other came around her waist, she felt his lips against her ear, his voice no more than a breath.

"You were getting fucked by our gunsmith, weren't you?"

"No!"

"While your daughter was getting fucked so were you. What a bad, bad girl you are."

"That's a lie!" She sobbed, "Who told you this shit?"

"Preacher Stone…"

Kate grew still, not understanding, "But, he's dead!"

"Of course he is, but the dead can still talk sometimes."

Blane threw her to the floor, the move coming so suddenly Kate didn't have time to brace herself and she landed heavily enough to wind and stun her.

The house was silent save for the soft creak of Blane's worn down boots as he ambled around her in a slow stiff-legged stroll.

When he stopped, she looked up and found that he was thumbing through a small notebook.

"The old preacher was quite meticulous. He recorded everything his parishioners told him," Blane tapped the notebook against the back of his hand, "every last detail. Would you like me to read his record of a conversation with you? Do you recall it, Kate, going to Preacher Stone, full of guilt and confusion about your sinful ways? Do you remember?"

Kate closed her eyes. She remembered well enough. The one person she'd told about her affair with John. It had been soon after the start of their relationship and she'd been racked with guilt about what she was doing. She'd turned to God for guidance and when she'd been unable to hear his voice she had gone to the Preacher for help.

He had listened. He hadn't judged or criticised. He'd been

understanding. Almost kind. He'd told her what she was doing was wrong and that God wanted her to honour her marriage vows. However, he'd added that only she could find her own path through the world, her own way to happiness and contentment.

She'd asked him if she was going to burn in hell.

He'd smiled then and said that if she did, she wouldn't be short of company.

She had gone away more confused than before. Shortly afterwards she'd started finding excuses to avoid going to church. When she'd seen the preacher on the street, he'd nodded and touched his hat and never said another word about what she'd told him.

He'd been kind and she'd liked him.

Then he'd raped her daughter.

"Where did you get that?" She didn't really care, but the words filled the void as she stared at Blane's boots.

"In the Preacher's house. Your husband was reading them."

Kate looked up, "Ash?"

"He hasn't been quite himself lately, has he?" Blane was still lightly tapping the notebook.

"Ash... has read that?"

Blane shook his head, "I found him in the Preacher's house, the old man had hundreds of these. All of Hawker's Drift's dirty little secrets are meticulously recorded. Your husband hadn't got to this one. Luckily for you."

"Why was Ash in the Preacher's house?"

"How should I know? He's your husband," Blane slipped the notebook into his pocket and squatted down in front of her, "but I guess that's not the only secret in this house…"

She noticed he had a few small hairs protruding out of his nostrils like tufts of wiry grass. They seemed incongruous for such a young man.

"Tell me, what do you think he would do if he read this notebook?"

Kate was going to insist Ash would never believe it, but that was just another lie. Ash would believe it well enough. Ash might even welcome it. He blamed her anyway. Blamed her for not waking up, blamed her for not saving Emily. He wanted to have someone to blame, especially now William Stone was cold in the grave and beyond his fury.

She thought of Ash in front of his Grandfather's mirror, scraping his razor along a leather strap.

Back and forth. Back and forth.

Yeah, he'd believe that old monster's words well enough.

"Are you going to show him?" She asked.

"Not if you give me what I want?"

"What have I got that you want?"

Blane looked at her for a good long while, his face as blank as stone. Then he smiled. Not a twitching little half smile, not a ghost of a smile, not something he twisted onto his face like an ill-fitting glove. A real smile.

It made her feel sick to the depths of her stomach.

His mouth gaped open to reveal faintly yellowed teeth, some broken, some blackened, some overlapping like ill-fitting tombstones in an overcrowded graveyard. Strands of drool, as fine as a spider's thread, stretched between his dry, cracked lips. His nostrils flared, his eyes bulged from behind narrowed lids and his eyebrows almost disappeared beneath his scalp.

Worse still was the noise; a wet, thick, snickering that bubbled up from somewhere deep within him and sounded as much like he was choking as laughing.

Kate felt herself trying to crawl away from him, but Blane scampered after her till she was backed up into a corner.

"Keep away from me..." she whimpered, pressing herself against the wall.

Blane lowered himself onto his knees, wiped the back of his hand across the slobber that had started to drip from his mouth.

"You're gonna be real nice to me Katie... real nice..." even Blane's voice had changed, the deep monotone replaced by a high-pitched, half-demented drawl. He reached out; his hand still wet with drool stroked her throat. Just a gentle caress, but it was enough to set Kate shivering.

"W-what do you want..." she repeated though she knew well enough.

"You're gonna give me your sweet cunt the same way you did to that nigger, or your loving ol' husband gonna find out what a whore he's married. And so will the rest of the town, and your pretty lil' daughters, though by then Ash may well have put you in the ground anyways. I got a feeling he'll take the news real bad..."

"Fuck off!" Kate jerked his hand away from her throat before spitting in his face.

She expected him to strike her, but instead he just kneeled there looking at her until his deranged smile faded back into the expressionless mask he wore to hide the thing he really was. He wiped the gob of spit from his cheek before standing up.

"Everything has a price..." he said slowly. His voice, like his face, returning to normal as he rubbed his hand clean on the front of his shirt "...and I have a real good memory when it comes to what I'm owed."

"Get out!" Kate spat though her voice sounded weak and broken as she sprawled at Blane's feet.

The Deputy nodded and retrieved his hat, as he sauntered towards the door, his boots still squeaking, he said, "You have a think about my deal. Next time I call by I suggest you work on your attitude some..."

He looked back at her from the doorway and gave her a slow, easy wink before disappearing.

Kate was faintly aware of the front door swinging shut behind Blane, but she was too busy hugging her knees and crying to be entirely sure. She didn't want to look up in case he was still there, his mad leering face snickering and gibbering as he hopped from foot to foot pointing at her.

Fooled ya!

She felt numb, soiled and terrified all at once. She wanted to crawl somewhere dark and stay there until the end of time. She needed to do something, she recognised, dimly, but her mind was beyond thought. She clasped her knees tightly, but she could still feel her hands shaking all the same.

Ash would probably kill her if he found out...

Back and forth, back and forth.

...and certainly kill John. She wouldn't have thought such a thing possible even a few short weeks ago, but he'd changed since Emily's attack. There was an anger within him that he was struggling to contain and if he found out she'd been in another's man's bed while Emily was being raped...

She let out a slow, miserable moan and thought about Blane. Not the impassive, emotionless young man she and everyone else thought he was, but the warped, twisted thing that lived behind his muddy, flat eyes. She thought of him touching her, those lips, hanging with drool, slobbering over her. That face! That mad, twisted, monstrous, demented face looking down as he grunted on top of her.

Kate fell onto her hands and knees. She tried to scramble up, but vomited before she could get anywhere near the door.

Unable to move Kate just stared at the puke on the rug through wet bleary eyes. Time, and pretty much everything else, lost its meaning. When she finally managed to pull her sleeve across her face and look up, she found Emily was standing in the doorway.

"Hun..." she managed to sniff. She should stand up, but she was afraid she would just fall straight back down again if she tried.

Emily stared at her, her eyes as flat as Blane's normally were through the bed-tousled hair that hung limply about her face. Her blanket, that she now took everywhere, hung from her fingers and trailed behind her. Her nightdress was stained at the front. It took her a moment to realise her daughter had wet herself again.

"I'm alright..." she tried to smile reassuringly but didn't think she got within a country mile of it. Emily, however, had already begun to trudge off towards the porch to stare at the backyard instead of the bedroom ceiling.

The Gunslinger

"I've never been on a rollercoaster," Amelia declared with a heartfelt sigh.

"Me neither," Amos muttered. Given he had no idea what a rollercoaster was he was pretty sure he'd never been on one. Whatever that involved.

"Think I'd scream and scream."

"You would?"

Amelia nodded vigorously enough for her bunches to bounce, "Be scary."

"Best to keep away from them then."

Amelia giggled and went back to devouring her candy apple.

Most of the town seemed to have turned out for the first day of *Billberry's Travelling Carnival*, save for Molly. The Mayor had said he hoped they would go when they'd bumped into him on Corner Park before Amelia had turned up. However, as Molly, probably rightly, had said, she wouldn't trust anything that came out of that asshole's mouth bar the spit.

Amos had also reminded her, several times, that he didn't think taking Amelia to the carney was a good idea. As he hadn't really been able to elaborate why, and Amelia had looked like bursting into tears when they'd suggested they weren't going, he'd relented.

He'd already worked out thirteen years of solitude and killing weren't necessarily the best preparation for looking after a little girl.

They'd strolled down the Tear towards the carney that had set up in the fields just outside of town. He'd elicited a few glances though some of them were probably made in Amelia's direction. Still, a little girl turning up on her own hadn't stirred much in the way of interest from the rest of Hawker's Drift. He was pretty sure in most small towns it would have generated at least some mild curiosity or concern. But here, nobody seemed any more bothered than if a pigeon had fluttered down onto their fence.

Amos had taken the chance of being alone with Amelia to ask her again about her family and how she'd arrived in Hawker's Drift. The little girl managed to avoid giving any kind of answer that he could make sense of. He didn't think she was being deliberately evasive; more that everything that had happened to her before arriving in town was just a half-forgotten memory, a dream that had slipped away with wakefulness. Maybe the trauma of the fever she'd suffered had affected her mind in some way.

A good clout on the head could make a man forget himself. Maybe fever could do the same. It seemed Amelia could only grasp fragments of her memories, though, in truth, she didn't seem greatly concerned.

Her life, it appeared, was just one big adventure, which, Amos guessed, was pretty much how life was supposed to be when you were eight.

Amos didn't know how many people lived in Hawker's Drift and the necklace of farms, ranches and homesteads that surrounded the town, but most of them appeared to be shuffling around the carney in generally good-natured revelry.

It was without a doubt the most people Amos had seen in one place since... well, he wasn't entirely sure. He tried to avoid the bigger towns and the ramshackle hell holes of the cities unless he had an extremely persuasive reason not to. And the only reason he had that good was a man named Severn.

A wave of nausea crashed over him and he gripped Amelia's hand tightly enough for the little girl to look quizzically up at him. He ground out a smile and tried to fix on an old Union flag hanging limply in the heat above a sharpshooting booth.

Too many people.

Jostling, hollering, laughing, joking, chatting all mixed with horns and drums and flutes. Carney men hawking games and attractions, mechanical organs spitting out cheery, steamy tunes, the clink of coins, the slurping of drinks, belching, coughing, clapping. And beneath that din, the other noises; the stray thoughts, the flaring emotions, the scattered memories, clattering and clamoring to be heard above the sounds everybody could hear. Whizzing about him like the blurred horses on the carousel. The mundane and the murderous, the happy and the sly, the wistful and the wicked all mixing together into a sickening, churning morass that made his head feel like it was going to explode.

Amos staggered into a man, catching his shoulder enough

271

for him to cry out.

"Hey, buddy! Watch out!"

"Sorry," Amos muttered.

"No worries," the man shrugged, his tone gruff, but amiable enough.

Stupid, clumsy cunt.

The thought slammed into Amos' skull. The man had wanted to hit him; to knock him to the ground and stamp on his head. It wasn't anything personal; the world was stuffed to the brim with dumb ass simpletons who deserved his wrath. But he kept it down and hid it behind a genial smile and a chuckle. At least till he was at home alone with his wife...

"Amos?" Amelia tugged on his hand.

He forced another smile, "Just felt a little faint... hot day."

Amelia looked at him in a way that made him think she was much older than her eight years and not much inclined to believe bullshit.

"Maybe I need to sit down for a bit... away from the crowd."

She nodded, pulled his hand and led him between two tents. He managed to follow her without tripping over any of the taut ropes and emerged into the relative peace beyond. As soon as he saw the empty grass pulling away to the horizon he felt better. He slumped down on his haunches in the thin band of shade behind one of the tents.

He took off his hat and was waving it in front of his face when a voice called out.

"You ok?"

He turned to see Cece emerging from between the tents,

her face hidden in the shade of an enormous, saggy brimmed hat.

"He doesn't like so many people being around," Amelia piped up before he could answer.

Amos peered at her. That wasn't what he'd told her. She was pretty perceptive for a little kid.

"Can't say I blame him, the whole town must be here," Cece crouched down next to Amos and Amelia, "you feeling better Miss?"

Amelia nodded.

"Do you remember me?"

"You came see me when I was sick…"

"That's right… glad you're all better. Have you been feeling dizzy or funny in your head at all?"

"Nope." Amelia shook her head wildly from side to side, before holding up her candy apple stick, the chewed remains of the apple core just about clinging to it, "Do you like candy apples?"

"Sure."

"Will you get me one when you go and get yours then?"

Cece laughed, her eyes sparkling and her nose wrinkling as she glanced at Amos.

"Quite the hustler you have here?"

Amos grinned but didn't reply. Cece was hunkering down close enough for the sleeve of her pale cotton dress to be rubbing against his arm, but thankfully he was getting nothing from her but the faint scent of lemon soap.

"What's your name?" Amelia asked, still holding the stick up least they forgot the lack of a candy apple.

"Cece."

"I don't know anyone called that."

"Short for Cecilia, but I like Cece better."

"Some people call me Amy, but my Mom don't like that..." her voice faltered as if she were struggling to recall something "...she says it sounds common."

Cece laughed, "Yeah, sounds like my mom..."

"What does your mom look like Amelia?" Amos asked after a moment's pause, "Just in case I see her around."

Amelia puckered her lips and scrunched up her forehead, "She's big... with lots of hair... much more than me... and... and... she's brown like me... and..."

She suddenly looked like she was going to burst into tears as she spun between Cece and Amos

"Why can't I remember what my Mom looks like?!"

Cece reached out and squeezed her hand, "It's just because you were very ill. It's what we call a *side-effect*, it may last a bit, but you will remember things eventually."

Amelia didn't look entirely convinced and Amos wasn't sure he was either... from the way Cece was looking at the child he suspected she'd emitted a "probably" from that sentence...

"Hey, why don't I go get you another candy apple?"

Amelia's face was immediately split by a broad and beaming smile.

Cece straightened up wearing the expression of someone who thought they'd just been played particularly well, "You going to wait here?"

The idea of heading back into the crowd made Amos feel cold beneath the sweat that was plastering his shirt to his skin and he gave her a nod.

"Can I go with Cece?" Amelia asked, already moving to the woman's side.

Amos doubted Molly would be entirely happy with the arrangement, but he knew Cece meant the girl no harm. Whatever her story was he was certain she had a good heart, and a few minutes alone would help him get his head back into some kind of order.

"Sure... but keep hold of her hand and no running off."

He glanced up at Cece and she gave him a little nod of understanding as she took the girl's hand. She'd take care of her.

"So, how do you like the carney?"

"There's no elephants, or rollercoaster or dodgem' cars, or..." he listened to the girl's voice until it was enveloped in the greater hubbub of the carney.

Amos closed his eyes and let out a long, slow breath.

*

"Sleeping it off?"

Amos awoke with a start. He'd only intended to close his eyes for a few seconds to clear his head, but found he had slid back against the tent with his chin on his chest. He had a vague recollection of snoring wetly and loudly.

He peered up at the bulky figure of Sheriff Shenan, who was looming over him, thumbs hitched into his belt, wearing an expression that fell some way between a scowl and a grin.

"Am I breaking any bylaws, Sheriff?" Amos asked, climbing to his feet. Damn this heat made everything much harder than it should be.

"Not so I can see. Just as well, my cells always get filled

up when the carney rolls into town?"

"Trouble?"

Shenan gave a little shrug, "Some folk get a bit boisterous and excitable; probably due to drinking all day in the sun and some new whores to fall in love with. You know how men can be?"

A lot better than most...

Amos settled for a little nod and looking about for Amelia and Cece, but there was no one to see this side of the line of tents that marked one edge of the carney, other than a young couple kissing by the fence. Or at least till they spotted the Sheriff glowering at them and they scurried off hand in hand.

"To be young eh..." Shenan muttered, his features softening as soon as the couple had ducked out of sight further along the row of tents.

"You seen-"

"That little girl of yours? Yeah, few minutes ago with the pretty singer from the saloon. Think she was trying to win a dolly for her," Shenan pulled a face, "cheaper just to buy one, these carney games are all fixed..."

"Don't suppose you got any news about her people?"

Shenan pushed his hat back a fraction and peered up at the cloudless sky, "Nope, can't say I have."

Amos followed his gaze, but there wasn't so much as a bird in the sky, just a profound and endless blue that would make him feel giddy if he stared at it long enough.

"So, she just appeared out of thin air?"

"Seems that way."

Amos' gaze dropped from the sky to look sideways at the

old sheriff, "That an unusual thing here?"

Shenan looked both thoughtful and uncomfortable, before sucking up some phlegm and spitting it through his teeth.

"Lots of folks turn up here. You did."

"And I got a saddle sore butt to show how I did it. But an eight-year-old girl?"

"Best just to get on with things. Live your life. Some folk turn up with no real idea where they came from, some folks turn up with the story of their lives piled in the back of a wagon. We take 'em in, give 'em a home, let 'em build a new life. Seems to work well enough. Mostly."

Amos stared at the Sherriff, "Everybody knows where they came from."

"Maybes, guess some just don't like to talk about it, that's all I mean."

He didn't think that was what Shenan had meant at all, but he let it pass.

"I'd better go find Amelia."

The Sheriff nodded, "Best to keep an eye on her, these carney folk..."

"What do you mean?"

The Sheriff cast a slow look around, but nobody was in sight, "They always made me feel a bit... unsettled. Found an old wagon parked up in the Small Field where they got their little carney town set up. Looks like a goddamn abattoir inside it. Dried blood everywhere. Told me it was someone died in childbirth, but..."

"But?"

"Women in childbirth don't spray the wall and ceiling with blood..." Shenan drew a finger across his throat "...a knife

277

across here though..."

An image of Megan's lifeblood spraying over the laughing face of the man who'd slit her throat came to him unbidden.

"Guess so. You investigating?"

Shenan shook his head and wrinkled his broad nose. "Not my jurisdiction. They'll be packed up and gone in a few days. Be glad of it too."

They made their way back into the main drag of the carney; a long avenue of tents and booths facing each other, thronged with people ambling – or staggering in a few cases – from attraction to game to food stall to beer and whiskey sellers.

Amos fought down the gorge in his throat as the miasma of souls washed over him again and he wondered how long it was going to take to find Amelia. He scratched his head and winced, looking back and forth while the Sheriff scowled at a couple of carney men with misbegotten faces and feathers hanging from their long hair.

However, he needn't have worried about catching up with Amelia. It turned out she was pretty easy to find once she started screaming...

The Widow

She hadn't much liked the idea of letting Amelia go off with Amos to the carney, but the girl had set her heart on going for some reason and she supposed Amos was capable enough of looking after her for a few hours.

She'd watched them amble down the street together, Amelia chatting in her usual incessant way as she held Amos' hand. She was probably old enough to not have to hold an adult's hand every time she went on the street, but she seemed to like it. Molly quite liked it too.

Amos, for his part, carried an air of perpetual uncertainty around the girl. It was like he didn't have a clue what he was supposed to do or say and worried that if he got it wrong something quite awful was going to happen. Like Amelia bursting into tears or Molly throwing heavy objects at him.

Once they were gone the house was awful quiet. She paced through it a few times, as much to fill it with the sound of her footsteps as anything else. What on Earth had she done before Amos and Amelia had rolled up on her doorstep?

Oh yeah, there'd been Tom.

She felt a familiar pang of guilt. Despite her disparate collection of woes, she'd felt strangely happy these last few days. She supposed it was just the keeping busy. Looking after a kid was a good way of filling up all the hours of a day. Then there was Amos. For all his peculiarities, she felt safe with him around. And she liked him. She trusted him. She... felt guilty about him.

What would Tom have thought about all this?

Knowing Tom there probably wouldn't have been a whole lot of thought. Probably would just have got mad. Or Surly. Or sulky.

She kept telling herself he was gone and he definitely wasn't coming back. Life moved on. Had to, no other damn way of going about it. Still, when it was slow and quiet, like the day was now without Amelia's laughter or Amos' strangeness, guilt would steal up on her and demand to know what the hell she thought she was doing. Being happy with her husband so fresh in his grave? With a mountain of debt to pay off, the prospect of the whorehouse looming and a creepy little lawyer determined to make her his wife.

Molly didn't like the feeling much so, after a good long bout of aimless pacing, she decided to face up to her guilt like any rational, intelligent, well-grounded person would.

*

"Whiskey. A large one."

Monty actually seemed pleased to see her. It was like she was an old friend who'd unexpectedly returned home after years away at sea, to be welcomed back into the bosom of their family as they gathered around a roaring fire to slap backs and catch up on old times.

Or everyone else was at the carney and he was just

grateful to see anyone he could flog whiskey to.

"Coming right up!" He beamed.

The saloon really was a morgue. Bright sunlight lanced through the big windows, illuminating the front half and the countless dust motes that swirled aimlessly in the air. The back of the bar was dark with shadow in comparison, the angle of the sun too steep to light up the interior reaches.

Other than Monty and a couple girls blowing smoke by the window the place was empty. Even the well-worn, ass-polished stools of the saloon's hardened barflies were deserted.

"The carney must be hurting your takings, Monty?"

"Fourth of fuckin' July..." he sighed, sloshing her glass with a deep and welcome measure "...worst day of the year."

"Why don't you just close up and go join the fun with everyone else?"

"Close?" Monty's chins shuddered with disgust.

Molly emptied her glass in one and took another fill immediately. She didn't feel in much of a savouring kind of mood. The whiskey's welcome was a hell of a lot sincerer than Monty's, but if she sat at the bar she'd keep 'em coming way too fast. She didn't want to be a steaming drunk when Amos and Amelia got home.

So, to his obvious disappointment, she waved away the opportunity to slump at the bar and help Monty with his takings. Instead, Molly headed towards the back of the saloon. Sippin' liquor in bright sunlight just felt kind of wrong anyway.

"You want to take the bottle?" Monty called hopefully.

"I'm good," Molly said, even if a whole bottle did seem like a splendid idea for a slow, quiet afternoon when Mr Guilt was plodding diligently about his business.

It was pleasingly cool out of the reach of the sunlight. She settled down in one of the booths at the very back of the saloon to sip her whiskey and do some thinking though all she ended up thinking was that she wanted more whiskey.

A bottle clinked against her glass.

"You look like you could use some more..."

Molly's head jerked up, she'd been staring too keenly at her glass to notice the saloon girl approach.

"I might not have wanted more."

The woman chuckled, "Don't worry it's on the house. We get an allowance..."

"Not all bad working here then," Molly muttered taking a swig as it seemed rude to make a fuss about free booze.

"I'm Josie..." the woman slipped onto the bench opposite and deposited the bottle and her own glass between them.

"Molly."

"I know who you are honey."

"Yeah... guess everyone knows me."

"Real famous," Josie smiled as she poured herself a drink, all the time keeping her green eyes fixed on Molly. Her hair was jet black and her skin pale enough beneath her paint and powder to suggest it had been a long time since she'd left the saloon. Her face had a slight gauntness to it that made her look hard and worn down, but her eyes held a warmth and intensity to them that suggested that life had not entirely broken her.

"Any tips to help a girl get by here?"

Josie sighed and fixed her a long steady gaze as she

sipped her drink, "Do anything else you can but this. *Jack's Saloon* really is the last stop on the line."

"That's what I figured. No offence."

"None taken, we all got our reasons for ending up here. Some better than others… so you might be joining us then? Heard what people said, but you need to take everything here with a large pinch of salt… and not just the tequila."

"I owe the Mayor money; if I don't pay him back…"

"It's not so bad here, just not the kind of thing you dream about as a little girl," Josie said with a sigh as she produced a tobacco pouch and begun to roll a cigarette.

"What did you dream about?"

"Damned if I can remember. You?"

"Getting away from my father."

"Not the first we've had here running away from that."

"What brought you here?"

Josie paused to light her cigarette with a casual flick of a match, "Dunno, just ended up here one day."

"You grew up around here?"

"No… long ways away… just a little place… you wouldn't have heard of it…" Josie's voice was suddenly as hazy as the smoke that drifted about-her while her eyes seemed to fade into the shadows.

"What was it like there?" Molly asked with a careful casualness.

Josie snorted smoke, "Can barely remember. Strange huh? Everything before I came here… it's kinda fuzzy like it was all a dream."

"Isn't that… odd? How old were you?"

"Seventeen, I guess."

"And you-"

"You sure ask a lot a questions… the men generally don't like that."

Molly stiffened but managed to bite down on one of her favoured retorts, "Just curious about folk…"

"The past's the past. Most folk ain't keen on talking about that, makes 'em edgy."

Only in this fucking town sweetheart…

"Sorry about your husband," Josie said after a long draw and a longer pause.

"You knew him?"

Josie shook her head, "Nah, he wasn't ever one of the ones that came sneaking in to see us when the wife was sleeping. Just saw him in here with you."

Molly glanced away, a couple of the regular drunks were staggering in, the novelty and excitement of the carney hadn't proved enough to keep them away from their usual roosts. Monty gave them the beaming smile of a man just reunited with a love he'd thought lost in a shipwreck years ago.

"Didn't ever notice him even talking to any of us. Think he only ever had eyes for you."

Now Molly blinked and looked at her glass.

"You mind if I have another one?"

"Knock yourself out," Josie grinned.

*

"Sometimes the dreams seem realer than this place…" Josie sloshed her booze about the bottom of the glass

She'd talked about men, the town, Monty and what it was

284

like to make a living from what God had chosen to put between her legs. The one thing she wouldn't be drawn on was her past.

Wouldn't, or couldn't?

Whenever Molly had tried to steer their conversation in that direction she'd got that same glassy look in her eye and her voice dropped to a hoarse whisper. Molly had put the thought into the back of her mind and wondered what it would be like for Amos, to sense the truth that people hid behind their words.

"Would have thought a place like this would kill any dream stone dead?"

Josie smiled, but didn't pull her gaze from the glass.

"I still have hopes of a good man and little place on the grass... even now. Soiled goods that I am and all." She downed her whiskey and then filled both glasses again. The bottle was emptying faster than was healthy.

"You must have some savings?"

"Sure. But money doesn't buy you the things you really want."

"Why not move on to another town, somewhere where people won't..."

"Know I'm a whore?"

When Molly couldn't think of a softer answer, she just nodded.

"I think about it. I got some money... but... it's a big world out there." Her eyes fixed on some point that didn't seem to be anywhere related to the world Molly lived in. "Feels like home now, even when I get around to quitting this place I can't imagine leaving Hawker's Drift."

"It's a hard place to leave..." Molly muttered.

"Sure is honey."

Seemed to Molly that Hawker's Drift should be a damn easy place to get out of, but maybe she didn't see it in the same light as everybody else did. Probably not the first time she'd been guilty of that.

"I'll stop doing this soon. I'll find a decent man and make a proper home; I still got some good years left in me."

Sounded familiar to Molly. Hadn't she said much the same when she'd been drifting from town to town swapping one asshole for another and never quite managing to find the life she wanted. She'd kept rolling the same loaded dice and being surprised when the same old numbers kept staring back at her. Even with Tom, she'd never been really happy, just maybe as happy as she was ever likely to get. Now he was gone... and she was back to rolling that old dice again.

Except this time, there was Amos. And Amelia too.

Maybe Hawker's Drift *was* a hard place to leave when you had something worth staying for.

Clink

Molly looked up, Josie was sloshing more booze. She really should stop. She should get up and go home while she still could without having to concentrate too hard to stop her falling flat on her fanny. But something held her in her seat – and it wasn't just the burn of the whiskey on the back of her throat either. There was something in Josie's bright green eyes, like she was saying one thing with her lips, but her eyes were screaming something else. Molly just couldn't work out what it was, but she had a hunch it was something to do with her past. Or the fact she'd drunk too much whiskey of course.

"Do you have dreams that seem... more real than this?" Josie's latest cigarette left a trail of smoke as she waved her hand towards the saloon.

Molly shook her head, "My dreams are all nonsense. Pink cats in rowing boats, castles of snow, chocolate rain, honest and decent men... you know, all the really impossible stuff."

Josie gave a little smile, but if faded away in a moment, "My dreams are strange, but they seem so damn real. So damn frightening sometimes. Sometimes I wake up with a scream and think they were real and this is the dream. Which don't go down so well if I got an overnight guest."

"What kind of dreams?"

Josie looked at her the same way Amos did. She assumed that meant there was some thinking going on.

"Sounds crazy..."

"Crazier than pink cats in rowing boats singing pirate songs?"

"Pirate songs?"

"*Pira-cat-ical* songs actually..." Molly giggled.

Josie was supposed to have groaned or rolled her eyes or something. She just stared blankly at Molly.

In fairness, probably not my best joke...

"Erm... so what *do* you dream of then?" Molly asked, after a moderately painful silence.

"Things that don't make sense," Josie said, looking elsewhere, "So real and vivid... there's one I have, over and over again. Always the same..."

"Maybe it means something?"

"I can't see how... I'm flying, in the sky, but not like a bird,

287

I'm sitting down looking out of this little window and I'm in this... carriage, and there's this noise, a deep constant thrum coming from all around me. The carriage is moving, side to side, up and down, every now and then. There are other people with me. Lots of them.

Down below is this city, but not like any real city. It's like a fairy-tale city full of these enormous towers. It fills up an island and this city stretches forever beyond the island, even though I'm as high as an eagle I can still see no end to it. A city big enough to house all the people in the world."

"Sounds... magical..."

Josie shook her head and drained her glass, "No, not magical. I'm terrified. So is everybody else. People are crying and sobbing. Screaming, praying, I want to run away, to get out of my seat, but there's nowhere to run. We are circling the city, getting lower and I can see these two towers, bigger than all the others, so tall they could touch the clouds. There's black smoke pouring out of one of the towers, not chimney smoke, it's on fire and there's a big hole on one side of it... I can hear someone screaming behind me "They're going to crash us, they're going to crash us!" I feel so scared and so helpless and... and... we're getting lower and the city is rushing past us ... then..."

"What happens?"

"I wake up."

"It's just a dream."

Josie looked even paler than usual as if the blood had been drained from her body. She stubbed out her cigarette with a violent little twist.

"No... I wake up in my dream... and I'm staring at the sky.

288

It's blue... a dark, dark blue. Like the sun hasn't quite gone up and I'm lying in the grass. There's just silence, no screaming, no roaring, no more voices. I sit up and look around. I'm here. Out on the grass. There's nothing to see but grass in any direction save for the figure of a man coming towards me. He's smiling and holding out his hand to help me up. Then I wake. For real.

"Who was the man?"

Josie blinked and bit her lip, her eyes rose from her empty glass before she whispered in a voice so low it barely carried across the table.

"The Mayor, it's the Mayor coming for me..."

The Songbird

"I like that one!"

The rag doll had bright red hair and appeared to have been stitched together by someone with only a rudimentary understanding of human physiology. It sat amongst a sorry looking menagerie of stuffed toys, mostly of indeterminate species, that could be won by knocking down pyramids of tin cans with three cloth balls.

"Why that one?" Cece asked.

"It looks like Molly!" Amelia giggled before taking a chunk out of her latest candy apple.

"I guess..." Cece wondered if there was a string you could pull in order to get the doll to start swearing at you...

Amelia was making big eyes at Cece over the rim over her candy apple. She got the distinct feeling that she was being played again.

"Well, maybe Amos could win it for you. He's probably better at throwing than I am."

And he can deal with a little girl's disappointment when it turns out some of the cans are nailed down...

Amelia nodded and accepted Cece's excuse with a world-weary shrug.

"We should go find him huh?"

291

Amelia nodded and curled her hand around Cece's without prompting as she looked back and forth through the crowd that was drifting along the makeshift avenue of games and distractions.

"They say the future is an unknown country..." a voice announced behind her. Cece looked around with a start and was surprised to find a tall dark-haired woman a few inches from her nose.

"...I say some people have a map."

"Erm..."

"I'm Giselle," the woman said, "I see the future and the past..."

Just a fortune-teller hawking some business, Cece relaxed and gave her a thin smile, "I'm sorry, we don't need to know the future."

"Of course you don't..." there was something close to a smirk on Giselle's face. She was in her late forties Cece guessed though the knowing in her onyx-dark eyes suggested she was much older. Her skin was a dusty-ochre, reminiscent of the warmth of a summer sunset. Her long jet-black hair was pulled severely back over her scalp and several large silver hoops hung from each ear.

"...but I bet you'd like to know wouldn't you?" Her gaze fixed on Amelia. The girl, who hadn't seemed much troubled by anything or anyone in the swirling, brash crowds of the carney edged closer to Cece and she felt Amelia's small, clipped fingernails dig into her hand.

If Giselle was clairvoyant enough to sense the girl's unease she didn't show it, her darkly painted lips split into a smile, "In your future I see a particular red-haired doll..."

She turned to the tin can booth. The silver bangles on her wrist jangled as she flicked a finger at the rag doll Amelia had been admiring. For a moment, her long painted nails looked like bloody talons and Cece found herself returning Amelia's squeeze of the hand.

The carney guy behind the booth had narrow, shifting eyes, a misplaced chin and haphazard shaving. He looked like the kind of man who would generally begrudge giving the grass the spit from his mouth for free. However, he grabbed the doll and handed it to Giselle without complaint or comment before spinning back towards a couple of prospective punters, a waxy smile nailed unwaveringly to his face.

Giselle pulled at her flowing skirts and crouched down before Amelia, the doll held out.

"Take it…" she said, her pencil drawn eyebrows stretching upwards.

Up close the doll looked even uglier, a dress made from a scrap of denim, its mouth just crude stitching and its skin a dirty gypsum white. It had two black beads for eyes. Both were already hanging loose enough from their threads to give the doll a look of garish, comic surprise as if it had been startled enough for its eyes to pop out of its head. The hair was lengths of red wool, hanging like dreadlocks down the doll's back, but carelessly enough placed to give the impression of a receding hairline. It looked like a mad clown in a dress it had made itself.

Molly's really not going to be flattered by that thing…

Amelia reached out a tentative hand and curled it around the doll, "Thank you…"

293

"What a polite little girl." As Amelia took the ragdoll, Giselle lightly held the girl's wrist, her eyes widening and her lips parting as she did so. It seemed a tremor rippled through the fortune-teller, a tremor strong enough to set her collection of oversized earrings, bracelets and bangles jingle-jangling like wind chimes in a shifting breeze.

"My Mommy always told me to say thank you."

"Of course she did my sweetness."

Giselle reached up and curled a hand about Amelia's cheek, each finger ending in a long blood red nail.

Talons, not nails, she could take someone's face off with those...

"What a delicious little thing you are," Giselle breathed, staring into Amelia's eyes, which had grown wide in return.

Cece shuffled, still gripping the girl's hand, but Amelia's grasp had become loose and felt like it would fall uselessly to her side if Cece released it. The woman was doing nothing wrong, just doting on a child like many women do, but Giselle made her feel queasy in some intangible way. Though her stitching was flawless and her dress much more flattering, she was just like the ragdoll Amelia was clutching. Neither of them had been put together quite right...

The crowd was still swimming by, laughing, jostling, pointing. There was a stink of sweetly frying onions in the still air, wood smoke too. A hog was being roasted somewhere. A heavily whiskered man sauntered past tearing at a slice of sourdough wrapped around a greasy slab of pork. A young woman was pushing a baby in a pram big and heavy enough to be pulled by a pony while the balding, freckled faced man at her side chatted animatedly. A teenager was running, his friend chasing him, dodging around a corpulently fat woman in an ill-advised striped dress and laughing manically.

Out of sight a penny whistle played and someone was *thump-thump-thumping* on a bass drum. The sun shone bright and hot enough for sweat to trickle down the back of Cece's neck even in the shade of her drooping hat.

Everything was movement and sound and colour and heat and stinks of food and humanity. Braying voices and feet shuffling on worn downtrodden grass. The bright garish colours of the carney folk mixing and blending with the generally drabber hues of the locals.

And yet...

Amongst the kaleidoscope of moving colours and forms she noticed several points of stillness. An old fellow in a jauntily cocked top hat, his long black coat incongruous and impractical in the heat. A huge man stripped to the waist, his barrel chest and pumped musculature glistening with enough oil to make his dark skin look like wet, slick obsidian. Another man, tall and sallow, his dark hair greased and combed into precise furrows and an arrow straight side parting. His Adam's apple seemed engorged, bobbing above his shirt that was fastened to the collar. A Chinese guy with delicately sculpted features. Others too, further back, just eyes amongst the moving bodies.

Tiger eyes in the swaying grass.

"I think it's time we got going, Amelia..." Cece said, her voice even and neutral. Or trying to be anyway. She looked about for Amos, but couldn't spot him in the throng.

"Oh, there's no hurry, is there Amelia?"

Cece was pretty sure she'd never mentioned the girl's name to Giselle.

"We really-"

Cece was cut off as Amelia suddenly jerked her hand free of Giselle and started screaming into the fortune-teller's face...

The Barber

Kate seemed to be becoming more agitated in direct proportion to Emily's descent into torpor. Perhaps it would all end with his daughter turning into stone and his wife bursting into flame.

He should be with them of course. He knew that. But he was finding more and more reasons to be elsewhere. The shop, errands, chores mostly. And listening to Mr Wizzle. He'd never felt himself a particularly pious or religious man. He just got on with what needed to be done; if there was a greater power in the world he was sure they could get along with their business just fine without Ash Godbold. He'd even been secretly relieved when Kate had lost interest in going to church. He'd never questioned her about why there was always an excuse not to go to church all of a sudden. He'd just been grateful.

Now he found the mad old clown's preaching kind of soothing and restful. It almost gave him a little peace and was infinitely preferable to watching Kate pace up and down the house, continually staring out of the window and jumping half out of her skin every time someone knocked on the door.

It was just fear of course; fear that someone else was

going to hurt their girls again. He'd tried putting an arm around her and telling her everything was going to get better. She'd just shot him a venomous look that suggested she didn't believe that crap any more than he did, before shrugging his arm off and storming out of the room.

He'd sat for a long time, not knowing what to do or say. Finally, he'd gone up to check on Emily, but her blank eyes hadn't even flickered away from the ceiling when he'd found her hand and squeezed it. He could feel her bones, sharp and angular beneath the skin. She was losing weight, fading from the world physically as well as mentally.

He'd stood over her bed, feeling about as useless as it was possible for a man to feel. Eventually, he'd blinked away his tears and gone to look for Mr Wizzle.

He'd found him standing on his crate by the side of the road down to Hooper's Fields preaching to the townsfolk trickling towards the carney.

It was a lovely day, the town had virtually shut down for the 4th of July and most everybody was ambling by in cheerful expectation of a day's fun at the carney.

In other words, nobody was interested in listening to a mad old clown telling them about the Devil in their midst. Ash, however, was finding himself more and more inclined to hear the man out.

"There is a Serpent amongst us!" Mr Wizzle declared, one wiggling finger raised above his head

"A Serpent that corrupts us all, that tricks us with its lies and deceits, that pets and comforts us like lambs being led to slaughter..."

"Ah, fuck off!" Jerry Jassawitz slurred as he ambled past

between slurps of the beer bottle that was keeping him going till he reached the carney. He was probably heading for the whores parked up in the fancy wagons at the back of Hooper's Small Field. Jerry wasn't the kind of man that needed to wait until nightfall to get blind drunk and screw prostitutes.

Ash sat down on the dry, scratchy grass on the opposite side of the road. The traffic heading down to Hooper's Fields was throwing enough dust into the air to parch his throat within a couple of minutes. The dust didn't seem to be having much effect on Mr Wizzle's throat, however.

Kendall Bratt was sprawled on the verge a couple of paces to Ash's right. His dog, Wally, sitting attentively between his legs, ears pricked as if he found the sermon as captivating as his owner.

Kendall was one of the town's small band of vagrants and he spent most of his days shuffling around town staring at things, many of which only he appeared to be able to see. He was a harmless old coot and got by on hand-outs and general charitableness.

In most places, men like Kendal were seen as little more than vermin, but in Hawker's Drift people were more tolerant. Maybe because there was less poverty here.

Ash remembered well enough rolling through town after town with his grandfather's chair and mirrors in the back of his wagon looking for somewhere that needed a barber. You would have thought there'd always be men in need of a shave and a haircut wherever you went, but nope. In most towns, he'd been peered at suspiciously and told there was no room for strangers, even the ones with half their Main

Street boarded up and deserted. In a couple of places, the message had been re-enforced by stern-faced men cradling guns.

Hawker's Drift had been different; thriving, alive and welcoming. The Mayor had come down and seen him on his first day. Told him how much the town needed a good barber, even found a shop for him and paid up the rent for the first three months to get him started.

He thought he'd stumbled onto paradise. Then he'd met Kate and had been damn well sure he had.

Now...

Kendal's mouth was hanging open, the way it usually did behind the twists and tangles of his long beard, the black shot through with veins of dusty grey. It was the kind of beard Ash would normally take professional offence at, but today he couldn't be bothered. He was starting to think there were far worse things in Hawker's Drift than unruly facial hair.

"Amen!" Kendal shouted, loud enough to make both Ash and a couple of passing townsfolk jump.

Mr Wizzle nodded and climbed off his preaching crate with a laboured wheeze. Ash hadn't actually heard much of the sermon. There wasn't much he was going to find out from the old clown's preaching, which mostly amounted to the kind of dire biblical warning of fire and brimstone many preachers resorted to. It was the implication behind the words that had caught his attention. The implication that something was rotten at the heart of this little too good to be true Eden of a town. Something that had ensnared his beautiful little girl and run a lot deeper than one mad old pervert dressed in the Preacher's black.

Ash and Kendal rose together. Without comment, he gave a little tug on Wally's string leash and the two of them headed against the flow of people trickling down from Hawker's Drift.

Mr Wizzle beamed as Ash came towards. Despite the indifference, insults and mockery he endured the old man seemed indefatigably cheerful. It was something to admire, Ash supposed.

"You heading up to the carney?" Ash asked.

Mr Wizzle tipped his derby to a couple of red-faced matronly women toiling in the heat as they passed them. By way of a response, they both started walking faster.

"That sordid den of iniquity and foulness? Of course."

"Mind if we walk up together?"

Mr Wizzle screwed up his nose and dabbed at his forehead with one of his multi-stained rags that passed for a handkerchief.

"Not at all... but I'll not be going yet."

Ash squinted down the road, which ran pretty much furrow-straight towards Hooper's Fields, where he could make out the garish tents and wagons of the transient little carney town shimmering in the early afternoon heat.

"Is a bit hot, I guess."

"I'll be seeing what there is to see once it's dark."

"Not preaching?"

Mr Wizzle shook his head vigorously enough for his derby to rock back and forth on his waxy pate, "There's none in that nest of sin who will listen to God's words."

It seemed to Ash there wasn't anyone much in town

301

either, but he held his tongue.

"I take it you're not going there to chance your arm against the strongman or kiss the bearded lady, though?"

Mr Wizzle didn't smile. Instead, his eyes fixed on the distant carney, half obscured in the haze.

"Every year I tell myself I'm going to find out what that carney is really all about. Then every blessed year I come here and preach to nobody much, look down that road and talk myself out of it. Every year I try to be less blind than the other souls in the town and every year I don't do what is required. My nerve fails me and I slink back to my shack, pull the blanket over my head and pretend all is well when I know that it is not."

"And this year?"

"This year my nerve is not going to fail me. There are answers down that road Mr Godbold. I swear there are."

Ash frowned. All he wanted to know was whether this town was safe for his girls, he couldn't really see how poking around a carney that only came to town a few days a year would help with that.

As if sensing his uncertainty, Mr Wizzle placed a hand on his arm and squeezed it gently.

"Come with me Ash, let's just see what there is to see. What's to lose?"

"And what's to find?"

"Maybe the Devil that hurt your girl?"

"William Stone is dead."

"That he is..." the old man dug his fingers into the meat of Ash's arm, "...but I don't think for a moment that he raped your daughter..."

*

It had never occurred to Ash that Mr Wizzle actually had a home.

He'd just assumed he was a vagrant like Kendal, scraping a living off the streets and the town's charity. Admittedly it was more of a shack than a home, but it housed a single bed, a wood burner, a rickety old chair, a washbasin (probably rarely used), shelves lined with books of all kinds. And jars of pickled eggs. Lots of them.

"I'm quite fond of pickled eggs," Mr Wizzle beamed, noticing Ash staring at the ranks of glass jars paraded on the rough splintered shelves.

"So I see..." Ash mumbled.

It was stifling hot inside and sunlight was snicking through the ill-fitting planks of the shack's walls.

Nasty draft in winter...

Ash shook the rather pointless thought away, "Why do you think Preacher Stone was innocent?" He'd asked the same question half a dozen times in different ways as they walked around the Tear to the Flats on the other side of town. Mr Wizzle's shack nestled among the outhouses, warehouses and ramshackle dwellings of Hawker's Drift's less fortunate residents.

He got the same kind of answer as he had all the other times he'd asked, "Be patient..."

Ash felt his temper starting to simmer but forced the lid back down on it. The old man was probably mad and this was a fool's errand, but nobody else in town was offering him much of anything by way of answers. Mad or otherwise.

Mr Wizzle nudged the room's solitary chair in Ash's

direction before rummaging through one of the shelves that was crammed with books rather than jars of pickled eggs.

Ash eased himself into it with a long nasally sigh that sounded a bit like steam coming from a boiling kettle. The shack had one window, just a pain of gauze between two drab rags that served as curtains. Outside a sad-looking mutt was nosing at something in the grass. It didn't hold its attention for long and the dog gave it a cursory pee before sauntering off to find something more appealing to sniff.

"Here!" Mr Wizzle handed Ash two hard-backed books as he lowered himself onto the edge of the bed. He was close enough for his knee to press against Ash's and the odour of deceased eggs to play across his face.

One book was black, the other red. Ash flicked through them; the light was poor in the room and his reading had been getting harder these last few years though he hadn't mentioned it to anyone. A barber with bad eyes might worry the customers. He knew he should get some eyeglasses, but the thought of them made him feel decrepit, the first outrider of old age bounding over the horizon.

However, even with the soft light and eyes that weren't as sharp as they once were he could see that in each book, written in the tight neat hand of an educated man, was a list of names. Most he recognised though some he didn't. The final name in the black book was "*Amelia Prouloux*" in the red one it was "*William Eustace Stone.*"

He stared at the Preacher's name a good long while before raising his eyes to meet Mr Wizzle's.

"*And?*"

The old man tapped a clipped, grimy fingernail on the

black ledger, "Arrivals..." then the red book "...departures."

Ash looked back at the ledgers, "All the people that have come and gone from town?"

"Indeed. Over, many, many years."

All of the names had either a tick or a question mark against them. Both Amelia's and Preacher Stone had a big black question mark.

"And these mean?"

"Well..." Mr Wizzle shuffled closer to him (Ash was even more convinced the wash basin was there purely for show) and tapped on a name in the black ledger., "...Cassie Winsky went to live with her cousin in Providence after her husband died. So she gets a tick."

Ash nodded, remembering a spindly woman with a hatchet face that permanently scowled at the world from beneath a bun of cobweb grey hair. She'd left town the previous year and he hadn't given her a moment's thought since.

"So?"

"I watched her climb up onto the stage and roll out of town whilst I was preaching. A few weeks later I took myself down to Providence to see how she was getting on."

"Cassie Winsky is a friend of yours?"

"She hurled a couple of tomatoes at me once, but I wouldn't really describe us as close..."

"Providence is seventy-five miles away. That's a long way to go to see a woman who throws fruit at you?"

"I do what I do. And actually it's closer to ninety."

"So... did she throw anything at you?"

He gave a phlegmy chuckle, "Nope. I was careful she didn't

see me, just made sure she was set up in town then turned around and came back."

"You didn't even stay?"

"You ever been to Providence?"

Ash couldn't say that he had.

"A couple of dozen cottages along a road that doesn't even bother to widen."

"Then..."

Mr Wizzle tapped another name with a tick against it.

"Joel Hellog?"

"Remember him?"

"Sure, old fella who'd never let me trim his ear hair."

"Uh-huh, passed away in the winter just gone."

"No great surprise, he must have been nigh on a hundred."

"Ninety-six."

"So?" Ash was expecting to see a wild goose anytime soon.

"Got himself a chill, then a cold, then a hacking cough, lungs filled up with nastiness, turned into a fever and he passed in his bed with his family about him."

Ash shook his head.

"He died naturally. Nothing suspicious about it. Far as I can see."

"So he gets a tick?"

Mr Wizzle beamed like Ash had suddenly become his star pupil.

Ash stared at the list in the red ledger again. Ignoring William Eustace Stone he tapped on another name, this one with a cross against it.

"Donna Bloom?" Ash screwed up his face, "Didn't she run

off with the carney last year?"

"So folks say."

"You think otherwise?"

"What do you remember about her?"

Ash shook his head, "Not much. Don't think I ever spoke to her. Can't even picture her to be honest. Didn't they say her Pa had been messing with her?"

"Who are "they" exactly?"

"People," Ash shrugged. His head was starting to hurt again.

Damn, it's stuffy in here.

The smell of warm eggs wasn't helping much either.

"People... *hmmmpf...*"

"So... you don't think she run off with the carney?"

"Donna Bloom was a waif of a girl, so pale and fair you could almost see through her, afraid of what little shadow she cast on God's Earth. She'd no more run away with a carney than she would fly to the moon."

"But if her-"

"Jez Bloom loved that girl. Loved her the *right* way. The way a father should. He never laid a finger on her I'm sure of it."

"How can anyone know what goes on in private?"

Mr Wizzle stared at him; his eyes were pale blue almost to the point of being grey and they peered out at Ash through puffy red folds of flesh.

"Oh, believe me, Mr Godbold, I really do know a thing or two..."

Ash rubbed his chin, "Well... the carney's back in town. Is Donna?"

"Not that I've seen. I mentioned it to the Sheriff... just to remind him. Folk have a tendency to be forgetful in this town."

"And?"

"I don't think Sam Shenan listens to me any more than the rest of town. But still, at least he doesn't swear at me; he's always had decent manners. Other than an occasional spit..."

Ash stared at the two ledgers balanced open on his lap and pointed to the black one.

"The arrivals?"

"Our latest newcomers; Amos and Amelia." Mr Wizzle tapped on their names at the bottom of the list, "Amos rode into town, not a lot of people noticed as it was pouring down something tempestuous, but I did. Rode into town on a weary horse with a lot of miles under its hooves."

"So he got a tick?"

"Uh-huh."

"Who is Amelia Prouloux?"

Mr Wizzle started to say something but checked himself and offered a smile instead, "A sweet little child. I found her wandering the street at night in a rainstorm – that big one that wrecked Marty Kideon's water pump. A little girl couldn't have just crossed the grass on her own, but nobody knows her."

"How does she say got here?"

"Doesn't remember."

"So she gets a question mark?"

"Everything out of the ordinary gets a question mark."

Ash cast his eye down the list of names. There were a lot

308

of question marks.

"Cecelia Jones?" Ash tapped on the next name on the list, which also had a question mark.

"Turned up in town, marched into *Jack's Saloon* and got a job singing."

"Unusual maybe. But not strange?"

"She has no horse and there was no stage that day."

"And does she remember how she got here?"

"Haven't got round to asking," Mr Wizzle admitted.

Ash's head was throbbing and he pinched the bridge of his nose.

"This is all fascinating and we could reminisce for days about the town's comings and goings, but I don't see how this is connected to Emily or Preacher Stone?"

"Strangeness." The old man said with a firm jerk of his head.

"Strangeness?"

"Lots of things happen in the world, most of them unrelated and of no great interest to anybody. A sheet blows off a clothes line, a cat falls asleep in the sun, a kettle boils, a baby cries."

"Yes..." Ash said after Mr Wizzle stopped speaking and stared at him.

"Now and then, an unusual thing might happen... say a horse drops dead in front of you, a bolt of lightning hits your house..."

Ash nodded again. He didn't have a clue what he was nodding at, but it seemed appropriate.

"And then very, very rarely. Maybe only once in your whole life you might see something *really* strange. Something you can't explain. Your Aunt Mabel standing by your bed a week after she died, a dog with two heads, fish falling out of the sky."

"Uh-huh."

"That's how the world works. Except out here in Hawker's Drift it doesn't work like that at all. Strange doesn't happen once in the bluest of moons..." he ran a finger slowly along the list of names in the red ledger "...it happens all the time. People arrive out of thin air and others disappear, healthy people drop dead and other people never seem to get older, people say things that could not have happened and then remember things they couldn't have forgotten. And then there is that carney."

"The carney?"

"A lot of these..." he stabbed a finger at the red ledger, "...left town around the time the carney was here. During or just before. Not all, not even most, but more than there should be if these were just the random comings and goings of life."

Ash had taken the girls to the carney most years and it had always seemed pretty unremarkable to him.

"It's just a carney – shows and games and juggling and... clowns..."

"You know it stops at none of the other towns out here? Not in Fellowes Ford, or Bridgeton or Muiro..."

"Guess the Mayor makes it worth their while."

A dark look crossed Mr Wizzle's face at the mention of the Mayor, before he muttered, "That's a lot of miles for a carney to travel just to get to one small town. Bad miles a lot of them, and they don't set down anywhere else in the vicinity?

310

Rather cover miles of road than pitch up and make some money? Smacks of strangeness to me."

"Guess they have their reasons. Other big payers to get to maybe."

"You remember Ziggy Shattir?"

Ash was going to say no, but it chimed distantly and he asked after some thought, "An old time rancher?"

"That's right, had a place way out of town. Shitty Shat-Here vulgar people called him. He had a bit of spite about him in his later years the ways some fellas do once they get into their cootage and their wife has gone to God. Underneath that though he wasn't really so bad. Always had a fascination for card tricks. He didn't come into town much, but when he did we'd sometimes sit outside and swap a few. Used to quite tickle him."

Mr Wizzle sat back on the bed and rolled his shoulders, most of the rest of him rolling with them.

"This was a good few years back, but one day we'd turned a few cards and I could see his heart wasn't in it. I asked what was bothering him and he just kind of shrugged. I didn't expect him to say much more. We weren't really friends; he just didn't see me as a mad fool best chased out of town. Anyway, after a lot of thinking he told me he'd lost a couple of his herd. Thought maybe one of his neighbours had helped himself to a head of two. So he'd gone out and hunkered down in the grass with a blanket and his shotgun to see what he could see. Which had amounted to not much for a couple of nights. This particular night he'd picked a spot close to the road and was surprised to hear wagons on the move. This was gone midnight and few people are about in wagons at that time unless they're in an awful hurry or up to shenanigans."

"Ziggy recognised the wagons quick enough. Guess he probably spat in the grass and cursed them for being queer carney folk, before taking a nip of whiskey and wishing they'd hurry on by as they were scaring off any of his neighbours from getting some well-deserved buckshot in their backsides."

"Well they trundled on by in their own good time, Ziggy told me he watched each wagon roll by and saw nothing much worth remembering. He stood up once the last one had gone by. He hadn't wanted them to see him as they'd just think he was either mad or up to mischief all hunkered down in the grass with just his old shotgun for company. He had a bit of a stretch, shook the stiffness out of his old bones and decided he'd had enough of staring at the stars with nothing but bugs for company. So he got together his gear and started back across the grass towards his place."

"Said he'd gone no more than a few paces when it struck him that it had gone quiet back on the road, all those wagons and horses, make a fair old noise usually. So he looked back to see if they'd stopped for some reason."

Mr Wizzle leaned forward and held his fist in front of Ash's nose before popping it open with an accompanying cry of "*Poof!*"

Ash just stared at him.

"They were gone."

"Gone?"

"Vanished, into thin air. *Poof!* Just like that!"

"Wagons don't vanish... he must have nodded off without

realising it and they'd disappeared from view. It was dark..."

Mr Wizzle shook his head, "It was a full moon, or near enough, you know what it's like on the grass Mr Godbold? You can see all the way to the horizon. Maybe you'd miss a man on a horse, but a whole wagon train..."

"He was an old man. You said he'd been out for several nights. He'd been drinking. It doesn't seem that strange to me."

"Well, Ziggy told himself much the same thing. He was a practical kind of fellow after all. He lay awake most of the night chewing on it, turning it over and spitting it out again, but whichever way he looked at it, he knew he hadn't taken his eye of those wagons for more than a minute or two. Nowhere near long enough for them to pass out of view, even at night. So, first thing he rode out to the road."

"It had been a wet spring and the rain had kept coming on and off right through to July, so the road was soft and muddy and he found the wagon tracks easy enough. All them heavy wagons churn up the mud real good and leave a track so deep and clear a blind man could follow them."

"And."

"The tracks disappeared too."

"Right where he saw them?"

"Uh-huh. Heavy grooves of churned up mud. Then nothing. No sign of the wagons pulling off the road, no sign of them turning round. Just gone."

Ash frowned. It was probably just a mistake or something to fool the gullible with. And third-hand tales were prone to become Chinese whispers. But still...

"And that's not the strangest part."

"No?"

"No. I decided to take a stroll out to Ziggy's place a few days later, as I'd been turning his story over in my mind and I wanted to ask him more about it..."

By Ash's reckoning, it would take a couple of days to "stroll" out to the old Shattir place from town.

"Found Ziggy working out back in his yard, he gave me a nod and muttered something about a new trick he'd figured out. We went inside and he poured some lemonade, but before he could fetch his cards, I asked him if he'd take me out and show me where the wagons had disappeared."

"He gave me a real strange look, "What damn wagons?" he'd cussed, rather unnecessarily if I'm going to be frank. Anyway, he point blank denied ever seeing any vanishing carney wagons or telling me any such story. He laughed and said I was going even crazier in my old age."

"Perhaps he was the one going crazy? An old man living out there alone on the grass? Happens."

"Maybe, but I noticed something when he laughed. Something I've seen quite a few times around this town over the years. His tongue was black..."

"Black..." Ash repeated, his eyes shooting up to meet the old man's again.

"Like a man who'd been eating a lot of liquorice. And maybe he had been. But I don't think so." Mr Wizzle leaned in close to Ash, close enough for his round, florid face to fill his vision.

"Tell me Mr Godbold, have you seen anyone with black tongues recently?"

Ash nodded.

314

"Twice."

"Your daughter and Preacher Stone?"

He nodded, "What does it mean?"

"It means there's far too much strangeness in this town... and it's high time someone got to the bottom of it..."

The Farmer

He hadn't known what else to do.

It wasn't an entirely novel feeling for Sye. A shovel and a pile of dung and he was fine, but anything more demanding he'd usually screw up and be left with a mess he couldn't fathom how to sort out.

He hadn't slept since he managed to lose the little black bottle in *Jack's*. His one and only chance to be with Cece - admittedly a thin, dumb-assed and damn unlikely chance, but a chance all the same – and he'd managed to screw it up.

How hard could it be to get a coffee across a room or keep a little black bottle in your pocket? *Really?* How fucking hard?

He'd retraced his steps back and forth along the bar with an increasing sense of dread and frustration, but they'd been no bottle. In the end, he'd had no choice but to take the unadorned coffee to Cece and go back to trying to woo her with his wit and charm. He'd, therefore, spent an uncomfortable and largely silent couple of minutes watching Cece sipping her coffee before she fumbled for an excuse to be somewhere else.

"My, my, you do look forlorn young man," the Mayor said from behind an enormous and entirely empty desk.

He really hadn't known what to do. So he'd come to ask the Mayor.

He hadn't been quite sure how to open this particular conversation, but luckily his usual honest to goodness assholeness kicked in and saved him from having to act like a sane, mature adult.

"I lost the damn bottle!" Sye blurted out. He sounded like he was about seven and couldn't find his favourite toy.

"Well, that was rather careless..." the Mayor's voice was flat, his expression blank and his eye was moving about no more or less than normal.

"I'm so sorry, I-"

The Mayor held up a hand, palm towards Sye, who took it as a sign to stop blabbering.

"Tell me what happened?"

Sye took a deep breath and stared at his scuffed boots before recounting in a hesitant voice how he'd poured the drops into Cece's coffee, but had walked into someone in his haste and dropped the mug. After he'd got another drink, he found he'd managed to drop the bottle somehow.

"I've always been a clumsy oaf..." he concluded.

"And who did you walk into?" The Mayor asked.

"Mr Smith."

"Which one? We have a couple in town I believe."

"The black one. The gunsmith."

The Mayor's eye became still.

"And you blundered into him?"

"Well... we kind of stumbled into each other really. I think he was drunk..."

The Mayor was silent for a good long while, his fingers

318

entwined in his lap, staring at Sye.

It was gloomy in the Mayor's office, the shutters were closed against the bright sunshine outside and the room felt stuffy and close, the scent of too sweet smoke was tickling the back of his throat. He'd paced around the square for a good hour before he'd worked up the nerve to go and knock on the door. He was starting to wish he hadn't.

He'd half expected to be sent away with a flea in his ear. The Mayor was a busy man, he assumed. But a sour-faced servant had ushered him straight in and led him to a little waiting room, where he'd clicked his heels for half an hour until the Mayor could see him.

Sye had never been inside the Mayor's residence. No reason why he should have been, such places were not for the likes of him. It was as grand inside as he'd expected. Everything clean and elegant and sparkling. Mirror polished floors, thick rugs your feet sank into like a meadow of fresh spring grass, silken drapes, enormous mirrors, crystal chandeliers. And that had just been the hall and the stairway.

He'd been ushered through to a relatively unadorned waiting room. He'd been too nervous to sit on one of the hard-backed chair lining the wall and had paced back and forth from the door to the window looking down on Pioneer Square.

A couple of times he thought he'd heard the distant tinkling of girlish laughter, but otherwise the house was entirely silent. Most of the town had gone to the carney, so there was little noise outside either. He kept staring at *Jack's* in the hope of catching sight of Cece, but aside from the

McCrea woman nobody came in or out.

He'd heard that Amos was living with her now, which had made him feel both relieved and jealous at the same time. Even a man with no cock could find a woman, but Sye Hallows...

"What happened after you dropped the drink? With the gunsmith?" The Mayor's words were softly spoken, but they snapped Sye's attention back well enough. He wished he knew whether the Mayor was pissed at him or not.

"Erm... we went to the bar, he paid for another coffee and beer for me... pretty decent of him really... then he went off... and I went to put some-"

"And you found the bottle was gone?"

"Uh-huh." Sye nodded and rolled his bottom lip between his teeth before asking, "Are you mad at me for losing the bottle?"

"Mad? Of course not. Love's passage rarely runs smooth does it?"

In Sye's experience nothing much ran smooth at all, but he wasn't going to contradict the Mayor, "I guess..."

The Mayor eased himself from his cavernous chair and ambled around his desk, "Don't look so worried young man. I'm not going to bite."

"I was worried that potion might be expensive."

"It has a certain... personal value. I do have something of an attachment to it, you might say, but it is not so difficult to come by."

The Mayor perched on the edge of his desk. He was wearing an immaculately pressed suit of fawn coloured wool and from the pocket he produced a small black bottle identical to the one Sye had managed to lose.

Sye fought the urge to snatch the bottle from the Mayor's palm so his fingers could caress that strange too smooth glass once again.

"Perhaps we should try a different approach this time..." the Mayor said, before curling his fingers around the bottle, his eye rising to meet Sye's gaze above his outstretched fist.

"A different approach?"

"Well, it might be best. We don't want anyone blundering into the path of true love again do we?"

"No..." Sye whispered, unable to take his eyes from the bottle protruding from the Mayor's fist.

"You know..." he mused, slipping the bottle back into his pocket, "...I think it's high time Miss Jones came over to sing for me again..."

The Gunslinger

Nobody paid Amelia much attention. A screaming child in a crowd is hardly uncommon and she garnered no more than a few cursory glances. As the little black girl didn't appear to be having her throat cut, passers-by decided it best to keep about their business and strolled on in the roasting afternoon sunshine. Those that did give the scene more than a second glance were far more interested in the pretty blonde singer from the saloon than the wailing child that was trying to bury herself in Cece's skirts.

Fewer people still noticed the crouching woman with the jet black hair and an abundance of bangles, even though she was quite striking herself in an austere and, perhaps, slightly unsettling way. None at all noticed the scattering of carney folk who were watching matters intently, eyes fixed on the child, bodies stock still, dark rocks unmoved by the crowd eddying around them.

Amos however, even as he barged people out of the way, noticed everything.

The woman didn't see him approaching, despite the curses of those he charged out of the way. There was a wrongness about her, just crouching on her haunches, long black skirts billowing about her, the faint trace of a smile

323

coating her painted lips. She was making no attempt to comfort Amelia with either words or gestures. She didn't look moved, or concerned, or even embarrassed by the child's screams which were distressed to the point of being frantic. There was no knowing glance at another adult, no attempt to sweep Amelia up and comfort her with smiles and kisses and affection, she didn't lay a hand softly on the girl and try to coo her to silence. None of the reactions you might expect from a woman presented with a distressed child. Not even the irritated sneer of a mean-hearted spinster.

There was nothing but a faraway gleam in the eye and something about her lips that made Amos think of a starving dog drooling in the sun.

He could feel them, even amongst the crowd. That same yawning emptiness he had experienced with the Mayor. Perhaps not to the same degree, but coming from all around, an echo bouncing back and forth in a dark canyon. He glimpsed Thomas Rum in his cock-eyed top hat, stooped a little over his cane, lips slightly apart. The jaunty smile of the conjurer and entertainer who'd pulled an apple from his hat for Amelia replaced by something distant and feral. He'd felt the same emptiness about him too, that day, though he'd said nothing to Molly. It was hard enough to explain it about the Mayor – the fact that some of the carney folk shared that same strangeness would just worry her even more.

And he had been right about not wanting to bring Amelia here.

Above all other things Amos knew he should trust his feelings.

He swept Amelia up with one arm and, without thought

324

positioned himself between Cece and the crouching woman as Amelia flung her thin arms around his neck. She was trying to say something, but the words were too muffled by thick, wet sobs for him to make out.

The woman rose with smooth, effortless grace; her eyes, dark pools beyond the reach of the burning sun, didn't stray from his. But Amos couldn't shake the feeling that all she was really seeing was Amelia.

"I'm Giselle," she said, "I see the future and the past."

Amos could sense the other carney folk moving far enough away to be engulfed in the crowd; their darkness lost amongst the mindless chatter and variegated emotions of the milling townsfolk.

"Not well enough to know you'd make a child cry?"

Giselle offered the barest of nods, "Children usually like me..."

Amelia had pushed her face into his neck and he could feel the stain of her tears on his skin.

"What did you do to her?" Amos demanded.

"Nothing, I just gave her a dolly. She is quite adorable. I meant no harm..." her dark eyes slid towards Cece for confirmation, who gave a non-committal shrug. Cece wasn't bawling her eyes out, but Amos could sense something had troubled her too.

"Is there a problem here?" Sheriff Shenan asked, arriving belatedly in Amos' wake.

"I don't think so," Amos lied.

"You sure about that son?" Shenan demanded.

Amos followed his gaze and looked down. His hand was resting on the polished sandalwood grip of his pistol.

"You know how kids are..." Amos forced a smile, uncurled his fingers from the comfort of his gun and wrapped both arms around the still sobbing Amelia.

"Miss Giselle," Shenan nodded at the woman, "Guess you must have some fortunes to read. A lot of gullible people in this town after all."

She turned her gaze, reluctantly it seemed to Amos, towards the Sheriff, "I just help the lonely and the lost Sheriff. Maybe you should come see me later; I could help with your grief."

Shenan's eyes narrowed, but before he could reply Giselle had turned on her heels and was quickly lost amongst the crowd.

The Sheriff watched her go before spitting through his teeth.

"Is she gonna be alright?" He asked, nodding towards Amelia.

"Sure..."

"Well... if I hear anything about her people..."

Amos nodded his thanks but doubted Shenan would be calling by with news anytime soon.

He nodded to Amos and Cece; he thought Shenan was going to head after Giselle, but he waddled off in the opposite direction instead.

"So what did happen?"

Cece shook her head, "I dunno. The woman gave Amelia a rag doll, she seemed fine at first then she started screaming..."

Amos glanced at the rag doll discarded on its back on the grass, arms and legs stiffly sticking out, coarse red hair and

326

a cheap homespun dress. For a moment, he saw Megan laying in the grass, sightlessly staring at the sky and he almost dropped Amelia.

"Are you ok?"

"Sure," he nodded, juggling Amelia to get a better grip, "she's pretty heavy for a skinny kid. Anything else happen to set her off?"

"I... no... nothing..."

She wasn't hiding anything, but her unease was based on intangibles. She'd sensed something wrong rather than saw or heard anything and most people didn't entirely trust such feelings, at least not enough to give voice to them.

"Well, I'd better get Amelia home. You staying?"

Cece shook her head violently, "No, I'll walk back to town with you. If that's ok?"

"Appreciate the company."

Cece scooped up the rag doll. It was a crude and ugly thing that Amos wouldn't have liked even if, for one stupid moment, it hadn't reminded him of his wife's corpse.

"You want this?" Cece asked, holding up the doll towards Amelia whose wailing had subsided to a few quiet sniffs. She shook her head before returning her face to the crook of Amos' neck.

Cece flung the thing aside without further encouragement.

They walked in silence through the crowd, passing a few of the carney hands as they went. Even though Amos got no sense of anything other than mundanity from them he was grateful to get out of Hooper's Fields and back onto the road to town.

"You think you can walk a little?" Amos asked Amelia as

the noise of the carney faded to a hum of distant voices and fragments of music at their backs.

"Sure…"

Once Amelia was on her feet, she immediately placed herself between Amos and Cece and curled a hand into each of theirs.

"You want to tell me what happened back there?"

Amelia sniffed and looked at each of them in turn before replying, "I got scared…"

"Was it the dolly?" Cece asked.

"No," Amelia shook her head, "it was the monsters."

"Monsters?"

Amelia looked up at Amos and nodded.

"The caves aren't empty… they have monsters in them…"

The Widow

"One of my regulars. I'd better go keep him sweet..." Josie curled a smile at a man fidgeting by the bar as she twisted out a cigarette, "...think I see more of him than his wife does. Still, at least I ain't got to make the bastard his dinner as well..."

Josie sloshed a final measure into Molly's glass, before taking both her tail and her bottle over to Hart Calbeck, who'd been waiting impatiently for her to finish up with Molly.

Molly had nodded her thanks for the booze and watched Josie sashay over. Hart was leaning back against the bar with a big old shit-eating grin smeared across his ruddy face. He swept a hand optimistically over his thin, sparse hair as Josie leaned into him, the whiskey bottle dangling from her fingers at her side.

She had to stretch up to whisper in Hart's ear. He was a big man, both in height and breadth and Molly couldn't help but think of Josie flattened beneath him like a squashed bug.

Hart laughed, slipped an arm around Josie's narrow, corseted waist and led her upstairs.

Molly could see why the girl had downed even more whiskey than she had.

Would she be smiling like Josie in a couple of months? All big teeth and promises and a skin full of whiskey to blur the world enough to make the prospect of Hart Calbeck grunting away on top of you bearable.

She found she quite liked Josie. She'd seen her around the saloon, but they'd never exchanged a word before. They inhabited the same space often enough, but they'd lived in different worlds. Up to now.

"Damned if I'm ending up in here..." Molly muttered, downing the last of the whiskey.

She was surprised at how much her head swam as she stood up. Didn't seem to matter how many times she got drunk, it still always managed to sneak up and take her by surprise.

She could see Monty out of the corner of her eye, watching her cross the room. Did he get freebies from the girls here? She should have asked Josie. She shot him a sour look and he went back to drying the glass in his hand. She didn't quite like the way he was forcing the cloth in and out of the glass. Was he leering at her?

She couldn't be bothered to shout anything suitable at him and pushed out into the square fast enough to leave the saloon doors quivering in her wake.

The heat slapped her with an open palm. She squinted into the harsh light. The square was mostly empty. A few dregs like Hart Calbeck were drifting in, but most of the town was still down at the carney.

Molly stood, or rather swayed, for a moment. She should

330

just go home. Sleep off the booze and wait for Amos and Amelia to get back. Maybe once the girl was asleep, she'd wrap her arms around him and tell him how much she wanted to feel her skin against his and she didn't care a damn about anything else.

Except... if she did and, even more unlikely, he didn't wriggle away, all she'd see when she closed her eyes would be Hart Calbeck's red, grinning face and all she would feel would be the weight of his blubbery carcass pounding up and down.

"Fuck this..." she'd said to nobody in particular, before stomping off towards Guy Furnedge's office.

*

The lawyer's office had been locked and the blinds were drawn down. Which she supposed, on reflection, was not entirely surprising given it was now late afternoon on the 4th July.

The little creep was probably down at the carney trying to find someone to tell him that they could see a fiery red-head in his future. However, while her blood was up (and heavily cut with booze) she wasn't going to give up that easily.

It was a relatively short, if rather sweaty, walk through the deserted streets of Hawker's Drift to Furnedge's house. It didn't appear any different from the outside since the wake and after slapping the gate open she stormed up the narrow path and pounded on the front door.

She hadn't really expected anyone to be in, but hammering on the lawyer's front door was a good way to let off some steam without getting thrown back into one of Sam

Shenan's cells.

When the door opened and Furnedge came blinking out into the sunlight, it occurred to her that she needed to say something.

"Molly..." Furnedge gave a fey little smile and looked so unspeakably pleased to see her that most of the venom that had bubbled up during her visit to the saloon instantly evaporated.

"You shit-faced little bastard!"

Well, most of it anyway.

Furnedge tried to reply, but no sound emerged as his lips puckered back and forth like a freshly caught fish on a riverbank. Molly shouldered her way past him and into the hall. It was too damn hot to stand on the doorstep and the business of blackmail was generally best done in private.

The windows were open in the front room, where Lorna had once entertained her friends and most of the wake's guests had congregated. The curtains twitched and flowed in the modest breeze that flitted through the house.

The room appeared to have been stripped half bare; most of the furniture, paintings, books and bric-a-brac that Lorna, presumably, had filled the room with were gone.

There were a few piles of books and papers scattered about and Molly noticed thin films of dust in the corners of the polished wooden floor, illuminated by the afternoon sunlight spilling through the open windows.

She spun on her heels as Furnedge followed her into the room. He was wearing a white shirt beneath a grey vest, both were crumpled and his tie was half undone. His hair was sticking up slightly at the back. He'd always struck her as a fastidious and careful dresser, but he had, like the house about him, become dishevelled.

"Molly..." he said again. His tone not that of a man who'd just been sworn at by a drunk woman barging into his home.

"Guy..."

"I've upset you, I see," he slumped into one of the remaining chairs and looked up at her. The light caught the lenses of his spectacles and the smudged fingerprints that were smeared across them.

"We have matters to discuss."

"I've been in love with you since the moment I first saw you..."

Molly wasn't quite sure what to say. She knew she should be spitting blood at the creep, but there was something so sad and lost in his voice that it bled the last of her anger away.

He snorted a half-laugh and looked away with a shake of his head, "I've been a fool to think I could buy your affection, but love makes..."

"Assholes of us all." Molly finished for him.

"Yes, I suppose it does." The lawyer pinched his nose and took off his glasses. His eyes looked small and beady without them. The bruising around his eye had faded a little, but his complexion was as bad, if not worse, than the last time she'd seen him. He didn't seem to be himself at all. He didn't even smell of anything vaguely peculiar.

"I'm not going to marry you, Guy," she said after a pause, remembering why she was there and trying not to be distracted by the fact he seemed to be reducing into a pathetic little heap before her eyes.

He put his spectacles on and stared at his feet; he wasn't wearing any shoes or socks.

"Would it really be so terrible a thing?"

"I don't love you."

"Did you love Tom McCrea?"

Molly sucked in air through her flaring nostrils. Perhaps she should sit down too. It would make it harder to slap him.

"What is that to you?"

"I used to watch you around town. It was always the highlight of my day to see you. You never seemed... entirely happy. That always gave me hope that one day..."

"My husband would die?"

Furnedge's narrow eyes darted away from her and Molly lowered herself into a straight-backed unfussy chair by the door.

"Marriages end for all manner of reasons. It was just... just a daydream, A fantasy. I knew a woman like you would never be interested in me."

"A woman like me?"

"Beautiful..." Furnedge blushed and held her eye for only a moment. He stood slowly as if his joints hurt and crossed the room to stare out of the window overlooking the street. The voile drapes swelling and falling before him on the breeze's whim.

"Besides, I was married. You were just a distraction to idle away the quiet moments when Lorna was not screaming or throwing things at me. But nothing that could ever be realised."

"Yet here we are; both our spouses dead and you trying to force me to marry you."

334

"I'm not forcing you, Molly. I don't think anyone could force you to do something you did not want to."

"Will you still love me when I'm a whore?" Molly demanded.

Furnedge's profile hardened in the diffused window light, "I do not wish to see that happen."

"If you actually did love me don't you think you would do anything to stop it happening?"

"Women like you don't marry men like me unless it's in their own interest to do so..." he turned his head towards her, the light glinting off his spectacles concealing his eyes "...but if you did. I would make you happy. I would make you safe from the world."

Molly felt her teeth grinding together, "Like you kept Lorna safe?"

Furnedge looked back towards the window, raised his chin and clasped his hands together behind his back, "She was very sick... she was beyond anybody's help."

Molly rose to her feet and stood behind the lawyer, she could make out another fine house across the road through the voile's haze, but nobody was about.

"I know what you did Guy."

"Did?"

"That little black bottle you poured into her booze..."

Furnedge grew very still, she couldn't even see him breathing, the only movement was the drape flowing and rippling before him, the breeze making the fabric caress the lawyer's legs.

"You killed her, didn't you Guy? You killed her so you could have her money?"

335

"No," Furnedge breathed, the word barely audible above the hiss of the voile's seam skimming back and forth across the polished floorboards.

"You killed her so you could have me?"

The lawyer turned on his heels; for once his eyes were wide, bulging from their puffy sockets.

"I did not!"

Molly took a step back; little gobs of drool had collected in the corners of Furnedge's mouth as his lips quivered. For the first time, Molly considered accusing a man of murder alone in his own home might not have been the wisest thing to do.

Whiskey drinking for you...

"I can see the guilt in your eyes Guy..." actually she could see nothing but two bloodshot eyeballs and pupils reduced to tiny piss holes by the bright sunlight. But she was confident enough in Amos' talents to bet he was feeling as guilty as hell. And maybe a bit scared too.

She took another step away from him.

"You want the whole town to know what you did to Lorna?"

Furnedge's lips were making silent little fish gasps again, but no sound came out.

"You want to people to be whispering about you being a poisoner?"

"You don't know what you're talking about," Furnedge hissed now and the spittle danced in the corners of his mouth.

"Was it worth it Guy? Getting all her money? Are you happy now?"

"Molly!"

336

She kept her eyes on Furnedge as she backed carefully towards the hallway. He'd never looked dangerous before, irritating and unnerving sure, but never dangerous, but now he looked half way mad. There was a fair chance the billowing voile might have knocked his slight frame to the ground, but she thought it best she made her farewell. Though she wasn't quite finished.

"Pay the damn Mayor off and I'll never breathe a word of it, Guy. Hell, I know she was halfway off her rocker, but murder is still murder."

"You don't know anything..."

"Don't I..." she smiled then, a big you-just-bet-your-life-I-know kind of smile "...a little black bottle Guy. A little black bottle poured into Lorna's booze. That wasn't medicine now. Was it?"

Furnedge was sweating, a slick cold sheen across his waxy skin. If he hadn't done anything, he was doing a real bad job of looking innocent.

"No. It was murder. And if you want it kept between us, you know what to do..."

Molly had backed out into the hall, but Furnedge had stopped following her. He was standing with his feet apart and his fists clenched at his side. His mouth had become a colourless slash across his flushed, sweating face. He was shaking, not just his hands but his whole body.

Would it count as murder if he keeled over with a heart attack? He looked distinctly unwell now.

She leant into the room and gave him her friendliest and most engaging smile.

"Please, do let me know if you're conducive to my

proposal..."

Then she slammed the door in his face and got out of the house as quickly as her legs would carry her.

The Clown

Mr Wizzle always gave a sermon in Corner Park. Sometimes it was late afternoon, sometimes early evening. It depended on the weather and the time of the year, but pretty much every day, even if it was just for five minutes and all he did was read out a Psalm or two. He liked to be dependable, even if no one much depended upon him save a couple of vagrants and folk who were more touched in the head than he seemed to be.

There was even less likelihood of people listening to him today than usual with *Billberry's Carnival* in town. Even so, he carried his preaching crate down Main Street despite the heat and the lack of an audience. It was what he did.

The town was deserted and he stuck to the shady side of the street, whistling as he waddled. When he noticed the three figures coming in the opposite direction he put down his preaching crate and waited. When they were close enough he beamed and doffed his hat.

"Miss Jones, Amos! Little Amelia! How are you all this fine day?"

Amos nodded a welcome, while Amelia, who looked a little puffy-eyed and was holding on to both adult's hands, favoured him with a smile bright enough to melt the hardest

339

of hearts. Cece Jones just looked bemused.

"Oh, please forgive me," he said, remembering she'd never actually met him before. He found people often got perplexed if you knew their name and they didn't have a clue who you were, "I'm Mr Wizzle."

"Pleased to meet you." She was very pretty and very sensibly dressed in a modest navy blue cotton dress and a drooping wide-brimmed hat. He was pleased to see the young lady's morals had not been corrupted by Monty Jack's palace of vice and debauchery.

"Are you with the carney?" She asked.

"Oh, no!" Mr Wizzle gave his lapels a sharp tug before clarifying her confusion, "I'm with God's circus. Do you like pickled eggs, Miss Jones?"

"Erm... not really."

"Pity"

With a huff and a protest from his knees, he crouched down in front of Amelia, "And what has my favourite little lady been doing today?"

"You're funny!" The girl giggled, before extracting her hands from Amos and Cece's grasp and throwing her thin, dark arms around his neck.

Mr Wizzle wasn't quite sure what to do. Children usually ran away from him and as she stepped back he found something had gotten in his eye. He blinked a few times to clear his vision.

"Hey, a pretty girl should have a flower? Why don't you have a flower?"

Amelia shrugged.

"Well, let's see what we can do about that..." he held up

his hand and snapped his fingers in front of her nose. As she blinked, a paper flower appeared in his hand, which he gave to her as she squealed and clapped her hands in delight.

"Thank you! It's beautiful!"

"Just a little thing," he smiled and straightened up with a grimace, remembering an old black woman sitting in the grass he had given a paper rose to not so long ago.

"Did you go to the carney?" he asked, glancing at Amos when Amelia's smile faltered.

"It was scary..." she said, staring at the rose with eyes that were focused on something else entirely, "...they put Lucas in the black wagon..."

"Who is Lucas, Amelia?"

"I don't know, but he's all alone now."

Mr Wizzle glanced at Cece and Amos. The gunslinger looked blank though a slight frown fluttered across the young singer's brow for a second.

"Miss Jones, would you mind going ahead with Amelia, while I have a quick word with Amos?"

"Of course," she smiled, took the girl's hand and carried on down the street, when Amelia looked back Mr Wizzle jiggled his fingers at her.

"We're right behind you beautiful!"

The cloud that had crossed her features when she'd spoken about the carney lifted and she giggled.

"What happened?" Mr Wizzle asked once they were out of earshot and the pair of them started ambling along behind.

"Something spooked her. A woman, fortune-teller I think."

"Did she say something?"

"No, gave her a dolly and when she touched her Amelia

started screaming like murder."

"Did Amelia say what scared her?"

Amos looked at him for a moment, his eyes dark in the shade of his hat, "She said there were monsters..."

"At the carney?"

"I think so."

"What did she say, exactly?"

"There are monsters in the caves..."

"Monsters..." Mr Wizzle nodded.

"Does that mean something to you?"

He shook his head, "But it means something to you, I think..."

Amos pursed his lips and stared ahead at Amelia and Cece. They were laughing; a young woman and a child laughing in the sunshine. What could be more natural and good than that? Even in this town.

"Makes me think I shouldn't have taken her there."

"And Lucas? The black wagon?"

"No idea... She didn't mention that to us before."

"Are you a curious man, Amos the Gunslinger?"

"Not as a rule."

"I'm going to take a look round that carney tonight. I've always felt there was something rotten about it. Something wrong."

Amos glanced at him.

"You want to find out what really spooked that girl and if it's any danger to her?"

Amos nodded.

"Yeah, I think I do..."

The Fortune-Teller

Giselle sat in the hot oppressive shadows of her tent, languorously waving a fan before her.

Her eyes lingered on the crystal ball before her; as big as a man's head and infused with a spider's web of milky-white gossamer threads. How many times had she stared into it whilst gripping the hand of some ignorant little monkey and telling them about their past and their future? Too damn many...

It was an impressive thing, she supposed, not that she'd ever seen anything in it other than her own distorted reflection.

She got what she wanted from the touch of their hands; sometimes she didn't even need that. All their pointless little lives spread out before her; unedifying cocktails of petty hatred, ignorance, simpering lust and dumb jealousies for the most part. But she endured it. Having to touch them, see them, breathe their fetid air and hear the dull, flat pounding of their weak and useless hearts. She endured it all for the one or two times a year she found someone, or at least a link to someone, who was worth a damn to them.

Like the little black girl.

She shivered despite the heat and felt the need turn inside

her.

Giselle looked up as the flap of her tent, or mystic grotto as it was officially known, was pushed aside and the harsh, hateful sunlight flooded in.

She let her welcoming smile fall away when she realised it wasn't another fool come to give her coins and, possibly, so much more.

Stodder Hope was an ugly man. Even by the standards to which she had so miserably fallen he was an insult to her eye. A nose that had been busted so many times it didn't know which way to go, broken teeth, scars twisting across his face, neck and shaved scalp, a long and tangled beard that hung to his chest.

She had never quite understood why she let him fuck her.

"Mr Rum wants to see you," he growled, the shadows mercifully rushing back in on his coattails as the canvas flap fell back in place behind him.

"*Mr* Rum?"

"He's the boss."

Well, not exactly.

"What does he want?"

"He's the boss."

"Is he pissed?"

"He's always pissed."

Giselle had to concede he had a point.

"Is he more pissed than usual?"

Hope ran a hand through the knots of his beard, "Kinda..."

The gunslinger eased himself into the chair opposite uninvited. He was a big man, tall and broad of beam. He was

345

strong and powerful with it. A lot of stamina too. Giselle could testify to that.

For all his qualities and uses, and even Giselle would admit he had some, he'd never been a verbose or descriptive man, which was one of the things she grudgingly liked about him. As much as she could like any of the little monkeys anyway.

She'd been expecting Rum to drop in after the spectacle with the little black girl earlier. If he'd sent his dog to summon her rather than come himself, he must be really pissed. Hawker's Drift belonged to the Mayor, they all knew that. He might throw em a bone at the Dark Carnival once a year, but a special little girl like that... she should know better than to covet his cattle in public.

And, of course, she did. She just didn't care anymore.

"Tell him I'll come see him later."

"Before the Dark Carnival?"

She nodded, yeah, she'd see him before the fun started. She wasn't planning to be around for the show after all. She was tired of their silly games. The others might be satisfied by the worship of a few dozen addled little monkeys, but she wanted more. Much, much more.

Stodder Hope was still sitting across from her. Staring.

"Is there something else?"

"Just seeing if you need me..." his eyes narrowed a fraction "...for anything else?"

"When I need you, I'll let you know..."

Hope didn't move. For a little monkey, a brutish, ugly one to boot, he was finely attuned to her desires. There were times when she despised the pleasures this flesh of hers craved, other times she gave into them eagerly. She would have said there was little else left to please and amuse and distract her anymore, but that made her life sound as empty and pointless as the little monkeys she despised.

"You're a disgusting animal. I hate you," she spat.

Stodder Hope smiled his shattered-toothed smile, even though she was pretty sure he knew she wasn't speaking entirely in jest.

He reached over and took her hand; his touch was as coarse as old weather-cracked leather.

"Tell me, what do you see in my future?"

"Nothing but pain and suffering."

"Much the same as my past then..."

She knew the things he'd done; she'd seen them, plucked them from his tiny excuse for a brain and turned them over in her hands. All the glistening, dripping treasures that his memory held. Murder, rape, theft, betrayal, cruelty, wanton violence all interlaced with an unending fury at the world.

Maybe that was why she tolerated him. His anger mirrored her own. She could understand it. The only difference between their anger was that Hope's was channelled solely into violence, while hers had always motivated her to greater things. Anger was the spur that drove her to pull herself above lesser beings in order to find her rightful place, even when she'd had to clamber over a mountain of corpses to do it.

And yet here they were together; trundling endlessly across this forsaken dying land, doing the bidding of others.

When she didn't say more, he reached over and squeezed her breast, no expression on his face as she winced. There wasn't a scrap of gentleness or subtlety in this man. She was just a piece of meat he liked to put his cock in. Even though he knew what she was, more or less. Perhaps that was why he kept coming back to her in preference to Mallory's obliging whores.

"Come to me later, in my wagon," she said, making no move to push his hand away.

He shook his head, "Now."

Giselle thought about telling him what she'd decided to do. She wasn't sure why. He was just a little monkey after all and the world was full of them, for the time being at least.

Would he serve her as easily as he served Thomas Rum? She had no illusions about love or devotion or any other such nonsense. Stodder Hope would follow whoever paid the higher price; it was just a matter of what he valued more highly. On balance she thought he'd give more weight to Rum's gold than he would her body. So she had dripped words into his ear instead and let his little mind run with them. His greed would serve her purpose well enough.

No. She didn't need him. She didn't need anyone. If she'd remembered that lesson maybe she wouldn't have ended up here, travelling the paths of this world to do the Mayor's bidding.

"I said later."

Stodder Hope let his hand fall away. He stared at her before rising to his feet. He came around the table one slow step at a time. When he was looming over her, he started unbuckling his belt.

"I say now..."

She could break him like a twig if she wanted. Perhaps it

348

was the fact that he knew it as well as she did that made him attractive. Stodder Hope's other quality, besides his relentless fury, was that he had no fear. Fear was something she usually liked in others, but she found the complete absence of it in his soul rather arousing. He was stubborn too. He wouldn't go unless she threw him out, which she could do with a flick of her wrist. Most of the carney folk she could control as well as Rum and the others could, but not Hope. He was immune to the black candy; too damn pig-headed for it to bend him to their will. It was usually a problem when they run into a little monkey like that, but not Hope; he knew what they were and served them well enough all the same.

Giselle stood up without another word, turned her back to the grizzled gunslinger and bent over the table. She watched her eyes narrow and her lips part in the distorted reflection of the crystal ball.

There were times she hated the flesh she was in, but there were moments, every now and then, when she liked it just fine...

The Gunsmith

It was too hot an afternoon for swinging an axe.

John could feel his heart pounding as he bent forward, hands on knees, sucking in air through his nostrils. Sweat was trickling down his naked torso and dripping from his face in thick, glistening beads. His arms were aching and he guessed they would stiffen up real nasty later.

Nobody knew how old he actually was and, as often as not, that included John X Smith too.

The sun was fierce on his back, he felt like a joint of meat being slowly roasted. It was a damn fool's errand to be chopping wood at this time of day. A sensible man would have waited till the evening or got up at dawn the next day to get the job done.

Maybe a sensible man wouldn't be too afraid to stare at a black stain on a table top too.

His heavy-topped table was being slowly reduced to kindling, save for the part that was stained midnight black by whatever had been in the bottle he'd smashed to smithereens with a hammer. The remains of the bottle, the fragments that weren't still embedded into the table top anyway, he'd collected up (wearing his thickest, heaviest gloves), and deposited in the large metal bin that the table would burn in.

It had near broken his back just to drag, shove and manhandle the table up the stairs. It was thick oak and he had no recollection of how he'd even managed to get the thing down in his basement in the first place.

Several times the thought had struck him it would be much easier to simply brick his basement up and seal that stain in there for eternity. But he wasn't sure a layer of bricks would be enough to ever let him sleep soundly again.

Why do you burn us?!

No. Fire was definitely a much better idea.

Whatever that stuff had been he wanted no atom of it within his home.

He closed his eyes and sucked in more air. He hoped the sound of his heavy wet breath would be enough to drown out the memory of that black goo screaming when he'd put a flame to it.

Screaming like a tortured child...

He straightened up, pulled his already sodden handkerchief from his back pocket and wiped the sweat from his eyes.

The job was nearly done, just split the last few bits of table top around the stain and then those big old hefty legs and he'd be done. He'd fill up the bin with kindling and get a fire going. When it was nice and hot, the legs could go in, maybe with some lamp oil to get it really kicking. The stained wood that he'd been hacking around would go into the inferno last and then he would see if that stuff had anymore scream left in it.

"John..."

351

He jumped and spun around, clutching the axe in front of him. Kate's eyes widened and she stumbled back a couple of steps. He'd been so damn focused on that freaky bottle he hadn't heard Kate let herself into his backyard.

"Shit Kate..." he tossed the axe aside "...you scared me half to death!"

Kate stood staring at him for a moment, blinked a couple of times and then burst into tears.

Damn, I hate it when they start crying...

There were things men were supposed to do in these situations he knew; a hug, a squeeze of the hand, some soft words, a bit of concern. He'd always been lousy at all of them, but, he supposed, Kate had more reason to cry than many of the women who'd started blubbing in front of him over the years.

"You shouldn't be here..." he said the words softly, but he could see they stung her all the same. She looked terrible, her eyes were so red and puffy these clearly weren't her first tears of the day. Her hair had barely seen a brush and there were small cascades of stains down the front of her dress.

"I know... but I've got nowhere else to turn..." she wiped her sleeve across her eyes and then honked into a handkerchief.

John retrieved his shirt and pulled it on; the days when he had the kind of torso he liked to show off to girls were long gone.

"We'd better go inside." His yard wasn't overlooked, but you could never account for prying eyes.

He ushered her up the short flight of steps that led into the kitchen behind his store. "Anyone see you come in here?"

He asked once he'd closèd the door behind her.

She shook her head, "Everyone's at the carney."

"Including Ash?"

She shrugged, "I don't know where he is most of the time."

She stood, twisting her handkerchief into a snot-damp snake, looking wretched.

John pulled out a chair at the table. The kitchen wasn't as messed up as his basement workshop, but it wasn't exactly homely either and the mortal remains of several meals still lay where they had fallen. Kate sat down with as much comfort as a cat on coals, but her eyes were too glassy to take in the carnage spread before her.

He buttoned up his shirt, which was already soaked with sweat, pulled out a chair and shoved enough crockery aside for him to rest his forearms on the table.

"Kate... I know you're going through a tough time, but you can't just turn up like this. People will notice. People will find out."

She swallowed, glanced at him then looked sharply away like there was something in her eyes she didn't want him to see.

"Someone *does* know..." she said eventually. Her bottom lip quivered until she bit it.

"How? Who?" John X's heart sank a little though it was hardly a complete shock. In a town this size secrets rarely stayed that way unless you were exceedingly lucky or exceedingly careful. A résumé of his life would quickly reveal he'd rarely been either. All that mattered was that Ash didn't find out, the man had been slowly unravelling since Emily's assault. He'd heard Ash had even been hanging out with that

353

mad old clown that had taken a shine to Molly and Amos. He doubted Kate's husband would take the news of her infidelity with much benevolence.

Kate went back to twisting her hanky until John reached over and laid his large hand over her two smaller ones. The veins in the back of his hand were standing out like the roots of an ancient gnarled tree bursting from the soil. Fuck he was old.

"Kate... tell me?"

A watery, transient smile trickled across her mouth and she found his fingers and squeezed them, "Deputy Blane," she whispered, the name evaporating the smile in an instant.

John raised an eyebrow. There was a long list of nosy, gossiping, busy-bodies he would have wagered as having noticed something they shouldn't have. Blane would not have been anywhere among them.

He actually felt slightly relieved. Blane wasn't a gossip as far as he knew. In fact, he never said a word more than he absolutely needed to. Maybe he would keep his mouth shut, particularly if he had a little man to man chat with him.

"Has he told anyone?"

Kate shook her head and John squeezed her hand.

"Maybe he won't... he doesn't strike me as a gossip... how did he find out about us? Are you sure he knows anything?"

"He knows," she snorted, "Trust me, that bastard knows."

It was unusual for Kate to swear; she was fraught beyond endurance and looked like she hadn't slept in days. John only knew two remedies for worries – sex and booze – and even he would admit they both tended to be distractions rather than solutions.

"When we... started..." Kate looked up at the ceiling and blinked back her tears "...I told Preacher Stone about us."

"You did *what?*" John's eyes widened and the words came out colder than he had intended; cold enough for Kate's wet eyes to snap back towards him.

"I felt... guilty... he was a man of God, I thought he could help me."

These people and their fucking guilt-trip God...

"And did he?"

"Think I wanted him to rant at me, to tell me I was a sinner and to stop immediately. That was what I was telling myself anyway. But he didn't."

"Maybe he wasn't all bad," John snorted, regretting it even before Kate could glare at him, "Shit, sorry, that was a dumbass thing to say."

"Yes..." she mumbled, tugging her hands free of his.

"Anyway, how did Blane find out?"

"Seems the old preacher wrote everything down. My little confession too. Blane got hold of them and... well, he has it all in black and white."

"And he told you this?"

Kate lowered her head and went back to twisting her hanky after giving a curt little nod.

"Why?" John frowned, gossips usually reserved their tattle-tales for their victim's back not their face.

She took a big gulp of air and looked up, she'd sucked the colour from her lips and her hands were shaking so much she dropped the hanky-snake and clutched her sides instead.

"Because he wants to fuck me!" She vomited the words up

355

like a rotten fish that had been poisoning her guts. Her head jutted forward as if she could spit them out further and faster from her body and be free of the wretched bilious taste of them.

"He's blackmailing you?"

Kate nodded and raised a hand to her mouth to stifle a sob.

That's the thing about people, they never stop surprising you.

Blane was cold and quiet, but he'd never heard much of a bad word about him. Nobody was much inclined to stand a beer for him in the saloon, but other than his detached demeanour, which most seemed to put down to shyness rather than aloofness, he'd heard little bad about the man.

But then most people were fools and inclined not to notice the monsters that walked amongst them. John X had always suspected there was something foul simmering beneath Deputy Blane's hat.

"What are you going to do?"

"Do?" Kate stared at him above her hand, "I have no damn idea what to do. That's why I came to see you. I haven't got anybody else to turn to?"

John had worried she was going to say something like that.

Sheeeet....

"You could speak to Shenan... he seems an honest guy..."

"Aren't you listening?" Kate hissed, "If I do that Ash will find out! My daughters will find out! Everybody will find out! Ash is half out of his mind already – he'll try to kill both of us."

"Ash isn't a violent man, he-"

"Ash *wasn't* a violent man."

"Has he-"

"No... but... his hurting so bad and... shit, I don't know. But I can't risk him finding out... I just can't."

"Perhaps Blane's bluffing, maybe..."

Kate shook her head violently, "No, you didn't see him. He's insane..."

"Insane?"

"I'm not exaggerating, it's like... like there's this different man inside him and when he came to my house he let this man... no... this creature out, this mad, gibbering thing. You didn't see it John, but I'm telling the truth, everything changed about him, his face, his voice, even the way he moved. You know he has this kind of stiff, jerky way of walking, like his joints are all rusty, even that changed he became... loose... all... damn it I can't explain it! But that man is evil John. I know it and I'm so fucking scared!" The last few words came out as a strangled wet sob as Kate slid from the chair. She would have sprawled out across the floor if John X hadn't caught her, hauled her to her feet and put her arms around her.

She fell against him, great whooping sobs muffled by his chest. He ran a hand through her hair, which was knotted and greasy instead of its usual beautiful softness that had always aroused him so much when he'd buried his face in it.

He had no idea what to do or say. She was clearly traumatised, hardly surprising given what her family had suffered and now being blackmailed by this bullying little asshole looking for a cheap, nasty thrill from a vulnerable woman.

When his relationships went sour, which usually happened around the time a girl got pregnant or her husband started looking at him funny, he usually found it better to keep out of sight for a while. Let things blow over and if it didn't, make it right as best he could. Right for himself of course. It wasn't as if he could run away from town. That's what he'd always told himself anyway. He'd come here to wait all these years and it turned out he needn't have bothered because now he was too damn scared to do what he'd come here for in the first place.

Stupid old man...

He patted Kate and whispered a few meaningless words in her ear. He did like her, always had. He just didn't want to get involved in this kind of shit, but, she was right, Ash was unravelling. If her husband came for him, he'd probably have to kill him to stop him and he didn't much fancy the gallows. So he'd have to get involved, as much as he didn't want to.

John held Kate tight and looked over her shoulder to the kitchen window. Outside he could see the remains of his work table propped up on its side. The big, black stain clearly visible in the bright sunshine. It hadn't soaked into the wood any, its colour hadn't faded. It was utterly black. So black it seemed to repel the sunlight itself as if a wet, slick, slice of the night had latched onto the table and refused to let go even in the heat of a bright summer afternoon.

The stain didn't have any discernible pattern; it didn't look like a face, or a dog, or an umbrella or a woman dancing. Just an amorphous, blob of nothing, a random stain, dark and black, but otherwise unremarkable.

All the same, he was pretty sure it was a damn sight more evil than young Arthur Blane would ever be.

The Gunslinger

Kennion's Dairy had been deserted when he'd arrived. Given it was after midnight that was hardly a surprise.

Amos leaned against the fence post and watched the empty road. He was early anyway and he made good use of the time looking up at the stars, spread across the sky above a kissing moon rising in the east. That and trying to figure out why he was so mad at Molly.

It wasn't her being drunk. It wasn't her trying to kiss him. It wasn't even that her words had softly glowed the colour of honey or the way she had kept looking at him with big liquid eyes. It had been entirely because she'd been stupid enough to go and see Guy Furrnedge on her own and blackmail him.

Extortion was an art and despite Molly's many talents and charms he doubted she had the experience to do it properly. Besides, it was dangerous. A blackmail victim, even one whose body weight doubled in a rainstorm, could be dangerous. And he *was* a murderer after all.

Amos let his eyes drop from the star-dusted sky and stared at the tufts of grass sprouting around the base of the fence post instead. Crickets chirping interweaved with a slight breeze that rustled the grass, but otherwise the night was silent.

Amelia had been asleep by the time Molly had come home; flushed, breathless and whiskey-scented. Luckily Cece had already left by then. It had only been a fleeting visit; he sensed she was torn between wanting to talk about what had happened at the carney without Amelia in earshot and getting out of the house before Molly came home. Self-preservation had won out.

He'd wanted to tell Molly what had happened, but she hadn't let him get a word in as she'd recounted her visit to Guy Furnedge. She hadn't mentioned the time she must have spent with a whiskey bottle beforehand, but Amos was able to fill in those blanks in her day easily enough.

Amos had wanted to snap at her. Annoyed that she'd been so reckless. She should have left it to him to deal with Furnedge – threats and intimidation were much more his field of expertise.

He'd stayed his tongue, not because he wanted to avoid an argument but because of the fear and worry that had bubbled up out of him as he'd listened to her.

He cared about her.

Why was that such a shock? Other than for the fact he'd cared about nothing and no one for thirteen years. He knew he was drawn to her. He knew she made him wish even more fervently than usual that he was still a man. He knew he wanted to help her and protect her and keep her safe.

But he hadn't known he could fear for her.

He hadn't feared anything for so long. Not pain, not loss, not hardship. Not Severn and his killers, not the thin rider slouched upon his pale horse.

But he'd feared for Molly then. Feared for what might have

361

happened to her, what might still happen to her.

So he had said little and struggled to feel less. When she'd tried to nuzzle up to him he had shrugged her off like he usually did, as much as he craved to let the honey warm light of her words and her feelings scour his broken body and leave him feeling clean.

She'd gone to check on Amelia, not in anger, but in resignation. When she didn't come back, he went up and found her curled around Amelia, one arm thrown over the girl and snoring with a low throaty rattle.

He'd closed the door and sat downstairs till the night came and the clock's hands edged past eleven, then he'd let himself out and snuck away hoping Molly wouldn't wake and find him gone.

"What are you doing here?"

Amos wasn't used to being startled, he was usually aware when another soul was close, even if it was a soul closed to whatever gift he had. He looked up with a start, he had been thinking so deeply about Molly that he hadn't either seen or sensed the figure come down the road from Hawker's Drift.

"Waiting for a fat old man in a bad suit."

Ash nodded and stuffed his hands deep into the pockets of his loose-fitting pants. Amos had the feeling they were curled into fists.

"You?"

"The same..." he replied, looking back and forth between the road and the gunslinger.

His eyes were sunken and dark, he looked like he'd lost weight the fast and nasty way a sickness can strip fat and muscle from a man's bones. Withering him and hollowing him out. Grief and anger could do much the same as disease, Amos knew well enough. Probably was a disease, if truth be told, and it had infected Ash Godbold down to the marrow.

"A midnight trip to *Billberry's* carney?"

Ash nodded again.

"Why you interested in them?" Amos jerked his head down the road to the cluster of lamps and fires that flickered out in the deep dark black of the night.

He looked like he wanted to snap back that it was none of his damn business and Amos was pretty sure that was the gist of his thoughts. Instead, he sucked in a deep breath and spat it out along with the words, "I wanna know if it's safe for my girls... this town... Mr Wizzle..."

He shook his head and flashed a humourless grin across his round face, tightening the loosening flesh for a moment. "Shit, can't believe I'd ever think that old coot was anything but mad."

"Even the mad can be right. Once in a while."

"S'pose... why you here?"

"Same as you."

Ash cocked an eyebrow.

"Seeing if this place is safe for..." he was going to say "my girls too," but he stopped himself "...Molly and Amelia."

Ash didn't ask who Amelia was. Maybe he'd heard. More likely he didn't care.

They stood in awkward silence. After a few moments of half-hearted pacing, Ash hoisted himself up onto the fence outside the dairy. He sat with his legs dangling, like a boy with a fishing rod waiting for his friend before heading off to try their hand at landing some brook trout.

Amos left him to stare across the dark fields.

...why you here?

It was a good question. He should be back in the house, especially since Molly's visit to Furnedge, but there was something wrong about the carney. In the same way there was something wrong about Hawker's Drift.

The caves aren't empty... they have monsters in them...

Amelia's words filled him with a deep unease every time they flitted through his mind, something they'd being doing unbidden ever since she'd uttered them.

Was it just a coincidence that Amelia should articulate the same sensation that he had experienced? That disconcerting sense he'd first felt around the Mayor, then Thomas Rum and again with the carney folk that afternoon. Like standing in front of a vast, dark cave and knowing there was something inside, even though there was no sight, sound, smell or taste of it. Something malevolent watching him from the pitch perfect blackness of a cave.

Monsters...

If he could sense such things, was it so unlikely that nobody else could? Was he unique in all of the wide, wide world? He'd never met anyone else who could do what he could, but that didn't mean they didn't exist.

His mother had claimed such a talent of course and they'd scrapped a living for years from her staring into the lines in a stranger's hand. He'd thought she'd been entirely bogus from the day his father had, entirely to his mother's amazement, walked out on them. Perhaps, after all she'd had a trace of something, a something that he had inherited and Death had enhanced.

And maybe Amelia had the same thing?

And she'd sensed something about the woman Giselle that had scared her enough to send her into fits of screaming.

"At last..." Ash's sigh brought his attention back to the present. Following the barber's gaze, he could make out the figure of a plump old man waddling up the road in the gossamer light of the moon and stars.

"At last," Amos agreed.

*

"You're wearing a different suit?"

Ash was still perched on the fence as Mr Wizzle reached the gates of Kennion's Dairy. The old man had indeed changed out of his customary attire in favour of a sober dark suit. It might have been black or navy blue, it was hard to tell under starlight, plus a white collarless shirt and sturdy boots.

"I've never seen you out of that suit..." Ash sounded as shocked as a young boy finding Santa Claus wearing overalls and smoking a pipe.

Mr Wizzle, who had also replaced his derby with a soft cap, folded his hand over his large belly.

"Gentlemen, when one is engaged in the business of shenanigans, it is better not to look conspicuous."

"We're going to a carney ..." Amos said, "...it's the only place in the world you *wouldn't* look conspicuous..."

Something that might have been within spitting distance of a grin flittered across Ash's face.

"Hmmpf..." was all that Mr Wizzle offered by way of a

reply, before continuing along the road without further comment.

Ash slid off the fence and fell into step alongside Amos as they followed the old man.

"What, exactly are we looking for tonight?" Amos asked.

"Strangeness," Mr Wizzle retorted, eyes fixed on the lights of the carney.

"You seen his ledgers?" Ash asked when nothing further was forthcoming.

"Ledgers?"

"Guess not."

"And we have a plan?"

"We are three gentlemen seeing what the carney has to offer as amusements at this late hour..." Mr Wizzle let the two younger men fall in at his side, "...and we shall see what there is to be seen without most of the town getting under our feet.

A deep frown creased Ash's brow, "You mean we're going to visit their whores?"

"Of course not! Though that is what we will tell them if challenged."

Ash looked deeply unhappy, "I wouldn't want Kate to get to hear such a thing and think it true."

"And *nobody* is going to believe I'm visiting whores..." Amos added.

"We sharn't be there long. Just enough to sniff around in the dark for a bit."

"Did we really have to wait until midnight to do this?"

"Of course..." Mr Wizzle insisted, giving Amos a sideways glance before adding, "...everybody knows that monsters are easier to spot in the moonlight."

*

Hooper's Large Field was deserted; the booths were closed, the tents emptied, the prizes taken away. The faint acrid scent of gunpowder from the fireworks that had lit the sky earlier as the town had marked the 4th of July still tainted the air.

Celebrating the independence of one country from another had always seemed a strange thing to Amos, particularly given that neither existed anymore.

They had passed a few stragglers heading back to town, they'd either given them knowing glances or glassily kept on staring ahead as they struggled to put one foot in front of the other. But the carney itself was deserted, the only movement a few greasy wrappers caught on the breeze.

"Why did you need us for this?" Ash hissed.

Mr Wizzle pulled off his cap and run a hand over his scalp. His tufts of hair had been tamed with hair wax and comb. He looked almost entirely normal. After a moment's pause he replied, "I've always been too scared to come on my own."

"Great..." Ash Godbold was evidently coming to the conclusion this hadn't been one of his better choices.

Laughter flitted down from the Small Field where the carney folk had their wagons. It was also where they'd sell drink and girls and other pleasures to punters who had a taste for such things.

They kicked around the Large Field for a while, examining the booths and tents, the rides and attractions. The painted horses of the carousel bared their teeth in maniacal grins, wide eyes staring sightlessly into the night as they passed.

Amos had spent a lot of his youth around carnivals and fairs as his mother tried to eke out a living from the gullible with her tales of imminent good fortune and handsome strangers. Nothing struck him as strange or out of place, but then he hadn't really expected anything to. There was rarely anything unusual about rope and canvas, wooden boards and faded flags. It was the carney folk themselves that unnerved Amos and they were all gathered over in Hooper's Small Field by now.

After finding nothing of note other than that Barney, one of the regular barflies from the saloon, had taken a vacation from his stool to lay face down between two tents, snoring wetly with his trousers around his ankles, they moved towards Carney Town.

Nobody paid them much heed. Locals were scattered about amongst the carney folk, most were as drunk as skunks and a few were a lot worse.

The carney folk were lounging around outside their wagons. Some had beer and liquor for sale, others trinkets and jewellery, the remains of food tables were being cleared away, though a few derisory blackened sausages drooping from sticks were still available.

A figure lurched out of the shadows between two wagons, bare-chested and wide-eyed. His torso and face were whitened with chalk dust and he wore a belt of raggedy fox tails around his waist. His lips were a slash of red across his chalky hairless face.

"Welcome to the Dark Carnival!!" he cried, loudly enough

for Ash to flinch and step away with a start. The man laughed, his gaping mouth revealing front teeth that had been filed to points before he bounded off down the street formed by two rows of wagons and a smattering of tents.

"Well, he seemed rather excitable," Mr Wizzle smiled, though it fell a little short of his customary beam.

"What's the Dark Carnival?" Amos asked

"Where all the freaks live I guess..." Ash snapped back, without looking at him.

Some of the carney folk certainly looked outlandish, but Amos got no sense of anything particularly untoward; a few stray images, mostly involving beds, but nothing else. No darkness, no shadows, no monsters...

A group of young women wearing little more than corsets and smiles were huddled together passing a bottle on the steps of a wagon carrying the sign *Mallory's Fine Strumpets.* When they spotted the three men approaching they whistled and waved. Beyond the wagon a large tent had been erected. Presumably for the business of entertainment.

"Fallen women..." Mr Wizzle warned, holding out his arms at either side to halt his two companions, "...I should intervene!"

The old man pulled a Bible from his pocket and clamped it against his belly with both hands, before striding over to the girls to offer advice about their immortal souls.

Ash looked forlorn. He glanced back and forth between Mr Wizzle and Amos before deciding the old clown and a gaggle of drunken prostitutes were preferable company to the man he had only recently tried to kill for raping his daughter.

A deep throaty laugh made Amos turn around. A woman

was sitting in a rocking chair by a wagon opposite *Mallory's Fine Strumpets*. She wore a long dress of tattered dark red lace and a derby perched upon her blonde curls that was so battered and sorry looking it could have been a hand me down from Mr Wizzle.

"You gotta admire a man with convictions..." she was smoking a thick cigar and she waved it in the direction of the old man.

"S'pose..."

Amos nodded at the empty stools next to her, "You mind."

"Sure... but I ain't for sale or for saving if you got any such things on your mind."

"Nope – not got much use for either women or God these days."

Her cigar flared fiercely as he eased himself down next to her. She was pale, thin and pretty in a painful kind of way. Her skin was the colour of fine undisturbed dust and her powdered eyes looked like vivid bruises in the flickering light of a long tar torch impaled into the ground.

"That sounds like a sorry tale."

Amos rolled his shoulders and asked her name.

"Clarice," she replied through a cloud of smoke.

"Amos."

She gave him the slightest of nods, though her eyes stayed on him, peering from behind half-closed lids.

"Where you from Clarice?"

"Bitty little nowhere place way down in the Carolina Low..."

"You're a long way from home."

"Everyone here is a *loooong* way from home honey..." her

370

voice was a slow liquid drawl; molasses dripped from every vowel.

"I guess... sure is a ride to get out here."

Clarice just smiled; her lips were dark red against her pale, dusty skin, the same colour as her dress. Her eyes rolled across Carney Town's drag as the girls broke into uproarious laughter. Ash looked like he wanted the Earth to gobble him up.

"Why'd they call this the Dark Carnival?"

Her eyes moved back, slow and languid, "'Cause the pleasures here are darker. A man takes his wifey and kiddies to the Day Carnival an keeps em entertained, but he creeps back here under the moon for his own pleasures."

"What's on offer?"

"Oh, just about anything a heart might desire. A girl, a boy, a nip, a smoke, a sniff, a snort, a turned card, a rolled dice. However a man cares to burn his money, we got a fire stoked and ready for him..."

She reached out and run a long red nail along the shaft of the tar torch, her eyes, which were absolute black between the hoods and the shadows, stayed on Amos.

He caught a whiff of desire, but it was hazy and unfocused, like looking at someone through the smoke of a campfire on a summer evening. Her mind was addled, he couldn't see nor smell any booze, but something had fogged her to the verge of stupor.

"What the fuck are you doing!"

A man cried out, Amos glanced over as he started shooing Mr Wizzle away from the girls. He was tall and sallow and wore his dark hair greased with a razor straight side-parting.

371

His Adam's apple, which looked large enough to be an actual apple, was bobbing up and down in agitation.

"Mallory..." Clarice whispered through her cigar smoke.

"The girl's pimp?"

"Among other things."

Amos stared at him as he glared at Mr Wizzle and Ash, who was tugging the old man away. He was used to a few coarse words after all and didn't seem much inclined to pass up on the opportunity to tell whores that they were all going to hell.

He felt it. Not as strong as before. Not as strong as with the Mayor and Rum, but the same dark, emptiness that wasn't quite empty. A hollowness in the earth that was home to something best unseen.

"What other things?" Amos pulled his eyes away; suddenly grateful Mallory had turned his attention to scolding the girls.

"Bad things..." Clarice pulled on her cigar, long and hard, hollowing her cheeks. When she exhaled, Amos noted the cigar butt was red with her lipstick, which had worn away on the inner part of her lower lip revealing the skin beneath.

Skin that was slightly blackened...

The Widow

Molly awoke with a start and took a moment to realise what the loud noise had been. "Fucking 4th of July..." she muttered. Then remembered Amelia was snuggled up against her.

"Oh shit..."

She grimaced.

Looking after a child is a lot fucking harder than I imagined...

Amelia didn't stir; her only reaction was the faintest sigh of a snore.

Molly looked up from the bed, she had fallen asleep without drawing the curtains and the softness of the night illuminated the bedroom. Nothing appeared to be wrong save the familiar thumping in her temples. Her hangover had kicked in early.

There was another distant whoosh followed by the retort of an explosion. For an instant the room was a fraction brighter and the shadows a fraction darker. It was only a dumb firework from the carney, but Molly found herself slipping a protective arm over Amelia.

She should really undress and get under the blanket with the girl, but she just lowered her head back to the pillow.

The night was warm and even the thought of moving was enough for her temples to throb a little harder.

Molly remembered Amos instead and immediately wished she hadn't.

Wincing made her head throb even more.

He'd been distracted when she'd returned, belatedly, from seeing Guy Furnedge. Amelia had already fallen asleep in a chair when she got back. She had the feeling Amos wanted to talk to her about something, but once she'd put the girl to bed all she'd wanted to do was tell Amos about her visit to the lawyer's home.

Amos had been staring distantly out of the window. Thinking again no doubt.

"I told Furnedge he was a murderer this afternoon," she'd blurted, trying rather unsuccessfully not to smile. It probably hadn't been the smartest move to go on her own, but it had felt good to finally do something about Tom's debt. For the first time in weeks she actually thought she might not be going to work for Monty Jack after all.

"You did what!?"

Evidently Amos hadn't thought it the smartest thing either.

It hadn't been an argument, not quite, but he hadn't been pleased. In fact, he hadn't even been within pissing distance of pleased. She'd felt deflated. Probably much like a house cat proudly depositing a dead bird at their owner's feet only to receive a boot up its ass instead of a scratch behind the ear.

She hadn't understood why he was so annoyed at first and it irked. She'd got herself out from under a rock that was as big and ugly as Hart Calbeck. Furnedge would pay off the debt, she was sure he would. She might lack Amos' strange gifts, but any fool could see the guilt staining the lawyer's face.

She'd felt her anger rising which wasn't a good thing even when it wasn't fuelled by booze. She'd been ready to let rip, she'd felt her lips press hard together and her heart start thumping. Her hands began to wave about and she was fixing him one of her meanest, beadiest stares.

Then she got it.

He's scared for me. And he's scared because...

And the anger had gone. In a heartbeat. Like it had never existed. Had that ever quite happened before?

So instead of swearing and stamping her foot at his dumbass inability to see she'd done the right thing and taken charge of her own destiny. She'd smiled and managed to get her arms around him before he'd had the chance to slide away from her.

She'd felt his whole body go rigid, but he'd held her, awkwardly and tentatively perhaps, but he had held her.

She had put her head against his chest and dug her fingers into his back and, like a drowning sailor clinging to a rock, she hadn't wanted to let go. He was quiet and strange and, if she was going to be brutally honest, a killer. But he made her feel safe and all she wanted was for him to hold her and make the world seem, for a few minutes at least, a less terrifying place.

For an instant she really thought he was going to let her kiss him, but he'd just pulled away muttering something incoherent. He'd gone to stare out of the window, leaning on the frame hard enough to turn his knuckles white.

She hadn't felt hurt or angry. She hadn't snapped or sworn at him. She just wished he would, just once in a while, hold her and kiss her. She'd smiled at him and said something about checking on Amelia.

He'd nodded and hadn't looked back.

Molly had thought to just lay by the girl for a moment. She hadn't expected to fall asleep.

She hadn't expected to cry beforehand either.

*

Molly awoke again. They'd been no firework this time and her head was marginally less thuddy. Amelia was mumbling and twisting in the throes of a dream.

"*Sssshh hun...*"

Molly rested a hand on the girl's shoulder until she quietened and grew still.

Molly lay there for a few minutes, listening to the silence beneath her heartbeat. Her throat was dry and she hadn't brought any water for the night up to the room.

Satisfied Amelia was sleeping deeply again, Molly carefully disentangled herself and padded downstairs. Although she was thirsty she looked in on Amos, the only time he seemed to be able to stand her being close to him was when he was asleep. Several times now she had crept down in the night and snuggled up to him on the floor. He had barely stirred and she had laid there and thought about how life might be with Amos in it.

The room was empty. The pillow and blankets he used still folded and unused.

She hadn't upset him that much. Surely?

There was a clock on the mantle, a battered old thing in a scratched walnut case, but it kept time well enough. It was too dark to read it, but she carried it over to the window and pulled back the drapes. It was gone one in the morning.

Where the hell was he?

Still clutching the clock, she looked around the room for a note, but there was nothing she could make out and she didn't want to light a candle or lamp just in case there was.

Molly walked through to the kitchen to fetch a drink. Amos' washed shirt was over the back of a chair waiting to be stuffed back in his saddlebag that sat in the corner of the kitchen.

He wouldn't have left them. She felt a sense of relief and realised she was still clutching the old walnut clock to her chest. He must have gone for a walk. People who think too much tended to do peculiar things like that.

She crossed to the sink, intending to put the clock down before pouring herself a drink. As she did, she happened to glance out into the yard, which was lit by only starlight and a thin crescent moon.

A figure was standing there.

Molly jumped, tossed the clock up into the air and managed only to catch it at the second attempt, pulling it against her stomach as she crouched down. After placing the clock on the floor, she peeked back over the sink, expecting the yard to be empty and the figure to have been no more than a trick of shadow and moonlight.

Nope. It was real...

It was a woman in a flowing black dress, head raised and

378

staring upwards. Her dark hair was pulled back across her scalp and tied into a single long ponytail. She was older than Molly but striking. Sharp features not tempered by the softness of the night.

She should bang on the window and tell her to scarper. Molly didn't recognise her and there were plenty of scarier looking people in this town, but Molly sank to the floor instead. She sat with her back against the sink, knees drawn up to her chin clutching the old clock.

She didn't want the woman to see her. She didn't want her to lower her face and see Molly standing in the window.

As much as Molly tried to tell herself it was just some harmless loon staring at the sky she didn't want to be seen. There was no good reason to be standing in a woman's yard past one in the morning. As Mr Wizzle would probably have said, the woman was clearly involved in shenanigans...

Molly thought of Tom's gun, locked in the drawer upstairs. She was no kinda shot and would as likely hit her own foot as anything else if she had to actually fire it, but she had a hunch it would feel more reassuring in her hand than a battered clock.

Placing the clock on the floor Molly thought about crawling back across the kitchen to the hallway and then bolting upstairs. She even got onto all fours.

This is ridiculous.

It's just a woman. An unarmed woman locked outside. Maybe she was just lost or needed help. Or had been knocked on the head. She was being stupid. And if she did try anything Molly could easily run upstairs and get Tom's gun before the woman could batter her way into the kitchen.

Molly took a deep breath and peeped back over the sink.

The woman was gone.

She let out a long breath and then leant forward over the sink to see if she might have moved along the back wall of the house and out of sight. She couldn't be entirely sure nobody was lurking in the shadows from her angle, but the yard looked empty.

How had she even gotten in? The back fence was high and the gate locked. Molly had never believed in that shit about leaving doors open for your neighbours.

Maybe she'd forgotten to lock the gate. Maybe Amos had left it open if he'd gone that way to walk. Although the front door would have been a more likely way to leave the house at night, Amos could be peculiar at times.

Molly took her drink and placed the clock back on its mantle, before returning to bed she inspected all of the doors and windows downstairs. There weren't many and they were all secure. She'd check the back gate tomorrow.

Amelia was still sleeping, just as she'd left her.

Molly locked the bedroom door just to be on the safe side. She thought about Tom's gun in the drawer and decided to leave it there. A small child, a firearms inept woman with a hangover and sleeping, were probably a more dangerous combination than a strange woman lurking outside a locked house.

Molly finally checked the bedroom window, which secure as it could be and was about to let the drapes fall back when something caught her eye outside. It was the dark-haired woman again, standing in the middle of the street this time, head raised and staring directly at the window. She had no expression that Molly could see and her eyes were lost in shadow. A breeze was ruffling the hems of her skirts, but otherwise she was completely still.

Amelia started to moan and mutter. Mostly it was incomprehensible, but one word she caught clearly enough.

Monsters...

Molly let the drape fall aside and hurriedly backed away from the window.

"Amos, where the fuck are you?"

The Songbird

The Mayor had put in another request for her company.

She'd been expecting a quiet night with most of the town at the carney. Monty was in such a bad mood as he prowled about the near empty saloon that she thought he might even give her a night off.

Instead, he'd told her curtly that the Mayor wanted her to sing for him and she should be over at his residence for nine.

"A special occasion?"

"Yeah, he has his own 4th of July celebration planned."

"Really?"

"You think he tells me his plans?" Monty had snorted as he'd ambled towards the doorway to fret about the lack of customers walking through it.

Cece wondered if he'd buy that she had a headache. That wasn't going to work. Time of the month maybe? Somehow she doubted that was an excuse that would ever wash here. Just ignore it?

He'd probably send one of his goons over to find her.

And she really should be trying to find out who the hell he was even if it wasn't why she'd been sent here. Not directly anyway. Find out what there was, note the differences and map the connections. Be curious.

Well, the Mayor was certainly a curiosity. And as he hadn't tried anything last time she doubted her virtue would be in any particular danger.

She'd sighed and retreated to her room to rest.

It didn't appear that she had much of a choice.

*

Pioneer Square was quiet as she crossed it, few people were about and those that were paid her little heed.

She noticed the gunsmith sitting outside his store, enjoying the warm evening light and staring at nothing in particular. Her eye lingered on him as she crossed the square, she couldn't shake the quiet nagging feeling that he looked familiar. Obviously she didn't know him, but he reminded her of someone she just couldn't place. As she watched, he rose to his feet and hurried inside.

Cece turned her attention back to the looming pile of the Mayor's residence. She had tried not to think too much about who he might be and why he was here. She'd always been reasonably good at sweeping things under whatever convenient rug came to hand. Even when they were big and unsightly enough to leave a huge lump in the middle of a room, she usually found a way to look in the other direction and whistle.

However, from time to time, you had no alternative but to lift a rug up and take another look at what was there. That's what the residence felt like. A big, gaudy rug she'd managed to sweep the Mayor under. When he was in there, out of sight and out of mind, she'd been able to avoid asking herself how the hell a man in this town would know the words to a

Rolling Stones song?

Observe and record. That's all she had to do. Someone else could figure it out when she got back.

"Ah Miss Jones, we've been expecting you..." the Mayor's manservant, who quietly gave Cece more of the creeps than the Mayor did, ushered her in with a welcoming sneer.

It was a beautiful evening, the air was warm and the light of the setting sun was hazy and golden. The kind of evening that warmed both your bones and your soul.

As soon as the door slammed behind her Cece felt cold. The windows were large and still uncurtained, but the light that fell through them carried not a hint of warmth.

Symmons, she was pretty sure that was his name, placed an unnecessary hand on the small of her back and indicated which way she should go with the other before following her.

Shouldn't he be leading the way?

Cece couldn't shake the feeling he was lingering behind just so he could stare at her backside. If she turned around quickly enough, she suspected she'd catch him licking his thin, bloodless lips.

There was no sound in the house bar the clicking of Symmons' boots on the hardwood floor.

From her extensive wardrobe Cece had picked the same unfussy, seduction killing number she'd worn on her last visit. She hoped the Mayor would get the message if he did have any plans for misbehaviour.

"Allow me..." Symmons breezed past her once they reached the polished oak doors that led to the Mayor's drawing room where he, presumably, entertained the great and the good of Hawker's Drift. Quite why he needed such a big room, she couldn't imagine.

The Mayor was slouching on a daybed between Felicity and another woman she hadn't seen before. A brunette with pouty lips and a small upturned nose, whose eyes seemed just as unfocused as Felicity's

"Miss Jones sir..." Symmons announced. The Mayor smiled but didn't see the need to stand up. She supposed she was just the entertainment after all. Cece glanced at the two girls, neither of whom could technically be described as being fully clothed.

Well, some *of the entertainment anyway...*

"I'm so pleased you could join us on such short notice," the Mayor purred after waving Symmons away.

"It was a quiet night. I'm surprised you're not at the Fair like the rest of the town?"

"Oh, I showed my face early. To be honest, I find it all a bit too brash and loud. But the people seem to enjoy it, so one mustn't be churlish."

Cece remembered Amelia screaming and talking about monsters, not to mention the way some of the carney folk had been staring at them till Amos had turned up. She would have added creepy to brash and loud.

"So," Cece looked at the piano, "you would like me to play?"

"Indeed we would... but first a little drink-" he held up his hand when she started to protest, "just one to humour me, Cecilia. Please."

His eye had stilled and was fixed pointedly at her.

She forced a little smile; it wasn't like it was going to do her any harm. She had quite the tolerance after all.

"Well... just the one."

The Mayor beamed, "Jennifer go and get our guest a drink."

Once the brunette had slowly disentangled herself from the Mayor she moved with the slow, deliberate steps of someone who had to actively try to remember just how the business of walking worked.

"What do you have?" Cece wanted to sit at the piano, it somehow felt more secure than standing on a luxuriant rug to be inspected by two sets of languid eyes and a single piercing one.

"Oh, something very special... just give it a try."

"I'm quite particular."

The Mayor favoured her with a knowing smile. He turned his attention to twisting strands of Felicity's long blonde hair about his fingers rather than give her a reply.

Jennifer returned with a large brandy glass with half a finger of amber spirit sloshing inside it.

"You will love this inside you..."

Her long hair had been tied loosely up save for a few long strands that hung to her bare shoulders, she let her deep hazel eyes hold Cece's as she handed her the glass. Jennifer's fingers entwined with hers for a moment before she smiled and pulled away to fold herself back onto the daybed with the Mayor and Felicity.

She eyed the glass. She could smell the spirit fumes without even having to raise the drink.

"French brandy," the Mayor explained, "Which is very rare these days, given the state of the Old World. But I'm sure you know that."

Cece smiled and knocked back the drink in one.

"It was more of a drink to be savoured slowly."

"I'm here to play the piano – but thank you anyway," Cece blinked, not quite sure why she had thrown the drink down her neck so quickly and feeling slightly giddy from it already. That would pass soon enough. If he thought he was going to get her drunk, he was going to be sorely disappointed.

"Should I start?"

The Mayor held up his hand, "Just a moment Cecilia, I'm waiting for one more guest. He'd be very disappointed to miss the start of your performance; he's quite a fan of yours. Almost, how would you say it "Back East" – a groupie?"

That's a word that shouldn't exist here...

"How intriguing."

The Mayor extracted himself from the daybed and the trailing hands of Felicity and Jennifer that fell reluctantly away from him as he stood. He took the glass from her hand and the aroma of sweetly scented smoke in her nostrils made her head swim further.

"I don't think I should have another..."

"No Cecilia, it's strong stuff," the Mayor lightly gripped Cece's arm to steady her. She hadn't even realised she'd been swaying until that point, "...it's sweet, sweet candy."

"I'm sorry?" Cece blinked again, her vision seemed to be blurring slightly as the Mayor took the brandy glass from her. The bottom of the deep bowl appeared to be black. How strange.

"You're such a long way from home, aren't you?" The Mayor's voice seemed to reverberate, forcing its way into her skull through the pores of her skin as much as her ears and then echoing about her brain

"Yes..." she replied, her own voice distant and small compared to that of the Mayor's "...home's Back East."

"Of course... Back East... that's the other side of another world isn't it Cecilia?"

"I suppose."

The Mayor's hands were holding her elbows, his skin felt smooth to the point of slippery, though not entirely unpleasantly. It did seem a little odd that his touch should feel like that, particularly given her dress had long sleeves. Very impractical on a summer's evening. But that didn't matter.

"You must be lonely... so far from home... from the ones you love..."

"Love?"

"Someone must love you, Cecelia. You're too beautiful to be unloved."

Although he wasn't standing that close to her, no closer than a modest clinch at a formal dance in fact, the Mayor's single eye filled her vision almost completely. It was as dark as the deep, deep woods at midnight, with only the barest sliver of a silver moon to glint through the all-encompassing blackness. Now she did feel giddy. Like she was going to dip head first off an enormous precipice.

"Who loved you, Cecilia?"

"Quayle..." she heard herself say.

"But you know you're never going to see him again, don't you?"

She found herself nodding, unable to move her eyes from the Mayor's gaze.

Distantly she heard giggling.

Must be those two girls. Are they still here? Dunno, can't see them...

"There's another man who loves you, you know?"

"There is?"

"Oh yes."

"Do you love me?"

What am I saying...

The Mayor laughed, a roll of distant thunder heralding a rain she wanted to drown in. Her legs didn't feel entirely right, if the Mayor wasn't holding her so tightly with those smooth, slippery hands of his, she was pretty sure she would be on the floor. Which would be silly.

"My love is so great and bountiful it encompasses everybody... but that is not what I meant."

"Who... who... loves me?" She wanted to rest her head against the Mayor's chest, she felt so ridiculously tired, but then she wouldn't be able to stare into the pit of his eye. Which wouldn't do at all.

"Sye loves you..."

"Oh him... he's just a boy."

"No, no, Cecelia. He is very special. You just haven't seen him properly. Haven't looked at him properly. Your mind has been full of nonsense. Full of unimportant things. You don't need to worry about them anymore."

"I don't?"

"Oh no. You're never going to go back. You're going to stay here in Hawker's Drift with the man you love. With Sye Hallows."

"I... don't..."

Cece felt her head swim and held on tighter to the Mayor. Her focus went completely for a moment and when it returned it was so badly blurred the Mayor seemed to have two eyes instead of one, except the second one wasn't an eye at all. It was a pit from which smoke curled softly about her, a pit which glowed faintly orange from a fire that writhed deep within it.

"You love him. You want him. All that matters is devoting your life to him and bearing his children. If you do, you will be happy. And that is your heart's desire isn't it Cecelia? To be happy. To be home, to be where you belong. To be at peace."

"Yes…" the smell of scented smoke was growing stronger, strong enough to taste. As it curled away from his second eye it seemed to be reaching out, delicate tendrils that pushed into her mouth and nostrils. And the smoke did taste ever so sweet.

Sweet as candy…

Dark Carnival

The Farmer

Sye had always felt uncomfortable on the rare occasions his Ma had cause to get out the good crockery. A life time's experience of being a cack-handed ass had always made him nervous of being around any object that was either valuable and/or breakable. When they were both he got decidedly twitchy.

He sat bolt upright in the middle of the room clutching his knees and trying not to look at the things the Mayor had furnished and decorated it with. Just in case a stray glance might be enough to send something priceless tumbling to the floor and smashing to a thousand pieces.

The Mayor seemed to have an entirely excessive amount of things that looked both valuable and breakable.

Two statues of naked ladies stood upon plinths either side of the door. He was really trying hard not to go near them. From where he sat, they both looked a bit like Cece. They were stretching their arms above their heads and looking down at their exposed breasts as if they found them as captivating as Sye usually did when it came to lady's breasts. Not that he'd ever seen any up close of course.

Hopefully, that would change soon.

Sye gulped and knocked his hat from his lap. At least that

wasn't breakable.

The room wasn't particularly big and it seemed he had been sitting in it for hours. The Mayor had told him not to worry, Cece would come to the house and he would take care of *matters*.

Sye assumed matters involved getting her to drink from a little black bottle before some damn fool managed to lose it.

He'd been told to wait in the room, which consisted of a window looking over the back of the Mayor's residence, a single chair, and a number of all too breakable-looking objects scattered about on tables, bookcases and shelves. He'd paced up and down the room to start with, waiting to be summoned, but had quickly decided to sit in the hard-backed chair that had been placed slap bang in the middle of the room. He guessed even he wasn't too dumb to take a hint.

The sky out of the window was a dark evening blue by the time the door finally opened and the Mayor's manservant entered to room. He was a tall, wispy fellow with a long straight nose he forever seemed to be peering down. Sye didn't like him much to be honest, he seemed rather too snooty, particularly after all the trouble he'd been to wash the smell of cow dung off.

"The Mayor has asked for you to come through," Symmons announced from the opposite end of his nose.

Sye's stomach did some acrobatics, but he managed to get to his feet and move forward without any mishaps.

Part of him thought this still had to be some kind of a joke. Symmons would take him to a grand hall where the whole town had gathered. They would be falling over themselves laughing and pointing as the town's official new gullible idiot walked in wearing his best suit, boots and gormless grin.

Love potion indeed...

Well, it was all a bit too late now. He stared at the back of Symmons' neck as he led him down a short corridor towards a couple of imposing doors. With every step he wanted to turn around and run. Either this was a joke and he was about to be made a fool of or he was tricking a woman into loving him. Somehow.

It would be better to run. Or at least hide. And be miserable forever.

Stop being a fool.

It was just a nudge, that's all. Just a little push in the right direction. He just needed a chance to show Cece how right they were for each other. How happy he would make her. That was all. Nothing more. Not really.

Symmons was at the door turning towards him, pulling a face that was part smile, part sneer.

A Smeer? A snile?

"Just got through sir... the lady's been prepared for you..."

An image of Cece on a giant silver platter with an apple stuffed in her mouth floated in front of his eyes.

"Thank you..." he managed to mutter, placing a hand on the door knob and staring at it, not sure if he should twist or push. Or turn tail and sprint back down the corridor.

Symmons cocked an eyebrow and continued to peer at him in the manner of a large flightless bird. One part curiosity, one part hunger.

Sye found you had to turn the knob to make the door

work.

The room beyond was large though probably nowhere big enough to fit the whole town into. As it was, there were only four people inside.

Two young women who he was absolutely sure he'd never seen around town were draped over a daybed, and each other, intently watching the Mayor who was standing between the girls and Sye with Cece propped up against him. The Mayor had one hand on Cece's arm and the other was fiddling with his eye patch.

"Good evening Sye..." the Mayor beamed. He looked pleased with himself.

"Is she..."

"Cecilia is perfectly fine... just a little groggy."

The two girls on the daybed, one blonde, one brunette, both beautiful and wearing loose black silk dresses that left little to the imagination, giggled in tandem.

Sye crossed the room in small hesitant steps till he reached Cece and the Mayor. Her head was lolling on the Mayor's chest and her body seemed too loose and limp for her to stand up unaided.

"What have you done to her?" It looked like he'd poured a hell of a lot of strong liquor down her throat, but he thought he'd ask anyway.

"I've made her see sense..." the Mayor looked down at Cece though he would have seen little but her blonde curls "...look Cecilia, its Sye, he's come to see you... I think you've got something to say to him haven't you?"

Cece's head turned slowly in Sye's direction, her hair had fallen about her face and she regarded him for a moment as she rested her cheek against the Mayor's chest.

"Sye... I've missed you..." she slurred the word slightly and she was looking at him as if she wasn't entirely sure who he was, but none of that mattered. Not really.

"You did?"

She nodded and bit her lip, "I've been so foolish about you, I see that now..."

The Mayor pulled away from her and gently spun her towards Sye, "Just hold her for a few minutes... she is just having a little turn. The way women do. It will pass very shortly and then..."

The Mayor may have said some more, but Sye was no longer listening as Cece took a couple of tottering steps that ended in his arms.

He held her tight and let a multitude of sensations wash away his amazement in her letting him put his arms around her. He revelled in the feel and the scent of her. The softness of her hair, the way her breasts squeezed against his chest, the small neat perfection of her waist, the heat of her breath on his skin

And the enormous erection that threatened to drain all the blood from his body.

Sye pulled away a little from her and she looked back up at him. She was smiling, the way he'd always dreamed she would one day smile at him. A soft, gentle little thing that promised so much more as they stared long and deep into each other's eyes.

"I love you..." she whispered eventually "...I don't know why it took me so long to see it, but I do Sye, I really do..."

Sye thought he might faint. Or jump up and down or run

down Main Street whooping and waving his pants around his head.

This is what happiness feels like.

"I love you too Cece... I love you so much..." Sye knew he was grinning so madly he was in danger of splitting his face in two, but he didn't care. He didn't care about anything, he just pulled her close to him and cradled her head against his chest.

"She will need to sleep soon," the Mayor said, suddenly standing at Sye's ear.

"Is she-'"

"She is as well as she has ever been. She is in the arms of the man she loves after all. Isn't that the place every girl wants to be? However, she is tired, but tomorrow..." the Mayor curled a knowing smile "...oh tomorrow young Sye, she will be so damn full of vitality she'll sing all day for you and I swear it'll be the sweetest song you ever did hear!"

"Thank you..." Sye replied, still grinning as he stroked Cece's soft, soft hair "...I don't know how I can ever repay you."

"Repay me? Oh phooey! I just like to ensure true love finds its way over the hurdles of life. I'm an old romantic I guess..." the girls on the daybed giggled in the distance "...it brings sunshine into my soul it truly does. Nothing makes me happier than giving someone their heart's desire..."

Cece was looking up at him and Sye thought maybe he shouldn't be discussing this with the Mayor in front of her, but her gaze was so soft and dreamy it was clear she only had eyes for him.

"So... what happens now?"

"Now?" The Mayor held out his hands, "You want me to give you the talk about the birds and the bees?"

Sye shook his head.

"Let her sleep and tomorrow you can start practising."

"Practising?"

The Mayor leaned in and whispered in his ear, "Practising making babies Sye. I got a good feeling you and this girl are gonna be making a whole heap of em for my town..."

Dark Carnival

The Deputy

He wasn't particularly surprised that she'd gone to see the old nigger.

It wasn't as if there were many other people she could turn to and people, particularly women, had a habit of going to people when they were in trouble. It was one of the many facets of human behaviour that Blane had never really understood. A trouble shared... A friend in need...

Glib little words to dress up the weakness of folk. Blane couldn't remember asking for help in his entire life. Well, not since childhood certainly and even then he'd been an independent and self-reliant little boy. If shit happens, you deal with it. Deal with it the best you can. If that means blowing someone's brains out or running to the hills or frightening some fool senseless, so be it. But as soon as you brought someone else into your dilemma you limited your options, you weakened your position, you had to account for their morality instead of just your own.

Maybe poor Katie would feel better for sharing her woes, but it wouldn't solve her problem. Did she think that old man was going to intervene? And even if Smith did, what could he do that would help her other than killing him? Nothing else was going to stop his fun. No matter which way round he peered at it, he couldn't see the blacksmith turning to murder to save his lover's honour, or marriage or even her life.

He hadn't stood by any of the other women he'd fucked (and they'd been quite a few of those) when things had become difficult. Nope, John X Smith struck him as a man who didn't give two hoots about anyone bar John X Smith.

Blane could admire that in a man as much as he could admire anything. Take what you wanted from the world, hang the consequences and walk away from the mess with a smile and a whistle when the fun was done.

That's how he'd lived his life though he greatly doubted his kind of fun would have been shared by the blacksmith.

He'd been watching Kate. Sometimes discreetly, sometimes not. He liked her knowing he was around. He loved seeing her stew in her own fear and humiliation. It was the kind of marinade he particularly enjoyed watching his meat cook in. Made the eating real tasty in the end.

She hadn't seen him when she'd gone into the nigger's store. My didn't she look the state? Seemed she hadn't slept in days, poor thing!

Blane was in the Sheriff's office; he'd drawn the short straw and had to man the desk while the rest of the deputies sauntered around the carney pretending to find men with painted faces amusing. Yeah, he'd been real unlucky.

The only downside had been having Old Shit Shenan around as he hated the carney about as much as Blane did. Still, he'd mostly kept to his office and left him in peace. Probably mooning about his dead wife some more.

He watched her skirting around the square in hurried

401

trying-too-hard-to-look-normal steps. Lucky for her Pioneer Square was about as deserted as it was ever likely to get. She didn't go right up through the front door; instead she ducked into the alley that ran down the side so she could get into the backyard. Yeah, that looks way less suspicious than going in the front door and coming out with a box of shells. Stupid bitch.

He watched the store for a while, but decided against having a little mosey on by. He'd let her have some leash for the time being. He was in no hurry. She was gonna cook real slow and juicy for him.

He pondered whether or not the old nigger would fuck her while she was there. Be all consoling and then help himself to a piece. Maybe. He had a reputation after all. Many folk didn't like the gunsmith on account of his niggerness, but it didn't bother Blane none. In his experience, black folk made just as good killing as white folk. Regardless of the colour of their hide, everyone screamed like a pig when you stuck em hard enough.

Kate came back out after twenty minutes or so. Which didn't seem much time to beg for help and get fucked, so Blane guessed Smith had played the gentleman and just listened. That or he shot his load real quick for an old fella, which didn't seem likely given the number of women he'd ploughed about the town.

Her head was down and she walked fast. Blane wasn't an expert on these things, but she didn't look any happier than when she'd gone in.

"Going to lunch..." he shouted, grabbing his hat. The Old Shit didn't reply. Probably having a nap. He had a lot of those, like some old folks do when they're getting ready to be dead.

Kate slowed a bit as she headed down Main Street, allowing Blane to catch up without having to break much of a sweat.

He wasn't planning to say anything, just give her a nice surprise when she glanced around.

She must have been deep in thought or her guilty conscience had been taking a nap with Sheriff Shenan, but she didn't look behind her till she got to the top of her road. Blane had made sure he was far enough behind her that she wouldn't have heard his scuffed old boots creaking on the boardwalk, but close enough that when she did turn around she'd be in no doubt who it was.

She looked sharply forward, but not before her eyes had grown so wide they might have tumbled into the dirt if they weren't on the end of cords. She scurried down her road like a rabbit heading for its burrow after spying a fox on the prowl. She didn't break into a run, but she walked about as fast as you could whilst desperately trying to look like you weren't. If any of Kate's neighbours happened to see her, they'd think she was in the most desperate need of the biggest shit of her life.

Blane kept his own pace, as if completely oblivious to the hurrying scurrying Mrs Godbold ahead of him.

After she had dived into the house, he strolled by, no slower, no faster. He was pretty sure she was peeking out from behind the curtains. He didn't smile for her, or raise his finger to his hat or tip her a wink. He kept his usual expressionless face. The one she knew now was only a mask.

He paused at the gate. A short path led to her front door. He thought about going in, but there was no reason to hurry things along. He peered at the window. Was that a flicker of movement? A cowering woman biting her knuckle to stop herself sobbing perhaps? Praying to her impotent god to make him go away, to leave her in peace, to do anything but walk those few paces to the front door and get his share of her.

He would, when he was good and ready. More importantly when she was good and ready too. But that wasn't today. He stared at the window, which was virtually opaque as it threw the light of the street back. He gave it a long knowing look so if she was peeking out she would think he could see her. See right through. See her naked and vulnerable and useless. He was going to get inside her head for a good long while before he got inside her legs.

He let a smile squirm out, just a tiny little slither of a thing, just for dear ol' Katie. Then he turned slowly around and walked back up the street feeling mighty pleased with life and the dark joys it offered.

He'd only had an hour or so to break Emily into pieces, but he was going to take weeks with her Mother. He was planning to do a real fine piece of work on her...

The Gunslinger

He wasn't entirely sure who started the brawl, as he'd turned back towards Clarice, but Ash and Mr Wizzle were plum in the thick of it.

A couple of men had appeared, hired guns, the type of men Amos recognised well enough. Security for the carney he supposed though they had the look of men more comfortable with breaking the peace than upholding it. Attracted by the hollering around Mallory's girls, they'd failed miserably in calming the situation.

Things had escalated in moments. As the two thugs had tried to grapple Ash several drunken townsfolk had waded in to help the barber, resulting in an almighty scuffle that was dragging in men from the length and breadth of Carney Town.

Mr Wizzle had shuffled back against Mallory's wagon. He was clutching his bible and trying to calm things down with a sermon that was attracting even less attention than his sermons usually did.

Amos took a step towards him, not wanting to see the old man take a stray fist, but Mr Wizzle shook his head and then gave him a wink and a slow smile.

Amos frowned, taking a moment to get his meaning.

"You gonna help your friends?" Clarice asked, still sprawled in her chair. Amos suspected she'd seen enough carney brawls in her time not to be overly troubled by the crunch of fist on bone.

Amos shook his head, "Nope... they're no friends of mine."

*

Things were quieter behind the wagons where the carney folk had pitched up their tents. Whatever thugs they had employed had been drawn towards the brawl, along with a lot of the other Dark Carnival revellers.

He picked his way between the glowing embers of campfires. Some were deserted, around others slumped forms shared bottles or dozed. Laughter cut through the night from numerous directions, from flirtatious giggles to near maniacal cackles. A man was singing spectacularly badly somewhere off in the distance.

Amongst the smell of burning wood and coal, other smells lingered; roasted meat, unwashed skin, hints of sweet gaudy perfumes, tobacco and pungent, acrid scents he could not name.

There were other things too. The things beyond normal senses glimmered, shimmered and sparkled around him in the darkness. Whatever his strange talent was, a gift from Death or something else, it was noticeably getting stronger in Hawker's Drift. Perhaps it was simply because he was surrounded by more people for a longer period of time than he had been for years. Perhaps it was being so close to one person. Perhaps the fact that he found that he had cares and feelings that he had thought long dead. Perhaps they were feeding his ability like air blown into a flame to make it burn brighter. Whatever the reason he wished it would stop.

It had almost overwhelmed him at the carney earlier, a cacophony of souls clambering to be heard inside his mind. Things were different at the Dark Carnival. Everything was muted; distant voices carried on a faltering breeze, the last light fading from a colour-washed sky, the scent of a woman lingering upon a sheet.

There was nothing coherent that he could focus on, nothing that could be made sense of. A couple of times he got the faint echo of dark, yawning, not quite emptiness that he associated with the Mayor and some of the carney folk, but they were not close. Those foreboding caves were out in the night somewhere and he wasn't sure whether he should be trying to get closer to them or run as far as he could in the opposite direction.

Actually he wasn't entirely sure what he was doing period.

Mr Wizzle had caused a distraction which had allowed him to slip away unnoticed. But a distraction for whose benefit? The carny's muscle or, as he was starting to think of them, the Monsters in the Caves? And now what exactly was he looking for?

There was a wrongness here. He sensed it. Amelia had sensed it. He was pretty damn sure Cece had sensed it too. Even that mad old clown sensed it. But no one else did, save maybe Sheriff Shenan, who'd seemed none too taken with the carney folk and Ash, who was just looking under every rock he could find for some kind of an answer. But was that wrongness a threat to Amelia and, by association, to Molly?

...there are monsters in the caves...

Yeah, he had the feeling that the carney was. Maybe not the carney down in Hooper's Large Field, the carney of candy apples and carousels, bunko booths and jugglers, but up here in the Dark Carnival.

In the diluted minds of the merrymakers, there was something else. A thread that weaved through the revellers and bound them together in need and want and desire.

He had no idea what it might be, but something kept coming back to him time and again as he picked his way between the tents and the fires. It came from the still forms clutching bottles as they stared glassily up at the stars. From the staggering figures momentarily silhouetted against the campfires. From the couples writhing urgently in the shadowy recesses. Just three words. Again and again. Three words that didn't make any sense, but bound carny and town's folk alike all the same. Three little words.

Sweet. Black. Candy.

*

There was something out beyond Hooper's Small Field.

It was hard to judge the distance in the night, but it was too far for any sounds to carry. Or anything else Amos' strange senses might detect. Another fire in the distance, a large one too. Not a farmstead ablaze, but a sizable bonfire.

It might have nothing to do with the Dark Carnival. Maybe some farmers were having their own 4th July celebrations, though they were well into the morning of the 5th now judging by how far the slivered moon had climbed up the slope of the star-speckled eastern sky.

Amos was resting his boot on the wooden fence at the rear

of Hooper's Small Field, the wagons and tents of the carney were all behind him. He stared into the darkness, the grass beyond the fence faded into the night and there was nothing else to see bar the distant fire and the cold flickering stars.

Someone screamed behind him, but Amos didn't bother to look back. He would have seen nothing and it wasn't the first scream he'd heard since slipping away from Mr Wizzle and Ash. Whether they'd been screams of pleasure or pain had been hard to tell and he had no inclination to find out more.

He was torn between walking out onto the grass towards the distant fire or skirting around the Dark Carnival some more to see if there was anything else he could learn while he was free of prying eyes.

He turned around to find a tall, slight figure behind him.

"Clarice..."

So much for no prying eyes...

"You looking for fun?" She took a step towards him. She was taller than he'd assumed, as tall as he was, though far slighter. She didn't look like she spent much of her day at the dinner table.

"I thought you weren't for sale?"

"I'm not. Just you seems like a man looking for something and there ain't much else to come looking for at the Dark Carnival other than fun ..."

"Guess I'm looking for fun then."

Clarice smiled, her eyes glistening in the darkness as she came close enough for Amos to smell the cigar smoke on her breath.

"Well you ain't got a sniff of a drink on you and you ain't been near no whores either. The gaming tents are way over yonder..." she jerked her head back towards the carney "...so you don't seem in any great hurry to lose no money. So what fun you looking for exactly honeybun?"

Clarice reached out and laid her palm flat against Amos' chest, long stem-like fingers pressing against his rough cotton shirt.

That kind of intimacy, particularly in Hawker's Drift where he seemed to sense things even more vividly than usual, would often result in a memory or an emotion cutting into his mind. With Clarice, however, as with the other souls he'd brushed past in the dancing firelight of the Dark Carnival, there was only a soft, blurred need. A faint, dry, musty stink escaping a shroud.

A memory did pop into Amos' mind, though. Not one of Clarice's, but his own. The day he'd arrived in Hawker's Drift, waiting by the road in the rain as the wagon bearing Tom McCrea's coffin trundled by with Molly, Furnedge and Preacher Stone in its wake. A terrible want had been emanating from the Preacher, a need for something that eased his pain, but more besides. The same want was coming from Clarice, albeit far less desperately.

Amos held her eye and placed his own hand flat over hers. Nothing more came into focus.

"I'm looking for sweet black candy."

Clarice's eyes opened a fraction wider then she giggled and quickly brushed her lips against his, "I didn't realise you were Chosen. I could help you..."

"Can you?"" Amos muttered. She was pressing hard against him now, hard enough for him to feel the weathered, splinted fence pushing against the small of his back. If Molly did this, he would be squirming to get away from her however much he wanted to put his arms around her and hold her, but he felt no compunction to push Clarice away. Instead, he placed a hand on each of her narrow hips and felt the bone through her skin. Still nothing came from her but faint unremitting desire. But not a desire for him, not predominantly anyway.

"It is like nothing else, is it...?" she breathed, her eyes flicking momentarily upwards and Amos felt a shiver run down her long, slight frame "...we are blessed. We are chosen."

"We are blessed, we are chosen..." Amos repeated. He had no idea what he was agreeing to, but he got no sense that Clarice suspected his cluelessness.

Clarice stared at him, her nostrils flaring slightly, before stepping back and producing something from a bag that hung from her shoulder.

It was a small black bottle.

"I only have a little left, but we could share."

Amos stared at the thing. It was just a bottle; small, opaque, unlabelled. Completely unremarkable, yet he wanted to hurl it into the grass. Something awful lived inside that bottle. He could hear it; squirming and chirping and hungry to be consumed. Hungry to consume.

"Where did you get it from?" He asked.

"Mr Qinn... you come from the town, do you get yours from Him?"

Amos nodded.

"I've heard his is the sweetest of all of them. You really must be blessed..."

"I am."

Amos looked off into the night and the distant fire burning out on the grass, not sure what to do or say next. Clarice followed his gaze and her lips parted enough to show the faint black stain beneath her lipstick.

"You… were heading there, weren't you?"

Amos nodded again.

She made a fist around the little black bottle as her hand dropped to her side.

"Take me with you. *Please?*" Urgency and desperation twisted her voice. Amos felt wave after wave of fetid heat wash over his skin. Finally, he got an image, soaked in want and desire. She wanted to walk towards that fire but knew that this time she couldn't, because she hadn't been invited and bad things happened to people who walked towards that fire uninvited.

"Have you been invited?"

She wanted to lie so much. Amos could taste it above the old cigar smoke on her breath, acrid and bitter, but she gave a hurried shake of the head and looked back over his shoulder towards the fire.

"Not this time… some of the chosen must stay here."

"Then I can't."

"I need to drink from the source. It is so much sweeter when it is pure," with her free hand she let her fingers entwine with his, "then you can fuck me while we are both full of their majesty and blessing."

"I can't take you," Amos said sharply.

She blinked and looked down, before sighing, "I know…"

"Go back, you don't want to anger them."

She nodded but looked unconvinced, before curling out a smile and holding up the bottle.

"We could still..."

"I've been invited."

"Of course..."

She took a step back, then another, "I haven't seen you here before."

"I... served elsewhere."

She nodded. "We all do as we are bid. For Him."

"We do."

She smiled again then hurried away to disappear amongst the pirouetting silhouettes of the Dark Carnival.

Once he was sure Clarice was gone, Amos turned back towards the grass and boosted himself cleanly over the fence. It swayed in protest under his weight, but he landed silently on the other side.

He stood staring at the distant fire, unconsciously he run his fingers over the smooth sandalwood grip of his gun before unclipping the leather strap to allow a fast draw. Then he set off across the grass.

It had been a long time since he'd needed an invitation for anything...

The Widow

Molly's natural instinct had been to lean out of the bedroom woman and shout at the woman to fuck off. It was a technique that had worked out reasonably well for her in the past after all.

Instead, she scurried over to the drawers and fumbled for the key to the top draw, the only one which locked. Finally finding it with her fingertips, she almost dropped it before finally getting the draw open and wrapping her hand around the comforting cold metal of Tom's old pistol.

It was a hefty piece of iron that she would struggle to hold steadily if she were to try and raise it with only one hand. Still, she instantly felt less vulnerable with it clasped in her hands.

"Monsters... monsters in the caves..."

Amelia was kicking off the blanket in the grip of whatever dream she was experiencing. Why couldn't she be having one of the cute ones involving horses or rabbits? It would be far less creepy.

Being careful to point the gun away from sleeping children, Molly walked slowly back across the room towards the sliver of soft light between the partially open curtains. She took deep, measured breaths and placed one foot in front of the other with far more precision than she usually took when stumbling across a darkened bedroom.

The street was empty.

She let out a slow, lingering breath and loosened her grip on the gun a little. Hopefully, the woman had ambled off to stare at somebody else's house and spook them witless.

Molly stood watching the street for a few minutes, but nothing much changed apart from the fact she no longer felt either tired or hungover. She'd never realised that simply being scared shitless could cure a hangover. She'd have to remember that one.

She eased herself down onto the room's only chair, which usually served no purpose other than to throw clothes over, not sure what she wanted to do other than wish that Amos was home. For a man that didn't say a lot, the house was unnervingly quiet with him not around.

Molly stared at the shadow encased bed and the small lump she could make out upon it. Amelia had grown still again and the only sound was the faintest sigh of the girl's breath.

Under the circumstances, a diligent and responsible adult would stay awake and ensure the crazy woman was gone and posed no threat to the sleeping, vulnerable child.

Molly, however, realised she hadn't eaten anything and her stomach had seemingly come to the same conclusion as it grumbled with more gusto than Amelia was managing with her occasional muffled snores.

There was some bread in the kitchen, and a fair chance that something else resembling food might also be lurking about.

She gave Amelia another quick, and only marginally guilty, look before rising to her feet. She was halfway to the door when she heard something. She wasn't entirely sure what that something was, but it sounded awfully like it had come from downstairs.

Her stomach gave a little lurch, distracted suddenly from protesting about its emptiness, and she paused long enough to tell herself she was being stupid. The windows and doors were locked and bolted. It wasn't anyone's idea of a fortress, but she was damn sure no one could have gotten in without breaking glass, splintering wood and generally making enough noise to alert an armed and vigilant guard. Or even Molly McCrea with a big gun.

Absolutely no way.

She crossed to the bedroom door, pressed her ear against the wood and held her breath. Nothing. The house was silent and the only imminent danger appeared to be getting a splinter in her earlobe.

Still, her hand rested reluctantly on the key.

You really need something to eat?

"Damned if I'm gonna get scared in my own home..." Molly muttered to herself and unlocked the door. Amelia mumbled something as the lock clicked but didn't wake.

Molly passed through onto the dark landing, making sure the gun was pointing nowhere near her feet, just in case she managed to inadvertently fire off a round.

She should light a lamp. She was pretty sure it'd be much harder to spook herself witless if she could actually see further than the end of her nose. Though of course it would make her a lot more visible if someone was lurking

418

downstairs.

There's no one downstairs. You bolted everything. Even Amos would have to thump on the door to get back in.

She edged forward to the top of the stairs; she could just make out the bannister as it plunged down into the gloom.

There was another creak.

Molly bit her lip and moved her weight from one foot to the other.

"Amos?"

She was *pretty* sure he'd have to have knocked to get back into the house and nothing rose out of the silence in response to her hopeful call.

Molly found the first step of the stairs with a prodding toe and eased herself down onto it. The wood creaked under her weight and she winced at the noise for no obvious reason. If someone – like a strange dark-haired woman for example – was lurking in the house, her calling out for Amos had already alerted them she was up and about.

She continued edging down the stairs, one step at a time. The door to the kitchen was open and what little light the night offered was dusting a ghostly grey upon the hallway's shadows.

Molly kept a candle on a table by the front door and she fumbled lighting a match and then the candle while juggling Tom's gun. When the little yellow flame finally took it half blinded her and her eyes watered a little as she held the candle out before her and waited for her eyes to readjust to the light.

Eventually she edged down the corridor, each step pushing the darkness away, but only a little. As she reached the door to the drawing room, another noise came. This was one she recognised, though. Not a footstep on floorboards or the random sigh of the house settling on its frame, but the sound of the rocking chair in the next room.

Creak... creak... creak...

Molly froze. She remembered the Mayor sitting in that chair and how creepy the creaking noise had been while he'd been rocking back and forth in it. This was far worse.

Was it the Mayor? That fucker had a habit of appearing when no one was looking after all. But, no, she didn't think it was the Mayor this time. He hadn't been standing outside her house earlier. If someone *was* in that chair, it was a woman, a woman with dark hair and a striking, sharp face.

The front door was shut and bolted, the only other way in, save breaking a window, was the back door. Molly glanced down the hall towards the kitchen, but it was just a black square beyond the small pool of flickering candle light.

She stared at the drawing-room door. Checking the kitchen would put her back to this door and whoever was on the other side of it. And it would also put them between her and Amelia.

"Who's there?" She hissed at the door; her voice and the candle flame shook together.

Creak... creak... creak...

"I know someone's in there... I've got a gun. If you don't say who you are, I'm going to fucking use it!"

Molly thought if she were sitting in a dark room rocking in someone else's chair she wouldn't have been much put out by a threat carried on such a weedy, reedy, quivering voice either.

"Dammit, who's in there?"

...the monsters in the caves...

Molly shoved the door open and stumbled through without dropping either the gun or the candle, both of which she held out before her. The candle offered a wan yellow light that could only partially push the shadows back into the far corners. However, she could see enough to tell the room was as empty as she'd found it when she'd come down earlier.

It would have been enough for her to blow out a long, relieved breath, lower Tom's gun and curse herself for a fool... if the chair hadn't still been rocking back and forth. Rocking as if someone had just sprung from it and rushed out of the room. Except she was standing in the only door and she was damn sure no one had rushed past her.

There wasn't a whole lot of furniture for someone to hide behind in the room and it only took a few faltering steps for her to be sure the room was empty.

Creak....... creak...... creak......

Or, rather, it was empty now.

She turned slowly in the centre of the room, gun and candle still both before her, still both shaking. Nothing was amiss, nothing was out of place, save for the gently subsiding creak of the rocker.

Molly's eyes returned to the chair. When it finally grew still she approached it. One cautious step after another, as if she needed to lay a hand on the smooth varnished wood just to make sure there really wasn't somebody still sitting in it.

She paused, frowning slightly as she placed the candle on the mantle above the fire. There was something sitting in the chair. Not a person and not something that could have

421

rocked it back and forth, but something she was pretty sure hadn't been there before.

A cheap rag doll was propped up against the back of the rocker like a drunk slumped against a wall. The crudely stitched misshapen face seemed to be set in a grimace as it's beady eyes stared back at Molly in the candle-light.

Amelia had gone to the carney earlier. Amos must have gotten the ugly thing for her. The man did have a soft heart under that scarred and hardened hide of his after all. Shit taste in toys, but a soft heart all the same.

But it hadn't been there earlier, had it?

She bent down and scooped it up, it was coarse and lumpy. She doubted such a poorly made thing would last more than a few days scrutiny under the rigours of a child's imagination. Its eye beads were loose and the red wool of its hair was already unravelling.

"Hope you didn't have to pay anything for this piece of shit..." Molly muttered.

She didn't like the thing though she knew she was just being irrational. It was only a cheap doll. Still, if the fire had been burning in the hearth, she would have thrown it into the flames without a second thought. Instead, she went to toss the thing into the farthest corner of the room.

That was when the candle went out.

Molly gave a little gasp and stepped backwards in shock as if the night had physically slapped her face. The darkness engulfed her completely; the candle-light had robbed Molly of her night vision and what little soft light from the moon and stars snuck into the room were lost to her.

A draft must have caught the candle flame and blown it

out. She couldn't actually feel any draft and she hadn't noticed the flame dancing and flickering beforehand, but what else could have happened?

She was torn between trying to find the candle and re-lighting it and scrambling back up the stairs.

Where had she left the matches?

On the little table in the hallway, where they usually were she guessed. Coming down the stairs she'd had enough night sight to make out the rough black iron candlestick and find the matches. But now she'd be working on touch alone unless she waited for her eyes to adjust back to the absence of light.

That seemed a little pointless. It was her home after all, so it wasn't like she was going to get lost in the dark. And there was nothing down here after all.

Molly edged towards where the door should be.

...creak...

She'd imagined that. *Right?* It might have sounded like someone settling themselves back into the rocker now that pesky, irritating candle had been blown out. But it wasn't. Obviously it wasn't.

She took another step towards the door.

...creak...

"Who the fuck is that?"

The words were softly spoken as she twisted around, but her heart was suddenly pounding so hard it felt like it was bouncing inside her chest like a lunatic about his padded cell. She still couldn't see anything, but she was damned if she was keeping her back to that chair.

...creak...

423

Was the only answer to come out of the darkness.

Molly took a step backwards. Sweat was greasing the grip of Tom's gun. Did she really want to start peppering a rocking chair with slugs in the middle of the night?

"Answer me or I'll shoot!"

Sure, why the fuck not.

...creak... creak... creak...

Molly let go of the ragdoll so she could grip the heavy old piece of iron with both hands, but the doll didn't drop to the floor, it clung to her wrist instead. Then it squirmed.

She staggered backwards till she hit the wall, trying to shake the thing off her. She could feel it's urgent struggles to hold on, lumpy jointless arms and legs wrapping themselves around her wrist as she waved her arm about.

Was that a gasping noise? Was the thing gasping for breath as it clung to her?

She couldn't use her free hand to prize it off without dropping the gun and she didn't want to try to pull off the doll while she still held it as she'd probably shoot herself. So instead she smashed her wrist against the door and the thing gave a wizened little cry.

Then it bit her.

She couldn't see it, but she was damn sure that's what it had done. It felt like tiny little knives cutting into the flesh of her wrist.

Ragdolls don't have fucking teeth!!!

They didn't come to life either as far as Molly knew, but something was sure as hell clinging to her wrist.

She crouched down muttering "Fuck!" over and over as the thing chomped at her flesh. Placing her hand on the floor she found the doll with her toes and pinned it to the floor before standing up and tearing it from her wrist.

There was a ripping noise, the kind you might expect a rag doll to make, accompanied by a high-pitched scream you certainly wouldn't. The thing let go of her wrist and she straightened up. She could feel it squirming beneath her foot and she ground her heel into it, using her other foot to find the limbs that were thrashing about and trying to paw them away.

She was panting and sobbing too much to think about the pain in her wrist or the fact that this simply couldn't be happening. The only other thing she was aware of was the creak of the rocking chair which seemed to be gathering pace as if somebody was mightily enjoying what they were seeing.

There was another ripping sound, followed closely by a thick wet plop and then the pressure and struggling beneath her foot ceased as if something had burst.

A smell came up out of the darkness, something acrid and sickening; the stench of rottenness, the stink of sulphur. The whiff of brimstone.

...*creak... creak... creak... creak...*

Back against the wall Molly gripped the gun two handed and raised it towards the rocking chair, she thumbed back the hammer and a woman laughed.

"Fuck you..."

Molly pulled the trigger and the gun made a hollow, metallic click.

She'd forgotten to load it.

She stayed slumped against the wall, the unloaded gun still directed, rather pointlessly, towards where the now silent rocking chair was. Molly decided to try another approach.

"Who are you? What do you want?"

No reply came bar Molly's own panted breath.

If someone was sitting in the rocker, they were awfully quiet.

Molly was about to throw the unloaded gun at the chair and run upstairs when a noise did come.

A creaking noise again, but not from the rocking chair, it was upstairs in the bedroom. The sound of footsteps on floorboards.

Molly scrambled to her feet and ran for the stairs as fast as the darkness allowed. Knocking one table over and bouncing off several walls until she found the stairs and took them two at a time. Slipping once and landing heavily on her wrist.

The room was still in darkness, but her eyes could see the curtains had been pulled back to stir on the night's breath. The window, which usually screeched like a banshee if you opened it, was agape.

"Amelia!" Molly gasped, flinging herself down and frantically patting the sheets.

The bed was empty and the little girl was gone...

Dark Carnival

The Barber

It had felt surprisingly liberating to punch him in the face.

He'd connected cleanly with his jaw, which was square and covered with patchy bristles, and his head had snapped back hard enough to send his hat, an incongruously small peaked cap, flapping to the ground.

The sensation of the man's shoulder crashing into his midriff as he'd barrelled into him and taken him staggering into the side of a wagon had, admittedly, been rather less satisfying.

He was dimly aware of figures lurching around him in the flickering torchlight. Their grunts and cries mixed with a scream from one of the fallen women who'd been so disinterested in Mr Wizzle's concern for their immortal souls. At first he thought she must have taken a stray blow before it came again and he realised it was a scream of laughter.

He supposed to someone who was used to drunks pawing at them, men knocking seven bells off each other might seem quite amusing.

Ash twisted away from the square-jawed oaf who'd taken it upon himself to crack open his head for little apparent reason. He managed to get a good firm grip on the thug's coarse cotton shirt and then rammed his head into the side of a wagon. His assailant went limp, which was *very* satisfying.

Ash spun around to find someone else to hit.

This was so much easier than being stuck at home with nothing to do but watch helplessly as his family disintegrated. He felt all the rage and impotence that had built up since Emily's attack flowing out of him. He couldn't turn back time, he couldn't undo what had been done, he couldn't even make a single goddamn thing better for his girls. But he could sure as hell hit meatheads and if feeling this good was a sin, then so be it.

Another mean looking viper was squaring up to him, he had a half-assed beard too; clearly the carney lacked a good barber.

He was aware of other figures swinging at each other all around him along the makeshift drag of Carney Town. Some of them he even recognised from his barber's chair. He wasn't entirely sure how it had all escalated into a mass brawl. One minute a guy who he'd taken to be the girls' pimp had been shouting at them, then a couple of thugs had waded in and pushed Mr Wizzle hard enough for the old man to have to stagger to keep his feet. Ash had stepped in and pushed one of them back. Then... well, then it just got a bit confusing and now he found himself surrounded by brawling figures. He wasn't sure if there were any actual sides to the fight, not that it really mattered as he was happy to hit just about anyone.

He'd never been a man much taken with violence, but he was starting to see it had its attractions.

He'd just ducked under his latest assailant's wild swing

and sent him to his knees with a powerful punch to his guts when someone tugged urgently at his sleeve. He growled and swung around only to find Mr Wizzle.

"Time to move along Ash," he grinned.

Ash was half tempted to hit him anyway and blame it on a red mist later, but he dropped his fist after only a moment.

"Fun's just started," he managed to say, though his feet were following the old man who still had hold of his arm.

They ducked between two wagons and left the brawl behind them.

After a few minutes and a couple of trips over tent ropes Ash slowed the pace and Mr Wizzle, panting heavily, did the same.

"That was... unexpected," Ash managed to say, wiping a sleeve across his face and surprised to see it come away dark with blood.

"It is a sorry state that men are so quickly reduced to violence..." Mr Wizzle stooped and placed his hands on his knees after checking that no men of violence had thought to chase them "...although it can occasionally be convenient."

"Convenient?"

"While the carney henchmen were engaged by our little distraction Amos was able to slip away unobserved."

Ash looked back and forth between the old man and the flickering lights of Carney Town. He had forgotten about the gunslinger in all the excitement.

"And why did we need to provide a distraction for him?" Ash pinched his nostrils and then wiped away the blood that was trickling from his nose, "A bloody distraction at that?"

"Amos has more of a nose for sneaking about and sniffing

things out. He is a talented fellow in fact."

"I assume he's fast with his gun, but otherwise-"

"Otherwise our friend the Mayor wouldn't be keeping such a close eye on him."

"He is? And he's our friend?"

Mr Wizzle straightened up and patted Ash's arm.

"Trust me... we're getting to the bottom of things," he nodded, adjusted his hat and started to waddle off towards town.

Ash dabbed at his nose some more. He didn't feel they were getting to the bottom of anything much.

"Why don't you think Preacher Stone hurt Emily?" he demanded, chasing after the old man. He'd let things be in the hope that their midnight jaunt to the carney might reveal something he didn't know. Now that they were heading home and he'd found out nothing other than the therapeutic power of violence he wanted a straight answer. Or at least a straighter one.

Mr Wizzle stopped and turned back to face Ash, he could just make out his crumpled features in the darkness. Carney Town's fires were at their back and Ash could make out the buildings of Hawker's Drift atop the low-slung rise of the Tear silhouetted against the stars ahead of them.

"Because I saw him that night and he was in no condition to hurt anyone."

Ash grabbed his arm, "Why didn't you tell me this before?"

Mr Wizzle raised an eyebrow and left it there till Ash eased the pressure on his arm.

"Because you would have blurted something out."

"Damn right I would have done – you should have told the

Sheriff-"

"And ended up swinging from the Judas Tree myself perhaps?"

Ash blinked at the old man.

"We have dangerous foes ranged against us Ash," he swept a hand out towards the night that surrounded them, "the very forces of darkness itself!"

Ash let that one pass; he still wanted answers, "What did you see?"

"The Preacher was passed out all night; he'd been acting strangely for a long time. I was keeping my beady eye on him as I do with all the strange and Godless shenanigans of this town."

"Drunk?"

"No... something else..."

Ash found his hand had curled instinctively around the little bottle that he'd found in the Preacher's study. It had remained in his jacket pocket ever since, despite reminding himself several times he should throw it out.

"He could have come to when you weren't looking?"

Mr Wizzle shook his head forcibly enough to set his jowls wobbling.

"He was curled up on the floor, naked. Writhing like a mad, tormented thing, weeping, laughing, gibbering words that... did not sound like they were of this Earth. Demonic words."

"Demonic..." Ash repeated, keeping his eyes on his feet as they plodded through the grass, all the time his thumb was rubbing the smooth, black glass in his pocket. "How did you see this?"

"I peeked through the window. Regularly."

"Do you make a habit of that?"

"Only when God requires it. I do not look into lady's bedrooms, if that's what you mean?"

"If the Preacher was... possessed... wouldn't that explain him attacking Emily?"

"Perhaps. But I spent the evening around the church. He never left his home. Eventually, he grew still and slept curled up on the floor. He was still there in the morning. I am sure he never left and I'm sure he didn't rape your daughter."

Ash walked in silence for a moment, letting the old man's words sink in and trying to decide if he believed them. Or even wanted to believe them.

"What made the Preacher act like that? Was he mad?" Ash asked when he felt he needed to say something, but didn't want to ask the obvious question.

"I think he was driven mad... by this..." Mr Wizzle produced a little black bottle. Ash's fingers snapped away from the identical bottle in his pocket.

"You got that from the Preacher's house?"

To Ash's surprise, Mr Wizzle shook his head, "No... from someone else. You'd be surprised how many of these little black bottles there are floating around Hawker's Drift. And everybody who has one thinks they are the only one... as far as I can see."

"What's in it?"

"I shudder to think. This one is empty. I've never found one that wasn't bone dry. I suspect it contains some form of opiate to addle the mind, but whatever it is it seems to be highly addictive and I've got a feeling it'll turn your tongue

433

black if you drink it."

"So... someone gave it to the Preacher and Emily-"

"And a lot of other people in town."

"...this stuff?"

"So it seems."

"But who? And why?"

"I can make a pretty good guess as to the who, as to the why..." he shrugged and looked back at the fires of the carney dwindling behind them into the darkness "...I'm hoping Amos might be finding out a few answers for us tonight..."

Dark Carnival

The Sheriff

He'd pretty much lived above the Sheriff's Office since his wife had died; he much preferred it to the neat little house he'd shared with Elena. He had a couple of cramped rooms that were cold in winter, hot in summer and noisy whatever the weather thanks to the comings and goings below.

They weren't much, but they were all he needed. He visited the house he still thought of officially as home as infrequently as possible. Just long enough to air it, make sure nothing had come loose and no critters had broken in. Then he hurried back to work and the pokey little rooms above it as fast as his legs would carry him; which was nowhere near fast enough these days.

There was a small garden at the back which he avoided even more than the house itself. It had reverted quickly back to grass and weed without Elena to love and care for it. Much like he had, he supposed.

He didn't sleep too well these days. When he did, he tended to toss and turn from one ill-remembered dream to another until he was eventually shaken to wakefulness. Occasionally, he would dream of Elena, and those dreams would be golden, or so it seemed when he tried to cling to the memory of them in the darkness. Sometimes the dreams would be memories, sometimes things that had never happened, sometimes just nonsense. Sometimes she wouldn't even feature in them directly, but he could feel her close by, watching him from just outside his field of vision.

He liked those dreams, those little moments, those echoes of the life he had once had. They were the only times he was ever happy. He would wake and find a smile painted on his face; at least until he reached out in the darkness to find that the bed was empty and Elena was three years dead. Sleep would never come again and he would stare into the night trying to hold onto the memory and hope that it was some message or sign or something of worth that she had come to bless his dreams. Then he would lie there until the tears had dried cold upon his face before pulling himself slowly from the covers to face another day alone.

A fist pounding on your door in the small hours generally filled people with either dread or fear. To Sam Shenan, however, it was always a relief as he knew it would provide an escape from rolling back and forth across his crumpled empty bed until dawn.

A knock on the door meant he could distract himself from his loneliness with someone else's problem. He groaned as he threw his legs onto the floor all the same. His body was old and over-used and not necessarily in agreement with that sentiment.

"Coming, damn it!" He yelled, only just managing to pull his pants on in the darkness without landing face first on the floor.

He left on the soiled old shirt he slept in and strapped on his gun belt as he navigated the stairs. He doubted anyone intending to shoot him down in the middle of the night would be polite enough to knock first, but he had some professional pride. The idea of being hauled out of bed to be killed without his gun at hand just plain irked him.

As it was, he heard the voice accompanying the knocking before he made it to the bottom of the stairs and guessed he wasn't in much danger of being shot on his own doorstep. Shouted and sworn at maybe, but not shot.

"Mrs McCrea..." he sighed as he opened the door, still patting his hair down as if she, or any other woman, would give a hoot about his appearance.

"She's been kidnapped!" Molly shouted at him.

"Who-" Shenan began before thinking better of it and ushering Molly inside. If she wanted to report a crime, even at this Godless hour, it was better to come into the office and do it properly. Besides, given her usual volume she'd wake his neighbours if he left her on the street. And as the Sheriff's closest neighbour was the Mayor that probably wasn't the best idea.

Shenan managed to light a lamp and then fumbled through his key chain to unlock the Sheriff's Office proper. The office was only manned overnight if some miscreant was in the cells. Currently, the town's collection of miscreants were all still down at the carney getting shit-faced drunk, so the cell block was as deserted as the rest of the place.

"Sit," he ordered as she began to babble again. He didn't bother taking her through to his actual office at the back, no one was here to overhear them so the nearest Deputy's desk would do just fine.

Molly looked far too agitated to sit. However, the Sheriff

reckoned she was much less likely to swing at him, spit at him or throw the one lit lamp at him if she was perched on her butt instead of pacing about in front of him.

"Sit!" Shenan repeated, easing his own hide down onto a chair to show her how it was done. He glared right back at her when she gave him one of her looks. He'd always been tetchy when he'd been called from his bed, regardless of whether he'd actually been asleep or not in the first place.

Molly's lips were pressed tight together, something he suspected was no mean feat on her part, but she managed to plonk herself into the chair without shouting anything at him. Once she was settled, however...

"You've got to fucking find her!"

The Sheriff rubbed his eyes, maybe getting shot would have been a better outcome after all.

"Find who?"

Molly gave him the kind of look reserved for the blind drunk or dead stupid, "Amelia, of course."

The little girl Amos had kept coming to see him about for news of her people.

"What happened?"

"She disappeared..."

There were sheets of blank paper in a neat pile, he really should be writing this down. Instead, he leant back into the chair and felt his heart sink down into his guts.

"Go on."

"She was asleep in bed when I went downstairs... I heard a noise... when I went back, she was gone."

He'd heard stories like this before, variations on a theme anyway, and he'd always done what was asked of him by friends and loved ones. Usually, some motive for a disappearance bubbled up when he started poking around. Sometimes there was none. The only thing that had ever been consistent about these cases, other than that there were far too many of them for a town this size, was that nobody ever saw or heard from them again.

Not usually a child, though?

No, he couldn't recall anyone so young disappearing before. Never little children, never old people either for that matter.

"And when was this?"

"A couple of days ago... thought I'd wait a bit before looking for help," Molly snapped.

"You're not being real helpful here..."

Molly fidgeted in her chair, her nostrils flaring as her eyes held his. At least she didn't say anything more.

"You said you heard a noise downstairs?"

She nodded and dropped her eyes. Molly stared at her left wrist, rubbing it as if something was irritating the skin.

"Was anything amiss?"

Molly's eyes rose back to his and for the first time she didn't look blazing angry. She looked scared.

"I... dunno... I was sure there was someone in my front room, I could hear the rocking chair... creaking... thought I could anyhow, but when I went in there was nothing..."

Her eyes slid away again, the way folks sometimes did when they didn't quite want to tell you everything. Not lying, just not everything.

"I need to know *everything*, Molly?"

"The candle blew out, I got spooked in the dark, that's all.

Why aren't you out looking for Amelia?"

Because we'll never find her...

"It helps to know where to start looking. Is there anything else? Did you have an argument with the girl? Was she upset? Could she have gone looking for her people? For her Mom?"

"No," Molly shook her head hard enough for her curls to fly about her face, "someone took her."

"Any idea who?"

"A woman, I think. She was hanging around my house. In my yard and then in the street outside."

"Who was she?"

"Look we really should be-"

"Molly! Who was she?"

She gave another shake of her head, "I didn't recognise her."

A suspect? There was never usually a suspect...

"It was dark, I didn't get a real good look..." Molly bit her bottom lip and scrunched up her eyes, which made her look much like a little girl herself, "...but she was tall, dark hair, pulled back across her scalp, a long ponytail I think..."

"Lots of jewellery? Bangles and stuff?"

"Yeah, I think so," Molly's eyes snapped open and she leaned forward, "you know her?"

"Not exactly... but sounds like a carney woman I spoke to... saw her with Amelia this afternoon."

"What the fuck was she doing?"

"Didn't Amos mention it to you?"

"Didn't really speak to him much today. What happened?"

"Don't rightly know, but the girl started screaming

something terrible when this carney woman, Giselle, gave her a ragdoll."

Molly's eyes widened a little further, "She gave Amelia that ugly bitch of a thing? I thought Amos had bought it for her."

Shenan frowned, "Amelia threw it away, scared her half to bits. Well, either the ragdoll or Giselle did, wasn't quite sure which."

Molly was staring at her wrist again, "She couldn't have thrown it away... it was sitting in the rocking chair when I went downstairs. Right before Amelia got taken."

"So this woman left a ragdoll and snatched a child?"

Molly jumped to her feet, "Whatever she did, we need to find Amelia..."

Shenan nodded and hauled himself to his feet, "Yeah, well, guess I'll take a ride out to the carney. That damn thing goes on all night so it's not like I'm gonna have to wake anybody up."

"Right let's get going," Molly turned for the door.

"Hey, you ain't going anywhere!"

"Amelia is my responsibility, I'm-"

"You're going home, in case the girl did just wander off... sleepwalking or something. Anyway, you can't go to the carney; it's outside the town limits remember?"

"Shit..."

"Go home Molly. If she's there, I'll find her."

"You going on your own?"

"I'll grab a couple of my boys on the way. If I'm lucky, I might even find some of em still sober."

"But-"

Molly was still protesting as they left the Sheriff's Office, and all the way across Pioneer Square and while Shenan saddled his horse in the stables. He was pretty sure she was still protesting as he galloped off across the square towards Main Street.

God, I'm too damn old for this...

The Fortune-Teller

"Don't do anything stupid," Thomas Rum had growled at her.

She'd snorted and tossed her hair, before spinning on her heels and retreating to the tinkling accompaniment of the silver bangles dancing on her wrists.

Rum wouldn't listen to her. None of them would. They'd keep on doing what they were told to do until they'd all withered to nothing or had forgotten entirely what they had once been. They were content to roam the roads and follow all the paths of the world to do His bidding for all eternity.

She was different. She always had been and she suspected they all hated her for it. And if they didn't hate her they feared her. Which was at least better. She'd been privileged and feted once, destined to rule, born to it, nurtured for it. Her birthright. And she'd given it all away to follow Him, and follow Him she had, right to the bitter end. To this wretched place of mud, and stink and weak corrupting flesh.

Don't do anything stupid? I did something stupid a long time ago and I'm still paying the price.

The child was sleeping as she carried her across the grass, the weight negligible in Giselle's arms. She could have held her for days without breaking a sweat. Her strength far exceeded the insubstantial vessel of the flesh she wore and the girl would make her stronger still. Much stronger.

She was tired of being weak. More than tired, worse than tired. She was bored of it. It served no purpose. He had a plan, but it was boring, dull, unimaginative plan. A plan that would take too long and probably wouldn't work anyway. She had other ideas. He could stay and scratch out some meagre existence, but she was stronger now. He had grown weak and soft while she had quietly reaped what meagre bounty the road could offer and she had supped deep.

Giselle looked down at the child, her dark skin bleeding into the night, and this one could be supped very deep indeed.

She'd felt her day's out from Hawker's Drift. A deep and low resonance beyond the horizon, a resonance that called her and demanded her attention, a resonance that made her soul ache with want and need.

Giselle had watched the others, Rum, Mallory, Qinn, Hester and Arlton, but they'd had no sense of her. Even between them they weren't attuned enough to sense at that range. By the time they had felt something, it was lost in the buzz and hum of what Hě had collected already in Hawker's Drift over these past decades. Enough for their mouths to water, but not enough for them to realise that there was something extra special on the plate this time.

Collected for himself while he sent the rest of them out to roll and rock and sway in those hateful wagons for month after intolerable month. Crawling from hole to cesspit, from slum to hovel, from ruin to wasteland, pretending to entertain the little monkeys while they searched for the precious amongst the worthless flesh in this slowly dying, broken civilisation. If that wasn't too grand a word for it.

They'd realised when the girl came to the carney, though. Yes, she'd seen those hungry, sparkling eyes and known that want well enough, for she'd felt it herself for days.

She should have kept her distance. It had been a mistake to approach her, to touch her. She was sensitive enough to feel Giselle's hunger, though, of course, nowhere near intelligent enough to comprehend those feelings or have any understanding of what she was.

"Don't do anything stupid," Thomas Rum had said later. He knew, she suspected, if anybody did then it would be him. She didn't care anymore. She had harvested diligently and carefully for all these years. Bringing back enough for Him to be happy, but she would not live on the scraps He threw them anymore. Let the others dance around the flames and rut with their acolytes at the Dark Carnival. She had other plans.

It was time for a new god.

She had loved Him once and it had cost her everything. She had been blinded by his power and magnificence. Young and foolish, weak and needy for his love and approval. She had betrayed everything for him and for what? To be cast out and exiled till the sun bloated red and scorched this ball of mud and shit to a blackened cinder.

No, not anymore. While he played at being a farmer growing a petty empire from the poor dirt of this land she had been feeding as well as she could. Now she was strong, stronger than any of them because they went without so He could sow and grow his seeds. Now she was strong enough.

The child stirred in her arms, wriggling for a moment before Giselle reached in and dampened her mind again. She filled it with dreams of flowers, horses, cute little bunny rabbits and the other meaningless shit that soothed these pitiful monkeys.

When she was still again, Giselle continued. The grass hissing against her skirts as she ploughed on beneath a sky that blazed with stars. The energy coming from the girl was intoxicating, and the temptation to suck her dry was almost unbearable, but she knew better. There was a nexus a few miles ahead and it would amplify the harvesting tenfold. It would have been quicker to ride, but Giselle had always hated those stupid, stinking beasts even more than the little monkeys. Besides, it was an aching pleasure to deny herself as she cut through the grass. A time to savour what was to come, to bathe and bask in the child's energies.

The best meals were never hurried.

The Gunslinger

Men were waiting out in the darkness. He could taste their souls on the wind.

Amos paused, closing his eyes against the little there was to see and ignoring the cricket's incessant chirping that was the only sound beside the sighing breeze. Guards, patrolling between Carney Town and the distant fire to keep out the inquisitive; somebody was being serious about their privacy.

Though perhaps not serious enough.

Each man was alone and spaced out a little too far from the next. They were bored and tired and not expecting anyone to be slipping through the grass in the small hours. He opened his eyes and plotted a path between two of the shimmering souls. The stars and kissing moon cast some light, but not enough to make out a single figure at the distance the guards were keeping from each other. He veered a little towards the left as he was sure that man was dozing, or pretty close to it, and walked slow and smooth.

No shout came out of the darkness to challenge him and he moved on towards the fire. The land this side of town was largely unfarmed and left for cattle and horse to graze. There was nothing to see but the toss and sway of grass heads turned silvery under the starlight... and the single flickering light of the silent flames ahead drawing him onwards.

He'd emptied his mind as he walked, discarding thoughts with each step; Molly, Amelia, Severn, the Rider on a Grey Horse, the Mayor, Megan. The only time he found anything close to peace was when he was out on the business of dark work. When his mind had to be clear to taste souls and divine the intentions of men. When he needed nothing to come between mind and eye and gun hand.

He sensed the guards slipping behind him till they were lost in the great empty night, then nothing for a good long while. Nothing but the flames growing bigger and more distinct. Then came the souls ahead of him. Fuzzy and indistinct, blurring together like watercolours running down a canvas. He recognised the sensation well enough, the people ahead were drunk. Very drunk. So intoxicated they barely knew who they were or what they were doing. The thought that he might be walking for miles just to find a bunch of drunken bums slumped around a fire flittered across his otherwise empty mind. It was a thought he dismissed as soon as he started to sense something else. Something he'd become familiar with ever since he'd rolled into Hawker's Drift.

Monsters in the caves...

He couldn't recognise one from another, but he knew those not quite empty echoes reverberating around a vast malevolent darkness belonged to the Mayor and some of the carney folk, so he guessed they were all there.

Amos stood for a moment. He could see now the fire was a large bonfire, no mean feat in itself out in this vast virtually treeless plain. He could make out – just – figures moving in front of the fire, as indistinct as the colour of their souls draining into one another.

"Just who the hell are you people..." Amos whispered. No answer was forthcoming on the breeze so he resumed walking.

He guessed he was going to find out pretty soon.

*

Well before the light of the fire started holding the night back Amos hunkered down and started crawling through the long grass.

He moved a few yards at a time. Pausing to make sure he hadn't been spotted. He might be well hidden from sight, but the grass heads swayed about him no matter how carefully he moved. It was unlikely anyone would see him. Not so much because it was dark and the grass was moving in gentle ripples beneath the night breeze's caress anyway, but because the people around the fire seemed far too preoccupied with their orgy to notice anything much.

Naked figures writhed around the fire in greasy, frenetic knots, coupling in all possible combinations.

Amos wanted to look away, for all kinds of reasons, but he forced himself to watch in order to try to understand what was happening. He'd never seen an orgy before, so had no idea if this was what generally went on. Even before Severn had mutilated him, his sexual experiences had been limited to a handful of women, and he certainly hadn't had any afterwards.

Even from where he lay in the grass he could see the participants were heavily intoxicated, their expressions were vacant, eyes glassy and movements jerky. As he'd sensed earlier, their souls were blurred and ill-defined through lust and whatever they'd been drinking.

Amos assumed that they were all carny folk as he didn't immediately recognise anyone from town. Though he couldn't swear to it given the short period of time he'd been in Hawker's Drift and the fact people could look remarkably different when they were butt-naked and shit-faced drunk.

Beyond the rutting bodies, on the opposite side of the fire, other figures sat watching events, in the middle was Thomas Rum, still wearing his crooked top hat and dark glasses. His expression was blank and he stared directly into the fire.

There were four others sitting either side of Rum. On his left was a heavy-set black man, his bald head glistening in the firelight, who Amos recognised from the carney that afternoon. On his right Mallory the pimp-master, who must have ridden to get here ahead of Amos though he could see no horses. On Rum's right were two empty chairs and then a woman, young and bored looking, dark ringlets falling about a round ochre face as she fanned herself with slow, lethargic strokes. Next to her a young Chinaman with delicate, sculptured features and long straight hair. In the flickering light cast by the fire, Amos couldn't be sure if his mouth wore a faint smile or a twisted sneer, either way it never left his face.

Amos waited, letting other people's lust roll over him and trying hard not to be repulsed by it. He'd never been a moralist and the cruelties of his life had ensured he wasn't much of a Jesus man either, but there was something so base and animalistic in what he was watching that he felt sickened to whatever was left of his own tattered soul.

Did he need to be watching this? So, the carney folk liked to pass their time a bit differently to most. That didn't help him much, didn't answer any questions, didn't mean Molly and Amelia were any more or less safe.

Yet he stayed. Because, beyond the lust and lascivious, drunken hunger, there was something else out there, beyond the flames, something centred around Rum and his companions.

The monsters in the caves.

The rutting showed no sign of abating. Whatever they'd been drinking hadn't sapped anyone's strength; nobody rolled away spent and panting. They just wriggled and crawled from one partner or partners to the next. Each welcomed wordlessly with eager mouths and fingers to draw them in.

And then they stopped.

There had been no word or command, but each figure disentangled itself from another and turned to face Rum and his companions. There was a moment's shuffling, but no one spoke, no one giggled or laughed or looked furtively at their fellows. No one staggered away for a bottle or a piss. In fact, for a drunken orgy Amos noticed there weren't any bottles strewn about. No other kinds of detritus either save little piles of clothes scattered across the trampled and flattened circle of grass. Otherwise, all that had been brought to the party were seven chairs and the remains of an old wagon that had been butchered with axes into a pile of firewood

Each figure rose to their knees, all facing Rum and with their backs to Amos. He expected some kind of speech – he wasn't entirely sure what a speech at an orgy would consist of – but nothing much seemed to happen. Rum still stared into the fire, the Chinaman continued to smile/sneer, the bored young woman made rhythmic swishes of her fan, Mallory and the heavy-set black man sat, statuesque and unmoving.

Amos noticed the lust had faded from the kneeling figures. In fact, everything had faded from them. He got no sense of anything. His gift, for want of a better word, tended to ebb and flow, stronger some days, weaker on others, more sensitive to some people's souls, non-existent to blanks. However, with thirty-odd people around the fire he should have sensed something, as he had up until a moment before. If they hadn't been kneeling, he would have suspected they had all fallen asleep.

All he could sense on the night's warm breath was that strange emptiness and the feeling that something malevolent was watching him from the dark shadows within.

Thomas Rum looked up from the fire and the flames mirrored momentarily in his dark glasses. His head turned towards the empty chair to his right, the bored-looking young woman glanced at him and offered a shrug. Rum's mouth twitched before settling into a hard pressed bloodless line.

A figure appeared out of the darkness.

The Mayor.

The seated figures rose as one, their heads bowed while the kneeling onlookers dropped their heads to the ground until the Mayor took the middle of the seven chairs. In turn each of the figures, Rum, Mallory, the black man, the bored-

453

looking woman and the effete Chinaman kneeled before the Mayor and kissed his hand.

The Mayor stared glassily into the fire, acknowledging none of them.

Amos felt a cold twisting chill ripple across his skin as he realised the crickets had fallen silent.

The Mayor spoke once the others had taken their seats, but even in the utter silence of the grasslands his voice didn't carry. He spoke for several minutes, but Amos didn't catch a word and he found himself reluctant to crawl closer. When he had finished each of the others bowed their head and the instant their eyes were averted his gaze flicked to the empty chair. Then he raised a hand and flicked out a wrist. A moment later two figures appeared out of the darkness.

Amos tensed so suddenly he felt his boot claw at the hard, dry dirt beneath the grass and he found he had pulled his gun without any realisation of what he was doing. He was trembling and he had to bite down on his lips to stop himself crying out.

The first of the newcomers was a girl in her late teens; fair-haired, skinny and pale-faced save for two rose flushes on her cheeks. Her eyes were blank and she shuffled into the light of the fire dressed in a simple smock, her legs and feet bare.

It wasn't the girl that had so startled him, though. It was the figure that walked behind her, one hand clamped on her shoulder; a tall, bald man with a broken nose and a thick, rough beard that hung to his throat.

He didn't know the man's name and he hadn't seen him for thirteen years, but he recognised him well enough all the same. It was a face he'd never forget for he'd been one of the men who had raped Megan while Severn had pushed his pistol into Amos' temple and hissed into his ear.

"See what ya did Mister? See what ya did?"

Amos screwed his eyes shut and sucked in air through his nostrils; the scent of grass and burning wood tickled the back of his throat. He found his holster and slipped the gun back in place before he risked opening his eyes again. He could put a slug in the bastard's head, a tricky shot with a pistol from this range, but he was pretty sure he could pull it off. And for a few seconds he might know some peace. Then what? There were thirty other people around that fire, plus the guards scattered out on the grass, not that he'd need to put a bullet in all of them to get away. Getting away would be easy; it would be where to go next that would be the hard part.

No, he wouldn't kill him now. Maybe other members of Severn's gang were working gun for the carney. Maybe Severn himself. That didn't seem likely; Severn wasn't the kind of man who worked for anyone bar himself. But the bearded man might know where Severn was, or where he'd been. He'd know *something*. Amos doubted he'd be much inclined to tell him. Not at first anyway. But Amos could be damned insistent when he came to asking questions...

Then he'd kill him and any of the other scum who might have ended up with Thomas Rum and his freaky carnival.

So he would wait until the bearded man wandered off into the night, then Amos would follow him and when they were alone the two of them would get reacquainted.

He didn't notice the Mayor give a little nod to Thomas

Rum, nor the fact that the Carney King moved towards the girl without his cane or the slightest hint of a limp. He didn't really see the way the flames reflected from the blackened lenses of his glasses so brightly and was only dimly aware when the old man tore the girl's smock from her body with one effortless tug.

He only noticed what was happening to the girl when the other figures moved, blocking his view of the bearded man, and formed a circle around the girl. Then Severn's man was alone and making no move to join the others. Amos guessed he was just a hired gun and not invited to the main party. He was still in too plain a sight for Amos to grab him, but he began to shuffle sideways to circle around the fire and get closer to him. Hopefully, he would be leaving alone. Amos didn't want to hurt anyone else, but if it came to it, he'd do what needed to be done. He'd spent thirteen years hunting Severn and his scum. He wasn't going to let one of them get away now, for Megan's sake, for his sake, he'd do what was necessary to see that vengeance was done.

He paused and looked back up at the fire through the stems of softly swaying grass, there was a noise. A humming, faint and high-pitched, but clearly discernible against the eerily silent backdrop of the night.

He eased himself back down onto his stomach, frowning until he realised the sound was coming from the naked, kneeling onlookers. None were moving, not in the slightest, which struck Amos as odd. Nobody fidgeted, or scratched, or tossed their hair. Nothing. Just humming, only that wasn't quite right. It was more like holding a note the way someone learning to sing might. Except the pitch didn't waver and there was no variation despite so many different throats making the noise.

There was something else too, something coming off the kneeling onlookers where there had been nothing before. It was the warm honeyed glow of adoration and love. And he was pretty sure it was directed towards the Mayor.

Just what were they going to do to the girl?

Amos' eyes flicked back from the kneeling onlookers. He'd assumed she was just another part of the orgy, but the spiders were crawling in his skull, the way they did when something was very, very wrong. Her back was to him so he couldn't see her face, but she was as unmoving as the others.

The Mayor, still seated, was saying something more, but he was still too far away for the words to carry. After a moment, Mallory and the Chinaman took the girl's arms and pushed her to her knees in front of Rum. She didn't resist. Thomas Rum smiled at her, a hungry, leering smile as he begun to unbutton his shirt. The Mayor looked on, impassive and unmoving.

Amos shook his head and begun to crawl again, just some old pervert's game, not his business. Amos didn't care, he only had eyes for the bearded thug who had raped his wife all those long empty years ago.

He moved carefully, a few yards at a time, only looking up to make sure his man hadn't moved. He hadn't, he was staring at nothing in particular, his face set, but not blank and glassy like the other onlookers had been as they'd uncoupled from their orgy. He just looked bored.

Amos hadn't been paying Rum much attention; he had no

great desire to see the old man sucked off by a teenage girl. His only interest was in ensuring nobody had spotted him and if these degenerates were all still transfixed by their seedy pleasures then it was probably fair to assume nobody had.

Amos froze again. His mouth suddenly dry as his fingers scratched involuntarily at the hard packed soil. Rum was bare-chested and his head thrown back to look at the stars, his jauntily tilted top hat still somehow sitting upon his grey hair.

The girl was on her knees, craning up to suck at the old man. Not at his cock, though, which as far as Amos could see was still buttoned up in his trousers, but higher up.

Amos squinted and resisted the urge to crawl closer to be sure he was seeing what he thought he was seeing. With a sudden yank, Mallory and the Chinaman pulled her away from Rum. The girl gave out a sudden howl of pain and rage. She tried to throw off the two men and get back towards Rum, but she was dragged unceremoniously away, thrashing and kicking like a five-year-old in a tantrum, leaving Amos with a clearer view.

The girl had been sucking on one of Rum's nipples, one of the six black nipples the man had in two vertical rows of three. The two nipples you would expect to see and two more below each one on his ribcage and stomach. The girl had been sucking at the lower left one and Amos could make out a viscous black trail smeared down from it across Rum's white, wizened skin.

As the girl thrashed about Amos could see the same black smear across her lips and chin.

Sweet, black, candy...

Thomas Rum nodded and made a quick flicking motion with his hand and Mallory and the Chinaman hauled the girl to her feet. Her howling had reduced to a moan and her limbs went limp as she was dragged like an old drunk back before Thomas Rum.

The hum of the onlookers stopped instantly.

The girl was surrounded now, Rum, Mallory, the bored-looking young woman, the heavy-set black man and the Chinaman; as one they reached out and placed a hand upon her head.

For a moment, there was only silence.

Then light.

All five threw their heads back as white twisting light streamed through their fingers. Some shot towards the stars but most flowed like curling snakes up the arms of the five to be sucked into mouths that were gaping unnaturally wide.

The air crackled with strange energies as if a thunderstorm were about to be unleashed from the clear night sky. Amos felt the hairs on his arms rise and his breath became laboured, it seemed there was no longer quite enough air left to breathe. The blazing fire slowly dimmed, the flames faltering and reducing to leave only hazy smoke and glowing embers.

Amos gave a strangled little gasp, there were figures all about the grass; translucent, ephemeral dreamlike figures of every colour and hue, flitting in and out of existence. None of them ever quite coalesced enough to be recognisable as an individual, but all were unmistakably human figures; some walking, some running, but mostly just standing. All glowed and twisted with every conceivable colour, none made a sound of any kind.

Amos watched one, a shimmering figure of blues and purples stroll through the crowd of kneeling onlookers, none of whom twitched a muscle, before fizzing out and fading to nothing.

He turned to find a figure sitting a few feet from him in the grass; he got the impression of a boy, hunkering down and up to mischief. Oranges and yellows swirled and flickered in clouds of emerald green. It was like the colours he sometimes saw flitting around people, the colours that gave him an insight into their mood and mind and intentions, but far more vivid. The colours he thought of as souls for lack of a better word. Colours that mingled with his other senses to give him his strange gift, but he got no sense from these figures. Perhaps the faintest flicker of happiness from the boy, like the final spread of colour from a setting sun. Was that a grin on the ill-formed face? A boyish smirk?

The figure faded back into the night before he could be sure.

One by one all of the figures did the same. Some were replaced by others for a few seconds before disappearing too until all were gone and Amos felt a strange sense of loss and sadness settle upon him.

He looked up at the ring of five around the girl, there was still a faint column tracing into the sky, but that was fading too.

Hadn't he seen something similar the night he'd spent outside the Mayor's ranch before he'd been arrested for the attack on Emily Godbold?

As the column faded to nothing, the fire leapt back to life and the crickets resumed their chorus.

The five let their hands slide away from the girl and each took an unsteady step backwards.

The girl stood for a moment before collapsing. Except there was no girl anymore, just a withered, desiccated thing of shrivelled parchment yellow skin and white hair.

Rum flicked a wrist towards her before turning his back and returning to sit beside the Mayor.

The bearded man, who had remained unmoved and seemingly little interested in events, passed Rum without comment, scooped up the remains of what had been a young girl only a minutes before and strode towards the fire.

Amos couldn't be sure but he thought he saw her fingers twitch and curl around the man's wrist before she was tossed into the fire, which engulfed her body as showers of sparks flew up into the dark night sky. He turned without pause and strode back to Thomas Rum's shoulder.

Ever the faithful dog...

Rum smiled and buttoned his shirt, before clapping his hands. As one life returned to the onlookers, who dropped onto all fours to scurry and scamper across the flattened grass towards Rum's four companions, each of whom were removing their tops to reveal six black glistening nipples.

Amos could watch for only a moment as the naked forms swarmed over them, like blind newborn pups eager for the teat.

Amos pulled his revolted eyes away and looked beyond the writhing figures with black smeared faces to Thomas Rum and his dog.

He could worry about that poor girl later and he could worry about what the hell he'd just seen later too; just like he could worry about Molly and Amelia later.

None of that mattered anymore.

Amos knew someone else was out in the darkness beyond the flickering firelight now. A thin rider sat upon a pale horse, his soiled coat flapping on the night's breath. A figure whose head lolled against his chest as he sat slumped in a sun-cracked leather saddle.

Death was watching him from atop his grey stallion and he was mighty happy. A contented chuckle that sounded like old dry bones being rubbed together bubbled up from his throat, while a beam sparkled deep down in the bottomless black pits of his eyes. Yes, Death was well pleased with the world right now.

Amos the Gunslinger had dark work to do...

Hawker's Drift

Book Three

The Paths of the World

By Andy Monk

In the Absence of Light
—
The King of the Winter

A Bad Man's Song

Ghosts in the Blood

The Love of Monsters

Hawker's Drift
—
The Burden of Souls

Dark Carnival

The Paths of the World

Other Fiction
—
The House of Shells

Further information about Andy Monk's writing and future releases can be found at the following sites:

www.andymonkwordsandpictures.co.uk

www.facebook.com/andymonkbooks